The Wo...
Who Ran

Sam Baker grew up in Hampshire and after a degree in politics at Birmingham University became a journalist, going on to edit some of the UK's biggest magazines.

For six years she was Editor in Chief of *Red* magazine, where she set up the Red Hot Women Awards recognising achievement across politics, science, tech, the arts, media and charity, as well as championing support for Refuge, the charity for victims of domestic abuse.

In 2015 she co-founded and launched The Pool with Lauren Laverne, the online platform that makes inspiring and original content for busy women.

Sam is married to the novelist Jon Courtenay Grimwood and lives in Winchester. When she's not working or writing she escapes by devouring crime novels or watching box sets.

Follow her on Twitter @sambaker

Sam Baker

The Woman Who Ran

HARPER

Harper
An imprint of HarperCollins*Publishers*
1 London Bridge Street
London SE1 9GF

www.harpercollins.co.uk

This paperback edition 2016
1

First published in Great Britain by
HarperCollins*Publishers* 2016

A catalogue record for this book is
available from the British Library

ISBN: 978-0-00-746435-7

Set in Meridien LT Std by Palimpsest Book Production Limited,
Falkirk, Stirlingshire

Printed and bound in Great Britain by
Clays Ltd, St Ives plc

MIX
Paper from
responsible sources
FSC C007454

FSC™ is a non-profit international organisation established to promote the responsible management of the world's forests. Products carrying the FSC label are independently certified to assure consumers that they come from forests that are managed to meet the social, economic and ecological needs of present and future generations, and other controlled sources.

Find out more about HarperCollins and the environment at
www.harpercollins.co.uk/green

To Jon, as ever

Prologue

Paris, late August 2012

I wake to the sound of someone choking. It takes me a moment to realise it's me; my body convulsing like a child shaking its parent awake in the deepest hours of the night.

Just in time, I roll sideways, bile splashing on the floor beside me. Acid burns my throat, and my eyes sting shut against billowing smoke the second I try to open them.

The smell of burning is all around me. The air filled with a buzzing, brown noise I know I've heard before.

Electrics burning and fizzing perilously.

An acrid stench. The unforgettable telltale smell of singed hair, flesh . . .

The memory plays at the edge of my mind. Teasing, torturing. I snatch at it, but it slips away, replaced by the heat that claws at my throat and sears my lungs.

Where am I?

It takes me a second or two to realise. Shock reduces me to choking. In what used to be my bedroom. On what used to be my bed. Naked.

I attempt a breath, gag on it, and try to suppress the panic that rises along with the bile. Nothing makes sense. Not my being here. Not the thick, dark smoke clouding the room and hiding its high ceiling.

Everyone believes fire crackles and rages from the start. A Hollywood idea of a fire. It doesn't, not really. Not at this stage. Not yet. Fires like this take hold by stealth, then, when they've got you, in their own time, when they're good and ready, they let rip.

The seconds preceding that sound like this.

That's how I know I still have time. A few precious seconds, maybe a few more.

If I can only make myself *think*. If I can only make myself *move*.

My brain is as thick with smoke inside as the room is without.

'Move!' it shrieks. 'Run! *Move!*' Or maybe it's me who shrieks. My voice is sucked into burning oxygen and absorbed. Legs buckling, I force myself up, head swimming dangerously, body swaying as the heat sends me crashing to the ground. Here, at least, with hot cheek to cold tile, there is air.

One lungful, two, three . . . I suck in as much air as my burning lungs can stand and try to think. My clothes . . . Where are they? Why aren't I wearing them?

Blindly I crawl round the bed, one hand in front of the other, towards the heat, the only way out, until my hand hits cloth. I grab at something – a T-shirt, then

2

thicker fabric, jeans, rivets searing my fingertips as my hands close on them.

Keep moving.

I drag myself along the wall until brick gives way to wood. Pulling myself up, I twist the metal door handle hard, screaming as my palm blisters. Heat billows around me and flames burst in behind, as if they've been waiting, vampire-like, to be invited.

I plunge into sickly orange fog, flames crackling now. An ominous crack across the room makes my heart lurch. I close my eyes, blinking against the smoke and stumble forward. Thinking only of the door, I begin to count.

Willing myself to be calm:

One, two, three . . .

As I fumble on, my hand lands on something *wrong*. Warm and soft, it gives beneath my weight. I gasp, and hear a whimper, like a kicked puppy. The noise, faint as it is, comes from me.

Scrambling backwards, I force myself to look. Through streaming eyes, I can just about make out the shape of a body, curled in on itself, in the corner between me and the door.

Despite the flames, my skin is suddenly ice; the fine downy hairs on my arm bristling even as I smell them begin to singe. I can't bring myself to touch him again. I can't make myself turn away.

Move! My brain urges. *Get out!*

I glance back. As I do, flames erupt behind me, blackening the rug and scorching my heels. Finally, my body obeys. Reaching for the handle to the corridor beyond, I hurl myself through.

PART ONE

The Stranger

'I would not send a poor girl into the world, ignorant of the snares that beset her path . . . nor would I watch and guard her, till, deprived of self-respect and self-reliance, she lost the power or the will, to watch and guard herself.'

Anne Brontë, *The Tenant of Wildfell Hall*

1

SCANDAL-HIT HOSPITAL THREATENED WITH CLOSURE

Upper case, 124 point. Headline framing a picture of a dilapidated red-brick Victorian hulk, surrounded by a rash of outbuildings all stuck on over the last half-century. A seventies extension here, a Portakabin there. Paintwork peeling, signs with letters missing – *ardiology, out-patien s* – and that was before you started on the state of the equipment inside. Rumour had it – well, the rumour behind this latest crisis – that the families of long-stay patients were being asked to bring their own meals and take away soiled laundry. Beneath it a rogue's gallery of administrators and hospital managers whose neglect and cost-cutting had contributed to its place in the NHS's last-chance saloon.

'Not bad.' Gil Markham stood back to admire his handiwork.

As front pages went, it wasn't his finest, but it would do. It ticked the boxes. A real story, with real implications for the local community. Everyone knew someone who'd suffered as a result of the hospital's decline, or knew someone who knew someone. It was like that round here. The last place in Britain where news travelled just as fast via garden fence, front doorstep and public bar as it did online, if not faster. Even that – a love of good old-fashioned local gossip – wouldn't be enough to save his beloved paper.

Gil sighed, glanced over his shoulder to make sure no one had heard.

A hospital closure wasn't the swansong he'd had in mind, but he could leave with his head held high. No small achievement for the end of August. He could just as easily have ended up with a silly season story or a hospital visit from a minor royal. He'd done enough of those over the years.

'Boss –' one of his subs appeared at his side – 'it's short. Want me to pad it on page four or shall I find a filler?'

Gil rolled his eyes. 'How short?'

'Hundred, hundred and fifty, thereabouts.'

'Hell of a lot of padding. Got anything else?'

'This just came off the wire.' The sub – a temp, Gil couldn't remember his name, if he'd ever known it – handed him a printout. 'Reporter, bit of a hotshot back in the day, missing after house fire.'

Gil perked up. 'Local angle? Got family round here? Leeds? Bradford?'

'Nah, fire was in Paris.'

'Paris? I don't call that local.'

'Steve says he was a trainee at the *Mirror* same time as him.' The sub indicated an old hand on the news desk. 'Reckons he was born Sheffield way, moved south when he was a kid . . .'

'Still, a bloody long way from West Yorkshire.'

The sub shrugged as Gil balled the sheet of A4, lobbed it in the general direction of the recycling bin and missed. Both men watched it bounce across the floor and roll to a halt by the printer.

'Pad it,' Gil said. 'But no fluff. Full names, ages, marital status – bung in some details about that last MRSA scandal, if you need it – that sort of thing.'

While the sub filled, Gil skimmed the two tiny pars below the headline, removed a widow and tracked back the sentence, more out of habit than necessity. Any reader whose attention span was too short to turn, as directed, to page four, would find all they needed here. If he had to hazard a guess, Gil would put that at upwards of 90 per cent of them. Made him wonder if it was worth bothering with page four at all.

'Good to go?' the sub asked as Gil speed-read the end of the story. Fluffy, but not too fluffy. And, like he said, no one would read it anyway.

Gil nodded and the sub's right hand shifted slightly, his finger twitched, and the page vanished from his screen. The move was barely perceptible. All that work and then . . . Gil tried not to let it gall him. His last front page sent to the printers and that was it?

He knew it made him sound like an old fossil – he was, practically Palaeolithic – but he missed proper print. He wasn't asking for hot metal, he wasn't that much of a dinosaur, although he'd liked the linotype machine when he was an apprentice on Fleet Street. The smell, the noise, the *commitment* of real print. The sense that, once you'd decided, that was it, there was no going back. It was a big decision in those days. What you thought, what you chose to go with, it mattered.

Digital was too easy.

Don't like it? Change it. Try this, move that. Up a type size, swap the headline with the picture. Better before? Put it all back where it was then. No problem . . . After all, by the time this was printed, it would be old news, already replaced several times over by something newer and more exciting online. Truth was, he was glad to be retiring five years early. No one bought a paper nowadays, not like they used to. Give it a few months and they'd be giving the thing away. If they bothered printing it at all.

'So, what's to say about Gilbert Markham?'

As if on command, Gil began to slink backwards. Shoulders drooped, head down, making himself as invisible as possible. Not easy when you're six four, but over the years he'd turned shrinking into an art form. The glasses helped, he found. One of the reasons he'd never bothered with contacts. If he could only drift as far back as the bar he could fortify himself with another pint. He'd need another, and a chaser, to get through this.

Fat chance.

'Come on, Gil,' someone from the sports desk shouted. Gil tried to remember the man's name, if only to mark his card, but it escaped him. 'It's your big moment, get yourself up there.'

Nev, that was it. He looked like a Nev.

Thank God there wasn't literally an up. Gil had never been one for a stage. Up at the front of this crowd, in the back room at The Cricketers was bad enough. Nev's jeer was joined by a second from one of the subs and a combined third from half the news desk; until even Gil could see he was making more of a spectacle of himself by refusing.

'So,' the new editor repeated, 'what's to say about Gilbert?'

'For Christ's sake,' Gil muttered, pushing his way to the front of the room, grudgingly accepting the affectionate pats that greeted his passage. 'Call me Gil. Haven't been Gilbert since I accidentally burnt down the Boys' Brigade hut when I was seven.'

'Gil joined the *Post*, back in . . .' The man paused, making no pretence of not looking at his hastily unfolded notes. He'd only been there six months, less. He hardly knew Gil. Why would he, when most of his time was spent cutting staff and trying to deal with falling circulation, the crash in advertising revenue and the paper's transition to digital?

'Back in . . .'

'1985,' Gil supplied, taking his place at the front and instantly dwarfing the younger, squatter man. 'Probably around the time you were in primary school.'

Gil remembered his first day clear as a bell, like it was yesterday – and all those other clichés he expected the subs to strike out. Life flashing before your eyes . . . Wasn't that meant to be when you were dying? From where Gil now stood it was same difference. London had been wet and sticky that summer; the worst combination. Jan, pregnant with Karen, was hot, heavy and worried. It wasn't an easy pregnancy. If he were being unkind, he'd say Karen started the way she intended to go on: bloody-minded and difficult.

Lyn was due to start junior school, house prices in Greenwich were soaring, and riots bubbled under the urban sprawl. Jan's mother was never off the phone worrying about the safety of her only daughter and granddaughter; though they lived nowhere near Brixton, or Tottenham for that matter, and trouble was brewing in Liverpool and Manchester, too. London was different, apparently. His own mother wasn't much better. The decision to move back north to head up a news desk, have a higher standard of living, better schools, a house twice as large for half the price, eventually made itself. He cracked when Jan accused him of not worrying about his kids having a safe place to grow up, a decent community, decent neighbours . . .

The things her mum said Gil was trying to deprive her of for the sake of his blessed career.

Working on a national was working on a national, but when the job on the *Post* came up it was too good to turn down. Trouble was, he'd been there ever since. Risen to Assistant Editor/News; covered when the boss was off (holidays, Christmas); pulled more than his fair share of lates in Jan's eyes. Editors came and went, but the top job eluded him, time and technology moving faster than he had a mind to. When he'd joined, the public image of a journalist was a hard-bitten hack in a trench coat with a book of off-the-record contacts. Now it was run by suits, marshalling whichever twelve-year-old with a camera phone happened to be in the right place at the right time, and was happy to sign away their rights for exposure.

What a cliché he'd been back then.

What a cliché he still was.

'You with us, Gil?'

The editor was frowning; the rest of the room had fallen silent and was staring in a way that made Gil uncomfortable. Tolerant was the only way to describe the expression on the younger faces. Like he was an elderly relative at a difficult funeral.

'Senior moment.' Gil mugged at the news desk. 'Comes to us all, guv.'

'Glad to be rid of you then, mate.'

'Give me a gold watch and I'll race you to the door.'

'Ah, about that: what's five letters . . .' He was grinning. The new editor never grinned. It should have been a warning. '. . . and ends in E-X?'

A smile broke across Gil's face. He knew head office would see him right. Tight bastards these days, dicking around with pensions, changing contracts for the worse, but he'd put in the time and they knew that. From his jacket pocket, the one furthest from Gil, the editor produced a box, black leather or something that would pass for it. Emblazoned across the top in foil was one word: *Timex*.

The room dissolved.

'You really think we'd send you off after twenty-seven years with a couple of warm pints and a Timex?' That the younger man's cuff had ridden up to reveal a Rolex Day-Date didn't make Gil feel any better. Gil was meant to say, *No, of course not*. Set himself up for the next fall.

New guard and old locked eyes. There was no hint of a smile in either of them. No mutual respect. No amicable passing of the baton from one generation to another. 'Yeah,' said Gil, loudly enough for the rest of the room to hear. 'I think you would.'

2

With the solid weight of the door between her and the outside world, Helen breathed more easily. Now she was inside, the dregs of last night's migraine nudged its way forward, bringing the exhaustion that always accompanied a night spent in fugue. Crossing the grand entrance hall into the ancient kitchen – a shrine to sixties Formica, probably state of the art once – she filled a glass with cloudy water from a rusting tap, pipes hammering as she did so, before fumbling in her bag for aspirin.

For a full migraine she'd need stronger pills. But these would take the edge off the aftermath. *Stronger pills . . .* Helen's sense of ease slipped away. On the worktop beside her bag lay a dead packet, each of its sixteen plastic pips squashed flat. She squeezed each one anyway, one after the other, heart sinking further with each pip. Empty. Every single one of them. *Shit.* She closed her eyes and felt the room lurch as the nausea of the night before washed back. This had nothing to do with side effects. In her hurry to leave, she'd forgotten to get a new prescription. Without it . . .

Helen downed two aspirin, took a third for luck, and leaned against the huge butler's sink. She counted down from ten, trying to imagine her next attack without the drugs. If she was lucky it might be weeks away.

If she wasn't . . .

Using what little daylight remained, Helen began a tour of the house. It wasn't necessary, logically she knew that; but she'd been doing it almost as long as she could remember. It was a stupid ritual. One of many she'd adopted over the years. Whether for luck, safety, or as some sort of offering to a god she didn't believe in, she wasn't sure. Art had mocked her for it often enough. 'What do you plan to do,' he'd asked once, 'if you find a psychopath lurking under the bed?' She'd bitten back her first retort and just shrugged. She didn't have an answer then and she didn't have one now, but she looked anyway. Everyone had their decompression rituals.

Doors, windows, under beds, were hers.

Shuddering, she pushed Art from her mind. She'd feel better once she'd checked the locks, she always did.

As she passed the door that led to the pantry, a noise stopped her. She froze on the spot, listening intently. There it was again. Small but insistent, growing gradually louder . . . A scraping, like a branch on a windowpane, or fingernails on a blackboard. Leaning on the handle, Helen pushed open the door and jumped back. Whatever she'd been expecting, it wasn't a mangy black tom glaring at her from the middle of the pantry floor, hackles up in fury. The room was dank and smelled of mould, the result of endless drizzle seeping through the missing diamond of the lead window that the cat had obviously used to break and enter.

The two faced off.

'Stay, if you want,' Helen said after several seconds in which it became clear that the cat had no plans to back down. Her voice sounded louder than she'd expected and they both jumped.

Eye contact broken, the cat hissed, showing yellow fangs, and darted towards the window.

Beside the pantry, a second door led through to several outhouses, the nearest of which doubled as a utility room. Beyond was a courtyard. In one corner, below tiles that obviously leaked, was a carriage. It had probably been a prized possession once. Today it was a ghost, rendered pale by decades of bird shit from pigeons in the rafters above. An arch through the rear of the courtyard led to a walled garden with a lychgate gate onto the Dales. At least, according to the letting agents' details.

She'd seen pictures of Wildfell before she arrived, of course. The courtyard garden, a couple of ostentatious family rooms. It looked big, which didn't matter, and remote, which did. She wanted somewhere she was unlikely to be bothered by neighbours. But now she was here and in, and could see the house in all its ruined glory, it was vast. Far larger than she knew what to do with. More run-down than she'd been told. And far closer to civilisation than the letting agent had let on, situated on the cusp of the moors and the Dales. Estate agents lied, it seemed, and so did photographs.

The red-brick Elizabethan frontage was built on to something even more ancient. According to the details, it had been a prep school in the post-war period; a boarding school for boys up to thirteen, which shut for undisclosed reasons. In the eighties it tried – and failed – to become a conference centre. In the early nineties it shut again. Though the agent didn't say so, she suspected it had been shut on-and-off ever since. Family dispute, was all he said when she asked why the house didn't just get sold to developers. Certainly, he had seemed peculiarly keen to let it to a single woman in search of somewhere quiet to work.

Dusk was falling as she locked the door to the outhouse, feeling its flimsy lock rattle in a way that cranked her anxiety up another notch. Then she retraced her steps to the entrance hall. Like everything else in the house it was huge and faded, several doors leading off.

A vast dining room with a mahogany table that would seat twenty at a squeeze. A study with walls lined with antelope heads. A billiard room with a table torn to reveal a heavy slab of slate beneath rotting baize. A red ball sat alone at the side. Helen slung it into the pocket as she passed and it fell through the threadbare net, landing with a crash that made her jump, before rolling away across the marbled floor. The air of abandonment was even more apparent in the drawing room, where a chandelier, two sofas and five chairs were all shrouded under sheets. A huge, gloomy portrait of an imperious man in breeches and knee boots glared down from above the fireplace. The hairs on her arms rose, as if the temperature had dropped a degree or two when she walked in. Not damp like the pantry, more . . . chill. Wrapping her

18

arms around herself, Helen rubbed at them in a futile attempt to warm up. Then she checked the windows. They were all shut. She pulled the curtains anyway, drab and heavy with dust. Anything to obscure the gloom outside.

The house seemed endless. Big rooms giving on to smaller rooms giving on to staircases, which in their turn gave on to a hidden underworld of servants' pantries and store cupboards that Helen decided to ignore, bolting the door firmly top and bottom when she returned to ground level. Upstairs were bedrooms; her own, chosen late the previous night by default, no better or worse than any of the others. It was huge, its ceiling so bowed she feared it might fall in at any moment. As she paced its floor, her boots squeaked on utilitarian grey-blue carpet, at odds with the rest of the bedroom furniture, an assortment of hideous hand-me-downs from elderly relatives who wouldn't take no for an answer.

With the light fading, Helen flicked the switch and a bulb flickered to half-life, barely concealed by a too-small panelled lampshade. In the darkening window, her reflection watched her make her inventory; black eyes sunk in a pale face that seemed to hover against the gloom, until she snuffed it out with the flimsy curtains. An old dark wood chest of drawers stood in one corner, two careless coffee rings interlocking on its surface. A wardrobe with a bevelled oval mirror between its double doors almost matched the chest of drawers, but not quite. Against the end wall sat the bed, little more than a single, in which she'd woken that morning.

Above it hung a portrait of a boy of about seven with blond ringlets and velvet knickerbockers, standing on a windswept moor with a long, low outcrop of rock behind him. The boy was smiling, a beam so full that Helen almost looked over her shoulder to see who he was looking at.

Visiting the servants' floor above just long enough to confirm it was empty, Helen locked the door that led to it and every other bedroom door that had a bolt or a key. The more of the house she could shut down, the less daunted she'd feel.

At the end of the corridor, she stopped on the threshold of a smaller drawing room, its windows overlooking the forecourt. The room was tiny by comparison, its furniture relatively sparse, just a sagging armchair and rotting sofa made almost decent by a huge Indian throw. A thread-bare Turkish rug hid most of the carpet. Over the fireplace was another painting of the same boy, a year or two older, in knee boots, his smile replaced by a scowl. In spite of the painting, the room felt, if not good, then calm. Wandering back out on to the landing, Helen decided not to lock it.

Satisfied the house was secure, she returned to the kitchen and set about unpacking her shopping. What had she been thinking, buying so much stuff? She'd gone intending to stock up on store-cupboard essentials: coffee, tea, milk, bread. A bottle of vodka. Now this. She'd even bought running kit from the sports shop next to the supermarket. That, at least, might be useful.

It was only as she lifted the last two bags from their soggy resting place on the hall floor that she noticed what was left of a note. It lay where her feet must have trampled it when she came in. The pale blue writing paper was good quality; the sort intended for proper letters; the kind that came with matching envelopes, and an unheeded lesson in the art of thank-you letters from a well-meaning relative. This sheet, though, had been folded in half, edges aligned. The words *Mademoiselle Graham* barely legible in unfamiliar handwriting. Biro, not ink. Just as well, given how soggy the paper was.

Eyeing the letter, Helen felt the knot in her stomach tighten again. Nobody in her world had handwriting that neat. Nobody she knew sent handwritten, hand-delivered notes instead of emails. Come to think of it, nobody called her Mademoiselle Graham. Nobody called her Mademoiselle anything. Clearing a space on the cluttered kitchen table, and smoothing the paper flat, Helen strained to make out blurred words scarcely a shade darker than the paper.

Dear Mademoiselle Graham,

I hope you are settling in well to our beautiful village. On the first Thursday of every month we have a 'social' at The Bull public house. As I gather from a friend at the letting agency that you will be with us for some time, we thought you might like to join us next Thursday and get to know your neighbours. We are a friendly bunch!

You will be welcome any time from 6.30 p.m. You'll find The Bull on the right as you enter the village from the direction of Wildfell. You can't miss it!

Looking forward to meeting you.

Yours,

Margaret Millward, Mrs

Balling the wet note, Helen hurled it at the sink.

You can't miss it!? She could and she would.

There's always one, she thought, slamming tins and packets randomly on to shelves. Always. It's the law. Wherever you are in the world, whatever you're doing, every town/settlement/encampment has a self-appointed busybody who makes it their business to winkle you out. Although they call it 'making you welcome'.

Worse, according to what remained of the address, this one ran the local shop, which meant she'd have to run the gauntlet whenever she needed a pint of milk.

Helen made a mental note to start drinking her tea black.

Back in the kitchen, she fished around inside the Sainsbury's bags until she found what she needed and headed upstairs to the bathroom. No Formica here, just an enormous cast-iron bath supported on lion's feet and brass taps that would have cost a fortune in Paris unless you had a lucky break in a *brocante*. Above the loo there was a window that looked over the lichen-clad slate roof of an outhouse, probably the pantry or an as-yet-undiscovered utility room. She didn't remember opening the window; but then she scarcely remembered anything of the past few days.

Peering at herself in a fly-specked mirror, Helen examined her face more closely. So ghostly pale as to be almost translucent, freckles fading, just the faintest hint of broken veins lining her nose; shadows, the baggage of endless nights of insomnia, circling already dark eyes. She was in there somewhere. Right now, it was hard to say where. Her long hair was a bedraggled mess; ends split and highlights growing back to their original reddish-brown. She'd never liked blonde, but Art did. And, well . . . she no longer had to please Art.

Helen flinched.

Tearing open the box of hair dye, she mixed the dye and developer in the tray provided, spread it evenly through her hair with a plastic comb, stumbling at each knot, then sat on the loo seat counting off fifteen minutes by her watch.

When her time was up, she unhooked the rubber shower attachment from the tap and shucked off her jumper, stopping briefly to look at the bruises braceleting her upper arm. They were fading now, yellowing at the edges, blurry orange in the middle. Wind blew in through the window and she shuddered.

With the dye rinsed off, she slid the nail scissors from their packet and began to cut; cautiously at first, then more confidently. Hardly expert, but it would do. By the time she'd finished nearly six inches were gone. Her wavy hair now stopped just below her shoulders. At a glance she looked almost like someone she recognised.

3

It was haunted, so they said. The big house. It was definitely haunted. Well, so those who believed in such things said, and even those who didn't partake of old wives' tales knew someone who knew someone who'd seen something where the lychgate met the Dales at dusk. Or maybe it was just a trick of the light and an ale or two too many. Everyone in the village had an opinion, and everyone agreed you had to be an outsider or stupid or have money to burn, probably all three, to rent an Elizabethan wreck no one with two legs had inhabited in years.

The gossip had started before the woman's taxi pulled away that first night. Not that Gil saw the taxi or even knew there'd been one until he dropped into The Bull for his pint and a ploughman's. He had better things to do with his time than stand in the window twitching his curtains. And besides, there were enough in this village to do that for him.

Truth be told, it got on his nerves. The constant minding everyone else's business for them instead of looking to your own. It was getting on his nerves now . . . Well, Margaret Millward was as she served him in the General Stores. *The Times* for news, *Mirror* for the cricket (plus he had a soft spot for a good tab), the *Post* out of loyalty, the *Mail*, well, just because . . . He knew he could have got them all online hours earlier but he liked the sense of occasion, the heft and rustle of a paper with his morning coffee. A pint of semi-skimmed and a jar of instant balanced precariously on top of his pile of papers. He'd need twenty B&H from behind the counter. Logic said if he bought one pack at a time he could only smoke one pack at a time. Logic was flawed like that.

'Arrived two days ago,' Margaret Millward was saying as she rang up the cans of beans and frozen fish fingers of the woman two ahead of him. 'Keighley radio cars . . . So she must have caught the train to there. Going to need a car if she's planning on staying long. You can't get far round here without your own transport, mess they've made of the buses.'

Revolted by the gossip as he was, Gil couldn't help being impressed by Mrs Millward's powers of deduction. Thirty years at the wordface of local journalism, and the village grapevine – of which Margaret Millward and her husband, Mike, who owned The Stores, were both root and branch – could still teach him a thing or two. Even with the steady flow of tourist traffic there was barely a face passing through she didn't clock.

Missed her vocation, Gil thought idly. Or maybe she hadn't.

'Could be just another walker,' the fish-finger buyer was

saying as she rummaged for a scrawled-on ten-pound note. 'Couldn't move for them in The Bull last night. Even with the weather turning. Boots and rucksacks and those stupid poles.'

'Why take the big house?'

'A rich walker then. More money than sense, that's for sure.'

Gil recognised the woman's face but he couldn't place her. He'd seen her in town though, over the years; had two girls slightly younger than his, he knew that much. Remembered her from some PTA cheese-and-wine thing Jan had bullied him into. Pretty sure they'd never spoken. Neighbours had been Jan's remit.

'Bet she's gone in a week. Would have thought the rooms at The Bull would be a bit comfier than that old wreck.'

'She'll stay,' Mrs Millward said confidently. 'She paid up front in lieu of a deposit. You're not going to walk away from that kind of money, are you? Gwen went in to give it a bit of a once-over on Monday. Said you could feel the damp right through to your bones. And the dust . . . well. Part of the furniture, it's been there that long. Not to mention the atmosphere. Awful quiet, Gwen said, just the house going about its business, you know how they do, them old houses. Wouldn't catch me up there on my tod in the middle of the night, thank you very much.'

She shuddered theatrically.

'That's just an old wives' tale though, isn't it?' said the woman, looking less certain than she sounded. 'Nothing about a bad atmosphere that a good airing can't cure.'

'I wouldn't be so sure,' Margaret said. 'There's something about that place that can't be shifted with a bit of an airing. There's plenty that's tried.'

The woman made a noise that could have been assent or disgruntlement, Gil wasn't sure.

'Had to make do with a bit of a vacuum, Gwen said. Well, it would be. Damp, I mean. Been empty for years. Decent-sized place though. Terrible waste, if you ask me.'

No one did, Gil noticed, but that didn't stop her.

'People today, they're spoilt. A place hasn't got as many bathrooms as bedrooms, they're not interested. Someone should gut it, turn it into flats. That'd sort it.

'Two pound thirty-four love,' she said, without breaking off her monologue to serve the customer before Gil. There was no disputing this one was a walker. His two-pound-thirty-four's worth of boiled sweets and bottled water should have been clue enough. If not, his hiking boots, cagoule in traffic stopping orange, green rucksack and 'stupid pole' certainly were.

'And how are you today, Mr Markham?' Margaret put on her best voice, as if Gil hadn't been listening to her regular one for the past five minutes.

'Not bad, thanks. And it's Gil,' said Gil, as he had repeatedly since he moved back to the village where he'd been born. He dumped his shopping on the counter, the barricade from behind which – day in, day out – Margaret Millward held court.

'Twenty B&H?' she went on, as if he hadn't spoken.

'Please.' He nodded.

'Matches?'

He nodded again.

27

'What a place to stay,' Margaret Millward continued as she handed both over. 'Makes you wonder, doesn't it?'

No, Gil wanted to say. It really doesn't.

That was the problem with the village. One of many, in Gil's opinion. More with every passing day. God only knew how Jan had put up with it all those years. But then, she hadn't, had she? Or she'd still be here. Only now, two weeks into his retirement, was Gil finally beginning to understand why. Strange, if you thought about it, given how long he'd lived here. Although *living here* was a bit of an exaggeration, in light of the hours he worked and the weeks he spent in hotels covering conferences and strikes, train wrecks and natural disasters. Owned a place here then. Two cottages knocked into one, with the work overseen by Jan after they moved in . . . Gil caught an image of Jan, back in the day, pregnant with Karen, bloody great hole in the living-room wall, her and Lyn, six, maybe seven, knee-deep in brick dust, dust-smeared faces split by grins . . .

He pushed the thought down, hard.

More than half his life spent living in a place he hadn't really lived in, leaving in the dark and arriving home in the dark. Hardly surprising that he hadn't noticed what a bloody difficult place it was to go about your business without someone wanting to know what you were doing and why, and when you'd done doing it so they could ask questions about that. Some might find it endearing, comforting even. Gil didn't. Not now. Not ever.

And Jan certainly hadn't.

'Go indoors, shut the curtains, turn the light off, sneeze, and next time you go in The Stores someone will ask how your cold's doing.' He'd thought she was exaggerating the first time she said that. She wasn't. She was making a point. She'd been big on that. Unfortunately, he hadn't been big on listening. He should have noticed when the moaning stopped. Should have known it was a sign and not a good one. But he hadn't. And if he had, somewhere in the back of his mind when he got home gone eleven after a late shift, he decided to pay it no attention. He'd been glad of the peace. If he'd noticed, he might have realised she'd found someone who was listening. When she left, she took the kids. Well, Karen. Lyn had already gone. Best part of twelve years now. Gil could still remember Karen's face, dark-eyed and hopeless, staring from the rear window as Jan pulled away, barely glancing in her wing mirror to check the road was clear.

Back home, Gil boiled a kettle, loaded two heaped spoons of Nescafé into his biggest mug, added a healthy slosh of semi-skimmed and a heaped teaspoon of sugar and set himself up at the kitchen table with that day's papers. Years of night-editing meant he found fault with almost every one. Lazy, most of the headlines, predictable. He knew all about house style, but would it have killed them to make a bit more effort?

Reading this lot wouldn't take long. An hour at most, and that was stretching it. He'd never been so aware of time crawling as he was now. Never had enough hours in the day before this; always hurtling somewhere, always promising to be somewhere he wasn't, always late, always letting someone down. Not any more. He'd tried taking the kitchen clock from the wall. The ticking bugged him, that and the fact Jan had bought it, like most things in the house. But it left a dark ring of dust round a faded yellow circle and he couldn't be bothered to repaint the wall, so he'd ended up putting it back. The little hand on the ten and the big hand on the one.

Five past ten.

Ten oh five.

Ten a.m. and five minutes.

Six minutes now.

One hour and fifty-four minutes until The Bull opened.

'Looking smart today, Gil – hot date, is it?'

Gil gave his suit the obligatory glance, shrugged as if surprised to find himself wearing it, and forced a grin. 'You never know,' he told the landlord. 'Ready for anything, me.'

'Usual, is it?' Without waiting for the answer, Ray turned to reach for a pint jug. It wasn't a question. Any more than the comment on Gil's suit had been. Dark blue, pinstripe, the suit was one of three Gil wore in rotation. Always had done. He'd contemplated casual the day after he got his all-singing, all-dancing bloody Timex; contemplated it for about three and a half seconds and still couldn't believe it took that long. Gil was a suit man and always had been. He looked like someone's dad in a pair of jeans, and those chino things were worse. He'd decided right there and then he'd be buried in one of his suits; and there wasn't a damn thing anyone could do about it because suits were all he owned. Let them laugh, propping up the bar in their Pringle jumpers.

It was the same every day. The suit, the gag, the pint of Sam Smith's.

Gil forced himself to relax. This was life now.

Assuming he wasn't about to take an old geezer's gap year, and he wasn't. Gap years were for kids who didn't know better and rich pensioners, ditto, and people who liked their adventures carefully orchestrated. Gil was none of those. There was always golf . . . If he had a tenner for every time one of this crowd suggested he join them at the nineteenth he could afford to take that gap year. That said, hell would freeze over before he was the proud owner of a V-neck sweater and a five iron. Time to get used to it.

Put up or shut up.

The Bull was filling up. It was a nice enough pub, not a bad place to call your local, not bad at all. A picturesque pub in a picturesque village on the edge of the picturesque Dales. It had enough oak beams to make for a pretty postcard and Ray wasn't above a few horse brasses, if that's what the tourists wanted. He also wasn't above sticking a few pence on the price if he didn't recognise you. What the incomers didn't know wouldn't hurt them.

There was brisk trade in B&B and bar snacks. Looking round, Gil could see a fair few strangers now. The usual mix of sightseers stopping off for a pub lunch on their way to or from the abbey and walkers on their way to see the Scar or on their way back from it. Then there were 'the regulars'. The lunchtime regulars differed from the evening ones. They were older, for a start; retired locals with or without 'the missus'. Gil knew them by sight. Some of them he knew better than that. When Jan was still around he'd been to their houses; the obligatory dinner parties, anniversary celebrations, alcohol-fuelled New Year's Eves, when he hadn't been able to wangle a late shift. All that stopped when Jan left him. Whether they'd stopped inviting him or whether he'd just stopped bothering to go without her to bully him, he wasn't sure. A bit of both, probably.

Gil took his pint, his suit and his paperback – Rankin today, only one more to go and he'd be done with Rebus and have to find a new curmudgeon to spend his days with – to an armchair in the corner, as far away from tourists as possible. Through the rain-streaked window, he could see his usual table, standing empty in the corner of the courtyard; wood sodden, fag butts swimming, he was sure, in the brewery ashtray put there by Ray in a futile attempt to stop Gil grinding his stubs out on the cobbles. Far enough away from others not to have to make small talk, close enough for people watching.

He caught himself: usual table.

Christ on a bike, he'd be getting a hobby next.

4

She didn't sleep that night, not really. Nor the next. Each night passing broken and jumpy, pitched on the very edge of the promise of sleep until a moaning joist or yawning floorboard dragged her back from welcome darkness just as she threatened to slide over. The yelp of a fox or whatever other animals haunted the Dales, the scraping of a branch and the scrabbling of tiny rodent claws in the rooms above her head, made her start and turn uneasily, neither fully awake nor asleep. On the plus side, no sleep meant no nightmares.

Sometime in the middle of the third night – or was it the fourth? Helen had lost all track of time – the rain eventually stopped. Perversely, when it did, she was finally napping, caving to exhaustion in the neither-one-thing-nor-the-other hours before dawn. The first she knew was when she emerged from an uneasy doze to a cracked ceiling moulding flushed pink through a triangle in the curtains. The jaundiced light of the previous mornings ousted by its healthier outdoorsy younger cousin. From the leaf-stuffed gutters outside her window the occasional drip of water on to stone slabs below. Nothing more.

She'd never bought that red sky in the morning shepherd's warning business. Waking to a pink-tinged sky always gave Helen hope and, in spite of everything, today was no different. Within seconds she was up, floral quilt kicked to the floor, rotting curtains thrown wide, the Dales blushing under her gaze.

Suddenly, she had to be outside. There was something freeing about slipping into trainers and turning your back on everything. Optimism surged through her as she rifled in the carrier bags that still contained her new running kit. Without stopping to think, without checking the time, she ripped carelessly at the tags that swung from her new running bra, cheap knee tights and wicking top, and slid her feet into the trainers, wishing she hadn't forgotten to get socks, and grabbed the door keys from the floor beside the bed where she'd left them after her final midnight tour of the house.

In less than a minute Helen was out of the house and halfway down the gravel drive, not so much as a backward glance when the door crashed to, rebounded and then clicked shut behind her. At the end of the drive, she turned left, away from the village, and ran squinting into the low sun. The road was quiet, not even the distant growl of traffic. She was used to running on urban roads, with no real protection from the traffic, but even here, in this relatively remote part of the country, she didn't fancy meeting a lorry head-on. It was half a mile before she came to a gap in the drystone wall that would let her into the rocky fields. Clambering over the stile, Helen felt her knee complain. She hadn't run for more than a week and she hadn't stretched properly, or at all, before she left Wildfell.

'Serves me right,' Helen thought as she felt the muscles in her calves tighten and a familiar burning begin at the front of her thighs. So what if the fresh air bit at her still-sore lungs? Ignoring the aches, she ploughed on, something remote and forgotten flickering to life inside her, the hint of a smile playing on her face.

These new aches were her aches. No one else put them there.

Despite the early sun, the air was chill, freezing the sweat on her shoulders and spine. The sky hung low overhead, but the horizon promised a bright day and the stony fields were drier underfoot than she'd expected; the air cleaner and clearer than any she'd breathed for a long time. Maybe it was the break in the weather, or the surge of euphoria that often came with the departure of a migraine. Maybe it was simply the exercise, the sense of purpose and structure that running always gave. Whatever, her optimism wouldn't be suppressed.

Don't get carried away, Helen told herself. Things that were easily given were just as easily taken away. It was only a sunrise, after all. One pretty sunrise meant nothing.

For an hour, Helen ran. Slightly unsteady, at first, then gaining confidence, she kept the sun in her sights so she could turn her back on it to find her way home. It wasn't an easy run, the fields far from smooth, but she'd done tougher. Strangely, the rockiness helped; as she ran, increasing her strides to keep pace with the landscape, her thoughts were reduced to nothing but the ache in her muscles, the pumping of her lungs, where to place her feet and how to navigate boulders and rocks without losing pace. You can do this, said the endorphins seeping into her bloodstream.

You can do this.

Her calves and thighs now burned in earnest. Her punishment for failing to warm up properly would be harsh, but there was no point stopping to stretch now. Sweat marbled the top that had claimed it would wick sweat away and her newly dyed hair was plastered to her forehead. Putting her hand up, Helen was relieved to see the sweat came away clear.

It was only when the road was far to one side and she felt confident she was alone – no walkers, climbers or birdwatchers in this early morning world – that, for the first time in a very long time, longer than she could bear to consider, Helen realised she felt entirely safe. Ahead was a long low cliff jutting from the dale. Looking closer, Helen recognised the rock from the painting above the fireplace in the upstairs drawing room; the rock on which the boy in the bedroom portrait stood. The Scar, according to a little brass plaque fixed to the painting's frame.

Part from superstition, part for luck, she ran up the sloping grass. From this side, the cliff was deceptive, the dale rolling and surging benignly, like the back of a sleeping giant. Only the occasional cluster of boulders puncturing the grass as the Scar rose beneath her feet.

Helen knew she must look like hell but she didn't

care, she felt better than she could remember. The endorphins were doing their work, flushing out the last of her migraine, reducing the nausea to a memory. Slowing to a halt, she dropped forward, resting palms on bare knees and watched sweat drip from her newly tawny fringe and spread a Rorschach blot on rocks at her feet.

Several minutes passed as she hung there. Not looking, not thinking, just breathing. And listening.

She'd expected total silence out here on the Dales, but she was wrong. In the near-distance a crow called and overhead the shadow of something wheeled far above. She didn't know enough about birds to recognise it; but she knew hawks wheeled. Several fields away, black-faced sheep bleated. Behind her, she felt, rather than saw, a small shadow shift. Then it was gone. Another bird, probably, moving quickly overhead. Everything else was still and, gradually, her heart rate eased and her breathing slowed.

When eventually she righted herself, the landscape took her breath away. A handful of paces in front of her the ground dropped away, plummeting perilously. In the distance was the crag that gave the village its name. Somewhere in the opposite direction loomed the skeleton of an ancient priory. At least, according to the old guide-book she'd found in a drawer at the house. It was well beyond her vision, though. This bit of the Dales was famous. People came from far and wide to see it, which was why she'd chosen it. Just another tourist, as far as anyone else was concerned, albeit one staying longer than most and a little further out of the way.

*　　*　　*

The idea solidified on her run back to the house. She badly needed Internet access, a new email address, possibly several. She needed to teach herself to appear to be someone else. She'd seen people do it often enough. It couldn't be that hard. What she needed – what she should have bought before leaving London – was one of those three-month so-many-gigabytes pay-up-front things you could slot into a laptop. Something anonymous. Art had known about stuff like that. Using a virtual private network to tunnel safely through filters and blocks and leave no traces. If he could learn it, then so could she.

It all seemed so obvious; Helen couldn't believe she hadn't thought of it earlier. Mentally she thumbed through the cash she'd sewn into the lining of her rucksack. There was enough there for a few more months, if she was careful. She'd need a car, something very cheap and short-term, bugger-all MOT and turn a blind eye to the insurance. And a vaguely decent phone. Not the pay-as-you-go flip-top handset that had been the very cheapest she could find at the time. If she wasn't choosey she could probably stretch to a laptop too, something basic, to upload her pictures. They'd all come with her, on a couple of USB drives at the bottom of her camera bag, along with the old 35 mm Leica, a present from her dad for her twenty-first, and a tiny digital Canon point-and-shoot she'd bought on a whim passing through some airport or other.

Behind her the sun split the horizon. Still tinged with pink, still auguring ill for shepherds. Searching for a hint of warmth on her skin, she turned and watched as the black speck that was the hawk wheeling endlessly in the distance suddenly came to a halt. For a split second he was hanging there, an almost invisible speck in the sky, then he plummeted, dropping hard and fast on his unsuspecting prey.

5

The new tenant of Wildfell House didn't show up. Of course she didn't. Gil had known she wouldn't. Why would she? He was disgusted with himself for even being there, let alone noticing who else was.

'This is what you've come to,' he muttered, as he made his way back up the empty high street to his cottage five pints later. 'The village sodding social. And you didn't even have the excuse of writing about it. You'll be signing up for the WI next.'

He lit his last remaining cigarette and inhaled sharply. There'd been a large turnout tonight. Gil had been surprised to push open the door to The Bull at 6.45 p.m. and find the lounge bar already heaving with people who'd more usually be tucked in front of the television with the last of supper on their knees, wondering if they could get the washing up in before *Corrie*. There was not a chance of claiming his usual table, not a chance of any table at all.

Unusually large and unusually prompt, according to the gossip Gil eavesdropped on as he waited at the bar to be served. Catching Ray's eye over a cluster of women, most of whom he hadn't seen before – middle-aged, middle-weight, middle-height, middling smart; just middling, not, Gil feared, that he was one to talk – he signalled for his usual.

'Busy tonight.' He was starting to get the hang of small talk. Never been any good at it with the suits, and not that good at it now. But he was learning. *Typical*, Jan would say, just when it's not important any more you decide to bother. Gil shrugged inwardly. If it got him his pint ahead of the others . . .

'Always packed on social night.' Ray tipped the tankard and they both watched the opaque brown liquid slide down the inside of the heavy glass. 'Didn't expect to see you, mind. Not really your thing?'

It was framed as a question but Gil knew no answer was expected. They both knew why he was there. The same reason the others had turned out. Idle curiosity in most cases. Active, intense curiosity in the case of Margaret Millward. Tonight was special. A one-off. They were hoping for a guest of honour, the mysterious new woman up at the big house.

'Mr Markham, what a pleasant surprise!'

Sweeping his change from the bar, Gil pasted a smile on his face and turned his attention to the woman at the centre of the cluster wedged between him and the bar.

'Gil,' he said. 'Please, Mrs Millward, call me Gil.'

'Gil,' Margaret Millward repeated. In her mouth his name sounded like a bad taste. She forced a smile of her own. 'I don't think you know Liza, do you . . . Gil?'

Shaking his head, Gil put out his hand to a small slim woman standing beside his interrogator. He didn't look at her properly, to be honest. More glanced in her general direction and smiled politely. He wouldn't recognise her even if they had met before. She looked utterly familiar and a total stranger; and not just because she'd obviously had her highlights done at the same hairdresser as every other woman in the village. Consequently her hair was the same ashy blonde over barely concealed grey. What was it they said? Blonde is the new blue rinse? To be fair, now he did stop and take her in, she was better-looking than her friends. Not like Jan, of course. Roughly Jan's age, though. Maybe two or three years younger. Quite smart too. Well turned out with a dark jacket over a fitted dress. Like she'd come straight from work.

'How do you do?' He tried not to stare over the top of her head; but a lifetime of being at least a foot taller than most women meant he couldn't help looking like he was feigning interest, even when he wasn't.

'We've met, actually,' Liza said, taking his hand and shaking it firmly enough to drag his attention down to her eye level. 'More than once. You won't remember.'

There was nothing to say. No point pretending otherwise.

'New Year's Eve, a few years ago, before . . .'

'Ah,' Gil nodded, saving her the trouble. 'Before my divorce.'

'No, actually, I was going to say before mine.'

'Oh, I didn't, uh . . .' Gil took refuge in his pint.

'Of course not. Why would you? Busy man, by all accounts.'

Gil raised his eyebrows. No need to ask by whose accounts. It was obvious. By the accounts of the woman standing next to her, smiling complacently. Margaret Millward was *this* far from patting her hair. One down, her expression said. And it suddenly dawned on Gil why she'd been so insistent he come. Nothing to do with the newcomer and everything to do with the divorcee standing directly in front of him. He was eligible-ish, slim-ish (instinctively Gil breathed in, hated himself for it), had his own house and most of his own hair. He was probably the only single man in the village under eighty who still fell into the 'Would' category, if he wasn't flattering himself. Turned out, he wasn't there for the entertainment after all. He was the support act.

The social started to thin out about eight, around about the time it became evident to everyone, even Mrs Millward, that the newcomer hadn't taken up her invitation. The usual conversations about golf, the parish council, and teenagers drinking cider and doing who knew what else behind the war memorial had dried up.

By nine, thank God, The Bull was back to normal.

The tables were dragged back to their usual positions in the corners and around the fake fire; a hard-core of evening regulars propped up the bar and a smattering of walkers tucked into assorted things with chips in baskets. Retro, they probably thought, little knowing The Bull had been doing things in baskets since Moses and wasn't likely to stop any time soon. Gil sat himself at his usual table, Liza's phone number scribbled on a bar

43

mat that dragged like a boulder in his jacket pocket. He hadn't asked, she'd offered, around the time she'd said she should be making a move and he'd said, 'See you again sometime.' Politeness, wilfully mistaken for intent. Social niceties always did get you into trouble in his experience. She seemed nice, it wasn't that. It was just that . . . Well, he wasn't looking.

'Well,' Mrs Millward's voice pulled Gil back, from the far side of the room where she nursed the same half-full glass of now warm white wine she'd been holding when he arrived. The same peach lipstick decorated the rim. 'I call that plain rude, don't you?'

'Maybe she didn't get the invitation,' her husband said gently.

Unlikely, Gil thought. For a second it looked as though Margaret agreed and was about to say as much, but then she relented.

'You could be right. I should have popped round again when she'd had a day or two to settle in. It's easy to get overwhelmed when you're new to a neighbourhood. Or she could simply have lost her way.'

Nobody pointed out that only one road ran through the village and the pub was on it. The same road that ran right past the gates to the big house. You could get lost, Gil supposed, but he couldn't for the life of him think how.

The next couple of days crawled by as most days had since the end of August. Gil got up with his alarm, as he did every day, dressed in his suit, as he did every day, and went to collect his regular order of milk, bread, papers, fags from the General Stores, as he did every day.

The only difference was the weather. Now the rain had finally stopped, the September mornings were growing darker, the evenings shorter, each day starting with dew and ending with an unexpected chill. He could see how giving up on things might happen. With nothing to make you, one day you might not bother to get up. Not until nine or even ten; and then the eight a.m. ritual would be broken. Would the suit be next? Just about flinging on his civvies in time for pub opening, barely managing to push a flannel round his face . . .

Yes, he could see how that could happen. A gradual erosion of routine that led . . . unintentionally his eye drifted to number 32. Since his wife had died, Bill's life had shrunk. The Bull was the atom at its heart. At noon Bill was at the door, waiting to be let in, back again at six. If the landlord didn't insist on keeping to the old hours, calling time at three Monday to Thursday, he'd probably never leave. As it was, Bill was always last out, drowning his dregs, calling for one more for the road and being gently refused.

Gil didn't examine too closely how he knew the minutiae of Bill's comings and goings, he just knew Bill made him uncomfortable.

Bill had kids, Gil knew that much. Presumably he still saw them. But why assume that? Gil had kids, but he wasn't exactly round Lyn's every weekend for tea. In fact, he'd be hard pushed to remember when he'd last seen her.

When he'd last heard from her.

Christmas, that would be. Plus a birthday card in May, the obligatory note saying you must drop over, you wouldn't recognise the kids, etc. . . . He never took it as a real invitation, hadn't for a year or two, maybe more. Then a text saying thank you for the kids' birthday cards (cheque for £50, recently raised from £40, accompanied by a feeling that probably wasn't enough and the definite sense he could no longer say with any degree of certainty how old they were).

Karen was another matter altogether. Gil didn't know where to start with her. He wasn't even 100 per cent sure what she looked like now; although since she'd been the spit of her mother as a little girl he imagined he could pick her out in a line-up. Truth be told, it depressed him just thinking about Karen. Oh, her mother knew her address . . . But then what? Turn up on Karen's doorstep and say he was sorry how things turned out? As far as he knew, he was no longer Dad to her. That honour went to the man who'd fed and clothed her for the past twelve years. 'The man who gave a damn.' That's how Jan put it the last time he phoned, her voice brittle, exasperated, done.

It was years ago now, but the damage, even then, was already done.

'Just get Karen,' he'd said for the third time in as many minutes, his hand gripping the receiver he'd used instead of his mobile so she couldn't screen his number. 'Just for five minutes. I haven't spoken to her for months.'

'Whose fault is that?'

'She could have called me. She's got hands, hasn't she? A mobile phone.'

Nothing. Silence. He didn't blame her. Didn't now, hadn't then.

'I just. Want. To speak. To my daughter.' His voice was rising, he couldn't help it, even though he knew the rest of the top table at the paper were pretending not to listen in.

The sigh on the other end, hundreds of miles away at the far end of the M1, must have been audible all the way to production. 'Well, she doesn't want to speak to you.'

And then, his big mistake. 'I have a right to speak to her. I'm her father.'

'She's sixteen. She gets to choose and she chooses not. You don't have any rights, not where she's concerned. And, even if you did, you're not her father, not any more. Kevin is. He's the man who gives a damn.'

The call ended with him standing at his office desk, breathing hard into the static of a dead line, his vision blurring and heart hammering as he thought of all the things he wanted to say. Like an idiot, not one of them was sorry. That conversation wasn't something he was proud of. Looking back, he wasn't sure how he'd let it happen. The same way he let everything happen, he supposed. Lost: one marriage and two children. One careless owner. It would take more than a Christmas card to put it right with Karen. God knew he'd tried that route enough times.

Up ahead, Gil saw Bill's familiar shape vanishing through The Bull's front door.

'Dot of twelve,' he muttered, side-swerving into the doorway of the General Stores. Sugar, that was it, he was out of sugar. If not sugar, something else. There had to be something he needed. Something that would stop him being through the door of The Bull five seconds after the local joke.

'It's not catching, you know,' Gil told himself. 'You can't get old and sad and unwashed and drunk by osmosis.' But he couldn't shake the fear that . . . Well, what if you could? He was only sixty-one. Bill Grimes had a good ten years on him, if not more. But somehow Gil was horribly afraid that Bill Grimes was his future. His ghosts of Christmases, springs, summers, autumns and pints yet to come. The spectre of the wreck Gil Markham could be if he didn't cave in and take up golf or book a cruise or do whatever it was retirees like him were meant to do to keep themselves sane.

Voluntary retirement, he thought bitterly. What a joke. Nothing bloody voluntary about it.

He bought sugar, in case he'd really run out, and a magazine about the Dales he hadn't seen before and suspected wouldn't be around for more than a couple of issues. Just as he was closing the door behind him, a battered Peugeot 205 squealed to a near halt. If there'd been a pavement the car would have mounted it. As it was, it lurched to a stop centimetres from his feet.

'What the . . .?'

'Sorry, sorry, sorry. I only just got this and its brakes don't seem to work very well.'

The young woman who threw open the driver's door, almost doing him a second injury, looked harassed, a bit like Lyn when she'd had her babies under each arm. Although this woman was minus babies. On second glance, she didn't look much like Lyn at all. For a start, Lyn was blonde, bottle-blonde these days, or had been last time he saw her, and this girl – woman, he corrected himself – had wavy brown hair to her shoulders, and freckles. She did have Lyn's slender build though, the same harassed air and perplexed V between her eyebrows that he'd already told Lyn would set into wrinkles with age. In her nondescript jeans, trainers and parka, without a scrap of make-up, she could have been ten years younger than his daughter. The lines radiating from her eyes suggested she was older.

'Or at all,' she added, as if she hadn't paused. 'Plus I'm a crap driver. And I hate cars.'

Gil started to smile, opened his mouth to tell her it really didn't matter, no one was dead, but she was already gone, pushing past him into The Stores as if working to a deadline. With nothing better to do, Gil followed.

'Back again so soon, Mr Markham?' Mrs Millward said it as if someone had pressed F8 on a computer keyboard and this was the default line. Gil forced a smile and was wondering whether he could be bothered to answer when he saw that she wasn't looking at him any more. Her mega-watt attention swivelling to the woman who'd entered ahead of him.

If Margaret Millward had been a teacher she'd have been one of those who could silence a class just by looking up from her desk. She had that effect now. Even Jeremy Vine, blaring from the radio behind the till, seemed to ratchet his voice down a little in defer-ence. 'Mademoiselle Graham?' There was a pause. A split second when every head in the shop – and there weren't that many – turned to look at the newcomer, then a beat, perhaps two, before he saw the woman's shoulders visibly tense through the thin fabric of her coat.

'It is, isn't it?' Mrs Millward's voice was triumphant. 'It's Mademoiselle Graham, the new tenant up at Wildfell. I knew we'd get to see you eventually.'

6

Who?

That was Helen's first thought.

She almost looked behind her, then she realised there was no need, everyone in the shop was transfixed by just one person: her.

As she opened her mouth and then closed it again, another thought occurred to her: How the hell did the woman know she was *her?*

Not that anyone with half a brain couldn't have worked it out by process of elimination, she supposed. Who she was, that is. But not what she looked like. How had this bossy little woman put two and two together and come up with Helen? In a village alive with passing traffic, which, for the past week, she had tried so hard not to be part of . . .

Not one to be put off, the woman kept staring pointedly. *Well?* said her expression. *Well?*

The small shop swam with faces. Helen felt the air constrict, her brain doing a go-slow while she tried to take them in. The blanking thing was an all too common occurrence these days. She couldn't think straight. But it was obvious which of the faces staring at her, watching and waiting, mattered. The busybody behind the till. Helen could tell just by looking that she – Margaret Millward, it had to be, she of the village social – was the very worst kind. Not harmless, that's for sure. Pathologically interested in other people's business; now examining someone pathologically interested in not being examined.

'*Oui*, madame,' she managed eventually.

Just her luck there were other people in the shop. Two old women, properly old, purple-tinged hair and dowagers' humps, both with wire baskets on flimsy wheel-along trollies. A young mum – young-ish, younger than Helen anyway – her old-school pram blocking one of three aisles. Then there was the man. The one she'd nearly run over outside. He was standing right behind her. Towering over her, not cowed by his own height, so she tried not to be. The fact he was lanky helped her not to tense. He was too close for comfort, but it wasn't his fault. In an attempt to physically remove herself as far as possible from Margaret Millward's orbit, she'd backed into his space. Close enough to see the pinstripe suit he wore was expensive, tailor-made. Close enough to see he wasn't as old as she'd first imagined. And close enough, she realised, for him to see how her fists had clenched, jagged nails cutting half-moons into the fleshy part of her palms.

'*Parlez-vous anglais?*' he asked.

The bossy woman behind the counter looked impressed.

Helen shifted from foot to foot, cursing herself inwardly. A loaf of bread for God's sake! Outed by a hankering for toast and Marmite. She should have been less greedy and stayed home, or less lazy and driven further. Either would have been better than this.

Margaret Millward was still looking at her, if anything, her curiosity piqued all the more by Helen's silence; head tilted to the side, ready to deploy sympathy and understanding the second Helen spoke.

What Helen wanted to say was, Fuck off. Mind your own business. She wanted to tell the woman where to stick her nose and her General Stores and her only loaf of bread and fresh milk for a five-mile radius. She didn't, of course. Hélène Graham wasn't a fuck-off kind of girl. She was *bon chic, bon gen*. Tough as nails, but with the *grandes écoles* manners of someone descended from someone with a metro station named after them.

Her Helen Lawrence fuck-you days were behind her.

'Yes!' she said brightly, ditching any pretence of a French accent. 'Fluently.' There was no point making life harder than it already was by having to pretend to speak pidgin English every time she ran out of milk.

It was as if the whole shop – even Jeremy Vine who'd been chatting to himself from the transistor behind the till – exhaled and started pretending to go on about its business; *pretending* being the operative word. They may no longer be looking, but Helen could tell every last one of them was listening. Even the man in the suit, who looked as if he'd escaped from an episode of *Yes, Minister* and wandered into *Emmerdale* by mistake.

'You must be Mrs . . .' Helen paused, pretending to search for a name that was on the very tip of her tongue if she could only . . .

'Margaret, dear,' Mrs Millward said, as Helen had known she would. They always did, her type. 'Margaret Millward. But you should call me Margaret.'

To her right, the man's shoulders shook and then he sneezed, a fake little atishoo, Helen thought, forced out, too little too late. 'Bless you, Mr Markham,' said the woman.

'Thank you,' he muttered.

At least, Helen thought that was what he muttered.

'We were very sorry not to see you, dear,' Margaret Millward said slowly, clearly determined to persist in her idea that Helen could not understand.

Helen stared back, trying to keep her face blank. Confused was the look she was after, but rude would do. Anything was better than what she felt, which was thirteen all over again and trapped in the school loos by one of those girls who had the teachers believing butter wouldn't melt. They were everywhere, life's Margaret Millwards: plaguing infants' schools and colleges, offices and school gates – who knew, probably nursing homes too. The type who, when you met them for the first time, looked you up and down, taking you in head-to-toe, every hair out of place, every scrap of mud on your boots, every stain you thought successfully sponged off. That type, thought Helen, but Margaret Millward's interest felt more dangerous. She wasn't looking for mud and split ends and smudged mascara. She was looking for the cracks below the surface. Although, God knows, Helen thought, there should be enough cracks on the surface to keep her going.

'I'm sorry,' Helen said, when it became clear that she was about to lose her second face-off of the week. 'You were expecting me?'

'Thursday evening.'

'I'm sorry?' she repeated.

'I sent you a letter. An *invitation*.'

Helen rearranged her face into its best imitation of sudden recognition. 'The blue letter?'

The woman nodded, looking halfway between exasperated and intrigued.

'Ah. I'm sorry,' Helen said. 'I didn't realise . . . The rain . . . it was destroyed. The ink was unreadable. My headaches were too bad. When they come I just have to lie in a darkened room and wait for them to pass.' Understatement of the year, but broadly true.

'Oh, you poor thing. You should have said. Shouldn't she have said, Mary?'

One of the old women waiting at the till nodded vigorously.

'Have you got a mobile number?' Mrs Millward asked. 'Might be useful for someone else around here to have it. In case you need anything. If you get headaches a lot, I mean. You don't want to be stuck out there in that huge house on your own, with no food or company. What if you need help? It's not as if you'd be able to drive, and it would be no trouble. Honestly, no trouble at all.'

Helen had to admit she was impressed. In another life this woman would have made a great journalist, of a certain kind.

'Thank you, but there's really no need,' she said. 'The signal out there is hopeless. But thank you, so much. That's very thoughtful of you. Really, though . . . when they come – the headaches, I mean – there's nothing anyone can do to help. I just have to stay in bed and get better. And eating . . .' Helen made a face that she hoped made it clear they would not want to know what effect eating might have. 'Eating is the last thing on my mind.'

Margaret Millward nodded reluctantly before saying brightly, 'Well, now you've found us, I hope we'll see you in here much more often.'

Recognising an order when she heard one, Helen pasted on her most polite smile. 'I'm sure you will.'

'And you will come to the next social, won't you?' Mrs Millward said, pressing her advantage as Helen sidled towards the bread shelf. Sliced white or sliced white. After all that, any locally baked loaves – assuming there had ever been any – were long gone.

'Of course,' she said, picking up a local paper and putting it down again. Instead she replaced it in her pile with a large bar of Galaxy and balanced a box of Rice Krispies on top. 'When is it?'

'First Thursday of the month,' the woman said, almost sharply, as if repeating the same instruction for an inattentive small child. Then she softened. 'But don't worry about that now. It's much too far away to remember. I'll drop a note through your door nearer the time. I'll bring a cake and we can have a cup of tea.'

With her heart beating against her ribs like a bird trying to fight free of its cage, it took Helen another five minutes to extricate herself.

Finally free, she flung her shopping on to the passenger seat. It took three goes to fire the engine into life and, when it started, it sounded like a bastard cross between a tractor and a motorbike. Still, what did she expect for £300 and less than six months left to run on the MOT? She'd taken the handbrake off and had it in gear when one of the old women barrelled out of the shop door and wheeled her trolley straight in front of the car.

Shit! Helen slammed her foot on the brakes, grateful that this time they worked. Mind you, the way she felt right then, an old lady or two would have been justifiable collateral damage.

The vein in her temple throbbed ominously. She couldn't face going straight back to the house. Huge as it was, it was still too confining. Even the thought of walls made her feel claustrophobic.

Helen had never been a popper inner, for tea or otherwise. Home was a sanctuary. Wasn't that the theory? A place you were supposed to be free from other people; their presence and their opinions. Even if it didn't feel that way to you – and Helen couldn't honestly say it ever had; except, maybe, once, for a short time as a small child – you had to respect people who did. Regardless of whether their home no longer had a roof or a ceiling or a front door, and there was a hole in the wall where the window used to be, and a pile of rubble in what remained of the kitchen, the overwhelming reek of cordite to remind them that this would never really be a home again. Despite all that, you could stand on the street and watch what was left of a family huddled together over a pan of boiling water, trying to rebuild some semblance of normality, some sense of home.

Not now.

Helen shook the image from her head. Even if she had known where home was, she couldn't imagine ever being there again.

The little Peugeot sped past the house without pausing. It clearly had no intention of pulling in, even if Helen had. But she felt no calling, no lure of kettle or sofa. None of the emotions that people often told her they associated with home. It was just a house, sprawling and empty. With little but climate, local language and location to distinguish it from other ruins she'd inhabited.

At the next T-junction the car took a right turn to Harrogate almost before she'd had a chance to decide. It was a bit of a drive but it wasn't as if she was short of time. She could stop there for the afternoon. Helen tried to picture herself buying a book and sitting in a tea room reading it, whiling away several hours eating toasted teacake and drinking Earl Grey from a proper cup and saucer, probably white and adorned with flowers, the sort of fine bone china you could bite through. Wasn't that the kind of thing people used to do? The kind of thing plenty of people still did, without smartphones or one eye constantly on the news sites?

She could picture the scene. She just couldn't picture herself in it.

At the crossroads for the abbey the car made up her mind for her and took the opposite turn. Whether it was the car or Helen, suddenly she knew she didn't need tea and cake and more people to watch. She didn't need smaller, she needed bigger. Something far bigger, far older, more significant than her.

*   *   *

She entered the village from the south, passing a caravan park and a car park, a hot-dog kiosk, a café-cum-gift shop, and a tawdry concrete block of public conveniences. The indisputable ugliness that tourism inevitably spawned. Clearly this wasn't the remote ruin she'd been hoping for. But the weather gods were watching over her and, as the Peugeot pulled into a space, the mizzle that had hung over the Dales all morning hardened its resolve, sending brightly coloured cagoules scattering for their coaches.

Shoving the ancient guidebook to Yorkshire into the glove compartment, Helen tossed the hood of her parka over her frizz, put her head down and beetled across the emptying tarmac into the village that surrounded the abbey. If her guidebook had been printed in the last century, not the one before, she might have known the priory was no longer the remote thousand-year-old ruin it described but the beating heart of a tourist centre, pumping the blood of outsiders and their credit cards around the surrounding villages and into the arteries of the Dales.

The priory, like the village that bore its name, and the countryside shrouding it, was schizophrenic. The face it showed the village was a working parish church, all neat grey stone façade, scrubbed and polished, surrounded by clipped lawns. More village green than thousand years of history.

There were no ghosts here. She should have been relieved.

Passing a blackboard bearing the legend, *Guided Tours 11 a.m. and 3 p.m.*, Helen glanced at her watch. It was nearly two. Lucky, she was between tours.

Beyond the sign, she skirted the abbey's soaring façade and ducked under a weathered buttress. As she cut around the side of the abbey, pristine stonework gave way to crumbling panels open to slate-grey sky. Here were the remains the guidebook had promised: a grand building left to decay after the dissolution of the monasteries in 1539. Its destruction accelerated by the valley's inhabitants who decided, not unreasonably Helen felt, that a deserted priory's stone could be put to better use in their own walls.

A last, bedraggled group of tourists hurried past, so bent on their search for somewhere dry to wait for the next tour that they hardly seemed to notice her. Perhaps the khaki of her parka rendered her invisible against the stone, compared to the primary reds, blues and yellows they were used to. Good. She'd had enough of people for one lifetime.

Tucking a stray strand of hair into her hood, Helen stuffed her hands in her pockets and walked into the squall. Back here, swept under the priory's neatly vacuumed carpet, were the jagged teeth of a ruin. Centuries of rain and snow had exposed the building's intestines to the elements, leaving them vulnerable and bruised. Arches soared skywards, their skeleton stripped bare of most of what made the building live.

The surrounding countryside was equally unpredictable: to the south the moors, to the north the Dales. One minute gently rolling hills and undulating greenery, almost chocolate-box pretty; the next rocks jutting through thin earth like bone, waters broiling a sinister stew in dark pools beneath. In front of her, tombstones tumbled like broken teeth before the graveyard dropped away towards the river.

Just as well. She wasn't looking for pristine.

Lining the walls of what little remained of the abbey's heart was a row of erratically spaced benches, dark with recent creosote, the kind of wooden two-seaters that littered suburban parks and riverbanks all over northern Europe. Clambering over a half-collapsed wall, Helen wandered idly amongst them. Up close, she could see they were scattered with dedications, the formal graffiti of engraved brass plaques screwed to the back of the seats.

Mary, 1910–2003, much missed.
For Margaret and Albert, together now as then.
This seat is dedicated to Ethel who sat here every day,
whatever the weather . . .

Ethel's bench was slick with rain, but Helen sat anyway, feeling the water soak the seat of her jeans, and gazed across the Dales in respectful silence. Was this the same view that Ethel had seen 'whatever the weather'? Who, if anyone, would dedicate a bench to her if she died? A year ago, even six months, she might have known the answer to that question. But now?

Closing her eyes, Helen took several long, deep breaths until she felt her heart begin to slow. Then she tucked her face as far back under her hood as her neck would allow. Invisible was a look she'd worked hard to perfect over the years. Professional necessity, personal choice. But she couldn't keep saying later, later had come and gone. It was time. Following one last, expensive taxi-ride to Bradford, the one that had made her the fifth careless owner of the battered Peugeot with questionable brakes and bugger-all MOT, she now had a second-hand MacBook and three USB dongles with enough pre-paid data to last a few months, plus a reconditioned iPhone she'd persuaded the laptop owner to throw in for another fifty. Tonight she would set up a VPN and go online.

Seized with sudden decisiveness, Helen fumbled in her pocket for her pay-as-you-go mobile and, before she had time to think – before she even had time to be surprised to find a signal out here – she keyed in a familiar number and pressed *call*, striding away through the ruins as she did so, stepping over a knee-height fence into the old cemetery and starting to walk in tight patterns through the gravestones.

'It's me,' she said when her sister answered. And then held her breath for what might come next.

'Helen!' Fran cried. 'Thank God!'

For a few seconds, all Helen could hear from the other end of the phone was someone taking several sharp, shallow breaths. She closed her eyes, listening as the breathing slowed. 'Fran,' she said eventually. 'Fran? Are you OK?'

'I didn't know. We didn't know . . . I mean, we knew there was a fire at the flat . . . and then you didn't call and we didn't know where you were . . .' Her sister stopped, suddenly composed. 'Where are you?'

Once a big sister, always a big sister.

'Resting,' Helen said. 'I just called to let you know I was OK.'

'OK? How can you possibly be OK?'

Now the initial shock had passed, Helen felt Fran's relief ebb away to be replaced by the lifetime's irritation that simmered between them. Whether separated simply by a dining table or whole continents and life choices, the friction had always been there. Twenty years on, more, the list of grudges was endless. Stolen Barbies, a broken Girl's World with blue Biro eyebrows, smashed Lego houses and vanishing homework blurred together with scoldings for crusts uneaten, lip gloss shoplifted and tittle-tattle told.

Were all siblings like this?

'Where are you?' Fran repeated.

'Just away, resting, like I said.' Helen meant it to sound reasonable, but it didn't come out that way. Instead she sounded petulant, bratty. The little sister she was.

'I didn't mean . . . geographically,' Fran was trying for conciliatory. 'I meant . . . You sound . . . echoey. And I can hear water.'

'I am by water,' Helen said. 'A river. Plus it's raining.'

It was, pouring now, a chill wind clawing at Helen's hood and driving rain into her cheeks. Her fingers had cramped around her handset, their tips white with cold. She examined her nails and listened to her sister's irritation on the end of the line. Not blue, her fingernails, not yet. If they turned blue she was in for another migraine. She shouldn't have let herself think about the fire. Not yet.

'Go inside then,' said Fran. 'You'll catch your death.'

Helen smiled.

'Yes, Mum.'

Fran smiled back. Helen could hear it. She was sure she could.

'I've been trying to get hold of you,' Fran said. 'I emailed dozens of times, and called, but your mobile's dead.'

'I lost it. This is a replacement.'

'You could have rung.'

'What do you think I'm doing?' Helen shrugged. The rain had crept inside her hood and was trickling down her neck. She cast around for shelter, but the ruins she'd been so enamoured with offered none. She tried to remember why she'd called.

'The police came round,' Fran said suddenly.

'The police?' Helen's voice was a whisper.

'They went to Mum's,' Fran said. 'They wanted access to your dental records and she called me. Helen, she was in a terrible state. We all were.'

'What did they say?' Helen asked, eventually. 'The police, I mean.'

She heard Fran take a deep breath. 'Helen, they said they'd found a body. She told them you couldn't have been there. You and Art had separated. Although we all hoped it wasn't permanent . . .'

Helen forced herself not to respond.

'That's what the concierge told them too. Well, that you'd moved out. And Monsieur was away somewhere. She didn't know where. That's why it's taken so long, apparently. The police just assumed the place was empty. And then they cleared the rubble and found . . .' Several hundred miles away Fran swallowed.

'Helen?'

'Uh-huh.'

'I don't think they think it was an accident.'

Closing her eyes, Helen tried to shake the fog that had clouded her brain since that night two weeks earlier. All she could see was an orange glow, the outline of a body slumped awkwardly in a corner, hear the brown noise of electrics crackling.

'Helen . . .?'

Helen swallowed hard. Tried to focus.

'They said that?'

'They wanted to know if Mum had heard from you. Don't you understand? It's been weeks since we heard. I told them that, you know, you travel a lot and sometimes go months without making contact. So if a week or two passed, well, that's you. But then we have the police on the doorstep asking about dental records, saying your – I mean Art's – flat burnt down a fortnight ago and no one's seen either of you since. Where have you been?'

When Helen finally found her voice, it came out small, more afraid than she'd have liked. 'Somewhere safe,' she said.

7

It played on Gil's mind all through lunch and for the rest of that afternoon.

Not so much his brief exchange with the French girl. *Woman*, he corrected himself. It had been made pretty clear to him over the years that women didn't much like being called girls; not by middle-aged-plus-a-bit men anyway. The girls at the paper told him he was patronising, even though he'd hear them refer to themselves that way seconds later. It wasn't so much Mademoiselle Graham's evident discomfort at Margaret Millward's forensic gaze. Who wouldn't be on edge finding themselves the centre of attention when they'd only gone out for a pint of milk? Although even then her discomfort had been extreme.

It was the conversation afterwards.

It didn't require investigative skills to tell she was thrown by the encounter. She dropped the bread when she opened the shop door, dropped the chocolate when she picked up the bread and took three attempts to start her wreck of a car. And then she stalled. Although that probably had more to do with her near collision with old Maude Peniston's trolley.

Even Margaret Millward wasn't that stress-inducing.

Frankly, Gil was irritating himself. He'd long since given up trying to read his book. It was new and he wasn't yet into it. Just a couple of chapters and he'd had to read both of those twice. He'd switched from Ian Rankin to Denise Mina when he'd run out of Rebus. Swapping Edinburgh for Glasgow mainly because of a Rankin quote on the cover. But he was doing that irritating thing of reading the same page over and over. Seeing the words while being too preoccupied to take them in.

On his third go, he gave up, downed his pint, wrapped his scarf around his neck, tucked the paperback into his pocket and raised a parting hand to Ray. Outside, he turned right instead of left. There was nobody about apart from an occasional car, but he made a point of not looking up as he headed out of the village. Someone would have noticed the break in his routine, he was sure of that. One of the twitchers. They'd doubtless grill him about it later. He wasn't about to encourage them by making eye contact.

With his long legs and loping cross-country stride it took less than ten minutes to reach the stile he wanted and veer off on a track signposted for walkers. If he kept moving at this rate he'd be deep in the Dales in under half an hour. Gil gave an involuntary shiver. He'd also be drenched. He wasn't dressed for hiking. Not remotely.

His suit shrieked office and though his well-worn brogues were more than up to the challenge, hiking wasn't the job for which they'd been made.

The drizzle was hardening, the wind growing squally and the cloud coming so low Gil felt he should hunch, or un-hunch completely and stand his full height and let the nimbus scrape his head at the point where his hair was thinning. Common sense said turn back; but Gil had no intention of listening to common sense. He needed to think. Indoors was hopeless. He felt . . . confined. More so, since the cottage was empty. The rooms were too small, the ceilings too low; he'd like to moan that the walls were too thin but, having seen the thickness of the walls Jan had taken a hammer to, he knew the only way you'd hear easily through that would be to tunnel through it. Hunching his head further into his neck, his neck into his shoulders, he pressed on, ignoring the give beneath his soles.

The gossip had been predictable enough, at least to start with.

'Well, what a piece of luck,' Margaret Millward was saying. 'If Mademoiselle Graham hadn't come in we'd never have known our invitation was destroyed.'

What was with all the *we*? Gil wondered. It was Margaret's social, Margaret's invitation, Margaret's injured feelings. As if anyone else gave a toss.

People's ability to believe what they wanted despite all evidence to the contrary never failed to astonish him. It was one of the things that had made his job so easy when he'd been a reporter. Self-delusion, a journalist's best, not to mention cheapest, friend.

'Hard to believe she's been living here over a week and

she's not passed through before,' said the woman with the pram. Youngish, blondish, skin so pale it was bordering on transparent, her eyes rimmed with tale-telling dark circles of four hours' sleep and night feeds. Gil thought she might have been at school with one of his daughters. Mind you, that went for nearly every woman in the village between twenty-five and thirty-five.

When he'd been gainfully employed he'd lived here for years without passing through. He could see the attraction.

'Looks like she decided against bringing the child then,' Mrs Millward said suddenly. That got everyone's attention firmly back where she liked it.

Child? Gil looked at her, mouth open. Where the hell had she got that?

'Not sure where I heard it now,' Margaret Millward continued, as if reading his mind. 'Gwen got it from the letting agent, I think, something about a little boy. But I've heard no mention of it since. Good job too, if you ask me. No place for a child, that big old house . . . No place for anyone.'

'Do you really think it's haunted, Margaret?' The young woman gave an involuntary shudder as she emptied her purse on to the counter and started counting out change. 'I mean, if someone's actually seen something up there, shouldn't the estate agent have told her?'

'I don't think they're obliged,' the store owner said authoritatively. 'Not legally. But you'd think they'd have a moral duty, wouldn't you? Young woman on her own like that, ought to have all the facts. Especially paying six months up front like she did. She'll have a hell of a time getting her money refunded.'

There were murmurs of assent and several other women nodded.

Gil turned away and rolled his eyes. Not that old Wildfell is haunted shtick again. If it wasn't one thing, it was another. The things some people could concoct to pass the time.

With his back to the wind, Gil struck a match, cupped its guttering flame in his hand and sucked until tobacco flared orange. Then he inhaled. Deeply. Nothing tasted as good as an illicit fag with no one hovering on his shoulder to keep count.

The Scar wasn't an arduous climb from this direction, even with nicotine-drenched lungs and brogues not built for the occasion with leather soles that slid in mud. He was barely breathing hard. The approach had inclined gently, rising to a well-trod path with steps cut into the rear of the Scar, and kept useable by planks at the back of each step, held in place by short stakes at either end. As he crested the top, the Dales dropped away, their swoops and hollows speckled with the red, blue and yellow of ramblers' anoraks, interspersed with patches dotted with white where sheep clustered together against the weather.

On a clear day the view from the Scar was breathtaking, no matter how many times you saw it. Today he could barely see as far as the next valley. The rain was settling in for the duration now, splattering his glasses and plastering his hair against his scalp. Blinking away water, Gil removed his spectacles, wiped them with the inside of his scarf, held them up to his eyes and frowned. The smears were worse. Reluctantly he turned for home. He might have walked a few miles to clear his head but he wasn't getting anywhere with his problem. Whichever way he looked at it – and he'd looked at it every which way – the gossip made little sense, no matter how many times he replayed it. His disquiet was at more than village idiocy. It was his village, after all; he was allowed to dislike it.

The woman's level of awkwardness wasn't natural.

Well, people with that level of social fear didn't usually enter crowded shops from choice. Mostly they worked hard not to leave their homes.

Something about her was definitely off.

Gil ran through the earliest rumours that had swirled around the village: that she was a French film star come here to die, a rich and recovering Swiss drug addict, a landscape artist in search of solitude and new views. Living all alone in that dodgy old ruin out on the Dales certainly fitted with that last theory.

Gilbert shook his head, scattering the rain on to his lenses.

He was as bad as the rest of them.

As he headed down the slope, Gil cursed the gossip for putting ideas into his head. Cursed himself for listening. But he kept playing the scene in his head one last time, from her near-failure to stop that ruin of a car to her panic at finding herself the centre of attention and not being able to start the car again. He was looking for a variation, a detail he hadn't noticed the previous five or six times he ran it through. Something that in the old days would have given him the story.

By the time he reached the main road the rain was coming down hard, puddles forming at the side where a pavement would be if there'd been one. Ordinarily,

Gil made a point of walking into the oncoming traffic. 'Better to see a lorry bearing down on you than only spot it when it hits you from behind.' That's what he used to tell his girls. And they'd roll their eyes, 'Da-ad.' And make who-is-he-and-why-did-you-marry-him faces at their mother. Today though, Gil hadn't bothered to cross. It entered his mind, but the puddles were worse that side, the road was deserted and his concentration was shot. Plus his suit was sodden, his brogues full of water and he wanted to be home with a whisky, maybe have a long soak and another shot at that novel. He patted his pocket. The paperback was sodden.

Why the gossip in the shop nagged at him, he didn't know. The certainty, he supposed. The willingness to construct stories without evidence. The way, these days, rumour became fact in seconds. *Stand it up*, that was what he'd been taught as a trainee: *why, who, where, what, when,* but above all *why.* That was what he'd passed on to the rookies on the news desk. Even if they did think he was an old fart for going on about it. Even if they did think Wikipedia counted as fact-checking.

Back. It. Up.

The gossips hadn't. They were simply certain. About the woman, about the haunted house, about everything.

Gil heard the car before he saw it. Only just though. He hurled himself into the hedge; grabbing a branch to stop himself going down, brambles scratching his wrists and tearing the knee of his ruined trousers. Something sharp swiped at his cheek as he fell and he felt rather than saw blood well to the surface.

'Fucking idiot,' Gil yelled as he pulled himself to his feet.

He waved a fist ineffectually at the back of the disappearing car. It was pouring now, the light failing and his suit was dark and getting darker the wetter it got. Only his hair was light and that was plastered to his skull. To be fair, the driver would have had little chance of seeing him, but that didn't lessen the pain in his knee. The car was shrinking away, moving into the dusk. Brake lights flared as it approached a bend and something in the rear windscreen caught Gil's eye. He squinted, whipped off his glasses, swiped at them, and squinted again.

'Gilbert, you silly old sod,' he muttered, as it vanished around the bend. 'Get a grip, get a hobby, get something.' All the same, he could have sworn he saw something – some*one*, a child, perhaps – staring at him from the back of the small, silver Peugeot.

8

By the time she arrived at the house, Helen was already regretting tossing the pay-as-you-go phone. It felt as if someone else had clicked the button to end the call, systematically removed the back of the phone, sliding out the battery and extracting the SIM, bending it this way and that until its spine snapped. On returning to her car, she'd reassembled the phone, turned it on and dropped it into a puddle, then extracted the battery, wiped both phone and battery on her sodden parka and tossed them into separate bins.

It had to be done. Helen loved her sister but she didn't trust her. And she was pretty sure the feeling was mutual. All it would take was one moment of weakness or moral rectitude, depending on your perspective. From Fran and Ian's perspective it would be the latter. It wasn't until she'd turned the key behind her in the lock and gone through her daily ritual of checking the doors and windows that Helen saw what should have been obvious out on the Dales: a smear, like golden jam, encroaching on her vision. Her fingernails, white earlier, were now turning blue.

'Bugger,' she muttered under her breath. Usually she had weeks, sometimes more than a month, between bouts of migraine. This time it was barely a week.

Pills. That was what she needed. If she was quick, she could head off the worst of it. Except the only pills she had were shop-bought and near useless.

The pills she needed were the ones Dr Harris gave her. (Ms Caroline Harris, she was a consultant now, dropping the *Doctor* the way consultants do.) Only the last of those was long gone. In the kitchen, the empty packet still lay on the counter where she'd tossed it in frustration days earlier. The pill fairies hadn't come in the night, it was just as empty as when she'd looked back then.

Removing her sodden parka, Helen hung it from the corner of the door to the pantry and lit the boiler, holding her hair behind her with her left hand as the match flared in her right. The gas gave a soft boom and at the edges of her vision, lightning crackled.

After the discoloration in her fingers the lights always came next. Usually she was too busy to notice until worse symptoms forced her to take heed. Her fingers, in the purple glow of the pilot light, looked waxy, a tallow yellow. Helen tried to calculate how long she had before the migraine really kicked in. As much as a day? Not at the rate this was moving in. Hours, more like. For an insane second she considered grabbing her camera and running kit and going back outside while a fraction of light remained. She'd taken some of her best pictures in this dead zone; pre-pain, post-sanity. Blurring vision, nausea and frozen fingers brought with them a remoteness that reversed the emotional binoculars she used to look at the world. What was ordinarily too close, close enough to terrify, became small and distant.

'Don't be stupid, Helen,' she muttered, imitating her mother. 'The last thing you need is to be out on the Dales, in the rain, in the full throes of a migraine without medication.'

Instead, she filled the kettle and made tea.

She'd made tea all over the world, usually as a way of thinking about something else. There was a mechanical and ritualised element to the British obsession with tea, Helen thought. It had started, her 'migraine thinking'. She never had these thoughts unless lights threatened the edge of her vision. Once they started she couldn't stop them until the full force of her migraine roared in. Then she'd shut her eyes, curl into a ball on her side and wait for the pain to stop.

She'd said exactly that to Caroline once. Caroline had given Helen one of her looks, before replying that when the time was right Helen might want to think carefully about what she'd just said.

Last time Helen looked, the time still wasn't right.

When the kettle had boiled, Helen took her mug and two pieces of hot buttered toast into the upstairs sitting room, using her laptop as the tray. She perched on a dust-stiff Indian throw on a rancid sofa in the upper drawing room of a decaying Elizabethan mansion and ate. There was a whole world of memories in the hot buttered toast.

Cut into fingers and then into quarters, with crusts on and crusts cut off. After memories of being given hot buttered toast after coming in from a wet and difficult day at the beach, and sitting next to Fran on the sofa and, for once, the two of them not arguing, and memories of eating it late at night in a road side café in Italy when she was covering riots and an election, came another. She was a teenager and her parents were out, Fran was at university, the house was Helen's, and the list of things she was forbidden to do was pinned to the fridge with an Anchor Butter magnet.

One of them stood beside her reading the list.

Tom Bretton.

She hadn't thought about Tom much over the last few years. Now he was in her thoughts constantly. She could still remember Tom's smile, ever so slightly lopsided, the way he made them a single piece of toast for breakfast, buttered it far more carefully than she would have bothered to and cut it neatly down the middle, while she made tea in two Greenpeace mugs they'd bought at a market stall the week before. Helen had done precisely what she'd been told not to do.

Gone to bed with Tom.

Nothing happened . . . Well, nothing beyond cuddling and the obvious. Nothing that would qualify as, *having done it*.

Half a piece of toast each was their breakfast.

Turning on the rusting electric fire Helen watched three bars glow fraudulently cheerful and wondered why it had taken her so long to remember. They'd broken up a few weeks later, just before exams. It was her choice. Looking back, she could remember the toast, Tom's Stone Roses T-shirt, the first time she'd understood the meaning of the phrase 'companionable silence'. But she couldn't remember why she'd ended it other than some stupid row about her being late, as usual.

As the fire heated up, the stink of burning dust took over and more dangerous memories flooded in. All Helen could see was that poisonous orange fog and the outline of a half-naked body curled away from her. Cracking the window open half an inch, she propped a book in the gap to stop it swinging shut, and felt damp and darkness flood in. Enough speculation. She needed to get online and find out for herself before the migraine made looking at a screen impossible.

As if sensing her urgency her second-hand Mac took minutes to crawl to life. Sliding one of her dongles into its USB slot, Helen drummed her fingers on its metal casing as she waited for it to connect. When it did, she typed **VPN** into Google and it offered a list of cheap providers. She clicked on the link for the first and realised cheap wasn't good enough. Cheap required PayPal or a credit card. She needed free. Five long minutes later, she'd found one.

After what seemed an unnecessarily fiddly process of installing, quitting open apps and double-clicking, an icon appeared on her desktop. Two more clicks and Helen was logged into the web through a VPN connection. Anyone looking – and there was no reason to assume anyone would be – wouldn't be able to see what she was looking at. Or, more importantly, where she was looking from. That was what Art had told her anyway, when she'd asked him why he bothered to file his copy from Iraq using one, instead of just sending it direct.

In the next fifteen minutes she had set up two anonymous mail accounts. She knew it was perverse to use her sister's old postcode as proof of a false identity; but Fran could just add it to years of perceived misdemeanours. And probably would if she found out. To check they worked, Helen typed **test** 1 and **test** 2 into the subject boxes and pressed send. Seconds later, two emails appeared in opposite inboxes. She punched the air in pride. Smiling in recognition at the brief glimmer of the old Helen. The Helen who could do anything she put her mind to.

Pulling up Google Search, Helen steeled herself and began to type.

Apartment Fire Paris 3eme

She hit return.

Within seconds a page of French newsfeeds, each accompanied by a brief report, had filled the screen.

She began to read, her progress painfully slow. Almost a year of living in Paris hadn't given her much beyond conversational French, but Google Translate did the rest, albeit poorly. Most of the stories were more interested in the damage that had been inflicted on a seventeenth-century building of historic significance than in the no longer famous English journalist who was thought to have rented the apartment but been away at the time.

Some words, though, it would have been impossible not to make out:
Témoin potentiel
Incendie
Cadavre.

9

Cadavre.

Somehow it sounded so much worse in French. Not that it sounded great in English.

Closing her eyes against the nausea pressing in, Helen leaned back against the mangy sofa and felt years of dust cling to her sweater. The jam was still there, etched on the inside of her eyelids. The lights could not be far behind. She tried to think but her brain turned to white noise whenever she tried to remember the night itself. It wasn't the migraine, although that wasn't helping. Something about the fire had played havoc with her short-term memory. Nothing but an orange-hued smog and the outline of a body. The hours immediately before and after that? Nothing.

Despite what the news reports said, what Fran said the police had told her mother, Art had been there, in the flat that night, Helen was sure of it. As sure of his presence in the flat that night as she was of her own. The question was, what the hell had she been doing there? And come to that, what the hell had he?

Through the migraine squatting in her brain, Helen clutched at the memory of the fire . . . tried to hold it . . . dropped it. Her mind kept drifting. Slipping back in time, not just weeks but years. Why, when she could remember heads ripped off tulips as a small child and that time with Tom as clearly as if it was yesterday, couldn't she remember a single hideous night less than a fortnight ago?

She stopped, tried a different approach, forcing herself to search for a similar memory of her husband. Something more distant. Something . . . fonder.

The man she'd studiously not thought about until she'd called her sister. Who not having to think about was a luxury she'd almost forgotten how to have. *I remember the first time I saw him.* That was what you were meant to say, wasn't it? Such a significant moment in your life was meant to have a momentous beginning. A moment, after which there was no going back. If there was that moment in her relationship with Art, she didn't remember it.

She didn't remember *him*.

Her mind was wandering now, but there was no point trying to rein it in. She'd been here often enough to know resistance was futile.

Like other clichés about firsts; first impressions counting, not judging a book by its cover . . . Well, they did count, didn't they? People did judge, didn't they? But there really weren't any first impressions with Art. She hadn't judged the book by its cover, because she hadn't even noticed the book, let alone read the inside flaps.

God knows she wished she had.

Things might have been so different if she'd only paid a bit more attention.

She'd been the only woman in Baghdad, that time, in a group of seven. They took three groups of two each out that day. Inevitably there was an odd one out; inevitably it had been her, the only woman. It was a coincidence, the colonel had explained, nothing to do with her being female. *Yeah, right.* She was the girl, she got left behind, on more than one occasion sent on a coffee run. So she'd got used to finding other ways. She always did. As usual she was too hell-bent on getting her picture, getting the picture, with or without permission, to notice anyone who might have been trying to make an impression. Art said later it was the fact she seemed not to notice him that caught his interest. He was put out when she said there was no *seemed* about it. She hadn't noticed him.

People always said there were two sides to every story. They had certainly said that about them. Art encouraged it, which struck her as odd, now she thought about it. Either way, his version always emerged on top. That was how it was. His version became fact. Love at first sight across a crowded diplomatic bar in a city of ruins after almost a decade of unrequited yearning.

How romantic. How false.

It was thinking of Art that made her do it. She wasn't sure why. Maybe some insane part of her thought there'd be something from him. That the reports were right and he was still alive.

No, he couldn't be. He was there. She knew it. She'd seen his body, twisted, naked . . . she swallowed . . . burning. She'd seen it with her own eyes.

Art was dead. And Helen felt . . . she felt nothing. Just numb.

Opening her eyes, she raised her head gingerly, and when the pain was no worse than it had been lying down, she swung her legs round and sat up. Washing down another three aspirin with the dregs of her cold tea, she woke the laptop and, going via the VPN connection, logged on to her email. Not the new, anonymous ones she'd just set up. The old one. The real one. She knew it was stupid, she did it anyway.

Reams of junk scrolled down her screen. Newsletters and digital updates. People trying to flog her Viagra and watches and give her a million pounds if she'd only send them her bank details right now. It was just a matter of time until someone cracked it, Helen thought as her mouse hovered over the list ready to delete. Suddenly she stopped. If someone was looking for her and saw her Gmail had been emptied they'd know she was there, even if the VPN did mean they couldn't find her. Instead, her eyes roved the list, searching for emails from a single address: ArthurHuntingdon@gmail.com.

Dead men didn't email, she knew that. But still she was relieved when she drew a blank.

Relieved.

Guilt washed in. Her husband – ex-husband – was dead, and all she could muster was relief. Her sister was a different matter. There were eight emails from Fran on the first page alone. Trying to ignore the migraine tightening its grip behind her eyes, Helen clicked on the most recent. Sent an hour earlier, subject line: **Something else**.

The email seemed to start mid-sentence:

> . . . Sorry Helen, pressed send too quickly, bloody hate this new track-pad thing.
>   I meant to tell you – or rather, I would have done, if you hadn't hung up. Tom Bretton came to see Mum.

Helen frowned. That couldn't be right. Why would Tom visit her mother?

> He said you called him late at night from Paris. There was a fire. You were crying, hysterical. You asked him what to do. He said report it and you said there were sirens and they already knew. He tried to get a number off you but you just hung up.

Helen read the paragraph and then read it again. She'd called Tom? In the midst of whatever had happened that night, she had called Tom. A pain stabbed her right temple and her hand flew to her forehead. The veins flared at her touch. Migraine or confusion, Helen no longer knew.

They'd been in touch over the years, had the occasional drink. But not since she'd started seeing Art. Art hadn't been big on old boyfriends. Why the hell had she called him?

> He wanted to know if we'd heard from you. If we knew how to get hold of you. He seemed worried,

said you were displaying classic symptoms of
shock. He's a doctor so I assume he knows. He
asked if you still had the same email address. I
told him you did, but I didn't think there was any
point emailing it. After all I've sent you dozens of
emails since we heard . . .

Skimming the rest to check there was nothing else,
Helen closed the document. The migraine was screaming
for attention now, refusing to be ignored. One more,
Helen promised, just one more. Then I'm yours. She
opened the one below, presumably the one Fran had
sent too soon. Subject: **Please open me.**

Dear Helen

Sorry I sounded angry earlier. I didn't mean to
scare you, but you must understand what an
impossible situation we're in. Can you imagine
how we felt when the police turned up? Terrified.
Mum's in a real state. I'm sorry, I had to tell her
I'd spoken to you. She needed to know you were
OK. Ian thinks I should tell the police you phoned,
but I wanted to check with you first. I tried to call
you back but the phone number you called from
was dead. Was it a call box? It didn't sound like
it. Please reply, Helen, or call again.
  We're worried about you. I know you say you're
good at being on your own, but if it's Art, the
body in the flat, well, you must be devastated. You
know I'm here don't you? Come home, we can get
this all sorted out. Then you can start to grieve

properly. I know you were splitting up, but you
were together five years. You married him for
God's sake. That must count for something . . .

Pushing the laptop away from her, Helen winced as
it skittered across the table, teetered on the edge, and
hit the floor. There was no need to read on. She knew
what it said. She'd heard it all before. *Lovely Art, charming
Art, what took you so long Art, so good for you Art, give him
another chance Art . . .*

From its spot on the rug, the laptop screen flickered,
its colours pixelating and fragmenting like the lights that
radiated across her vision. Helen crawled over and slammed
it shut. There was a smell too. One that hadn't been there
before. Not rancid or especially repugnant, just an under-
tone. It was familiar, but Helen couldn't place it. A musky,
dusky fragrance that she knew she'd smelt before. Smoke,
brick dust, cordite, burning meat . . . Helen winced, felt
her gorge rise. Everyone had their own personal migraine
experience, or so Caroline said. Smell was Helen's.

Shuffling backwards on her bottom towards the sofa,
Helen propped herself against it and closed her eyes,
forcing herself to breathe through her mouth. She'd long
since learnt how to close her nose. A fractured constel-
lation played both inside her eyelids and out. Inky
patches in negative where the viscose smear would be
if she opened them. The scent was stronger now. Even
keeping her breaths shallow, she felt her stomach swell
and a cold sweat break out on her forehead.

Blindly, she leapt up, scrambling over the armchair
between her and the door. It wasn't far to the bathroom, but she'd barely reached the landing before the

tea found its way back up her throat. She lunged towards the bathroom door, thrusting it open as fatty undigested toast splattered through her fingers and across black and white tiles. Slumping on the floor, she rested her forehead on cold plastic and scrabbled for the loo-roll holder. Spinning it until paper spooled on the floor beside her she began to mop blindly at the mess. She knew where she'd smelt that smell before.

She'd smelt it for the first time in Baghdad.

10

Sleep hadn't come. Gil had given it plenty of opportunity, putting off going to bed for as long as possible. He sat up watching television until the only things to watch were repeats of things he'd already seen, now with sign language. He'd drunk one pint too many in the hope of boozing himself to sleep, then knocked back two Nurofen with a shot of whisky when he got through his front door, then another two with another whisky. He'd read until his eyes drooped, the crime novel tumbling from his chest to the living-room carpet.

None of it helped. With his eyes open or shut, Gil saw the same thing. Bloody Helen Graham and a flash of something he couldn't explain as her beat-up old Peugeot vanished into the rain. At one a.m. Gil gave up and went to bed.

Even though his eyes had shut of their own accord as he tried reading on the sofa, the second his head hit the pillow he found himself wide awake. For an hour, maybe two, he stared through the dark at the unseen ceiling. When he wasn't staring at that he was watching the inside of his eyelids, where neon seemed to flicker. It didn't help that he ached like hell from being run off the road. The knee he'd twisted as he leapt out of her way throbbed in time to some unholy music, while his hands stung from grabbing the branch, its thorns having ripped his flesh. Kath at The Bull had insisted his cheek needed a stitch or two when he'd gone in there this evening, but he'd shaken off her suggestion and told her butterfly plasters would do.

After lying on his back, Gil rolled on to his left side and damned his swollen knee. Then on to his right side, via his front. When his cheek stung, he wished he hadn't. He even tried Jan's side of the bed. Something he never did.

He didn't really know what he'd seen. Probably nothing but a trick of the light in torrential rain at dusk. But he knew, suspect eyesight or no, that he couldn't have seen a child. Who was he to talk about children anyway? Fat lot he knew. Truth was, he only knew one thing about kids. He'd got it wrong. Whatever the magical *it* was.

Karen. That was it. The last time he'd seen his youngest daughter she'd been staring at him through the rear window of Jan's car, dark eyes brimming with tears. God, he was a silly old sod. He had too much time on his hands and not enough to do with his brain. Time to rectify that.

Before the light even started to change, before the very first early bird called the first note of that day's dawn chorus, Gil gave up fighting his insomnia, rolled himself out of bed, wincing as his knee took his weight, padded down to the kitchen and filled the kettle.

Opening the kitchen window, he lit his first cigarette of the day and inhaled. Then he leaned forward and blew the smoke out of the window into the morning mist. Another Jan-induced habit. Who cared if his house reeked of nicotine these days?

Spooked, that's what he'd been.

No other word for it. Common sense said, *Nothing to see here*. Only a bunch of old women with over-active imaginations and too much time on their hands. He was as bad as they were, Gil thought, stubbing his cigarette on the outside windowsill, something Jan definitely wouldn't approve of – and flicking the butt across his uncut lawn to fall with the others. Two weeks into retirement and he was giving credence to old wives telling tall ones, while fixating on a woman young enough to be his daughter, who clearly had no interest in having anything to do with any of them. He should be ashamed of himself.

Trouble was, there'd been something about the way she'd had to fight the urge to run when confronted by Margaret Millward's nosiness that caught his attention. Fists clenched so tight he could see half-moons cut in her palms, breathing so carefully controlled she could be counting away panic . . . There was a story there. He just knew it. Call it instinct, call it too much time on his hands. He'd never been wrong yet.

Well, not often.

He'd had a gran given to seeing things. Seeing things, hearing noises, agreeing with her cats that the spare room was best given a wide berth. As a teenager, he wasn't having any of it. Granny O'Donnell could keep her Hail Marys and her rosary. Her Mass every day and twice on Sundays. Her plaster saints and restless spirits. How his ma had ever been allowed to marry a non-believer was a mystery. More than once Granny O'Donnell had walked into a room, shuddered and walked out again.

Gil never paid much heed to all that until he and Jan went to Venice.

It was meant to be romantic. Four days off when Jan dumped the girls with her parents for a long weekend. Lyn had complained like hell, Karen had been too small to care. It would be nice Jan said, like old times. Not that they'd had the money for minibreaks in those days. Nothing to do except eat, drink, walk, have time for each other. It might have worked too, if the horse hadn't already bolted, emotionally at least. And if not for that ruddy monastery. Palazzo something or other.

No way was he ever going there again.

Jan liked a bit of history and Gil, keen to get in her good books after too long out of them, agreed to take her for her birthday. Turned out you could have too much history. For a start, the manager had double-booked the room they'd chosen. So instead of a first-floor suite reached by a sweeping stone staircase, with ten-foot ceilings, four-poster beds and antique, if mouldering, brocade curtains covering the Romeo and Juliet balcony overlooking an off-shoot of the Grand Canal, they got a door he had to bend in half to get through, a ceiling so low it scraped his head even in bare feet, and a room heavy with potpourri and dark wood furniture that dwarfed its proportions. If he'd been cynical, Gil would have said they'd been shoved in servants' quarters on a mezzanine above kitchens. It certainly smelt like it.

The room's ill-humour worked its sorcery within minutes.

No sooner were Jan and Gil through the door than they started bickering, slamming their clothes into the too-big-for-the-room wardrobes before snatching up their coats and storming out to find something to eat. It took fifteen minutes fast walking through Venice's back alleys for the oppression to lift. Somehow, they managed to salvage the evening and even joke about their room over a litre of the thinnest red he'd ever drunk and a shared bowl of blisteringly hot and oily arrabiata. By the time they left the little restaurant either they or the streets were weaving. Jan took his hand as they headed over a bridge and Gil felt his lost fondness return.

But the room's gloom was waiting for them. They scratched their way through teeth cleaning and make-up removing and lay stiffly side by side on a lumpy mattress. And then, because this was Venice, city of lovers, and this was what they were meant to do, they rolled in towards each other and made clumsy and wholly unsatisfying . . . you couldn't call it love. Jan slept after that, fitfully and as far away across the bed as she could manage. Gil didn't sleep, he couldn't. If the darkness hadn't been so dense, he'd have stared at the ceiling. A ceiling so low that he felt he could reach up and touch it.

He nodded off at some point. Must have done, because he was in the room but it was early morning, just before dawn and the furniture was new. Servants' quarters, back when the palazzo was young, to judge from the girl hunched at the foot of his bed, who was looking at him and sobbing. Her pregnant belly huge through a cheap shift. And then she was in the bed, legs splayed and he was standing at the end. There was blood and gore and screams. Gil could have sworn he heard a baby wail. And then, without knowing how, he knew the baby had been taken away and drowned; that the mother drowned herself a week later. When he woke the ceiling was crushing him. His mouth was wide, but not screaming.

The first thing he did was yell at the concierge. Then he yelled at Jan, who cried and said she hated birthdays and wanted to go home. Then he went out and found another hotel. A modernist cube, all right angles and straight walls and zero history.

Gil shook the fog from his brain and with it his memory of Venice and whatever it was he'd glimpsed for a second in the back of a car. Helen Graham was just a woman who wanted to keep a low profile, and whatever her reasons for it, they were nobody's business but hers. That house though, of all places, why would she want to stay there? Personally, Gil would have preferred the palazzo in Venice, and that was saying something.

Fags, papers, more coffee and Gil got on the Internet. Who she was could be easily solved. He cursed himself for not doing it sooner. Bringing up Google, he typed in 'Hélène Graham' and hit return. There were a handful. All French. One or two roughly the same age. None that looked or sounded remotely like her. Gil wasted an hour before admitting defeat. What if Mrs Millward was wrong about her being French? Although the woman had an accent of sorts, her English didn't sound French.

Typing in Helen Graham was even worse. As Google-fu

went, *first name* and *last name* wouldn't win him any medals, but you had to start somewhere. Hundreds of Helen Grahams. Sixty million hits to be precise. To narrow the search he clicked *Pages from the UK*, and the hits reduced to three point eight million. Then he did what he should have done at the start and put double quotes round her name. "**Helen Graham**" cut the number dramatically but still left dozens of search pages. Professors, academics, writers . . . The first ones up were those with obvious public profiles. She wasn't there. So he switched to Google images and flicked through endless unfamiliar thumbnails. She wasn't there either. Date of birth? Early thirties, he'd hazarded a guess. Maybe older but looking young on it.

Dob 1978, 1977, 1976.

He threw in 1979 and 1975 for good measure.

Doctors, dieticians, a historian. Directory Enquiries wasn't much more help. Over two hundred Helen Grahams. Thirty-four in London. Forty in Yorkshire, none anywhere near Wildfell. Even Gil knew landlines were a thing of the past. Lighting another cigarette he tried to think. He needed images. Bookmarking a few HGs that looked possible, he went in search of their pictures. The first, his favourite, was thirty-six years old. Any delight was short-lived. Her Facebook pages proved she couldn't look less like his Helen Graham if she'd tried.

In under an hour, he learned the private business of thirty-five Helen Grahams in their mid-thirties. Why didn't these people lock their accounts? They'd be posting bank details next; probably already had, given the drunken party pictures, ecstatic post-birth baby pictures, boyfriends, lovers, husbands and exes laid out for anyone to see. It was a stalker's paradise. Which was precisely why journalists loved it. Free pictures, free information and you didn't even need to get anyone's permission.

He was dismissing Helen Graham number 53 and starting 54 when it dawned on him that the whole world was on Facebook. Eighty per cent of the UK, or so he'd read. Scrolling to the search box, he began to type: 'K-A-R-E-N M-A-R-K-H-A-M' and hit return. Far less common name Markham. Nothing. Not one.

The next thought came to him slowly, sickeningly. Surely Jan would have told him . . . wouldn't she? He knew the answer to that even before he slid his cursor back to the search box and, with a sinking inevitability, keyed in the letters: 'K-A-R-E-N K-I-N-N-E-A-R'. Four hits. One in exactly the right bit of London. It was locked.

'For fuck's sake!' Slamming his hand on the desk, Gil winced.

Bloody thorns. Bloody idiot.

He pushed the chair back from his desk hard, stood up and sent it spinning across the room into the door. Sod's bloody law. He couldn't find Helen Graham but he was pretty sure he'd found his daughter. Just one bloody Facebook search away. Not that there was any way of being sure, since it was a locked account. Was she being a smart girl, her father's daughter? Although clearly she considered someone else her father now. Or was she trying to keep people out? A particular person, even. Maybe him?

There was only one way to find out.

'You sad bastard,' he muttered, as he began to open a Facebook account. But he wheeled his chair forward when he got bored of crouching and kept going. It took him five minutes to open the account and then he spent another twenty trying to work out what would make Karen most likely to accept his friend request. A lot of information or a little? Not that he had much hope of success with either. He gave name, location, birthday and occupation (ex-occupation, though he glossed over that). A pop-up appeared suggesting *A Few More People You Might Know And Like To Be Friends With* if he knew Karen. Scanning the list only confirmed he didn't really know Karen at all. He carried that thought through the morning and into the pub at noon.

By chucking-out time his daughter had still not responded to Gil's Facebook request. Not that he'd expected her to. Just hoped . . . She was probably at work, wherever that was. He'd long since given up berating himself for not knowing even the most meagre details of her life. He'd asked his ex-wife often enough, but Jan just said that was between him and Karen and refused to get involved. 'Why won't you tell me?' he'd wanted to yell. The one sure-fire way to end the conversation. Then it dawned on him. Her sister would know. How could she not? He wondered why he hadn't thought to ask before. It was almost three, so Lyn would probably be home, or down the shops, or maybe on her way to pick up her eldest from school.

Who was he kidding?

He didn't have the faintest clue where she'd be. He didn't know if she worked part-time or full-time or no-time. For all he knew, she could be on maternity leave. That thought brought him up short. No way would she have had another without telling him. Just before Christmas, that had to be when he'd last spoken to her. Nine months? Ten? A baby was possible . . . But no, she wouldn't do that. They got on better than that.

And there'd been birthday cards since.

They just weren't a clingy sort of family. That was all. Pressing *Lyn – home* on his mobile, he started walking. Out of town again. This time with one eye firmly on the traffic and a slight limp in his injured knee. *Paul, Lyn, Meggie and Alfie are busy right now*, said his elder daughter's voice after three rings on her home number. *Leave a message and Alfie will probably push the nice red button to delete it.*

Gil smiled, didn't leave a message.

It wasn't that he didn't want to forewarn her; but now she'd put that idea in his head about Alfie deleting messages . . . Well, he'd never know, would he? Scrolling down, he found *Lyn – mobile* and walked as he waited for the phone to connect. Too far into the Dales and he'd lose his signal. But he had a way to go before that happened. Five beeps, six, seven . . . More bloody voicemail. He was about to hang up when his daughter's voice kicked in.

'Hello? Dad? Hold on, I'm in the car. Give me a sec to pull over.'

Before he could speak he heard himself tossed aside, bounce once on the passenger seat and again, harder, on the floor. Gil winced, as if his own scarred cheek had just hit the ground. 'Just a sec, sweetheart,' he heard Lyn say. 'Mummy needs to talk to Granddad.'

'Gangdad.'

'Yes, that's right. You remember Granddad.'

Except he wouldn't, couldn't. Little lad hadn't seen Gil since he was a baby.

'Stay put, sweetheart. Mummy won't be a minute.'

Static crunched in Gil's ear as she picked him up again. Reaching a gap in the drystone wall, Gil heaved himself over the old stile, finding it noticeably tougher than yesterday, when he'd still been able to bend his knee. Several groups of walkers straggled across the valley in front of him, three or four abreast, swinging those damn ski sticks. Where had they come from all of a sudden? It wasn't even that sunny.

'That's better – I'm parked on the verge. Hang on . . . no, Alfie, stay in your seat, love, Mummy will be right outside . . . You OK, Dad?'

'Yes, fine, why wouldn't I be?'

A pause, followed by a small intake of breath. 'We-ell, let's just say you don't call every day of the week. You sure you're OK? Nothing wrong?'

Gil opened his mouth. Pot–kettle, he wanted to say.

He shut it again. He couldn't very well complain. Retiree with nothing to do objects because his thirty-something daughter with two kids and a job doesn't call him. 'Fair dos,' he said. Then, 'Well, I'm calling now. From the Dales. You wouldn't believe the number of walkers. Just thought I'd see how you are. How are the kids?' He managed to catch himself before he could add, 'Any more on the way?'

'We're good. Meggie's at school full-time since last week. Alfie's just started nursery. Mornings only. Godsend. Paul's busy at work. Me too. Dad . . .?'

'Yes?'

'You sure you're OK? There's not anything?'

'Yes, I said so, didn't I?'

'Yes, but . . . Well, it's just not like you to call out of the blue, like, for no reason.'

Gil took a deep breath. 'I thought I might, you know, take you up on your offer. That is if it still stands, of course.'

'Offer?' Lyn sounded confused.

'To take the train over . . . See the little ones. It was in your Christmas card . . .' He was losing his confidence now, wishing he hadn't called. He hadn't even got around to asking about Karen yet. Maybe this wasn't the time.

'Dad,' Lyn laughed. 'That was for Christmas! It's September!'

'Christmas soon,' he said, all too aware of how very pathetic that sounded.

'Of course you can stay with us. Meggie and Alfie would love it. Any time. Just give me some notice in case Paul's going to be away.'

Gil wouldn't mind that. His son-in-law was all right for a salesman. It wasn't like they'd ever really got to know each other. Only met a handful of times in the ten years Paul had been married to his daughter. If anything, he suspected Paul thought of Kevin as his father-in-law.

'Is that it, Dad? Only I'm on my way to pick Meg up from school and Alfie's raising merry hell in the back of the car.'

'There was one other thing . . .'

'Y-es.' Suspicion entered Lyn's voice.

'About your sister . . .'

Silence.

'I was just thinking. Wondering, if you had an email address.'

'You know I do and you know I can't. Karen doesn't want to hear from you. She knows where to find you. And if she wants to, she will. She was the youngest. She took it hardest. You know she did. Is this the reason you phoned?'

'No, love, course not. It's just, if I could speak to her, I'm sure we could sort it out.'

'Are you? I'd leave her alone if I were you.' Lyn paused, listening to muffled yells too far from the phone for Gil to make out. 'Yes, love,' he heard her say. 'Mummy's coming now . . .

'Dad,' she was back. 'I've got to go. If you really mean it about coming to visit, call me later with dates.'

11

It was better this time. In as much as when she emerged from her migraine Helen knew where she was and, for that matter, who she was and when it was. She knew it with such sharp-edged clarity it was shocking.

The house felt better, too. The bits of it she used anyway. Familiar, almost calm. The floorboards and joists had ceased their constant moanings, the scuttlings and scrapings had fallen silent. As if she wasn't the only one who'd been waiting for the storm to pass.

Helen wandered along the landing on colt-like legs, testing door handles and windows as she passed. Locked. All of them, apart from the one she'd wedged open with a book just before her migraine kicked in. The book was still there, half in/half out, its pages curled where pre-dawn mist had descended. The three-bar fire still blazed. Waving her hand in front of its bars to gauge their heat, Helen grinned. Blazed in the loosest possible sense.

Several years earlier she'd trained herself not to turn on gas or electrics when she felt a migraine coming on. Her chances of remembering to turn them off again were minimal. She hadn't expected yesterday's to roar in quite so fast. Normally she could predict, gauge their ferocity and closeness. But this attack had taken her completely by surprise.

Picking up the laptop from the upstairs drawing-room floor, she tucked it under her arm and went downstairs. Her legs felt weak, shaky, as if she'd been in bed for days, not hours.

Could she have lost a day, she wondered, checking the front door – still locked – and repeating the exercise with all the downstairs rooms.

It wouldn't be the first time.

In the kitchen, she found milk neatly returned to its shelf in the fridge, open but fresh. Bread, Marmite, jam, even chocolate. Piling it all on to the oak table next to the laptop, she broke off a square of Galaxy and put it on her tongue, counting slowly down from ten in her head as she let it dissolve while the kettle came to a boil and the laptop cranked itself to life. When it did, she broke off another square, feeling glucose seep into her system.

She flicked on the old Roberts radio she'd tracked down to one of the unused bedrooms, and stopped on the first station she found, surprised to discover it was noon, but at least she hadn't lost a day. The sky outside made it seem earlier; overcast but not jaundiced, not the yellow that polluted so many migraine hungover days. And the rain had stopped again. For once the lychgate and the woods beyond weren't obscured by drizzle.

Filling the teapot to the brim, Helen spread a thick layer of jam on hot toast and logged on to the VPN. Her fingers hovered over the icon for her real email. What had Fran's email said? *You called Tom . . . he asked if you still had the same email address . . .* something like that.

Why Tom, of all people?

One last time, she promised herself, then she wouldn't look again.

It had been years since she'd last emailed him but she knew the email address by heart, just as she did the phone number. TBretton@kingscollege.ac.uk. There were three emails that she could see, the first sent two weeks ago.

Licking jam from her fingers, she savoured its sweetness and counted back in her head. Yes, the day after the fire. The day after, if what Fran said was true, Helen had called him.

The email was short and to the point. More like a text.

Helen,

Are you all right? Stupid question, obviously you're not. I'm worried about you. Call me.

Txxx

She read it over again, hand hovering on the reply arrow. What harm would it do? He knew she was alive anyway and ten to one her sister would tell him she'd called.

Just one line: I'm OK, don't worry. Thank you. xxx

She ached to do it.

But no. She couldn't. It wasn't fair. On either of them.

His second email, sent a week later, was much the same. I'm worried. **Call me.** Just one kiss this time.

The third had been sent the day before. About an hour after she'd called her sister. 'Bloody hell, Fran,' she muttered under her breath.

Helen,

Fran called. She told me about the police. And other things. She doesn't know what to do. If you're reading this, you have to call me. Let me help you, Helen. Please.

Tom

Tom. Just Tom.

Helen logged off.

No more Gmail. That was the last time. Someone, somewhere would be able to tell she was opening her email, she was sure of it. It was too risky.

Fran was right. She was good at being alone. Just as well.

Half a loaf of bread, half a bar of chocolate and two pots of tea later the last shadows had lifted. This attack had been different. Shorter, sharper, wreaking havoc with little warning. Moving away as quickly as it had come, like a tropical storm. She hoped it wasn't going to set a pattern. Too many more like that would finish her, even with her medication. Her eyes skipped over the empty pill packet lying on the worktop and she groaned. There was another problem that hadn't gone away in the night.

She could sign on at the local surgery, but they'd want a passport or proof of address and she didn't have one, at least not in a name she was willing to use. Even if they didn't, and her local infamy was enough, could she persuade an unknown GP to prescribe Clonidine for a simple migraine? They'd want her to see a consultant, have tests. Caroline was her only option; and that meant going to London. It wasn't the expense that bothered Helen – not that she could really afford it – it was the risk. Helen trusted Caroline, she'd had to over the years, but she had no idea how far medical confidentiality stretched when it came to this.

Back upstairs, Helen dumped yesterday's clothes, fuggy with the sweat of sleep and the aura of vomit, on her impromptu washing pile on the bathroom floor and slipped into her running kit, point-and-shoot in one pocket, second-hand iPhone in the other. She'd been experimenting; using the phone for still life: half-eaten toast, muddy trainer, dishcloth kicked into a corner.

For years pictures had been the only thing she believed in. To tell a story, to shape the world, to change lives. Take Bill Brandt, or Brassaï's night photographs of the underbelly of Paris. Or Weegee, so keen to get his crime-scene shots that getting punched was simply part of the job. Famines, migrations, stories of human survival. A part of her envied the old hacks with their press cameras. The photojournalists, drunk on cheap beer, stoned on cheap drugs, and wired on adrenalin and lack of sleep as they brought in the photographs that took America out of the Vietnam War. Pictures made history.

Helen was proof of that. One photograph had given her a career. Another had changed her life irrevocably.

Helen's pictures had always been of people.

The human cost. Consequences, not conflict. Aftermath.

Big moments in otherwise small lives, or what remained of them. But now . . . she wasn't sure she could ever bear to photograph another face because of what she saw there. Innocence of how the world really was. Apart from those who had the misfortune to know, of course. Seeing that knowledge reflected back was even harder.

Helen was so deep inside her thoughts that she barely noticed when she left the road. She came to halfway across a field, instinctively giving the walkers' trail a wide berth. Grass squelched beneath her trainers, mud oozing into grooves as she cleared the field. It was dry now, but the air was damp, seeping round her windbreaker and under her sweatshirt. If her hair wasn't tied down it would be getting bigger by the second. The weather out here on the Dales was deceptive. Light that looked forgiving from behind a kitchen window hid a biting wind that chafed her face as she paced herself up the hill to the Scar, her head full of the faces that had haunted her pictures.

Taking out the iPhone, she switched it on, wondering if she would be able to get a signal on the cheap pay-as-you-go SIM she'd persuaded the shop owner to throw in for the price. Before she started, she dipped into her windbreaker for the scruffy Moleskine she'd taken from her nearly empty photo bag and scrabbled backwards through its pages until she found the number she wanted.

Ms Harris, Caroline Harris the consultant, answered the phone herself.

That was more luck than she deserved.

'Helen, good to hear from you,' she said, doing an excellent job of not sounding surprised. She was a busy woman; working both for the NHS and in private practice; appearing in court occasionally as an expert witness. Very busy. 'How *are* you?' Caroline asked. The enquiry was genuine. She'd become, not quite a friend, but almost, over the years; which was why, Helen told herself, she was prepared to risk trusting Caroline now.

'Been better,' Helen said truthfully. 'Been worse. Just come through a migraine.'

Caroline sighed. A sigh Helen knew she was meant to hear. They had an ongoing difference of opinion about whether what happened to Helen in the fugue state could medically be called a migraine. 'Where are you?' Caroline asked.

Grinning, Helen told her the truth. 'Standing on top of a huge outcrop of rock staring down over a patchwork landscape.' Helen could almost hear her consultant wonder if that was literal or a description of her state of mind. Deciding her call had gone on long enough to be traced, Helen cut to the chase. 'I'm out of pills.'

'Since when?'

Helen counted back in her mind. 'A couple of weeks. A month.'

'Long enough. When do you want to come? Tell me and I can make myself free,' Caroline said. 'Provided it's not Friday, that's operating day.'

They both knew she meant free for Helen. Caroline Harris's time was like gold dust. A minute later Helen had an appointment for the following Monday, plenty of time to decide whether to drive herself or take the train. Whether to tell her sister she was passing through London. Whether to contact the police.

Helen tried to distract herself by photographing the Scar, noting the time of day and the light in her notebook, shooting first with the phone, then with the point-and-shoot. Neither offered flexibility for exposure, shutter speed or depth of field and she struggled to muster any enthusiasm. The call to Caroline had left her empty. It was a feeling she recognised. A fall always came right after a high. The cold was eating at her and the sky looked less certain than it had. Helen wasn't the only one who'd been duped by the break in the clouds. The landscape below was alive with climbers and walkers. Even the sheep and birds were noisier than usual. Noisier than she'd heard since she arrived.

When she saw a school party slung out across the valley below – pairs of adults front and rear, marshalling a crocodile of small children in Smartie hues – she started photographing them, for no reason other than primary colours made a change from the more muted grass, rocks and sheep. Hidden behind her phone, she felt far less obtrusive than with a camera. Their erratic meander towards the crag warmed her, as she captured the four adults trying and failing to keep some semblance of a neat line.

She'd reeled off dozens of shots when she first saw the boy. He was standing with his back to her, not quite with them, not quite apart; far closer to her than the main group. The boy was small and dark and, somewhere on the day out, he'd lost his anorak.

He must be cold, she thought, shivering as she tried to zoom in. The boy didn't move in the frame. Helen swore quietly under her breath. What did she expect from a practically obsolete camera phone? But even from this distance Helen could see his clothes didn't look right. He looked separate, other, and not just his lack of coat.

Poor kid, Helen thought. She knew how that felt. Picked last for games, no one to sit with on the school bus, no one to hold hands with in the crocodile. Still, there was something about him that was familiar. She started back down the escarpment to get closer.

All it took was one child to trip.

One, perfectly positioned Jenga.

A smallish boy, near the front, took another down with him, or her. A girl, possibly. It was hard to tell, they were all dressed in bright anoraks and dark school shorts. The whole line concertinaed. The crocodile bunched at its head, the tail scattering into groups. They looked like nothing so much as spilt M&Ms. Helen cast about, looking for a single M&M without its primary-coloured coat.

There wasn't one. He was gone.

Frowning, she scoured the Dales below her. Where was he? Perhaps he hadn't been with them after all. Perhaps he'd gone with his parents. But there hadn't been any other adults between her and the school party. Helen was sure of it.

Head down, eyes on the rocks at her feet, she took the winding path at the back of the Scar at a sprint, feeling the jolt in her spine as her trainers slammed into dirt pounded hard by dozens before her. A couple coming towards her moved aside. The woman said something, something snipey. Helen didn't care. She was so lost in thoughts of the boy she almost missed seeing the man ahead. At least, she missed him seeing her. As Helen reached the final slope she picked up pace, close to flat out, pretty stupid this far from home.

As she tried to swerve, he tripped and fell into her path.

'Shit!' she felt her ankle turn on rock. Putting out a hand to break her fall, she landed awkwardly on her wrist, then elbow, somehow managing to wind herself with her knee. Blood rushed to her face as she hit the ground.

'Oh God, I'm sorry. I don't know what . . .' He stopped. Helen didn't look up, she was too furious; embarrassed and winded. *Don't look at me*, her body language screamed. *I'm fine. Go away.*

'Are you OK?' he sounded worried.

Glancing up through the frizz that sprayed from her ponytail, Helen scowled. 'Yes, fine,' she said, not really looking at him and not meaning it. She hauled herself up, swiping furiously at the mud that smeared her legs. But getting back on her feet wasn't as easy as she'd expected. When she put her weight on her ankle it gave.

'Here,' he said. 'Let me. My stupid fault.'

His hand was under her arm before she could resist. He tried a joke. 'Like Leeds in rush hour out here today.'

Helen knew she should smile, be polite, but she was too cross – and shaken.

'It's fine, really,' she said, through gritted teeth, trying to shake his hand from her without physically removing it. 'I just need to walk on it and I'll be . . .'

'Madame Graham?' she heard his voice change. 'I mean, Mademoiselle . . .'

She looked up and her heart sank. His face was familiar. His height. His spectacularly out-of-place suit. She wouldn't go so far as to say she recognised him exactly, but she knew she'd seen him before and that could only be in one place. To her annoyance, tears sprang to her eyes. Frustration balling in her chest. She groaned audibly and his face collapsed in misplaced worry. He thought she was in agony and he was responsible.

Let him think it. He was sort of right on both counts.

As he fussed and fretted and apologised, Helen gave in to the inevitable and let him take her weight. She could have limped her way home alone eventually, but why bother?

She could just imagine how they looked, lurching across the Dales. Her hopping, him half carrying her with his hand under her elbow rather than around her waist where she could tell he was resisting putting it. As they lurched three-legged through the straggle of ramblers, Helen swore inwardly. First a migraine, now this. Stranded in the middle of a field with no transport, one good leg, in the clutches of a concerned neighbour.

Trapped, and it was all her own sweet fault.

12

'Call me Helen,' she said eventually.

The first thing she'd said for half an hour. Gil took it as part apology, which it obviously was. 'My French pronunciation is that bad?' he asked.

'Atrocious.'

They'd made slow progress, the difference in their height not helped by the fact Helen alternated between leaning on him and trying to manage on her own. More than once, he'd had to resist the urge to suggest a piggyback or tuck her under his arm and carry her like a child. Not that he could. He might be tall, but he wasn't that strong any more and she wasn't that light. Plus, two falls in as many days meant his knee was killing him.

Finally they were stumbling past a mud-splattered silver Peugeot parked on the gravel in front of the great house. While Helen rummaged in her pockets for keys and undid three Chubbs on the front door, Gil looked around him. All these years and he'd never been this close to Wildfell before. Never paid the mansion that much attention to be honest. It was red brick, ivy covered. Faces carved in cheap sandstone around the main door were weathered Botox smooth. If you'd gone to central casting for haunted houses you couldn't have done a better job.

Gil eyed her car. He was pretty sure it was the one that almost hit him. It was definitely the one that she'd parked so badly outside the General Stores. There was no child seat in the back, and no sign of any of the rubbish that usually accompanies small children. Empty crisp packets, sweet wrappers, discarded toys.

The front door groaned as she opened it.

'Needs . . .' she started.

'. . . oiling,' he finished. For the first time a flash of a smile crossed her face, blue eyes lighting, before she turned her back on him and hobbled inside, flicking on a bulb that hung without shade from electric cord so old it was plaited.

'Welcoming, huh?'

Gil grinned. Winced.

She frowned. 'What happened?'

He put his hand up and realised the scratch on his cheek was open again. 'Oh that.' He looked at her, seeking a hint of recognition and finding nothing. 'Took a bit of a tumble into a hedge, that's all. Nothing serious. It's just a scratch.'

'Looks more than a scratch to me.' Her sudden change of tone surprised him. Efficient, maternal, bossy. The tone Jan had used to tell the girls it was time for bed, no arguing. 'You need to see a doctor. That probably requires stitching.'

He raised his eyebrows.

'What?' she demanded.

'You don't seem the type to interfere in other people's business.'

'I'm not, I . . .' then she laughed. 'Seriously,' she said. 'It looks bad, like it might be about to go a bit septic. Trust me, I know a bit about these things.'

They hovered in the doorway for a moment. Her just inside, balancing on one leg, supporting herself with one hand on the door frame. Gil standing awkwardly outside on the mat. There was no noise from within.

'Well, Mr . . .'

'Markham, Gil Markham. It's Gilbert but . . .'

'Gilbert?' Her mouth twitched.

He nodded. 'I know. Family name. Gil, really.'

She frowned, put her head on one side as if deciding whether or not he was a Gil. 'Well, thank you for helping me back, at least. But I'm home safe so I'd better let you go.' She put out her hand and he looked at it for a moment before realising they were meant to shake.

'Are you sure there's nothing . . .?'

She shook her head firmly, already beginning to close the door.

The doctor couldn't fit him in that day, nor the next, so Gil ended up driving to Keighley and spending three hours sat in A&E with the pond life of West Yorkshire, plus a few sick babies screaming the place down. All for two stitches, a prescription for codeine, questions about his drinking and a lecture on being more careful at his age.

At his age, indeed.

He seethed all the way home, putting his foot down on the dual carriageway just because he could. *You should take more care at your age.* What was it the nurse had said when he'd muttered some half-truth about taking a tumble while climbing on the Dales? You're lucky it's not worse. Rock climbing? At your age? In those shoes? She hadn't said any of those things; but she might as well have done. The way she'd looked at him. Like, if he was her dad, she'd be giving him a proper talking to and grounding him indefinitely.

This . . . regression. He couldn't stand it. Who wrote the memo saying at what point you started going backwards in the eyes of everyone younger? He was sixty-one, for God's sake. Harrison Ford was making Indiana Jones movies when he was older than this. Bruce Willis was still dying hard, or as good as. Five years ago, he'd been *grown up, successful, respected.* Although nothing perceptible had happened, he'd somehow become a man that nurses less than half his age could scold. Gil wanted to see the small print. He didn't sign up for this when he decided to step down from the news desk.

Gil had no idea how long the text had been there, flashing silently from his phone. He only knew he'd missed it. He discovered it when he got through the front door and tossed his mobile along with his keys on to the little table in the hall, which had been there since Jan decreed they needed a *telephone table*. The telephone was long gone.

Above the 'table', a kind of a semi-circular thing he'd never liked – too fakely old-fashioned in the way it fitted snugly against the wall – hung a mirror. It was oval, in the same dark wood as the table. Jan probably bought them at the same time. Since she'd moved straight into her new man's house, already fully furnished and on an executive estate with half a dozen similar, Gil kept telling himself he could throw it away if he wanted. Somehow, like the kitchen clock and reclaiming her side of the bed, he'd never got round to it.

Still, he wouldn't have cared if Jan had taken it. She could have taken the lot as far as he was concerned, so long as she'd left a bed and a telly. And even the telly . . . All that stuff was easily replaced and something about the idea of 'travelling light' appealed to him. He liked to think of himself as a man who was above needing things. But no, she hadn't wanted the telephone table, the television, the bed. She hadn't wanted much, now he came to think of it. Except the kids.

'Not really Kev's style,' she'd said of the rest.

Something along those lines.

'What makes you think it's mine?' he'd wanted to reply.

Maybe he had. That was possible. Not that the split hadn't been amicable enough; but there had been moments . . . Well, there would be, wouldn't there? Dismantling a marriage after twenty-odd years. And even saints snark. He couldn't remember the detail. It was a long time ago now. So the table and the mirror, and the bed and the telly, and plenty more besides, stayed. Ten years later, all that stuff was still here. Except the telly. Sometime in the last four or five years he'd found his way to replacing that with an enormous wide flat-screen thing the bloke in Curry's had convinced him he needed. Flicking on the overhead light, Gil blinked, examined the stitches, neatly tied and self-dissolving, and tried to look at himself impartially. Not much to see except floppy blond-grey hair and heavy black-framed glasses.

Without those he couldn't see a bloody thing.

Well, not unless it was very close, and even then not in focus.

Hanging his suit jacket on the end of the banisters, where it would stay until he put it back on again to go out, he picked up his phone and wandered into the kitchen. That's when he saw the envelope flashing on screen, with a number underneath he didn't recognise. Heart pounding, he fumbled to enter the pin-code to unlock it. It wasn't from his ex-wife or his elder daughter. It wasn't likely to be from his youngest, but he couldn't help hoping.

I don't know if you remember me, but we met at The Bull? I wondered if you'd like to have a drink sometime? Maybe dinner?

Liza x.

PS hope you don't mind, Margaret gave me your number.

Disappointment surged through him. Who'd he been expecting? Jan? Karen? Lyn? Helen Graham? That was hardly going to happen. And who the hell was Liza anyway? Margaret had to be Margaret bloody Millward. He didn't know any other Margarets. How in God's name had that Millward woman got hold of his mobile number? Christ, she'd missed her vocation. And had he just . . .?

Been asked on a date? By a woman?

Don't be such an old fart. It's the twenty-first century. He could imagine Lyn saying it. If he'd ever been able to have those kind of conversations with her, which he hadn't. Women asked men out all the time these days. He should be grateful anyone was interested. He tried to picture her, couldn't get her face. He did remember her though, sort of. Or he would if he'd been looking. The Liza was followed by a single kiss. It didn't mean anything, he knew. People did that these days. Everything was xxx. Texts, Facebook, emails.

See you later, kiss.

Dinner's in the dog, kiss.

You're invited to apply for early retirement, kiss.

Gone nine now. They'd be wondering where he was down The Bull; wondering if they should still be keeping his pint warm. Well, let them wonder. Gil tossed his phone on the kitchen table, not sure how to respond or even whether to respond at all. Turning on the TV produced some ITV crime drama just starting.

It would do. Squabbling women juggling families and crime-scene investigations. Made a change from dysfunctional old sods who couldn't hold down a relationship . . . Gil fired up his laptop, dragged a cottage pie out of the freezer and bunged it in the microwave. He bought them by the dozen. Hot, filling, vaguely passed for healthy. Occasionally, he could have sworn he saw a carrot. Flipping the top on a can of Sam Smith's, he sat down at the kitchen table to kill a bit of time with his good friend Google.

Seeing the old house up close had intrigued him.

He caught himself. Who was he trying to kid? It was

Helen Graham who intrigued him. That was the truth of it.

Three hours and three more cans later, cottage pie stone-cold in the microwave, Gil remembered Liza's text. Gone midnight was too late to reply. It would have to wait until morning. Not that he knew how to respond anyway. He'd been thinking of saying yes, but he'd probably have changed his mind by tomorrow. Couldn't think of a reason to say no; any more than he could think of a reason to go.

Somehow he'd managed to move enough to get those three cans of Sam's from the cupboard, but not to take his supper from the microwave. Bit of an art that.

He was still no closer to finding out about Helen Graham.

Her voice had an accent he couldn't place. Not French exactly, but something . . . International. European, maybe, more member of the global community than anywhere specific. And that comment she'd made about knowing a bit about wounds. Thanks to that he'd spent the evening down a blind alley with the medical profession. Wouldn't be the first time, although she'd been a nurse, and that was decades ago. BJ: Before Jan.

He'd even spent a bit of time exploring the history of the big house, as if to prove to himself it wasn't the woman that interested him. Trouble was, in the scheme of things, it wasn't that big. Not *significant* anyway. So there wasn't that much to tell. Owned by an old local family, the usual rifts over a couple of centuries. Then nobody but an old woman in the decades after the Great War. Gil put two and two together and assumed she'd been a war widow. After that, nothing much to report until that scandal that got the boys' school closed back in the nineties. That rang a bell, now he thought about it. Some local bigwig got it hushed up, if he remembered right. So there must be some extended family some-where locally with a vested interest. Since then, tenants had come and gone, but the last couple of years it had stayed empty. Not a word about a ghost, but that kind of tittle-tattle didn't tend to come from computers, it came from old wives and kids with nothing to do but smoke at the bus stop and break into empty houses at night and scare themselves witless.

There'd been no text from Lyn, no Facebook response from Karen. Not that he really deserved or even expected one. He hadn't given his daughters a moment's thought since he sat down, any more than he had Liza. There'd been no room in his head for anyone but the woman at Wildfell. The more he thought about her, the more convinced he became he'd seen her somewhere before. In the papers, on television, maybe a news site. Since she wasn't local and was far too young to have crossed his path back when he worked in London, those were his only other options. He thought about phoning the news desk, getting them to check the electoral register. Even picked up his mobile and started dialling the number. Then he imagined the laugh they'd have at his expense when he had to admit he couldn't give them any information apart from her name. Oh, and she was probably French. It was worse than useless.

Unless she was the daughter of someone he did know? That thought stopped him in his tracks for five minutes. Until it bugged him back into action. It was an itch he had to scratch. This was the twenty-first century, as Lyn never tired of telling him. Everybody could be googled. Even the insanely rich couldn't buy total anonymity. Off grid was for religious fanatics and Montana gun nuts, and that was it.

If Helen Graham was on Google, he'd find her.

13

By six thirty on Monday morning she was on her way to Leeds Bradford Airport. She didn't glance in her rear-view mirror as she pulled out of the driveway. She never did. She didn't know why. It was just a thing. Don't look back. Never look back. She wasn't sure what she thought she might see if she did, she just thought best not.

Her ankle shrieked whenever she leaned on the clutch, but she didn't want to leave her car at Wildfell overnight. Now she'd started having visitors, Helen didn't want it to look like she was in and not answering the door. Better to be obviously away. Perhaps it was unnecessarily elaborate to drive to the airport, leave the car in a long-stay along with thousands of others, and take a diversion through the arrivals hall to pick up a bus to Leeds station. She had no reason to think anyone was following her. Or even interested. But better safe than sorry.

Inevitably, the train was packed. Helen parted with £100 and wedged herself between a window too filthy to see through and a man whose hips devoured the armrest that supposedly divided their seats. Tray table balanced on his gut, cup of PG, debris of sugar sachets and milk cartons, scraps of pie crust, all clinging to its surface, 45 degrees north of comfortable.

Pulling out her phone, Helen aimed it randomly in his direction, pretending to be holding the screen up to the light, until she got an image she was happy with. Then there was nothing to do but stare through the dirt and hair-gel smeared glass and watch north become south, urban sprawl give way to suburban sprawl before, gradually, London started to make its presence felt.

Out on the Euston Road, she slung her holdall over her shoulder and limped in the direction of Harley Street. Still sore from the drive, her ankle was just about all right for walking. She was bored with limping, just as she was bored with silence and bored of being alone. When her ankle shrieked, she ignored it. When she couldn't ignore it any longer she downed a handful of painkillers. All around her, London was yelling, pulling and poking for her attention. Taxi drivers leaning on their horns, brakes screaming, cyclists swearing, pedestrians hammering on closed bus doors, telling the driver what they thought of his mother. A balding man wearing a sandwich board and carrying a megaphone damned Helen, and anyone else who cared to listen, to hell as she passed. Little does he know, Helen thought, hell and I are already pretty well acquainted.

She stopped, turned. Almost spoke.

But if she started Helen had a feeling she'd never stop.

She could tell him a thing or two about the Devil. Things like how the Devil had all the best tunes, and a smile as bright as a searchlight that went right through you until you worked out he turned it on and off like a switch; he had eyes that pinned you to the bed, the ground or the wall, for when you were both behind closed doors and his public smile was no longer required. He didn't even look like the Devil to most people. And it was when you discovered that most people didn't think he was the Devil, because he didn't behave like the Devil to them, that you knew . . . You really were damned. And then you realised if you were damned it didn't matter what you did, because you were damned already.

The man was staring at her now, megaphone poised. Pulling her phone from her pocket, she took his picture, twice, and saved it in a folder along with the train man before turning away, his damnations bouncing off her back like darts.

The day was warm, for autumn. Sun stripping coats and jackets from pedestrians.

Acrid petrol fumes and lunchtime food smells: kebabs, Chinese, pizza and burgers. The unavoidable stench of humanity – BO and piss, stale food, coffee-and-fag breath, last night's booze doing battle with Chanel No.5 and whatever celebrity fragrance it was this month. A kaleidoscope of odour that would flay her alive in the onslaught of migraine. Now it smelled of familiarity, anonymity, safety . . .

The sprawl of Euston gave way to the sedate Georgian streets of Marylebone. Only the traffic fumes and human smells remained. The streets were politely busy; an orderly queue of taxis and town cars flowed past, the only noise but for the hush of caught conversation. You would be able to tell this was where doctors practised even if you didn't know. It wasn't until Helen turned on to Devonshire Place, rang the bell of a red-brick townhouse and was buzzed in that she realised she hadn't once felt the urge to glance behind her since she got off the train.

'Helen! How are you? You look . . .' Caroline Harris, MD, plus a lot of other letters, shut her surgery door behind her and walked round to the professional side of her desk. 'Different,' she said finally, tilting her head.

'Hair,' they both said simultaneously.

'Fancied a change,' Helen shrugged.

'Your natural colour?'

Helen nodded.

'Suits you.'

Caroline flipped open a manila folder and made a note. Only friends to a point, Helen reminded herself. Caroline skimmed the page although, knowing her, she'd read and reread it half a dozen times already. She was expensive, unless you were on medical insurance, and then she was even more expensive. But Helen trusted her. She looked up to find Caroline staring at her.

Probably just as well she did.

'What do you remember?' Caroline said suddenly.

'A-About the migraine?' Helen swallowed. Already this was not going to plan. She tried to stop her eyes flickering in the direction of the door. Too late. Caroline had obviously noticed.

'Helen . . .' Fixing her gaze on Helen, Caroline reached down and produced a copy of the *Evening Standard* from her bag. It was folded open, into neat quarters, a column of also-ran news stories on top. Her expression neutral, she handed it to Helen and sat back.

The tiny, fifty-word filler was crammed into an inch at the bottom of the column. No picture, barely any headline. Easy to miss. Although Caroline hadn't.

A body, believed to be that of British journalist Arthur Huntingdon, 46, has been found after fire destroyed the building in which he lived in an exclusive Paris square. Huntingdon, who was last seen . . .

Helen swallowed and closed her eyes. The room lurched.

So it *was* him.

He was dead.

But why had it taken so long to be reported? She had a pretty good idea. By now, their dental records must have proved beyond doubt that the body was his. Or at least that it wasn't hers. And if it wasn't hers, it could only be Art's.

When she opened her eyes, Caroline was still staring at her. Her face expressionless. The sheet of paper in front of her blank but for the note about Helen's hair colour.

'Nothing,' she said, slumping back in the chair. There was no point lying. 'I remember nothing.'

The doctor stared at her. Not the way Art used to stare, silent and cold, with the intention of inducing dread, but thoughtfully.

'Is that true?'

'Entirely. I swear.'

Again Caroline made a note. 'Let me put it another way,' she said. 'What was your first memory?'

'Coming awake in the smoke. I didn't know where I was, but I knew I was going to die.'

Caroline's eyes widened slightly. She glanced at the couch behind her and Helen shook her head. She preferred to do this sitting up. That way she could pretend to be normal, that this was simply a doctor she was seeing about her migraines. Caroline had practised as a GP anyway, before specialising, and they'd dealt with illnesses and injuries along the way. She was allowed to do that too. 'The memory,' Caroline said.

Helen rubbed her forehead. Something was taking shape. It was there now. Shaken loose by the migraine, the shock of the article, or simply sitting opposite Caroline. The orange fog was starting to clear. 'I rolled out of bed, I was naked, I don't know why. I made it to the bedroom door on my hands and knees. There was smoke, flames . . .'

'Your husband – Art – was he in bed with you?'

Helen shook her head. 'No. I was alone. That's the . . . there was a body . . .'

Caroline looked at her. Her face was impassive. 'Where?'

'On the floor in the sitting room. I think that's where the fire had started. He was dead.'

'How do you know?'

'I know what dead looks like,' Helen snapped. 'He was dead. At least . . . I think . . . no,' she knotted and unknotted her fingers in her lap. 'I'm sure he was.'

'You saw his face?'

No, Helen thought. I didn't get that close.

She shook her head.

'And then . . .?' Caroline prompted.

'Nothing.' Helen said. 'Honestly, Caroline, nothing. The next thing I remember, I'm in London with my rucksack and a camera bag. I don't even remember how. Until now, I've been happy to remember that much.

'There is one other thing . . .'

'Oh?' Caroline's pen hovered over the pad.

'Only it's not a memory, so it probably doesn't count. My sister told me I called an ex-boyfriend. Tom? Tom Bretton? I think I've told you about him?'

Caroline nodded thoughtfully. She didn't seem as surprised as Helen expected. 'Why do you think you did that?'

'Your guess is as good as mine.' Helen tried for a smile. 'Probably better. I guess my subconscious has a sensible streak.'

Caroline didn't return the smile. 'I'm serious.'

'His was the only number I knew?' Helplessness was turning to panic. 'I don't know Caroline, honestly. It came as a total shock.'

Caroline pursed her lips and made another note. 'And how are you feeling now?'

Helen looked at her. Tried to work out what it was OK to say.

'Numb, mainly. You know . . .'

Caroline waited for Helen to continue. When it became clear she'd said as much as she was going to, the doctor sat back. Helen did the same, mirroring her. Her armpits were sodden, her back slick with sweat. She knew she stank of fear. Her fingers were folded so tight that bone showed through the skin of her knuckles. She couldn't bear to imagine what else she might remember.

Without being asked, Caroline fetched her a glass of water, passing it to her with a smile that said she was safe. Then, she looked serious, a little too serious, and put on her reading glasses before glancing down at Helen's file. 'Are you planning to kill anyone?' she asked.

Helen choked, then shook her head, relieved she hadn't said anyone *else*.

'Quite sure?'

'Quite sure.'

'Good. Are you planning to kill yourself?'

Helen looked at her in astonishment. 'Caroline . . .'

'I need you to answer the question.' Her voice was surprisingly stern.

'No,' Helen said meekly. 'I'm not planning to kill myself.'

'Good.' Caroline seemed satisfied. Taking off her reading glasses, she closed Helen's file. 'You're my patient,' she said. 'That is, you've been my patient before, and are, for the purposes of this, my patient again. Since you do not plan to kill someone, and you do not plan to kill yourself, I am free to keep what you've said confidential. Should either of those things change, I will have no choice but to consider committing you or going to the police. Do you understand?'

Helen nodded.

'Please say it.'

'I understand.'

'Good. Should you need me to go through what I've just said again, tell me and I will. Should you need to ask a question you think might lead to the authorities becoming involved, ask it in the abstract and I will answer it in the abstract.'

'Thank you,' Helen said. And she meant it.

'I do have one more question,' Caroline said after a moment's silence.

Helen knew what was coming. The same question had haunted her day and night since the fire. Since she'd left him. What was she doing back at their old flat?

Helen shrugged.

She didn't have an answer.

When Caroline dropped her at the receptionist's desk, Helen's bill and prescription for six months' Clonidine were already waiting. 'Take care,' Caroline said, kissing her on both cheeks. She squeezed Helen's shoulders slightly longer than usual before turning away. 'And keep in touch.'

Helen took the small white paper bag and sheet of A4 neatly folded in three and zipped it safely into the pocket of her rucksack. The relief she felt at having it was tinged with a pang of conscience. How would she pay for it? And how long would Caroline give her before losing patience altogether? Maybe it didn't matter.

When Helen looked up, she found the receptionist staring at her.

'Sorry. I was miles away. Did you want me?'

'I'm not sure if I should say . . .' The woman glanced towards the closed consulting-room door, considering. 'A man was looking for you.'

Helen's stomach lurched. 'What did he look like?' Her voice was a croak. The receptionist glanced at her strangely, then remembered her job. If she looked strangely at all the strange people who came in here she'd never stop.

'Blond,' she said. 'Medium build. Not tall, not short. Nice smile.'

Helen felt her body unclench.

'Very professional. Ms Harris shook hands and walked him to the door.'

'What did she say?' Helen asked. Her mind was racing. The police, it had to be. But why hadn't Caroline told her?

'She didn't,' the receptionist said. Then she hesitated before adding: 'Also, someone called asking if we had a contact number for you.'

Helen smiled tightly, hoping the tension in her jaw didn't show. 'Ms Harris spoke to him, too?'

'Oh no,' the receptionist said brightly. 'I did. He said he was an old friend and needed to get hold of you urgently, but your mobile was out. Did I have an address? He knew you saw Ms Harris. And I knew the mobile bit was true because I'd tried to call it myself. So I figured he must know you well . . .'

Her heart was pounding again.

'He was so insistent, I said I'd email you for him, pass on his details.' She was talking fast now, tumbling over her words. 'But then I thought, since you were coming in anyway . . . I'm sorry if I did the wrong thing?'

'It's fine . . .' Helen's pulse was racing. She tried to think straight. 'When was this?'

Relief showed on the woman's face. Helen was not going to yell. She had not broken any protocols. Well, she had, but she wasn't going to get into trouble. 'End of last week,' she said. 'That's the weirdest thing. The same day you called. That's how I knew your usual mobile wasn't working, because I tried to call you back.'

Coincidence. It had to be.

'Did you get his name?' For the first time, Helen noticed a yellow Post-it note in the woman's hand. She glanced down at it.

'Ridley,' she said. 'Mark Ridley.'

14

Somehow London didn't feel so safe any more. Sun reflected off the white stucco of the terrace opposite just as it had half an hour earlier. Taxis lingered, meters running, exhaust fumes creating a haze in the air. People strolled past, some heading for Regent's Park to take advantage of the weather, some just getting from A to B. All with the gait of those basking in the unexpected gift of a city in the grip of an Indian summer. A hundred metres away on Marylebone Road, traffic roared. Everything had changed and nothing had. Or maybe she just hadn't been looking properly before.

Helen knew better than to look like a person who didn't feel safe.

She didn't scan the street when she left Caroline's surgery. She didn't hug the wall. She didn't obey the voice that wanted her to keep one eye in the back of her head at all times. She walked down the middle of the pavement, she smiled politely but disinterestedly at strangers coming towards her, and she prayed like hell for rain and an excuse to put her hood up and her head down.

How much did anybody know?

Now a British paper had run the story it was only a matter of time before someone else latched on to it. Mark Ridley was a journalist. She should have known someone who knew Art – who knew her – would try to hunt her down.

It hit her like a bus careering out of nowhere side-swiping her off the pavement. One moment she was walking down the street, the next she was curled in on herself by iron railings, hands cradling her head as if attempting to hold in the tears that began washing over her in great, painful gasps.

She had no idea how long she huddled there, fighting to silence the wails that threatened to burst from her. Finally she caught her breath and steeled herself to glance up. No one was looking. Or, if they were, they were pretending not to. Certainly her side of the pavement was suspiciously empty. The crying jag had come from nowhere. It wasn't sadness, or despair, it was sheer bloody fury and impotence. Fumbling the pills from her rucksack pocket, she pushed one from its bubble through foil, looked at it, and then tried to put it back. When it dropped at her feet she had to resist the urge to pick the precious thing up, instead kicking it into a gutter and watching it tumble into a grate. Then she stood up, hooked her rucksack on to her back and made herself put one foot in front of the other. It didn't occur to her to worry about the state of her face.

They said dogs could smell fear on you.

Well, Helen thought, dogs had nothing on people. There was a type of person, usually a man, in her experience, for whom fear was a magnet. That man could spot fear from the other side of a packed room, from the other side of a packed city. If you were really unlucky, he might be the type of man who liked to nurture fear, create it where previously there was none, then feed it to amuse himself.

A man who was attracted to light, only to snuff it out.

Art Huntingdon was that type of man.

Mark Ridley was Art's best friend. If she and Art had separated in the usual way, then she would have lost contact. That was the way it went; friends divided down the middle like belongings, the friends that came with you into the relationship left with you. Mark came with Art. His sidekick, his partner in crime. At least he had been. Helen hadn't seen him for over a year; couldn't recall Art mentioning him in months.

She wandered the backstreets of Marylebone and Bloomsbury for the next hour, trying to find her fleeting sense of wellbeing and belonging. She scoured the pavements in search of them. They weren't there. London felt lost to her now. Her insane plan of maybe visiting a gallery – Tate Modern; she'd entertained ideas of the Turbine Hall – finding a restaurant and being *that woman*, the one who sat in the middle of the room, not at the edge, paperback propped on the salt cellar . . . Her plan was as hollow as her gut.

It was impulse that made her do it. That and the pain in her ankle. As she turned the corner on to Euston Road from Coram's Fields, a modern block loomed on her left.

A sign in the Premier Inn's window advertising rooms for £39. She knew it would end up costing more, it always did, but she could stretch to that. Exhaustion overwhelmed her. The promise of hot water, Wi-Fi, walls that weren't stained with damp and carpets that didn't feel sticky under her feet, the silence of a new build with nothing to say, was too much to pass up.

Six months ago – even six weeks – she couldn't imagine having considered this place a sanctuary, but she'd stayed in far worse. The receptionist was polite but disinterested, heedless of her absence of luggage and the puffy redness that must have ringed her eyes; paying cash didn't pose a problem and he didn't demand a credit card for extras since extras weren't an option. She paid a £10 surcharge to guarantee a room with a bath. It was worth every penny.

The room, when she reached it, at the far end of the corridor by the fire escape, was basic but comfortable. A small rectangular window, like every other small rectangular window in the building's façade, looked out on to Euston Road and the British Library on the far side. Below, traffic snarled and she cranked shut the double-glazed panel, pulling the blackout blind to shut it out, and with it what remained of the daylight. Slipping her laptop from her backpack, she put it on the desk along with the *Evening Standard*, and scoured the instructions for getting online. The luxury that was Wi-Fi, she'd almost forgotten.

Double-locking the door, Helen checked under the bed and in the wardrobe before turning on the TV; dozens of channels and a reception so sharp it was startling. The normality calmed her. A bed, a bath, four walls, only one door. Magnolia paint and mass-produced paintings. What could be safer? In the time it took to run what would have been an hour's worth of hot water at Wildfell, she kicked off her trainers and socks and sat on the loo seat massaging her swollen ankle and cursing herself for not thinking to buy a support. When the bath had run, Helen sank gratefully into the bubbles and tried to push the day's events from her mind, everything but the white noise of a game show cackling from the TV next door and the occasional ping of the lift.

When the water started to chill, she dragged herself, waterlogged but still pink with heat, from the tub, wrapped herself in a warm towelling robe, made herself a cup of faux posh instant and ate both packets of complimentary biscuits. Flipping open her laptop she logged into her VPN via the hotel Wi-Fi, before downloading Helen Graham's two webmail accounts. There was nothing, of course. Why would there be? Nobody knew the accounts existed. And yet the spam was there. How did they do that?

There was no alternative, she'd have to go back into her own Gmail account. Chewing the inside of her lip, she double-clicked.

Fran's name leapt out at her, dated yesterday. Subject line: **News**.

Hi Helen

I don't know whether to assume my emails aren't reaching you, or you're just not replying. I guess I prefer to go with the former. Anyway, something

happened that I thought you'd want to know. You
remember Art's friend Mark?

Helen spilled lukewarm Kenco on to the white towelling robe. Mark. Twice in one day? Even twice in two
days, it didn't add up.

. . . He said we'd met at your wedding, not that I
remember to be honest, I was so pregnant.
Anyway, he was ever so cut up about Art and
seemed desperately worried about you, so I
emailed to say I'd spoken to you . . .

Closing her eyes, Helen did the distraction thing
Caroline had taught her, counting as she pushed the
nails of her right hand hard into the flesh of the palm
until she felt them begin to cut.

Apparently he has some stuff of Art's you might
want? Anyway you should call him. Call me, email
me, something. I'm worried about you.

Love Fran x

Helen's first urge was to run. She could throw on her
clothes, check out and be at King's Cross in less than
five minutes. Safe back at Wildfell by one a.m. Two at
the latest. Indoors, with the doors locked . . . The hotel
dressing gown was on the floor; one leg in her jeans,
before Helen caught herself.

What, precisely, would that achieve?

Barricaded in Wildfell, where, she hoped, no one could

find her – and even that was feeling less certain by the moment. Forcing herself to sit on the bed, Helen breathed slowly. Started counting down from one hundred, intoning the numbers aloud into the room.

Ninety-nine, ninety-eight, ninety-seven, ninety-six . . . A documentary about food burbled to itself from the small, flat screen above the desk.

Eighty-nine, eighty-eight, eighty-seven. A siren wailed on Euston Road.

Seventy-six, seventy-five, seventy-four . . . The person in the room above turned on the shower.

Gradually her voice grew louder, more confident, drowning out the babbling in her head, the blood roaring in her ears. Flight not fight. When had that become her default response? What would teenage Helen say if she could see her older self now? Sitting alone in a hotel room, repeatedly checking the locks and scared of her own shadow.

She wouldn't recognise me, Helen thought. *I* don't recognise me.

By the time she reached zero, Helen was in control. She would spend the night here, as planned, and try to regroup. Art was dead, it was entirely reasonable for Mark to be upset; upset and worried. The way Tom was worried for her. Tom had dropped in on her mum, then called her sister. Mark had emailed her. Of course he had, he was a journalist, getting people's contact details was second nature.

Both sachets of instant coffee gone, Helen resorted to PG tips and turned her attention to the laptop, typing in two words for the first time since the fire: 'Art Huntingdon'.

The browser spun for a few seconds and then screeds and screeds of links started to appear on screen. Art's journalism, reports and front-line notes from Afghanistan had been syndicated the world over, Iraq less so, Syria not at all. But still the hits went into the hundreds of thousands. Facebook, Twitter, Instagram, Google Plus, Foursquare. He even had a LinkedIn page. When had he set that up? None of the photographs were recent. Six, seven years old or more. Showing him younger than she remembered. Thinner, with more hair, before age and career disappointment removed the arrogant flash of good looks.

An arresting black-and-white image brought her up short. He was leaning against a tank, in fatigues, wiry dark hair sticking up, hooded eyes staring directly into the camera. It was his expression that unsettled her, mocking, combative. There was no softness in his gaze, no flirtation. Only confrontation. Helen knew the picture all too well. She'd taken it. Although she hadn't felt entirely comfortable about it even then.

After ten pages and a glance at all the social media pages she could access, she'd confirmed what she'd already known. There was nothing at all for the last three weeks. For the weeks before that, she could tell you what he'd eaten for breakfast and what colour socks he'd worn.

How exposing it was to live life on the web was one of the things they'd argued about. Not argued, exactly. Arguing with Art was unwise. More, disagreed. Art believed his Internet presence was a sign of his place in the world, a way of recording his true worth. His accumulated value was not in the zeroes on his bank account (although he prized those too), but in digital dollar signs. Helen thought differently. Still did. There had been a time when she'd agreed with him. Not about money, she'd never cared very much about that; obviously, or she'd have had more. The status, though. Professional respect. Winning awards. That much had mattered.

They said war reporters were the surgeons of the newspaper world. It was the adrenalin surge of having other people's life stories in your hands, she supposed. Her response had always been the same: if reporters were the surgeons, then photographers were the snipers; high maintenance, aloof, riddled by doubt and driven by certainty.

And she hadn't known back then, hadn't worked out for herself, that there were two types of war reporter anyway. Maybe more, but she'd definitely met the two. There were front-line journalists that were out there to make a difference and the war junkies. Art had always been good at selling himself as the first . . .

The balance of power had been off from the start. Not the very start, as Art saw it, back when Helen was a rookie photographer and Art, ten years her senior, was already on his way to greatness. In his head, that was the start of everything. Seven years before they actually did. And it was that . . . time-lapse, that made him superior. She owed him, he joked, that night in Baghdad, for her very first front page. Without him, she'd never have been in Soho the day the nail bomb went off and never got that image. Beginner's luck, he insisted on calling it. Just as she owed him for the one she'd got earlier that day. It passed him by that there had been dozens, if not hundreds, of front pages for her in the intervening years. But he was so convincing, she'd half believed him.

He never tired of telling people how they met on her first job, casting himself as her champion and mentor. It was a role he relished. Within weeks of that first meeting, the one she barely remembered, he got his longed-for move to the foreign desk. Then 9/11 happened and Art became a name. A picture byline. Beating off job offers, industry accolades and sexual favours with a stick.

Or not beating them off. With the benefit of that telescopic lens known as hindsight, Helen finally understood why, after they got together, his sheets were always fresh the morning she returned from a trip.

By the time they met again, seven years later, Helen had gone from 'lucky beginner' to front-page regular. They'd make a great team, Art said, as he lay in her bed that night, painting a picture of mutual glory. But Art hadn't wanted a partner, not really. He wanted a handmaiden. As Helen's Google pages grew and his faltered, their relationship took the strain. The only difference being that when you searched 'Helen Lawrence' you didn't get her. Well, not much. You got her pictures.

It was around then Helen had started to wonder if the true mark of success wasn't invisibility. If the seal of a good journalist or photographer wasn't obscurity. How can you tell a story if the story simply becomes you? Art's growing obsession with social media tipped her over the edge.

You had to be *a force* to live life off-line, she told Art one evening. It required power to erase yourself from the world's search engines. They were sitting in the window of a bistro he liked behind Rue de Rivoli. In her head, Helen could still see the frontage, the stainless-steel tables covered with white paper tablecloths. She'd erased its name though. Imagine, she'd said, waving her fork as she warmed to her theme. Imagine having a lasting body of work that existed entirely beyond the name attached to it.

Only the truly great could ever achieve that.

Paris was quiet, that night. Winter settling in. A couple of tables of locals and that was it. The tourists began to vanish at the point it became too cold to huddle under a heater at a pavement table, holding a Gauloise in frigid fingers and looking convincingly like it passed for fun on Facebook.

It was only when silence crowded in that she looked up from her omelette. Art's steak was running red on his plate, a familiar cloud darkening his face. He laid down the serrated knife and looked at her. Blood pooled with oil in a lake of Dijon. He didn't speak. Just stared, his face expressionless, cold and hard. Nothing human behind the eyes that she could see. As though she had devalued his entire life's work in a single sentence. It didn't occur to him for a second she might have been talking about herself, her work, her dreams.

'I . . .' she started. 'I wasn't . . . I didn't mean . . .'

But he just stared, face white, lips a tight, narrow line, silencing her.

15

It wasn't Gil's imagination. When he next went into the shop, Mrs Millward was definitely giving him what could only be described as a *look*. If anyone should be bestowing 'looks', thought Gil as he bought his daily pack of B&H and made a point of ignoring her questioning gaze, it was him. Looks in his repertoire this morning might have included, How did you get my mobile number? Who the hell do you think you are, handing it to a total stranger? What made you think this was a good idea anyway? He was being old-school, Gil knew that. But mobile numbers weren't things you gave to just anyone. Not like landlines. Mobile numbers were personal.

Friends, families, colleagues.

Mind you, then no one would ever call him. The sourness of that thought made Gil feel better, but it didn't solve his problem. What to do about the Liza woman? He'd liked the look of her well enough. What he'd managed to remember, anyway. She'd been friendly, well turned out. It had been a while since he went out with anyone. Truth was, he couldn't think of a good enough reason not to.

Hi Liza, he tapped, once he was safely outside. **That sounds nice. Gil.** Pressing send, he immediately regretted it. *Nice?* That sounds *nice?* He shook his head, vaguely aware he looked like a mad man muttering to himself in a shop doorway. Less than five steps further down the street his phone buzzed.

Great, how about dinner Thursday? 8 p.m. at Genarro's? I can pick you up if you like? Lx

Was it too late to pull out? He could always say he was busy this week, maybe next. Find an excuse next week to postpone it . . .

Oh, what the hell.

Sounds good. I'll pick you up. What's your address? Gil.

He pressed send. The message bar was only three-quarters gone when he realised that in the space of three texts, an invitation for a drink had turned into a dinner date, with 'picking you up' and, therefore, 'dropping you off afterwards' on the menu. For the first time since Jan left, he felt the cold chill of the single man of a certain age on the rocky shores of dating. Gil shuddered.

It wasn't that there hadn't been other women.

There had, several. Donna, Meg, Maureen, Linda, the temp who'd covered in HR (that had been drink for both

146

of them), Angela, Chrissie . . . He stopped running through the list in his head. More than five, less than ten. Only Donna and Angela had been more than a couple of drinks and a warm bed for two lonely people of a certain age. It had surprised him, at first. Not to be too pleased with himself, but he'd expected to be beating them off with a stick. Single, not bad-looking, decent job, own place . . . He wasn't short of offers. Just not like that. Most of that list were even less keen to settle down again than he was.

'God no,' Maureen had said. Or was it Linda? 'Got my house, my kids are gone. Eat what I want when I want; watch what I want when I want. If I have my way, I'll never do anyone else's washing again.'

This, Liza, felt a bit different. It didn't feel like a drink, dinner and a bit of what Donna had euphemistically called companionship. It felt like she was after more. It felt like she meant business. Gil wasn't sure he was in the market for business. He'd just reached his front door when a thought occurred to him.

'Back so soon, Mr Markham?' said Margaret Millward, when the bell above the door brought her from the stockroom.

'Forgot to pick up some bits.' Gil ducked down an aisle to escape her beady stare. It wasn't easy, his head towered a good foot over the top shelf. He scanned the shelves, trying to remember what Helen Graham had picked up last time he saw her. Milk . . . the red label, he thought, skimmed stuff. The stuff that didn't taste like milk at all, changed the colour of the tea but that was all. Bread. Fresh loaves had just been delivered so he picked something crusty. She didn't seem the sliced white type. Earl Grey. She hadn't bought tea bags so he would . . . And nice chocolate. Well, as nice as the General Stores could provide. Then he scoured the fruit and veg and settled on a bunch of purple grapes.

'Visiting the sick, are we?'

'What makes you . . .?' Gil looked at his pile on the counter. The bloody woman didn't miss a trick. It was like some long-forgotten memory had kicked in. Not the bread and milk, so much as the fruit and chocolate. He was only short of a bunch of flowers. 'Not really,' he muttered. 'Just short of a few things.' As if to prove the point, he picked up a can of beans he didn't need and wouldn't eat from a nearby shelf and added them to the pile.

Wildfell House looked exactly as it had last time he was there. Silver Peugeot at 45 degrees to the front, tyre marks a tidal wave in gravel behind it. Curtains pulled part way across the front windows, like half-closed eyes. Not so much deserted as not yet awake. No light that he could see. No noise but crows wheeling above the trees in the field behind him, and the growl of an occasional lorry on the road behind.

Almost eleven. Not too early to knock. Not on a weekday.

There was a bell to the right of the heavy black door. Round, metal, ugly. Old-fashioned wasn't in it. It looked almost as old as the house, which was obviously not possible, since the Elizabethans didn't have doorbells, so far as he knew. Although it was certainly stiff enough.

Leaning on the bell, Gil thought he felt it shift slightly. He couldn't be sure if it budged, but in case it did he leaned on it again and listened. Was that an answering ring he heard inside? It was equally possible it was his imagination supplying the noise. He gave it ten seconds, made himself add another ten and leaned again. Still nothing. No movement from inside. No lights going on. He stepped back and stared up at the first-floor windows.

Most likely the bell wasn't working.

He rapped three times with the knocker, the tarnished face of a lion dead-eyeing him as he did so. Could she have gone for a walk? Gil tried to imagine her limping towards the Scar. Perhaps she healed quickly. Perhaps you had to be his age before injuries took their toll. If you could get over a hangover twice as fast when young why not everything else? He gave one final knock, bent down to put the provisions on the doorstep, cursing his wasted walk and wasted opportunity. Not to mention wasted money. As he unconcertinaed himself, he heard locks rattle on the far side of her door.

'Mr Markham?' Helen Graham opened the door just wide enough to stand in the gap. She was wearing what probably passed for pyjamas. Grubby grey jogging bottoms, an even grubbier T-shirt with a slogan too faded to read, beneath a slightly cleaner towelling robe once belonging to a Premier Inn.

'Mademoiselle Graham, Helen, I'm sorry. Did I wake you?'

A wry expression crossed her face. Not a smile but not exactly unfriendly. 'Don't worry about it,' she said, but she didn't open the door further. 'Went to London for a couple of days. Tired myself out. Also I don't sleep well. So when I do I just go with it.'

She certainly did look tired.

'I wondered how you were. I thought . . .' Gil picked up his offerings, feeling naïve, like a boy bringing an apple for the teacher and fearing it might be rejected. Gil Markham, sixty-odd going on six. Her gaze flicked from his eyes to the things in his arms and back again. Something flashed across her face. Irritation, maybe. Sadness, confusion. He'd overstepped the mark. Gil knew that already.

Then she did smile and her pallor lifted.

'Baked beans?' her mouth twisted.

'Isn't that what sick people eat, beans on toast?'

'Some sick people maybe. I'm not sick. I'm barely injured.' She took the tin and turned it round in her hand as if examining an exotic object. 'Can't remember the last time I ate baked beans.'

'Don't children live on baked beans?'

She frowned. 'Maybe. Not my specialist subject, I'm afraid . . . Fish fingers and beans sounds familiar though. I'm pretty sure I ate that as a child.' She looked at him. 'When I was in England, I mean. Visiting. I'm more of a black coffee and whatever's cold in the fridge person now.'

On the road behind him, a truck rattled. 'Shall I carry them in for you?'

'No need. I'll take them . . .'

Then she stopped, seemed to relent. 'I'm sorry. I don't mean to be unfriendly. Yes, of course, come in. You must be cold standing there. I'll make tea.'

The entrance hall was dark and panelled in heavy wood with enough split panels and woodworm to make Gil worry for the rest of the house. A huge painting of a stag at bay over an equally cracked marble fireplace was flaking to reveal canvas beneath. It could hardly be a Landseer original. Someone would have removed it. As Gil crossed in front of the wide stairs a draught tickled his hair, like a window opening above. For the first time he realised he might have interrupted something. Helen might have been with someone. Why wouldn't she? An attractive and mysterious woman like her. He glanced up, but the stairs doubled back on themselves and there was nothing he could see.

'Cold, isn't it?' she said, glancing over her shoulder. 'It's so big, even with three-quarters of the rooms locked up, I can't seem to get the place warm.'

The kitchen was surprisingly cosy by comparison.

'Nice,' he said, unthinking.

She turned, gave him that look again. In a different life, to someone she knew, she might have said 'Who are you trying to kid?' Instead, she just said, 'Really?' her voice rising in disbelief at the end.

'Well, yes, you know, relatively.'

Helen raised her eyebrows. 'I suppose I do spend most of my time in here. I guess that's why it feels more lived in.'

'Where shall I . . .?' he nodded at his pile.

'Oh, anywhere is fine.' She waved her hand in the general vicinity of a chair and Gil took it as an invitation to dump his offerings on the table and sit down. There was a laptop open, but dozing, on the scrubbed table, green light flashing as it almost slept. A mug with the dregs of coffee grounds. A copy of the *Evening Standard*. A *Metro*. As she sliced open the cellophane on the Earl Grey, Gil reached out and touched the mug. Not hot but definitely not cold. Not asleep then. Not even slightly.

Then he leaned over and picked up the *Standard*.

'Haven't seen one of these in a while,' he said, waving it at her.

She glanced over at him, her face suddenly tense. 'Oh, you don't want to bother with that,' she said. 'It's days old. Try the *Metro*, it's a bit more recent. Not much though.' In one smooth movement she slid the *Standard* from his hand and replaced it with the *Metro*, putting the former out of reach on a worktop.

For a couple of minutes, Gil pretended to flick through it. Both free, both full of nothing. He was buggered if he could see the difference.

'How's the ankle?' he asked as she put a mug in front of him and sat down at the end of the table, in front of the laptop. Her seat, he could tell. The place she always sat. The place he suspected she'd been sitting when he rang the bell.

She shrugged.

They sipped tea in silence. Not exactly companionable, but near enough. The kitchen had the feeling of a room that had known love once. Not recently. Not for a long time. Certainly not this century, maybe not even last . . . How did she stand it out here on her own? If she was on her own. Gil listened for sounds of someone else in residence. Nothing but scraping from outside the back door. The groan of the occasional pipe.

Helen didn't seem to notice the noise. She was staring into space, her hands hugging the mug like a hot-water bottle. She bit her nails, Gil noticed. Her cuticles were pink and raw. No rings on her wedding finger. No dent or pale skin to tell him one had been recently removed. Hands that looked older than she did. Faded freckles peppered skin so papery that blue veins showed through. They brought to mind the rumours of her being a famous French actress come here to die. He wasn't convinced, but something had brought her here.

You didn't choose to live alone in a ruin like this for no reason.

'Thank you,' she said suddenly into his silence. Gil jumped. If his mug had been full he'd have spilt it. 'Bringing shopping was kind of you. Not necessary. But kind. I've forgotten how to recognise kindness recently. To be honest, I was afraid you'd tell that woman in the shop about my fall and she'd turn up . . .' Helen caught herself. 'Not that I mean to be rude. Is she a friend of yours?'

'Not exactly . . .' he smiled. 'Don't worry. Your secret's safe with me.'

As the words left his mouth Gil felt the air ice around him. Her face, which had momentarily softened, shut down again.

'What I mean is, I won't say anything to Mrs Millward.'

'Thank you,' she said, but all familiarity was gone. 'I came here to get away . . . You know? For the peace and quiet. To work and think and . . . I didn't expect the gossip. That I would be required to socialise.'

Gil winced. 'Small towns are famous for gossip. Villages even worse.'

'So I've discovered.'

'Mind you, who needs a small town when you've got the Internet?' Gil joked, inclining his head towards her laptop, USB flashing in its side.

'Oh,' she said, following his gaze. 'I don't really look at the Internet unless I can't avoid it. I was just downloading something.'

'Not even for news?'

Helen smiled grimly. 'Especially not for news.'

Gil shrugged. He didn't get it. Why would you have two papers in the house and a USB dongle knocking around if you weren't interested in news?

'How long are you planning on staying?' Gil ventured. He had a feeling he was on borrowed time. Better to ask her now. If she threw him out, he might not get another chance. 'Reports differ.'

Her mouth quirked. 'Not sure,' she said eventually. 'A few months maybe. I'd hoped for longer, but to be honest, I'm not sure I fancy being here in January and February.'

'Can I ask what you're doing?' he didn't expect her to answer, but in for a penny.

'Here? I'm working on something. A project . . .'

'A book?'

She bit at an already sore hangnail. 'Possibly. I haven't decided what form it should take yet.'

'You're a writer then?'

Helen shook her head. Laughed. 'Can't write to save my life.' Squeaking her chair back, she pushed herself to her feet, picked up her mug and reached for his. As she did, her sleeve brushed the trackpad and her Mac lurched into life. Its screen saver flashed up with a password box obscuring the middle. A picture of a ragged boy, maybe five or six, sitting on a filthy doorstep, surrounded with rubble. Bare legs skinny and bruised, ending in lace-less plimsolls. He was playing with a plastic figure.

Slamming the lid with something just short of force, Helen smiled a quick tight smile and turned to the sink.

Gil's audience was over. But there was something about that picture, something haunting. It wasn't the poverty that made Gil's guts churn. It was the certainty he'd seen the boy before.

'That picture . . .?'

Helen Graham stared at him, eyes unreadable.

'The boy? Is he someone you know?'

She didn't answer, just turned and walked out of the kitchen and through the hall to the front door in silence, leaving Gil no option but to follow. She held the door so Gil could pass through it.

'Was he?' he repeated, feeling the door start to close on him before he was entirely clear.

He didn't expect her to answer. Then, just as the door was about to close, she stopped. 'Knew,' she said, when Gil looked back in surprise. 'He died.'

16

She locked the door behind him, more from instinct than because she expected him to return, then leaned against it and closed her eyes, taking comfort from the solid wood against her back, the sound of gravel crunching beneath his brogues. As his footsteps faded, her breathing slowed. It took an age for the sound to vanish altogether. His pace was heavy, solemn, and Helen was surprised to feel a pang of regret through the panic that had surged when he'd homed in on the boy. She was starting to like him. He reminded her of an old boss, one she'd had a lot of time for, and, though she'd never have admitted it, she'd been glad of the company. Until he'd started to pry.

What was it with this village?

Perhaps Gil was right. Perhaps it wasn't this village, perhaps it was all villages.

Not for the first time, Helen wondered if she should have stayed in the city.

A draught lifted the hairs on the back of her neck, and she shivered. Glanced around but she couldn't see the source. It was chill out here in the entrance hall, all rattling windows and gaping floorboards. Chill everywhere in this damn house. Dark, too, despite the fact it was gone noon and outside, behind the ever-present clouds hanging low over the Dales, the sun was high in the sky. Wildfell seemed impervious to weather. Like a black hole, it sucked in the light; a permanent February. Helen shuddered and wrapped the stolen robe more tightly around her.

Ever since she'd got back from London, the house had seemed darker, more forbidding. Not the comfortable sanctuary she'd conjured in her mind by the time she'd checked out of the Premier Inn, contraband robe complete with coffee stain in her rucksack. Unused rooms and corridors had grown shadowy. The mansion's quirks and quinks, always there, had grown noisier, more vocal, as if they'd regained their voice during her absence. There was no reason they should be silenced. It wasn't as if they expected her to stay. It wasn't as if she expected to. But still she couldn't shake the sense that when she entered a room, someone else left.

Well, she told herself, *someone* else probably did.

While she was away, the cat appeared to have moved in. He didn't think she'd noticed, but she had. A flicker at the corner of her eye, a tail vanishing round a door, a smudge of black on a window ledge, the occasional carefully positioned mouse corpse.

If that was what passed for company here, it would have to do.

Driven back into the kitchen by the cold, Helen moved

instinctively towards the kettle, then caught herself. If she had to drink one more bloody cup of tea she'd scream. Instead, she lapped the room, checking the pantry and the doors to the outhouse, opening cupboard doors and closing them again. Outside, the trees were beginning to shed their leaves. In a few weeks, the copse that protected Wildfell from the Dales would be bare, leaving the unkempt grounds looking even more deserted. On the other side of the window, a crow squawked. Helen jumped in surprise, banging her hip on the corner of the table as the bird took flight less than a foot from her face.

This was ridiculous. She had to get a grip.

Company. Helen Lawrence looking for company? That was a laugh. The fact she didn't need it, scorned it, even, was part of her psychological scaffolding. Something she knew about herself. She was good at being alone. Wasn't that what Fran had said?

Art, on the other hand, could do company. He was good in company. He could put company on and take it off like a mask. War reporters . . . Even former war reporters are not naturally gregarious. A tight group of comrades whose ability to fake it in larger groups got them through what they need to get through. As for her . . . she liked people, most people. But send her to a desert island for a week and she'd have said, fine, no problem. What she'd failed to notice before this, though, was that no matter how many out-of-the-way places she'd been, she'd always been surrounded by people: journalists, locals, villagers, officials, police, translators, soldiers . . .

Self-sufficient, maybe. A loner, no. Show her a strange city where she didn't speak the language, couldn't even read the alphabet, and she'd find her way across it. But there was a skill to being entirely alone. She was discovering now that she didn't have it.

The journey back to Wildfell had been uneventful, but she hadn't been able to shake the sense that she was being watched. At the station, on the train, on the bus to the airport. At the airport, though, the feeling had shifted a little and she'd put it down to paranoia. Even so, she'd taken a circuitous route from the bus stop to the long-stay car park just in case and kept her eye on the rear-view mirror on the long drive home over the moors.

Relenting, Helen made another cup of tea and then perched in front of the laptop, exactly where she'd been sitting when Gil arrived. Photographs flickered across the screen. Faces blurring until she stopped, attention caught by a colour, a pose, a moment in time that triggered a recollection. Some of the pictures had been filed geographically or chronologically, the rest she'd bundled on to the cloud in random folders before she left for her last assignment. The mess wasn't a problem, she could find her way around it. Better messy than destroyed. She'd come close to discovering that the hard way.

This morning, she'd been toying with a different sort of narrative. A way of putting them together that would tell a story that was theirs, not hers. Every so often an image caught her eye and she stopped, appraised it and added it to a collection. It was only when she'd built the first catalogue that she noticed it. So many children. When had she started focusing on children? It was the children standing in the ruins that made her fingers freeze. And women. Lots and lots of women. Some faces blank and hopeless, their homes destroyed, husbands dead. If the women were lucky, children clustered round their legs, hiding from the foreigner with the camera.

If they weren't . . .

Helen shuddered, tried to concentrate on her fingers skimming the trackpad, creating new folders and dragging pictures into them until gradually their story began to emerge.

The more life stories she could build, she figured, the less time she'd have to think about Art's.

Art had been dead nearly three weeks now and yet, the more time passed, the more she felt his presence. As if the removal of his physical presence had bolstered his psychic one.

Something clattered the other side of the door, and Helen froze. Sat stock-still, listened.

Just the hum of the fridge, the distant call of crows.

It was probably nothing, she told herself, turning on the old Roberts to obliterate the nothing, and returned her attention to the pictures.

His was a constant presence – Art's – and the boy's too. They seemed weirdly inter-linked, always there, always out of sight. Although that sequence of pictures had nothing to do with Art, quite the opposite in fact.

She had forgotten about the boy, more or less, until she thought she saw him out on the Dales. And she hadn't seen him since, although she'd felt him right up until she went to London. It wasn't just this house. The boy had been with her for years. As long as Art, now she thought about it. Not that she'd realised that, not at first. But the minute she uploaded the image and those button brown eyes looked up from his Power Ranger and fixed on hers, she knew it had been him all along.

She'd carried him home in her camera.

What was it about him that had caught Gil Markham's attention? She cursed to herself. It was a good picture, she knew that. Along with its twin, it had won her awards, another front page, more than one, in several languages. They had been everywhere for a time, those pictures. They had changed her life in more ways than one. Hardly surprising that someone who'd never met her before and knew nothing about their origin, might recognise them.

But Gil had seemed too interested.

She'd been telling him the truth about the Internet. She hadn't used it since she got back. The VPN had made her careless, given her a false sense of security. A security that had been taken away by a single tiny news story and two calls from Mark Ridley. Now the house she'd been so desperate to return to was beginning to feel like a trap of her own making.

Checking the USB had a signal, she logged on to her secure connection and typed in two words 'Gil Markham'. Then she opened a new page beside it and typed in two more words 'Gilbert Markham', making sure they were one and the same.

As the links appeared on the pages in front of her Helen's heart sank. Far from being a harmless friendly local, Gil Markham was a bloody journalist. A handful of local awards. Ex Fleet Street and now retired early, according to the most recent snippet she could find on the local paper's website. That didn't help. In her experience, a journalist with time on his hands was a dangerous animal. And Gil didn't look old enough to be retired.

Shit, she muttered under her breath, as she logged off. Just as she was starting to like him.

After that, Helen couldn't settle.

She was unable to shake the feeling that she was no longer alone.

Guilt, that's what Caroline would say. Banquo's ghost. There was no one in the house. Helen knew that. Whatever her 3 a.m. self thought. No Art, no boy, no friendly neighbourhood busybody. Apart from anything else, it simply wasn't possible, not with her intensive lock-checking regime. Then it occurred to Helen: if not someone inside then how about out? She eyed the kitchen window, looking for some telltale movement beyond, but all looked still. When she pushed back her chair, its wooden legs screeched on terracotta tiles so loudly it quite literally set her teeth on edge. Behind her, on the worktop, the Roberts radio had slipped into white noise without Helen noticing.

Clonidine would take the edge off her terror.

But she wasn't allowing herself to take the pills. Knowing they were there should be sufficient. Despite the slight shimmer of colours around her, the prickling of her temples and the sweat under her arms, Helen was determined to prove she could do it.

Helen caught herself. That was precisely what had kept her with Art. *I can do this.* She used to think stubbornness showed character. Now she suspected it simply showed stupidity. *I can do this* turned too easily into *I don't know how not to do this*. Becoming, *I don't know how to stop this.*

Passing the back door she flexed its wrought-iron handle from habit. Locked. Twice: Chubb and newly installed bolt. Through the pane of glass in the top half she could see another bolt, also newly installed on the wicket gate. Both products of her trip to London.

Helen didn't hear the scratching until she passed the pantry with its square of cardboard taped over the broken pane. Distant but persistent. It wasn't the first time she'd heard it. At night, usually. Mice she assumed. Or rats, which would be worse. Helen hated rats, more so since she saw the corpse of a woman in Syria who'd been tortured with them. This time, though, the noise was less scrabbly, more focused. On the larder's shelves were empty Kilner jars. On the floor a huge and filthy microwave dumped there and moved no further. By the time she reached the back the noise was gone.

A handful of seconds later, it started up again behind her.

Circling the kitchen, Helen strained her ears for the source. Flicking· off the radio, she skirted the room, listening at doors and opening cupboards. She could imagine how she looked. Mad as a box of frogs, make-up free, with her hair knotted on her head, spooking and stealthing around a gloomy room in socked feet, looking for the flicker of movement that told her a mouse had just left the building.

The scratching resumed, louder now.

Helen padded across terracotta tiles, cold even through her socks, and put her ear to the back door. It was there now. Right there on the other side of that door. The sound vibrated upwards, like nails on a blackboard. Trying to peer down through the filthy glass of the door in the hope of avoiding opening it, she saw nothing. If the noise wouldn't go away, then she could. She would take her laptop upstairs.

Against all judgement, she slid back the bolt, turned the key in the lock and twisted the handle. On the mat sat the black tom, tangled and filthy, tumbling from his hind legs, caught mid-scrabble. Helen didn't know much about cats – make that *anything* about cats – but he looked worse for wear than the last time she thought she'd seen him sneaking through the pantry window. Not emaciated exactly, but as if he hadn't eaten for a few days. When she bent towards him he hissed. When she stepped away, he tipped his head and mewled. Part wail, part plea, part bitter fury at life's lot. Then he tipped his head further, revealing a badly torn right ear.

'Come in or go home,' Helen told him.

The cat gave her a look. Then, before she had a chance to close the door on him, he slipped between her legs, through the scullery into the kitchen.

'Hey . . .' she started, almost forgetting to lock the door behind her. 'What do I call you?'

He glanced at her over his shoulder, expression amused.

'Cat? Ghost? Felix?'

Seeming to realise eviction was not on the cards, the cat launched himself up the stairs and then sat on the landing at the top, peering down through the banisters, as if waiting for her to follow. On the first floor his inspection was repeated. He paced the corridor, sniffing corners, vanishing into her little sitting room and reappearing several seconds later as if tracing some long-ingrained floor plan. In spite of herself, Helen watched, transfixed, wishing she had her camera to record his journey.

When he'd done the entire floor, he stopped at one last, closed, door. The door to her bedroom. He nudged at it with his shoulder, then meowed and looked back, as if to say, 'Come on, open it.' When she didn't move, his tail began to quiver.

Curiosity, plus a certain neurotic empathy, made her open the door for him.

It was when she pushed the door open that she noticed the air for the first time. It tasted stale, despite the fact it was the third most used room in the house. And chill too. Although the window had hardly been open since she'd arrived and the chimneybreast was stuffed with newspaper yellow with age.

She stepped aside to let him pass. He ignored her. Instead, he stared straight at the painting of the boy above the fireplace, the amber of his irises almost totally subsumed by pupils, his tail flicking faster as his irritation increased. 'In or out,' she said, stepping over him. 'There's nothing here but you and me and a tribe of dust balls.'

Even as she said it, she wasn't convinced.

Nor was the cat.

She watched, waiting for him to move. His sudden reticence unnerving when only a minute ago he had been inspecting the house with all the confidence of a previous owner who wanted to know why you knocked down this wall or replaced that window. When he still didn't move, she bent down, ready to pick him up.

As she did so, his spine arched in a fury, fur standing on end, tail suddenly huge. Then he yowled, a long shriek that chilled her blood, and sharp claws swiped out, slashing towards her face. Then he was gone.

17

Liza's house was exactly what Gil expected. Or would have been if he'd given it much thought. A small but neat new-build semi not far outside Keighley. One of the smaller properties on the estate but it must still have cost a few quid.

Pulling his Volkswagen up to the kerb, he turned off the engine, then sat for a moment, counting down in time with the engine's ticking. He wasn't nervous, not exactly. It had simply been a while and he wasn't sure how he'd got himself into this situation. A date indeed. He hadn't been great at this stuff at twenty. He was hopeless at it now. Even thinking the word made him wince.

For someone who didn't want to be on one, he'd certainly made enough effort. Smartest of his three suits straight from the dry cleaner, packet-fresh shirt (with creases to prove it), silk tie and polished Church's. He'd even been to the barbers. It was only the certain thought of Lyn laughing at him that stopped him buying Liza flowers.

Not that bothered, eh?

Just being polite. Manners, they're called. Didn't your mother teach you anything?

You leave Mum out of this.

That was another thing; he needed to stop having little conversations with himself. In his head was bad enough, but out loud? First sign of madness. Possibly second.

The car in the one-car drive was small, Japanese or Korean, with the look of an inflated yoghurt pot, reliable but dull. Red and, from where he sat, its paintwork illuminated by a carriage lamp over the garage, very clean. Made Gil realise how clean his wasn't. Scanning the interior, the mess took him by surprise. CD covers scattered in the well of the passenger seat, the Stones, best of; a bit of Bowie; early Floyd, the stuff he liked . . . At least she couldn't fault his taste. She might have more of a problem with the pasty wrapper and empty Coke cans, the Costa coffee cup from the other night at A&E, the empty B&H packet, and an old copy of the *Echo*, from the same night.

Scrunching his torso so he could reach into the gap, Gil started to pile the junk from the floor on to the seat. A tap on the window just above his head made him jump, banging his head on the glove compartment as he looked up. A woman was peering in. He stared at her blankly, before it dawned on him it was Liza. It'd taken him a second to recognise her. Another to realise his passenger door was still locked.

Flustered, Gil scooped everything up and tossed it on to the back seat before releasing the passenger door. 'I, er, was just . . .' He gestured at the now empty seat beside him. 'Making you some space. Then I was going to come and knock.'

Amusement flickered in her eyes. Whether at the mess or his discomfort, Gil wasn't sure. 'I was ready anyway, thought I'd save you the trip.' She swiped at the seat before smoothing her skirt beneath her and sitting down, handbag in her lap. 'Do you need me to direct you?'

The drive to the restaurant wasn't awkward. Liza was a talker, a journalist's dream. In less than ten minutes Gil discovered she was divorced, a few years now, had two children, a girl and a boy, both grown up, the girl married locally with two kids on the other side of town, the boy with his girlfriend in Bradford. All this before they reached the table.

At this rate, Gil thought, they'd run out of conversation before the starter arrived. Then he wondered if they actually had to have a starter; or whether he could get away with a bowl of pasta. Not being tight, just wondering how he was going to fill a couple of hours.

'What about you?' Liza said, after the waiter handed them both menus. 'Kids, I mean.'

Gil wasn't sure what she already knew and how much he wanted her to know. 'Same,' he said. 'Both grown up now. Eldest has a couple of kids, a girl and a boy, lives in Manchester. Youngest's in London.' Could he get away with that little?

'What are you drinking?' he asked.

'Nice suit,' she said. This was after they'd ordered what

Gil considered a good red, and his hoped-for bowl of pasta turned into starters, mains, bread and olives and, 'We'll see how we feel about dessert.'

Gil found he didn't mind as much as he expected. The being bossed around by a woman thing. In fact, he quite liked it. It had been a while.

'This old thing?' he shrugged.

'It's the one you were wearing the night we met?'

'Not the very one. Similar.'

'Oh, I wasn't implying you hadn't made an effort.' She seemed flustered. 'I thought I recognised it, that's all.'

'Let's just say I know what suits me. And that's what I wear.' Gil grinned, 'Day in, day out. All my suits look like this.'

He wasn't sure who was more grateful when the wine waiter appeared with the Barolo and everyone could go through the formalities of uncorking, pouring, sniffing and tasting. It was good Gil thought. It wanted to be, given it was the price of ten pints at The Bull, maybe twelve. He nodded at the waiter and watched Liza watch her glass fill with the smooth red liquid. 'Cheers,' Gil said, holding up his own when it was full.

She tilted her glass against his. 'Let's start again, shall we?' She put down her glass and held out her hand across the table. Unsure whether he was meant to kiss it or shake it, Gil shook. It was the hand of a fifty-something woman, just as his was the hand of a sixty-something man. If it was a test and he'd failed, then so be it. He'd never won a medal for chivalry and he wasn't likely to start now. 'I just meant,' she continued. 'I like the suit, it, er, suits you. Some men look good, you know, in suits.'

There was another silence that Gil realised almost too late he was meant to fill with a compliment. 'Thank you,' he said. 'You look lovely too. Nice dress.'

Liza picked at a piece of imaginary lint on the bodice. 'It's new. I mean, not new for now, just new in general. Don't have much call to wear it.'

Picking up her glass, she took a sip. And then another.

'Well,' she said, looking him square in the eye as if the Barolo had given her courage. She had nice eyes, blue, clear, subtly made up. All the hallmarks of having been 'one of the pretty ones' when she was younger. One of the girls at school who wouldn't have looked at lanky, gawky him. But she hadn't gone the same way as plenty of those girls, the ones whose pretty round faces had bloated by forty. Good bone structure. Plus, she was slim, but not so thin she had one of those necks that looked ten years older.

'I didn't expect this to be quite so difficult.'

Surprised, Gil glanced up. 'Didn't you? I did. But I suppose I thought you'd be a pro. The way you got hold of my number and asked me out like that.'

'God, no.' Liza shook her head, 'I haven't done anything like this for years. It was Margaret, she encouraged me.'

Gil said nothing. He didn't need to. His expression did the talking for him. Liza smiled. 'Not much of a fan then? You're not the only one. She's such a busybody. But she told me you'd been single for a while and seemed lonely. Sorry if that's not true. And I thought you looked nice. And, well, I hadn't thought that for a long time. Not since . . . sorry, I'm talking too much, aren't I?'

171

He shook his head. 'Not at all. Go on.' Maybe Margaret Millward wasn't too bad after all.

'Well, it wasn't a big deal, the divorce. It was sad, of course. Twenty-five years all in all . . . just fizzled out. But once the kids left it became pretty clear there was no point staying together for the kids. You know . . .'

Gil nodded and sipped the wine, tasting cherry and black pepper and maybe . . . Was that cumin? Whatever, it was good. When had he stopped drinking wine? He knew the answer to that. When he opened a bottle and drank the whole thing on his own. Too much of that and you were talking a serious habit.

'So there hasn't been anyone since?' he asked, as he knew he was meant to. Getting the hang of it now.

'Not really. Couple of dates. Horrible word, date, isn't it?' She paused, popped an olive into her mouth and chewed, spat the stone into her hand and put it neatly on the side of her bread plate. 'Well, you know, a few. But I don't meet many new people at work.' She pulled a face. 'Not that you'd want to go out with anyway. Married friends occasionally fix me up, divorcees, widowers, but you know, it's embarrassing if it's a friend of a friend and you think he's dull as . . .' Lisa shrugged. 'I don't mean to be rude, but most of the men I've met only want to talk about golf or football.'

'I can assure you I have no interest in either. Or any sport, for that matter.' Gil put his hand on his heart as if taking an oath, glossing neatly over the cricket. 'It's one of my USPs.'

She gave him a blank look.

'Unique Selling Points. Forget it. It's a work thing. A good thing about me, though, apparently.'

Inclining her head, she fiddled with the stem of her glass. 'And when you do, well, you know, meet a man you think might be nice, turns out they're only interested in one thing . . .'

'I have the same problem.' Gil said it without thinking.

She burst out laughing. 'Oh, poor Gil. All these women who want to get into your trousers.'

'I was serious,' Gil said, affronted. Talk about double standards.

'Right.' She rolled her eyes.

'I'm not kidding, Liza. I'm not complaining either, mind. I'm just saying, all the women I meet . . .'

A cynical expression crossed her face.

'And when I say *all*, I don't mean hundreds, or even dozens. I can count them all on one . . . OK, maybe two hands. Definitely not more . . . They all just want "a bit of company", which seems to be divorcee speak for a one-nighter.'

Liza laughed.

Noticing her glass was empty, Gil reached over and topped it up, refilling the top half-inch of his glass. The wine was good. Too good to stick to one glass. He wished he'd taken her up on her offer to give him a lift. 'They seem to think all men are looking for someone to cook their tea and wash their socks.'

'And are you?'

'Am I what?'

'Looking for someone to cook your tea and wash your socks?'

Gil shrugged, took a piece of focaccia, and tore it in half. 'It's been years since anyone else washed my socks,' he said. It came off more melancholy than he intended.

'Thank you. I had a lovely evening. Nicest in a long time.'

Somehow it was gone eleven and the Volkswagen was parked back under the street light outside Liza's house.

'Even the steak?' Gil smiled.

'We-ell, maybe not the steak. Remind me not to order medium-well next time if I want to be able to chew it.'

He pretended not to notice the next time and she didn't labour it. 'But the rest of the food, the wine, the company . . .' She caught his eye. 'Not that sort of company.'

'I didn't think . . .'

'I know you didn't. I was joking. And thank you, I really didn't mean for you to pay. I asked you out, after all. I'd have picked somewhere cheaper if . . .'

'We've been through this already. I won't hear of it.'

'My treat next time?'

There it was again. Next time.

Gil nodded slowly. 'OK.' He'd done it now. 'Your treat next time.'

Seeming satisfied, Liza put a hand on the door handle, then paused. 'I don't suppose you'd fancy a coffee?'

The offer took Gil by surprise. Especially after that comment about company. 'No, but thanks,' he said, seeing her face fall. 'That cappuccino's all the caffeine

I can take at this time of night. Plus, you've work tomorrow.'

Life's all-purpose get-out clause. Until you didn't have it to fall back on any more.

He knew he'd said the wrong thing. Her face was a picture: part disappointment, part hurt. He wouldn't have been surprised to see the windscreen freeze up. Then she cut through the ice to lean across the gear stick and give him a stiff, dry-lipped peck on the cheek, before bolting up the drive and indoors with the tiniest wave over her shoulder, not even a half-turn. Front door shut, lights springing on all over the house, before he even started the ignition.

'Nice work,' he muttered. 'That's got to be a personal best.'

The roads were quiet, a bright half-moon lighting his way through a cloudless sky. The first cloudless sky the moors had seen in quite some time. Once he cleared the dual carriageway and hit the country roads, he turned off the Stones CD mid-'Sympathy for the Devil' and drove in silence. It was a good night for driving, clear and bright, hardly another car about. So quiet and clear he was tempted to kill the lights and drive on with only the moon and a kaleidoscope of stars to light his way as he skirted the Dales. He didn't, of course. Too old and sensible and sober.

He'd have done it when he was younger.

Gil hadn't drunk that much, a third of a bottle, maybe a little more, but he'd been careful to keep Liza's glass topped up at the expense of his own. *Next time*, how had he got himself into that one?

He liked her well enough. Perhaps better than well enough. She was good company. Real company. Not, inverted commas, company. He'd had a great evening. If not one he could afford too often at those prices. The wine was good, the food better than anything he'd eaten in years. But it had all gone wrong back there. All because he fancied waiting for the second date. Or, more honestly, because he didn't want her enough not to wait.

It would be funny if it wasn't so bloody depressing.

There were ex-colleagues at the paper who'd say he was a bloody idiot. Not blokes he had much time for . . . But all the same. Shadows swooped around him as he took a left on to the road that led to the Dales. Not the most direct route back, he wasn't in the mood to be tucked up in bed just yet, and if he went home before he reached his exhaustion tipping point he'd only end up spending half the night on his laptop looking for the invisible woman, and the other half counting sheep or whatever animal taunted him from inside his head. Probably also a few minutes in the company of his faithful right hand.

Wouldn't that be ironic?

He didn't consciously take the road up past Wildfell. So he told himself. But that was where he'd ended up, anyway. He'd done stake-outs, stayed up all night, hoping to doorstop someone as they came home from somewhere they shouldn't have been, or left somewhere they should be. That was in the early days. There were more rules around that sort of stuff now. Just as well, he hadn't felt clean doing half the things he'd had to do to make his mark. Such as it was.

Well, such as it had been.

His car slowed, almost without Gil telling it to. He expected to see light seeping from between not quite closed curtains. It was late, but not that late. Anyway, she'd said herself, she didn't sleep that much. Not that he was planning to knock or anything. Glancing in the rear-view mirror, Gil slowed to a crawl before killing the lights and pulling in, easing on to the verge just before the gate so he could see up the drive.

There was no sign of life.

He didn't get out, what was the point? Instead he put the window down, lit a cigarette, tip flaring in the darkness, and sat in silence, staring at the ruined house. Curtains pulled across the upstairs windows rendered them blind. The glass above the top of the side door stared blackly at him like a dilated pupil reflecting the half-moon. He smoked and he waited . . . for what, Gil wasn't sure. A hint of movement maybe. A flicker of light. When none came, he lit another cigarette from the butt of the last before stubbing the old one into his car ashtray, like a proper addict.

Who lived in such a place anyway? Someone poor, or someone very rich. Someone able to make the choice, someone who had no choice at all. Gil knew he had a lead but couldn't tell which of those she was; and where that photograph of the child in ruins fitted in. He'd seen the picture before. He'd tried putting child and ruins into Google, and been swamped by the results. A thousand children. A thousand more ruins. More than he could bear to see. He was on the right track though; and there was something else about that photograph, something he'd forgotten or been not quite quick enough to notice. He'd remember it, though. And things would become clearer when he did.

There was a story here. He knew it. And so did she.

18

It was 6.03 when Gil awoke, with a crick in his neck and breath that tasted of one last B&H. Unfolding himself, he wiped mist from the windscreen with the sleeve of his jacket and started the engine, hoping she wasn't awake to hear him pull away. Bad enough that one of the twitchers would inevitably see him draw up.

He knew how it would look. A night spent in a cold car watching a darkened house. Great. Better they thought he'd spent the night with Liza.

He made himself wait a couple of days before he went anywhere near the old house again. Two days during which he googled every permutation of Helen Graham's name he could conceive of, and looked through more pictures of children in war zones than he could stomach. At one point, he wondered if he was obsessing so strongly because Karen still hadn't accepted his Facebook request, and anything was better than thinking too deeply about that.

Such moments of self-awareness were rare and Gil reminded himself not to have another too soon. The morning after, he drove out to Wildfell in daylight, having promised himself he'd simply knock at the door.

The milk he took wasn't a peace offering. More a practicality. Helen hadn't been seen in the General Stores for three days. That meant she'd probably need milk. Even if she didn't, he did. He couldn't drink coffee black; and he was hoping she'd let him stay long enough to drink at least one cup. It was the coffee he also took that was the peace offering. A decent medium-ground Columbian he'd driven into Keighley to buy. He'd been looking forward to drinking it for days. He just hoped she appreciated the gesture.

She was wearing running kit when she opened the door, her hair plastered to her head in damp tendrils, a towel in her hand.

'I'm sorry, I . . .' Gil said. 'I didn't mean to interrupt.'

She smiled, sort of. Well, her mouth twisted in an upward direction. For a second Gil wasn't sure she was going to let him in.

'Yes, you did,' she said, wrapping the towel around her head and stepping back to let him pass. 'Or you wouldn't be here. Come in anyway.'

Taken aback, Gil bowed his head and shuffled past. He felt every bit the foolish old man he was apparently destined to become. What was he thinking, dropping in like this, behaving precisely like the nosy neighbours she'd moved here to avoid? 'I brought this,' he said, when she'd bolted the door behind him.

'Milk!' Taking the carton and ignoring the coffee, she

headed for the kitchen. 'You must be a mind reader. It's just what we need, isn't it, Ghost?'

Ghost? Seeing no one, Gil turned to a rotting leather armchair.

'Not there!' she yelled.

He leapt up, but not before a filthy black tom had yowled crossly and leapt from the chair, lacing himself around Helen's legs. Holding the towel on top of her head, Helen unscrewed the lid from the milk with her other hand, took a saucer from the cupboard and poured milk into it.

'I don't suppose you brought cat food too, did you?'

Gil shook his head.

'Joke. Fancy a cup of your coffee?'

'Please. Where did the cat come from?' Gil asked when a cafetiere sat between them on the table.

'He's a ghost,' she said.

It had to be another joke. The ghost was lapping loudly at his saucer.

'You were a journalist, weren't you?' she said suddenly.

Gil looked up, startled. He nodded and she smiled at him.

'Newly retired, I gather. Most of your life spent on the best of the local papers? Some time in Fleet Street before that? A couple of awards? Took early retirement following the arrival of a new editor?'

Gil tried not to look nonplussed.

'I did some googling,' she said in answer to his unspoken question. 'It must be boring being retired.'

'It is,' said Gil, almost scalding himself in his hurry to finish his coffee.

* * *

'Silly old sod,' Gil thought, as he slammed the car into fourth and screeched past a pair of cyclists riding two abreast on the dale road, narrowly missing a delivery van coming in the opposite direction. 'Let her make a right fool of you. That'll teach you to stick to women your own age.'

But it wasn't that, and Gil knew it. He knew that was how it looked, that people in the village were starting to talk. Well, if they wanted to talk, let them. There was more to that woman than she let on. And anyway, he muttered, braking as he approached the centre of the village and then changing his mind and accelerating out the other side. He didn't care what they said, but he'd still give the General Stores a wide berth for a few days. What with fixing him up with Liza and noticing his 'fascination' with the widow, as she'd taken to calling Mademoiselle Graham, Margaret Millward was getting a bit too interested in his business for Gil's liking. Instead, he drove to the garage on the bypass to top up on B&H – two packs, to be on the safe side – a four-pack of Tetley's and a couple of pasties. He had work to do.

Back home, Gil went up to the spare room, pushing aside three coffee cups and two empty cans to make room for the new supplies, and turned on his laptop.

This time he didn't start with the woman but with the picture. That was where the answer lay, he knew it. He just had to go about it in a more methodical pattern. He began by searching for picture agencies, Getty, Rex, Icon, and started to explore their sites one by one, as he'd seen picture researchers do on the *Post*. There was no point searching by photographer, he already knew that would be futile; and he'd already tried guessing the war zone and approaching it that way to little avail. Instead he scrolled through reportage, global assignments and photojournalism, poring as image after striking image of human misery and its aftermath filled his screen. What could possibly make someone want to stand there and watch all this suffering, he wondered. Knowing, even as he thought it, his question invited the retort: What could possibly make someone want to become a journalist? The suffering was the same. Only the means of recording it differed.

He'd cleared five or six internationally renowned agencies and started on a smaller, edgier agency based in somewhere called Belleville when he saw it, or something like it: two small boys flicking skateboards with their heels in front of a burnt-out office block. The image wasn't identical, but it had to be the same photographer, he knew it. Even he could tell it was taken with the same eye. Ten, fifteen more photos, nothing.

Then he spotted the tabs at the top. He clicked Iraq and started again.

Three photos later he'd found it.

The boy was small and dark, skinny legs sticking out of too big shorts, a toothy grin and an outstretched hand holding a red Power Ranger. And staring out, over all of it, a pair of button brown eyes that Gil could have sworn he'd seen gazing from the back of a small silver car a fortnight earlier as it receded into the distance.

Gil stopped, took a swig of his beer, choked and slammed his hand down hard on the desk. Dammit, there it was, there was the picture. But he couldn't have seen the kid. Hadn't she said the kid was dead?

Impatiently, he flicked down the page to find the credits.

When he found them, he frowned. Copyright H. Lawrence. Who the hell was H. Lawrence? Sod this. His eyes ached from the screen and his brain was swimming, but he was hardly any further forward. He'd been so sure that picture would provide his answer.

This was doing his head in, as Lyn would have said. Taking a cigarette from the packet – his fifth or sixth since he'd sat down, but who was counting? – Gil picked up his lighter and half-empty beer can and went down into the garden. Sat on the bench under the kitchen window in the fading light, he tried not to notice how long overdue the grass was for a mowing.

H. Lawrence, he muttered between drags. Who the hell was H Lawrence?

Scuffing the filter underfoot, he headed back upstairs.

As he suspected, H. Lawrence, photographer, turned out to be female.

According to Wikipedia, Helen Lawrence was a prolific photographer, specialising in tough stuff. Only, she seemed to spend so much time behind her Leica he couldn't find a sodding picture of her anywhere. She was the right age, according to her wiki; not that you could rely on wiki. (How many times had he told the features desk that?) Her work seemed to date back to roughly the right time. But she definitely wasn't French. Her first picture, thirteen years earlier, was a gut-churning image of a victim of the Admiral Duncan bombing in Soho. Six months or so later, an archive story from January 2000 listed her as one of the cultural movers and shakers under thirty who would shape the next century. Even that didn't have a picture of her. It used the Admiral Duncan to illustrate her section.

Around 2007, Gil noticed, halfway down the fourth

page of Google images, the pictures stopped being of people, women and children mainly, and started including buildings. Make that rubble. Odd, he thought, reaching out to unwrap a pasty and noticing as he did so that it was dark outside, how she got the same emotion into both. Impressive as they were, the woman's pictures were getting him nowhere. Flicking back to the main page, Gil resumed reading.

Industry honours Lawrence.

Clicking on the link, Gil was bemused when the picture that unfurled on his screen was of a man in a well-cut dinner jacket giving the camera a look that screamed 'get a move on'. A glitch, it must be. Gil closed the window and tried again. Painfully slowly, the same picture emerged, too large to download easily. Then Gil saw her, half-eclipsed by the man. At first glance it looked as if he was hogging the frame. But when Gil wiped his glasses on his shirt and leaned closer, it became clear it was the woman who wanted to get out of the shot. The man was gripping her hand, hard, as if holding her in the frame.

The woman was Helen Graham, Gil was sure of it.

The picture was old, six or seven years out of date; and her hair was blonde and wavy, longer than she wore it now. It didn't suit her, Gil thought, made her look older somehow, harder. But it was her, he was certain. He read the caption for confirmation: *Photographer Helen Lawrence with her husband, foreign correspondent, Art Huntingdon.*

Gil punched the air. 'Knew it!' he hissed into the silence. 'Bloody knew it.'

He'd found her.

* * *

It took all his will power not to get in the car and drive to Wildfell, but too many beers and just enough common sense stopped him.

The pub, then. A whisky and one last pint to set him up for a long night. Gil pushed back his chair. Catching sight of his reflection in the dark window, and the debris surrounding him, he leaned sideways and yanked the curtain shut. Looking like that, he was going nowhere tonight.

'Come on, Gil,' he muttered, returning to the spare room with the last of the beers. 'You know the drill. Back it up. You know the who, and you've always known the where, but you still need the what and the why. What is Helen Lawrence doing at Wildfell, calling herself Hélène Graham?'

No one could hide on the Internet. Didn't they say that? Didn't this just prove that was true. There was one photograph of the woman, half-hidden behind her husband, more than half a decade old, and bearing a different name, and yet he'd found her. Gil had to admit he was impressed though. No Facebook page or Twitter or LinkedIn and whatever else the suits at the *Post* had been on at everyone to do.

She was her pictures. And that was it.

Nothing at all except one stray to give her away.

He found only one more. Taken, he imagined, on the same night. Cropped so closely you could barely see the top of the award she held in front of her. The look on her face was one he'd seen before, best described as uncomfortable. Her pic was part of a recent story so small it would barely have made half a sidebar on page seven.

Alongside was an arresting black-and-white image of a charismatic man somewhere in his late thirties/early forties in fatigues. The same man who'd glowered over his bow tie. This time, he was leaning against a tank, wiry dark hair sticking up, hooded eyes staring directly into the camera. Gil clicked on the picture and found himself on a news site. The paragraph was short and to the point:

A body, believed to be that of British journalist Arthur Huntingdon, 46, has been found after a fire destroyed the building in which he lived in an exclusive Paris square. Huntingdon, who was last seen over two weeks ago, was estranged from the photographer Helen Lawrence. Police also seek Ms Lawrence to eliminate her from their enquiries.

19

'I thought you might be here . . .'

She turned at the voice and saw Gil stopped at the stile behind her, holding one of the posts with one hand and bent forward as if catching his breath. 'Climbed the hill a bit too fast.'

'Were you looking for me?' She slid her camera into her backpack, trying to conceal her irritation. She'd hoped, by letting him know she knew his interest wasn't purely neighbourly, she'd be able to stall him a while longer.

He hesitated, just a fraction too long, and obviously knew it because he said, 'I was hoping to run into you, yes.'

'Why? Other than that you clearly enjoy my company.'

Gil blinked, and flushed a little more.

He looked around him, forgetting her question and his embarrassment, simply seeing the view; long stretches of rolling dale and gorse and the smudge of another world in the far distance. Helen was impressed. She liked people who could see. So many people couldn't. Most of those who could were like her and looked at the world through a lens of some kind.

'Just the retired journalist in me, I guess,' said Gil, calling her bluff.

Helen felt her face flicker, saw him clock it.

'You don't like journalists?'

She shrugged. 'I can take them or leave them.'

'But you've met some.'

When she didn't reply, he smiled. 'I thought so. Most people haven't. They think what they see on the TV is the truth. We're either scumbags or truth-seeking saints.'

Helen raised her eyebrows. 'And which are you?'

'Neither. For most of us this is—'

'Just a job?'

'You really have met some, haven't you? Do you know what they say about you in the village?'

'No, but I don't doubt you'll tell me.' He was driving at something. Helen wasn't entirely sure she wanted to know what.

'Half of them think you're a rock star.'

Helen contemplated pointing out that rock stars were an endangered species, about as common as snow tigers and white rhinos. A dozen still in captivity, maybe two. These days you might just about be a pop star but you were more likely to be a celeb, famous for five minutes, if you were lucky.

'Not taken with the rock-star idea?'

'And what do the other half think?'

'You're a rich bohemian. A painter or sculptor. But

then you'd be up here with your oils and easel, or down at the house with a chisel or a chainsaw attacking some block of wood. Instead you're up here with your Leica.'

They looked at each other.

'It's a good model,' he said. 'Old, but good. Serious.'

'I used to be serious about photography,' Helen found herself saying. 'A fixed focal length like that means you have to think.'

Once he found his feet, Gil went on. 'And it's discreet. If you didn't know better you'd think it was a toy. Our staff photographer was always after one of those. The editor wouldn't sign off on one and he couldn't afford his own. Then it all went digital.'

'This one is digital.'

Gil raised his eyebrows. It looked theatrical, intentionally so. 'That's the other thing they say about you. That you're a reclusive millionaire. Those don't come cheap, so perhaps they're right.'

'And how do they think I got my money?'

'Oh, various ways.'

'I bet.' Helen grinned.

At least he had the grace to blush, and even shuffled his shoes a little on the heather in a small boy kind of way. It hadn't passed Helen by that he still hadn't told her why he was looking for her.

'Well,' she said. 'Are you going to tell me why you're here?'

He seemed to be right on the edge of one thing, and then he paused and said something else, and she got the feeling, from the sudden hunching of his shoulders, that the words coming out of his mouth surprised him too. 'I'm avoiding telephoning my daughter.'

'Why don't you want to call her?'

He shrugged, and she could see he was tempted to leave it at that; but they were up on a windswept moor and this was a place for truth. She was putting what she felt on to her surroundings, Helen knew that. She even knew the name for it, pathetic fallacy, but it was true. Never trust someone who doesn't read, never trust someone who's not impressed by the mountains and the sea. She'd learnt that the hard way.

'I never know what to say,' he said at last.

'Hello,' Helen suggested. She wasn't being facetious. 'How are you . . .?'

'Oh, we can do that bit. It's everything else. Sometimes I write myself a list as if I'm about to go into conference, and I can hear myself working my way down it, ignoring her replies in my hurry to reach the next question.'

'When did you last see her?' she asked. He looked so uncomfortable, she almost felt sorry for him. Almost.

'It's been a while. She's busy and her house isn't very big and it's a huge inconvenience to them having me there . . .' Gil was gabbling now.

'And you don't want to go anyway?'

His eyes widened. 'You don't mince your words, do you?'

'Sorry.' She said it instantly and truthfully. He was right. Not that she'd ever felt the need to apologise for it before. 'I didn't mean to be rude.'

He shook off her apology with a shrug. 'How about you?' he said. 'Do you have children?'

'No,' she said shortly.

He pretended to study a witch tree that looked so picturesque that someone could have lopped off its limbs and twisted it intentionally. Without thinking, Helen reached into her backpack for her Leica, moving slightly downhill to find a better angle.

'I'm sorry . . .'

She stopped, her finger on the shutter button. 'For what?'

'That you never . . .'

'Oh.' She shrugged. 'I don't think about it. Really. Well, hardly ever. What about you? Have they brought you happiness?'

He waited while she took the shot, fidgeting from foot to foot.

'I'd better leave you in peace,' he said, when she lowered the camera.

Far from helping him muster the courage to call his daughter, she'd upset him. I wonder, Helen thought, cross with herself, what it would have been like to have a daughter to call. Would it have been something to look forward to, or just another chore? She was selfish, driven, focused – call it what you wanted – enough to suspect it might have been a chore. Not that she was ever likely to find out.

'I was pregnant once.' The words were out of her mouth before she had a chance to think better of it.

He turned back towards her. 'The timing was wrong?'

'I lost it. Two months after we married. We never tried for another.'

'Was that your decision? Or Art's . . .?'

Helen stopped, took a deep breath.

So, he'd done it. That was why he'd come.

She was surprised to find that she wasn't. It was the photograph of the boy that had done it. Deep down, once he'd seen it, she'd known from the way he reacted that it was only a matter of time. What difference did it make anyway? If it wasn't him it would be someone else. If anything, it was almost a relief.

They faced each other and suddenly a twisted tree and the long line of the Dales seemed a lot less important.

All she wanted was to be away from there.

She was moving almost before she was aware of it, walking calmly but swiftly down the hill.

'Helen, wait—'

'Leave me alone.'

'If you don't tell me you'll only end up having to tell someone else,' he raised his voice, so she could hear him over the wind. 'Another journalist, the police. Don't you want to put your side of the story? Why don't you tell me what happened? You know I can't just let this go . . .'

Afraid he was going to come after her, she walked faster, her body bent forward, fury and fear carrying her downwards.

Away, she had to get away.

As soon as she hit the shade of the copse that bordered Wildfell, she started running, vaulting the lychgate in two moves. She rarely used this way in, there was something sinister about the trees, they spooked her, but today the threat was behind her. She ran up the path and fumbled to get the key in the lock, slamming the door and locking it again behind her. In the kitchen, Ghost took one look at her and decided that if he was hungry he'd be better off feeding himself.

She looked around wildly. Coffee cups in the sink, breadboard on the side, Roberts radio chortling to itself.

It was starting to look something like home. Well, so
what? She didn't need any of it. She had moved before,
many times, and fast. She could do it again. She didn't
need anything she hadn't come with. Only her laptop
and her cameras.

Slamming the lid on the laptop, she scooped it off the
table and ran upstairs, taking them two at a time.
Grabbing her rucksack from the bedroom floor she
stuffed her clothes into the bottom, dirty mixed with
clean, running kit on top, and then went in search of
her charger. She needed to be somewhere else. But
where? She'd come almost to like Wildfell, she realised
with a shock. Even with its noises and shadows. Got
used to it, at least. Liked having the Dales behind her.
This had become about more than hiding.

Here, for the first time, she felt strangely as if she
belonged.

Not the people, not even the ramshackle wreck of
a house, certainly not her . . . It was the silence, she
realised. The silence and the space and the fact
Wildfell's ruin was nature's revenge for building a pile
on the edge of such a windswept wilderness. The holes
in the roof were storm damage. Wind had ripped the
biggest branch from the rotting oak tree. The wall
below the terrace was broken by subsidence. She'd had
enough of buildings split by mortar-fire and cars torn
apart and overturned. She never wanted to see a burnt-
out office block again.

Since the boy, that was all she'd photographed.

All she'd been able to photograph.

Broken buildings standing in for broken people. It was
easier to look at damaged buildings, to look at them and

see their damage. Marvel at the ruin; the firestorms and rain of shells that brought Beirut, Fallujah, Tripoli, Damascus to that state. You couldn't do that with people. It was easier to look away. What was it T. S. Eliot said? 'Humankind couldn't bear too much reality?' Something like that.

Below, Gil's feet crunched the gravel and Helen stood back from the mullioned drawing-room window where she was stuffing her laptop charger into her rucksack. Gil looked around as if genuinely interested in the fore-court, and then looked behind him, as if suspecting he might be followed, then she saw him straighten his shoulders and take a deep breath before disappearing under the portico to lean on the bell. Somewhere deep inside the house the old bell clattered and clattered again, the flat sound suggesting the bell was cracked.

She stayed frozen two steps away from the window, grateful for her obsession with keeping everything locked.

He pushed again, harder this time, and the notes sounded below, flat and dull. He would have to go away eventually. He couldn't stand there pushing the bell forever. He must know she wouldn't answer.

When she next looked down he was staring up and she stepped smartly into the shadows, while he kept staring, uncertain whether he saw movement.

Just go, she willed him. Please. Let me go.

If her thoughts were enough, he'd be gone. Instead, he rummaged in his pocket for a pen, then searched for paper. What kind of journalist doesn't carry a notebook, she wanted to shout at him. The useless kind. Except he'd found her, when she was trying so hard not to be found, so he couldn't be that useless after all.

In disgust, he pulled a receipt from his wallet and ripped off part of it, dropping to a crouch and began to write. A note, she presumed. He halted halfway through, his head tipped to one side as if debating what to say. Then he put it on the mat, or she assumed he did, because he vanished briefly, but the letterbox didn't clang, and then she heard his too-big feet crunching away down the gravel. That same slow, solemn pace.

She stood there for what seemed like hours to see if he came back. If he was waiting just around the corner to catch her when she came down. When fifteen minutes had passed without a sign, she cracked.

The note was simple, to the point.

I won't tell anyone anything before we've talked. But we must talk. Call me . . .

A promise, and what might or might not be a threat, depending on how you read it. There was a mobile number too. Below that an email address.

Why did he think she would talk to him?

How could she think she wouldn't?

Ghost padded up the gravel while she was crouched by the mat reading Gil's scrawl. He shot her a glance to check her mood had improved, and decided to brave it, slipping in through the open door to spare himself the effort of entering via the water butt and broken pantry window. She glanced at her rucksack lying in the doorway, and then at the cat, who was glaring at it with contempt, and sighed.

Where did she think she'd run to?

What was to stop him going to the papers? He didn't

seem entirely happy with his just-retired status, maybe he still had something to prove. This would give him a story. Even if he didn't, there was nothing to stop him going to the police. Her only option was to talk to him. That was how the press worked. Or that was how they wanted you to think it worked. Confide in them and you could control the story. Was that what Gil's ungainly friendship had always been about?

She dropped the rucksack back inside with enough of a bang to send Ghost halfway up the first flight of stairs and then slumped on to the floor.

PART TWO

The Boy

'Covering a war means going to places torn by chaos, destruction and death, and trying to bear witness. It means trying to find the truth in a sandstorm of propaganda . . .'

Marie Colvin (1956–2012)

20

The pub was already brightly lit and she could hear the noise from a suddenly opened door as two men tumbled out, talking loudly. Their conversation stilled as she passed and restarted, but quieter. She knew that if she turned they'd be looking at her, so she didn't. She pushed the door open and the chatter inside dipped, then resolutely kept going.

Gil was at a table in the corner, staring forlornly at the murky amber of a half-empty pint, a crime novel lying face down, spine broken, beside it. Taking a deep breath of her own, she slid between two men in golf jumpers and pushed her way towards him. If he wanted her to talk, then talk she would.

'I can't do this here,' she said when Gil looked up.

He opened his mouth and shut it again.

'We'll have to go back to the house. Wildfell, I mean. But you can't come with me. Obviously.' She inclined her head over her shoulder as if he wouldn't know what she meant. 'Give me ten minutes, then follow me.'

'No.' Gil drained his pint in one mouthful, propelling his seat backwards with his feet. 'I'll walk you.

'It's not for your sake,' he added, seeing her expression. 'Just don't want you changing your mind.'

Helen shot a sidelong glance at those clustered round a big table to one side, empty pint pots herded into the middle. The ones looking at her, and that was practically all of them, glanced away. 'What will they say?'

'Does it matter?'

She surprised herself by nodding.

Gil shrugged. 'You can understand my reluctance to let you out of my sight, surely?'

'Yes,' Helen said. 'I suppose I can.'

The entire pub watched them leave.

'Where do you want me to start?' Helen placed the cafetiere on the floor between them in the upstairs sitting room, before sliding her precious bottle of vodka from its perch under her arm.

She'd need it, even if Gil didn't.

He watched her pour coffee into a mug, nodding first when she waved the milk carton at him, and again before she sloshed in a hefty slug of vodka. 'At the beginning?' he suggested, when she handed him his mug.

She didn't return his smile. 'You say that like I should know where it is.'

From the way he looked at her, she could tell he was trying to decide whether she was playing games. 'Not me,' she wanted to say. 'One game-player is enough in any relationship.'

'What I mean,' Helen said instead, 'is *whose* beginning? Mine or Art's?'

For a second, he seemed to understand, but she recognised it for the old journalist's trick it was. He would sit and he would be quiet and he would be sympathetic and if she stalled he would prod just enough to get her talking again.

'D'you mind?' he asked, waving his pack of B&H at her. Helen pushed a saucer towards him with her toe, shook her head when he offered her the packet.

'Start,' he said when he'd had time to light up and inhale, 'with the Admiral Duncan.'

Helen swallowed hard and sloshed vodka into her own coffee, leaving it black. He wasn't bluffing after all. How much did he already know?

London 1999

It was my first day. I was late. I was always late. It was congenital. Actually, congenital was the last thing it was. Nobody in my family is ever late except me. I was late because I'd taught myself to be. Once learnt, I found it impossible to unlearn.

So I was late on my first day as junior photographer. Still not on contract; but, even so, a big leap up for a freelance who'd done nothing since college but assisting and the jobs no one else would take. All the obligation, none of the rights. I didn't know that then, though. Wouldn't have cared if I had.

The lifts weren't my friends either. One was stuck on six, the other had flat-lined. So I ducked into the stairwell, taking concrete steps two at a time. An unpleasant cold sweat had broken out under my shirt. There's no convincing excuse for arriving twenty minutes late on your first day. No excuse other than cutting it too fine, a tube breaking down, the heard-it-all-before usual that gets you an eye-roll, if you're really lucky, and first dibs on the next crap job to cross the picture editor's desk if you aren't. Bursting out of the stairwell, I bent gasping in the atrium by the lifts.

'Late?'

I jumped, cursing myself for not looking before collapsing in a heap.

The bloke at the coffee machine didn't even bother to take his cigarette out of his mouth when he looked me up and down. I don't know what he saw, because I didn't give him more than a cursory glance, but I doubt it was impressive. 'Don't sweat it,' he said, before turning his back on me and heading for the newsroom. 'They're still in conference.'

The picture desk was in a corner of the newsroom, some bollocks about light that anyone who knew anything about photography knew was going to make not the slightest bit of difference by the end of the coming year. Digital, you see. I'd dropped my rucksack and camera bag and just finished arranging myself nonchalantly on the corner of the picture editor's desk when conference emptied out. Thank God, it didn't take any longer, because I'd have started to snoop. A sleeping computer without a password is a terrible thing.

'Lawrence. You made it then.' The picture editor, top of his voice. All eyes turned to me, decided I was 'not interesting' and turned away. In less than a second, I was dismissed. Or maybe I imagined it. Either way, my new boss was clearly a twat.

'Get yourself a coffee,' he said. 'Machine's out by the lift. Get me one too. Milk, sugar. Then open that lot over there. Make yourself useful.' He indicated a small desk, half a desk really, hidden under an enormous pile of brown envelopes.

I opened my mouth to protest, I'd done the assisting thing, setting up lights, taping down wires, endless form-filling and filing . . . Then I caught the dare in his eyes, thought better of it and surprised myself. Already, I was learning you don't have to say every single thing that enters your head and I'd only been there ten minutes.

Slow news day. *The phrase was invented for ones like this. Saturdays bracketed by Easter and bank holidays when nothing happens except football and the paper starts filling up with comment and analysis of the non-events of the week. Busy for picture research, sod all to do if you're the not quite staff, not quite photographer.*

The morning was painfully quiet, made worse by the huge pile of collects *– pictures that needed to be returned to their rightful owners. Family shots from the seventies and eighties. Weddings, funerals, christenings, summer holidays, graduations, you name it. The kind of pictures that mean absolutely nothing to anyone but their owners. Dump them in the bin instead of carefully addressing an envelope and sending them back and you'd rip a tear in someone's life. A small one, maybe. A tiny tear in a life that was insignificant in news terms; one with no public voice, but still a life.*

'Lawrence! Job for you!'

I leapt up, bag in hand – keen keen keen. I don't know where I thought he was going to send me. Somewhere big! Somewhere important! Ten minutes later I was on a bus to Lewisham to photograph some woman for a triumph-over-tragedy filler that wouldn't even run if any real news happened between now and deadline. I didn't care. I had a commission. And, I told myself, even the legendary war photographer Margaret Bourke-White had to start somewhere. Although I very much doubt it was on the 89 to Lewisham.

As first jobs went, it was underwhelming. I only remember it because of what came next. It was just after half six, and everyone had pretty much given up on the day except for the poor sods who had to put the paper to bed. Dullest Saturday in the history of dull Saturdays. I was loading my cameras into my rucksack, one staff photographer was out, one was on holiday, one had sloped off early.

Then the news desk phone rang and all hell broke loose.

Phones began ringing off their hooks and suddenly everyone was moving and yelling, grabbing coats, Dictaphones, swearing about remaking pages. In amongst the furore I caught the words Soho and bomb. Nail bomb. Fuck! Nail bomb. *Also, somewhere in there, bloodbath.*

'Lawrence! Scrap that, whatever you were planning to do tonight, cancel it. Huntingdon! Ridley! Take her with you.'

'But, guv . . .' I didn't know which of them protested, but it was clear they didn't fancy taking a woman, and certainly not a newbie.

'You need a photographer. Lawrence is it.'

Well, fuck you too, *I thought, when I saw the look on their faces.*

The news editor turned to me. 'Get everything. Everything. *I mean it. If in doubt, cover it. And don't come back 'til you have.'*

I got the rest: Or don't come back at all.

'Come on!' The guy from the coffee machine – Ridley – was wedging the lift door open with his foot, an expression on his face that said he'd shut it on me, given half a chance. The other one was already in the lift ranting into his mobile phone. 'Get a fucking move on!'

Once in a cab they discussed strategy and swore at the traffic. Walk, I wanted to say. Better still, run, it'd be quicker. I forced myself to stay quiet. It was pretty clear they thought I was the weak link. As far as they were concerned they'd be better off with no photographer at all. A small voice in the back of my head was a bit too hasty to agree with them.

'Admiral Duncan's near Dean Street. Drop us on Shaftesbury as near to Dean as you can get,' Huntingdon told the driver.

'No chance, mate.' The driver shrugged. 'Gridlock up ahead, look. Locked solid. Bloody chaos. Police everywhere. Something going on?'

Listen to it, *I wanted to say. Instead, I yanked down the window and the shriek of approaching sirens rolled in, swamping the cab. Huntingdon ignored me, scowled at the back of the cab driver's head. He looked like he wanted to pull it off.*

'We could always get out and walk?' I said. Sick of being ignored, I directed the comment to Ridley, unable to keep the sarcasm out of my voice. 'Or, better still, run?'

Huntingdon looked like it was now my head he wanted, but he threw a tenner at the driver, leapt out and sprinted off. Point making, much.

'He's starting at Wardour, working back,' Ridley said, only the faintest hint of patronising in his tone. 'I'm starting this end, we'll meet in the middle. You stay with me. Photograph everyone I talk to and anything I tell you. We need colour and lots of it. Road blocks, ambulances, fire engines, stretchers, crowds. Cover the lot. And the injured. Plenty of injured. If we get back without them we might as well not go back at all.'

'How injured . . .?' I started to ask.

'How injured?' He gave me a look, one I was already coming to think of as a very news desk look. 'As injured as you can get.'

Old Compton Street was rammed. The noise was over-whelming, sirens wailing, voices screaming directions and orders. 'Stand back! Move! You can't come in here, sir! Over here! Move!'

And in amongst it, music still flooding from neighbouring bars. Howls of pain and grief undercut by the Backstreet Boys. Beneath it, more unnerving than any howl, was a silence I would come to recognise in the years that followed.

The silence of utter shock.

There was a smell too. I've always been sensitive to smell, but this . . . I'd never smelled anything like it, although I'd come to recognise that too. The flat, metallic smell of blood. Exhaust fumes fused with singed hair, burning flesh overlaid with Italian food, Chinese food, burgers . . . Flesh, both human and animal. Beneath that, the stench of alcohol where the opticals had exploded. All that, and vomit.

Bile rose in my throat and I made myself swallow it down. Ridley glanced over and rolled his eyes. That was what did it. I swallowed again, and turned away. Fuck you, *I thought,* fuck you.

It was almost too easy to lose him. So easy, I'm pretty certain he'd been hoping to shake me off. While he waved his press card in the face of the officer guarding the tape, I walked straight past with an ambulance crew. I should have felt bad about it, but I was too angry. Angry, and horrified.

'How injured? As injured as you can get.'

It played over and over in my head.

Almost an hour had passed since the bomb went off. Long enough for everyone to have convened on the scene; not long enough for anyone to have started doing anything other than the most urgent clearing up. There were photographers and journalists everywhere; all taking the same pictures, all asking the same questions, of the same people. What was the point of another shot of the blown-out pub? The first stretcher carried out? The policewoman with her hand over her mouth? The upturned bar stool in the middle of the street? I took those shots anyway. If The Times *had them and we didn't, I'd be out of a job as quickly as I'd found one.*

Weaving my way up Old Compton Street, avoiding eye contact with anyone looking remotely official, I realised the smell of fear and alcohol was overpowered by something else, something acrid enough to make me swallow down more bile. The scent of burnt coffee coated the inside of my nostrils. I'd never feel the same about percolator coffee again.

'There were people running out covered in blood, dust and bruises,' a dazed-looking man was telling an ITN camera crew, outside the coffee shop next door to what remained of the pub. I doubt he had a clue where he was, let alone who he was talking to. The only people running now were ambulance crews, shuttling stretchers to and from the Duncan. Those from inside still able to run had done that long ago. On the pavement opposite, a row of the injured, red and blue blankets draped over their shoulders, dressings held to their heads, sat on the pavement awaiting treatment. Their number was slowly growing as police ushered walking wounded from the ruins. Their expressions hollow, eyes dead with shock, T-shirts covered with blood or dust or both. If they noticed me raise the camera Dad bought me to celebrate my new job, their expressions didn't register it. Mine wasn't the first to capture them and it wouldn't be the last.

Soon, all that was left inside was the debris. The front of the Admiral Duncan was ripped away, shattered bar stools clogged the gutter, the shop windows opposite looked as if they'd been machine-gunned. The sheer devastation said more about what whoever did this intended than the occasional scream from someone being moved ever could. The emergency teams worked on: quietly, competently, moving through the rest of us as if we didn't exist. As I slipped past, trying not to get in the way of the rescue services, side-swerving other journalists, staying as inconspicuous as I could, rumours swilled round me that the dead had reached double figures. A paramedic muttered, strictly off the record, that the injured were into the hundreds. Far more people than could possibly have been packed into the small Soho pub, more than could have been passing by or drinking on the pavement outside. Once I thought I saw Huntingdon, but never Ridley. I kept my head down and made sure neither saw me.

At the far end of Old Compton Street, I slipped under a tape, past a police car locking off Wardour Street, and leaned against the window of the chemist at the corner, trying to catch my breath. When I looked up, I found myself staring into the open rear doors of an ambulance. Inside, blood was already soaking the bright white of freshly applied bandages. The man was shirtless, grime-splattered. The nurse looked up from her charge, saw my camera and her face changed; concern turned to loathing in less than a second.

'I wouldn't,' I wanted to say, 'I'd never . . .'

Before I had a chance to, she shut the doors on me. All that stared back at me from the blacked-out windows in those doors was my own lie.

I already had.

Adrenalin had carried me from London Bridge across Soho, through hundreds of torn-up lives. When I let down my guard, it deserted me, courage draining my body like air from a leaky balloon. It was almost eight o'clock and the light was failing fast. My eyes were sore, my neck ached, my hands gripped my camera so hard my knuckles hurt. I couldn't bear to see one more victim covered in blood, tread across another beach gravelled with broken glass. That empty expression, which I'd never seen before but already recognised, spoke of lives unutterably changed. I knew I'd never again shut my eyes without seeing it.

To my left I saw an open gate in the wall and stumbled through into what seemed to be a deserted playground. Except it wasn't a playground – no playthings, no children – it was a churchyard. And it wasn't deserted. It was one of those other-worldly pockets you can stumble across in every city; not particularly enclosed, but somehow eerily silent. Groups were scattered in twos and threes across the grass, some muttering to each other in a dazed blur, others staring silently into space, oblivious to the used syringes and cans left by its usual inhabitants. Every so often a siren would wail and someone would look up, confusion across their face, as if its sound was unexpected. In the far corner, where railings gave way to church wall, a row of benches stood concealed by trees. Concentrating on picking my way through cans and syringes, I didn't notice they were already occupied until I was almost upon him. On the furthest bench a man sat in shadows, the lightness of what remained of his white T-shirt contrasting with the gloom. His head was in his hands. Blood soaked through his fingers. I knew I should turn away, leave him to his misery, but I couldn't.

When my office mobile rang I killed the call without even looking.

Blood ran down his face from an open gash in his skull. Before today I'd never seen a wound beyond broken arms or grazed knees, but he wore an embedded nail like a stud beside one eye. His once-white T-shirt was bruising into grey and red.

His eyes looked right through me.

Not looking. Not seeing. Already dead.

'You should . . .?' I said. Should what? Get help? Get that seen to? I sounded as if I was talking to someone who'd cut his knee. He shook his head imperceptibly. Or maybe he didn't, maybe the movement was mine. Then his eyes dropped, staring into nothing, at a spot somewhere between where I stood and

211

his feet. I lifted my camera and quietly stole his picture. Then I left the churchyard, unintentionally kicking a discarded syringe ahead of me.

The picture made the front page. Of course it did. That one shot, the last of three hundred and ninety-eight.

'Thank God for digital,' the picture editor said when he saw how many I'd taken. 'Cost me a bloody fortune in film, that would.'

And I'd taken it almost as an afterthought. It was a lesson that shaped my career; never disregard the afterthought.

My one unintended, unsought picture; taken at the point when I was beginning to realise what I'd just done. Walk through a battlefield like a recording angel, leaving others to dispense care or charity. The man's name was Michael. Five years later we met for a drink when he was writing about his experiences and I wondered then if he wished he'd died. His lover did. The only person he'd loved in his entire life, before or since.

Huntingdon was furious. Ridley, only slightly less so. It was Huntingdon's call I'd killed.

Not furious because I got the front page. No, they were perversely proud of that . . . Suddenly I was their little protégée. My success was down to them. I owed them, for letting me go with them. Patronising arseholes. They were cross because their piece would have been 'even better' if we'd got a quote from Michael. If I'd answered the call they'd have known where I was and could have got one.

Thousands of words they recorded that evening, and not one from the man who made the splash. The only excuse for that, usually, was that the subject was dead. Why hadn't I stayed with them? Why didn't I call them? I didn't answer. I could have said he wasn't capable of speech. That would have been true. I could have lied about crowds. But I wasn't scared of them any more, and I wasn't much interested in their questions. I had one of my own. Why, when a man sat badly wounded in front of me, hadn't I gone for help?

Why had I simply taken his photograph and left?

21

An uncomfortable silence fell. It felt like several minutes but was probably only a matter of seconds. Gil finally broke it. 'And you and Art Huntingdon have been together ever since?' he asked. 'Since the Admiral Duncan, I mean.'

'God no,' said Helen, then stopped, realising how that must sound. How heartless he must already think her. There was a place for gallows humour and this wasn't it.

'That didn't happen 'til much later. Not 'til Iraq. Although, to hear Art tell it, I'd been pining for him the whole time. The man who gave me my big break.'

She noticed Gil glance down at her hands, and forced herself to stop endlessly twisting her fingers.

'But your paths must have crossed?'

'You'd think so. But no, not really. Art is, was, nearly ten years older than me. We hung with different crowds. You have to remember, I'm "just" a photographer.' She looked at him to see if he understood. If he didn't, he didn't show it.

'And then 9/11 happened and Art headed off on his path to glory. I don't even remember seeing him again until Iraq. I say "again". To be honest, I didn't recall him from the first time. There was a bloke, I thought he was an arrogant arsehole, that was the extent of it. Like I said, that memory, the one I've just told you, most of that – or at least Art's part in it – was Art's memory.

'It was another picture that got us together. Not the one on my laptop. Another one. Its twin, I suppose you'd call it.'

Iraq 2007

The small boy lay curled up in the shade of a peeling wall, his hair flopped across his eyes. In his hand was a Power Ranger, the red one. He was lovely, for all his striped T-shirt was filthy and his jeans frayed and his plimsolls two sizes too big. He must be, what . . .?

I leaned in towards the screen to study the picture more closely.

Five, possibly six. Small enough to look angelic and big enough to be a monster at home. He had what seemed to be a slight smile on his face.

So beautiful I could hardly stand it.

I was sitting in front of my laptop in a hotel room staring at the shot with tears streaming down my face. My hair was damp, the neck of my shirt clung where tears had leaked into my collar, but I couldn't stop. I wasn't even trying.

My fingers hovered over the keys. In my head I could hear

the voice of the American colonel who'd dropped by long enough to shake us all by the hand and tell us he was sure we understood the rules. We were journalists, the truth was important to us. It was important to him too, that's why he was fighting for it. His press liaison officer would be happy to discuss angles on stories before they were written and advise on suitable picture edits. I knew I should find him, go through the edit with him . . . But who knew where he was right now?

And more to the point, who cared? I didn't.

Taking one last look at the boy, I hit send and watched the RAW file begin to upload. I chose the best of the later shots and uploaded them too, then found one of the burnt-out truck and uploaded that. Finally, just for the hell of it, I loaded some pictures of the hotel pool.

The picture desk Skyped within half an hour.

'Helen.'

'You like them?'

'He's . . .' the picture editor hesitated.

'Beautiful?'

'That's not the word I'd use.'

Mostly the only pictures of children that got approved were the ones that showed them being given sweets or walking down streets with their mothers under the gaze of soldiers there to keep them safe.

'Tell me you have permission for this.'

I didn't even pause. 'I have permission for this.'

'Good enough for me.'

Skype went blank and I took one last look at the pictures arranged down the side of my screen and shut off my laptop.

That wasn't how the day began. But it was how it ended, pretty much, except for what came later. It began with us gathering in the hotel foyer to be given our groups and briefed for the day. The US army was big on briefing. We'd only been in their sector of Iraq for two days and had been briefed three times. This would be the fourth. A version of the same talk every single day.

The hotel floor was black marble and the walls were white. The marble of the floor probably thicker than the walls, which didn't say much; a crack showed it to be cardboard thin. A long glass mirror behind the reception desk reflected a foyer designed on the European model but a little more ornate and gilded. It was like a nineteenth-century French designer brought up in the Middle East had been given free run of a catalogue of late twentieth-century building materials.

'Penny for them, Lawrence?' I turned, taken by surprise. The English journalist was tall, broad-shouldered; his hair, salt-and-pepper grey at the temples, stuck out at all angles, as if he hadn't bothered to look in a mirror when he got out of bed. But somehow it worked. Along with his flak jacket hanging loose over his fatigues, it gave him a rakish air. And he knew it. In the forty-eight hours we'd been here, it was the first time he'd spoken to me. Even then, I didn't make the connection.

'Kitsch,' I said, indicating the décor.

'Kitsch?' he said. 'That's it? Kitsch? Glad I didn't offer you a pound.'

Further conversation ceased when an American major pushed his way through the swing door, followed a second later by a captain and a sergeant. There were seven of us. All American, bar a French photographer, Art and me. Six men, one woman.

'Good morning,' the major said. He looked around at the group, his gaze not quite meeting mine, but passing over my body which was hidden beneath a blue flak jacket with Press *stencilled above one breast and on the back. His sergeant's gaze*

was more openly curious. It didn't bother me, I was used to it by then.

'Three journalists, two camera crew, two photographers. Is that right?' His eyes singled me out, and I realised why he'd been avoiding looking at me until now. 'I'm afraid I've got bad news for one of you. We're taking three groups of two each. That's all we've got capacity for today. It's a bit rough out there and we've chosen our routes carefully . . .'

His voice was reassuringly normal, just the right mixture of authority and friendliness to let us know he valued our opinions, and the democratic freedoms a free press represented, but he was the one in charge and he was the one making the decisions.

Once upon a time . . . I thought to myself sourly, journalists went to war and risked being killed and were on their own, mostly. Until Vietnam taught the military that uncontrolled journalists wrote stories you didn't want written, took photographs you didn't want taken, and lost you wars; particularly if you let them photograph coffins coming home. So the embedded journalist was born. On the upside you got transport, protection, good and open access to the troops and press briefing. On the downside . . . Well, the downside was obvious.

The major ran through his briefing. Mentioned the escalating tension between Sunni and Shia, talked about a hospital recently reopened, a road out of town made safe, the number of new troops in the area. We were given a little background on why this increase was essential, how a surge now would help bring the violence to a close.

'Right,' he said. 'Let's get to it.'

The captain looked at a clipboard and muttered to the sergeant, who called out two names. The pair hurried over, listened and made their way outside. There were tank traps at either end of the short road that ran past the front of the hotel to keep suicide bombers away. A checkpoint on the way. Hired contractors armed with AK-47s patrolled the grounds. The hotel was a safe zone, inside another safe zone, and yet no one believed we were all that safe. But we knew we'd be a lot less safe with every checkpoint we passed.

Two more names were called, the pair grabbing their equipment and leaving the room. Three left. I was still waiting for the major to let me know I wasn't going.

'. . . And Mr Huntingdon.'

That was the last of them.

Huntingdon? It was only when his name was called that I realised who he was. Huntingdon – Art – cast me a lazily apologetic look. I scowled. He wasn't that sorry. Nor would I have been in his place.

'I'm not going?'

The major looked as if he always knew this moment was coming. The irritated and irritating English woman with the too loud voice. 'As I said, we've only got six slots.'

'You're leaving the woman?'

He consulted his own list as if to confirm that, yes, the others were indeed men. 'That's not the reason.'

'So, what is the reason?'

He looked as if he was about to answer, then remembered he didn't have to justify himself to anyone, let alone me. Instead he turned on his heel and marched out, flanked by his flunkies. I was halfway across the foyer myself, headed for the little garden at the back, and fucked if I was going to let them see my tears of fury. There were days I wished I was a smoker, this was one of them. When I returned a few minutes later, the room was empty and I was alone in the foyer with the lumpy-looking girl on the check-in desk. She was in her late teens or very early twenties, bareheaded and quiet. Each night, before she left, she put on a headscarf and a black robe that hid her jeans. I'd seen her do it.

'We have a swimming pool,' she said.

Until that point, I hadn't realised she spoke English, although I supposed she must do to be on the desk. The army had handled our checking in and it was the first time I'd heard her talk.

I looked at her astonished. 'Really? Where?'

'On the roof.' She glanced around the empty foyer, considering. 'The water's fresh. There are sun loungers and parasols. Would you like me to show you?'

I'd used three Iraqi lifts since I arrived and been briefly trapped by brown-outs twice. We climbed five flights of stairs, our feet echoing on the concrete. By mutual but unspoken agreement we paused on the third floor to get our breath and look out at mountains that began where the dirt-brown fields ended on the outskirts of town. I could see three farms, two bridges, and a grove of what might be olive trees. A village in the distance had a small white-painted mosque with a spindly turret.

'Through here,' she said, pushing a door open for me. A pristine pool filled with crystal-clear water awaited me. The tiles in and around the pool were pale blue, apart from deep blue detailing. The sun loungers were arranged around the edge, their thin mattresses folded into a neat pile beside the door. The umbrellas were closed, their canvas and spines pointing down like broken palm trees. In between them were actual palm trees, tiny stubby ones in terracotta pots.

Without thinking, I produced my camera. Shot the mattresses, shot a single sun lounger with its naked frame, another shot of a row of loungers and then stepped back to include the pool, ending with a shot of the pool and beyond it the village and the *mountains. A spiral of smoke rose near the village. Bomb, that was my first thought, but I'd probably have heard the explosion. A farmer burning off his fields, more like. Or the town rubbish dump. Either way, it didn't matter. It gave the view a slightly 'off' air and worked within the framework of the picture.*

'Could you sit there?' I pointed to the low wall that rimmed the roof terrace; lower than would be allowed in Britain. She shook her head.

'Please . . .'

The girl looked uncomfortable.

'You're afraid someone will see the picture?'

She nodded.

'Face away from me then.'

'Please . . . wait . . .' Before I could answer, she'd vanished. I could hear feet descending away from me on concrete stairs. A few minutes later she returned, out of breath, but wearing a scarf round her face and carrying the robe she wore to cover her jeans on the walk home.

'Now,' she said, shrugging herself into the gown. She came from the city, she told me. Until she came here she never used to wear scarves. But these days, it was best. Safer. I positioned her on the wall, her face turned to the curl of smoke in the distance and then stood so the village, the minaret and the edge of her face were in the frame. I fired off three shots. Then another three from a slightly different angle.

'Thank you.'

'You're welcome.'

I wondered if I should give her money and decided against, afraid of offending her. I'd leave some when I left.

I eyed the pool. The water was clear and, for all I knew, cool. I liked swimming. I hadn't packed a costume, but I could improvise. Swimming in a hotel pool in the middle of a city at war was a story in itself, I supposed. Only it wasn't the story I was there to get. Five floors below, the town was laid out around me. A square, smaller squares, old, flat-roofed houses and concrete office blocks. A market set up under canvas in a car park. Broken buildings and a burnt-out police station reminders it was fought over. I wanted to explore the narrow alleys behind the shell of the police station.

'I'd like to hire you.'

She looked at me.

'As a guide. I want to hire you as a guide.'

'What do you want to see?'

'What can you show me?'

'There are tombs. Ancient. Very ancient. And a fort. The British were here before. They built a fort. These days it's a ruin.' Her smile was wry, she didn't have to finish that sentence.

'Over there,' I said. 'I want you to show me over there.' She eyed me doubtfully. My hair was dark and curly, dyed almost black back then, my eyes brown. For once in my life it was better than being taller, thinner, blonder.

'They're coming.' The girl stood in the hotel lounge doorway.

We'd been back about an hour – just long enough for me to edit the film, send in the pictures and pull myself together.

'I ordered you, understand?' I told her.

She nodded.

'I told you that I had permission. I'd been told you'd help me. I was very firm. All right?'

'You said you had permission.'

'That's right. I didn't offer to pay you . . .' That was true, I hadn't. 'You took me to the old quarter because I told you that was your job. You work at the hotel. I'm staying at the hotel. Understood?'

When she nodded decisively I knew that was what she would say. That, and only that. I hoped it was enough to keep her out of trouble. I didn't care about being in trouble myself. Later, maybe. Then maybe I'd care. When my boss found out. When the MoD got on the phone to scream. Right now I was too cross with the men strolling through the door. They looked pleased with themselves, like they'd had a productive day. Only the major wasn't smiling.

'You went out.' He stopped right in front of me, Art was directly behind him.

'You could have been killed, Lawrence.' That was Art.

I did a double take, looked at him. What was it to him? OK, so there was a code, we looked out for each other out here, but that didn't stretch to this.

'I wasn't.'

'Where's your flak jacket?' the major asked suddenly and I realised, stupidly, I had left it up on the roof.

'It's hard to blend in with a flak jacket.'

'You're not here to blend in,' the major said. I glanced at the other journalists in their fatigues and patches, mostly still wearing flak jackets and at least one holding a television camera with the insouciance he might hold a weapon.

'Obviously not. Unless you want to blend in with the army. Then you'd be fine.'

Behind him, one of the Americans leaned in and muttered to the other, who snorted. Art flushed in embarrassment and I felt a pang of something . . . it wasn't his fault he'd been chosen and I hadn't, after all.

'There was a car bomb,' the major said heavily. 'You could have died.'

'I know,' I said. 'I was there, and I didn't.'

'You took photographs?'

'Of course I took photographs. I'm a photographer.'

'I'll need to see them. Tell me you haven't sent them through.'

'I haven't sent them through.'

He held out his hand and, without protest, I handed him my camera. Well, one of them; the Leica hanging from my shoulder. 'We'll talk later,' he told me. He walked back to where his captain was waiting, muttered a few words and they both turned to stare at me.

'Drink?' Art said when the others had dispersed.

I nodded, already drunk on adrenalin. It was my most impressive shot in ages. There had been plenty of others in the intervening years, but this was the first I could look at and say, You nailed the truth.

Also, I'd got the shot the proper way, not hand-delivered and rubber-stamped by the army.

The beer in the bar was another thing that came via the army. I wasn't sure of the arrangement but the beer was American and cold enough to make my teeth hurt. I drank down the first one Art brought me in unladylike gulps and swallowed a handful of pistachios, almost choking on an escapee shell. A television in the corner got satellite from the roof, and the Iraqi behind the bar, trusted because he wouldn't be there if he wasn't, turned it on and down, leaving it on rolling news at my request.

The bar was half full and Art and I were on our second beer.

'Shit,' one of the Americans said.

A talking head popped up and, in the corner, just above a ticker tape of rolling news, an agency headshot of me, so many years old as to be almost unrecognisable. Almost. My stomach lurched. I sensed what was coming. It was the shot the agency trotted out every time. The only one I'd been prepared to pose for back at the beginning before I knew better.

'Turn it up,' someone shouted, and the Iraqi behind the bar obliged.

On the screen was a photograph of a small boy, so beautiful and so serene.

His eyes were closed and he was curled as if in sleep, a plastic toy in his hand. There was no sign of the talking head now, but he could still be heard, explaining how I took the shot in the immediate aftermath of a car bomb. The photograph faded to be replaced by another shot. The boy from behind. Because the newsfeed was neither British nor American the shot was not pixelated; the back of his skull pierced by shrapnel, a little of his brains lay in the dirt. The things you didn't see from the front. Then a third shot, the photograph I took of the boy on my way into the quarter, my hair hidden by the headscarf my companion provided, my T-shirt under a maid's dress borrowed from the hotel.

The boy sat on a ruined doorstep half in sunlight, half in shadow, squinting shyly at the camera and holding out his red Power Ranger.

By the time the major stormed into the bar tears were streaming down my face. At the sight of a woman crying he stopped, appalled. Just as quickly he regrouped. 'You,' he said unnecessarily, pointing at me. 'We need to talk.'

When I returned fifteen minutes later, the others were talking quietly, the Iraqi barman had changed channels and Art was still at the bar, where I'd left him, at the bottom of his third beer bottle.

I almost didn't go back to the bar, to be honest. Many times since I've wondered how things might have turned out if I hadn't. If I had just done what the major ordered me to do, gone to my room and packed. Instead I decided to get blind drunk. I had my picture, I had my story and I was being shipped *out of there in the morning. Tonight I could do what the hell I wanted. And I already had an idea what that might involve.*

'You could have ruined everything,' Art said conversationally, indicating the empty stool next to him. His hair was even more tufty, like he'd been raking his hands through it as he digested the news.

'They're not shipping you out,' I scoffed, taking my first gulp of the beer he'd just handed me. 'Only the bad girl.'

'But they could have done,' he said. 'Come on, Lawrence. You know this game only works if everyone plays by the rules. What you did—'

'I got the story, is what I did. Isn't that why we're here? You think your uniformed friends are going to give you anything that isn't homogenised, sanitised and hand-delivered?'

For a second a shadow crossed his face, hooding his eyes. I recognised it suddenly for the look I'd seen in London eight years earlier. Although I didn't realise it then, it was one I was to see many times in the future.

Then it passed. His brown eyes softened, tiny lines radiating outwards where the skin was slightly lighter from his sunglasses.

'Too true, Lawrence,' Art said. Grinning, he drained his bottle and signalled for two more, even though I'd barely started mine. 'But then, from what I remember, you never were much of a team player, were you?'

I frowned.

'Admiral Duncan?' His smile dropped slightly.

'What a memory,' I said. 'I didn't recognise you until this morning.'

He looked taken aback, but let it pass.

We talked all evening. It was one of those nights when one beer turns to five and seven o'clock turns to midnight in the blink of an eye.

226

*There didn't seem to be anything we couldn't talk about.
Art seemed interested in me. More interested than anyone had
been in a long time. And the result was intoxicating. I found
myself telling him things I hadn't told anyone since Tom.
Stupid things, significant things, tiny details. He knew quite
a lot about me already, as it turned out, could name several
of my pictures, knew what I'd been doing since that night at
the Admiral Duncan. His irritation at my insistence that I
hadn't immediately been able to place him passed as quickly
as it flared.*

*It was as if he'd taken off his other self – the competitive,
angry, brooding, resentful one – with his flak jacket. This was
the real him, I decided. The one under the reporter's armour.
He was divorced, he said. He'd met his wife at university, they'd
split up, got back together, there'd been others for both of them,
and then she'd got pregnant and they married. He was twenty-
five and she was twenty-four, his daughter was fourteen, almost
fifteen, his son twelve. The kids lived with their mum. He didn't
see them as often as he should. He gave me an abashed look
and told me he knew what I'd think of that.*

'That marriage was a mistake from day one,' he told me.
'That's not just me saying that. Angie would agree. Well, maybe
day two. Textbook fuck-up. So here I am, nearly forty, two kids,
one ex-wife and maintenanced up to my eyeballs. How about
you?'

I shrugged. 'No kids. No ex. No maintenance.'

'Come on, Lawrence,' *he snorted.* 'No one? Don't give me
that! There must be a trail of broken-hearts in your sordid past.'

I laughed. 'Not really. Nothing serious. Not for a long time,
anyway. Ever since then, ever since I picked up my first camera,
I've been married to that.'

'Know what you mean,' *he said.* 'Sometimes there just isn't *room in one life for two great loves.' He paused, eyes locking on mine. 'Or that's what I used to think . . .'*

Somewhere between the beer and the vodka, the bar emptied and Art and I moved to a booth. Around about the fourth vodka I noticed his hand had slipped from the shelf of the banquette and was resting lightly on my back. Somehow it had found its way under my shirt. I had no interest in removing it. It was hardly professional, but I was leaving in the morning and since we hadn't found ourselves assigned to the same city before, it was unlikely we would again. It had been a while and I was lonely. I needed to lose myself in someone else's body. And I'd decided that body would be Art's.

There was another reason, too. I didn't want to sleep, and I certainly didn't want to sleep alone, because I knew every time I closed my eyes I would see a small boy, huge brown eyes staring at me. In his hand a red plastic Power Ranger.

It was gone midnight when the barman started turning off the lights around us. Art got up, tugging me with him, and led me towards the lift.

'Uh-uh,' I said, heading towards the stairs instead. 'I don't want to be stuck in a brown-out with you.' He followed me into the stairwell, letting the door clang shut behind us. The silence was absolute.

'Really, Lawrence?' he said, his whisper echoing off concrete. 'I can think of worse things.'

'Helen.' It came out almost a gasp. My cover, such as it was, blown. 'Not Lawrence. Helen.'

'Helen?' His face collapsed into a smile. It was, I realised, the first time I'd seen him really smile.

I let him manoeuvre me into the corner behind the door, so our bodies were wedging it shut. Not that we were likely to be interrupted. Vodka coursed in my veins and all I could feel was

the heat of his fingers through the thin cotton of my shirt as
he clasped my arm; firm, proprietorial. His physical proximity.
Taller by five or six inches. Broader. Warm, strangely. That was
my overriding impression. Heat. Then he put his other hand
on my other arm, pinning me to the wall, and stepped in close.

He dipped forward, brushing his lips against mine, his breath
hot on my face. 'I can think of worse things. Lots of them.'
When I didn't resist he moved back in, his lips harder now,
his tongue easing my mouth open as his hand grazed my nipple.

'Like what?' I managed, feeling my body make its decision
long before my brain.

'Come and get in the lift,' he said, releasing his grip slightly,
my skin still prickling under his touch. 'And I'll show you.'

When I woke the next morning, sun blazing through half-open
curtains, head pounding and my mobile vibrating relentlessly
on the desk to tell me the taxi for the airport was waiting
downstairs, Art was long gone. Fifteen minutes later, so was I.
I can't honestly say I expected to hear from him again.
One-nighters weren't a frequent occurrence. But they had
happened before, and part of me expected this one to follow the
usual pattern.

One long, steamy night thousands of miles from home.

A memory, for when the need arose. Another part of me
hoped it might be more. I was thirty and there'd been no one
who mattered in over ten years. No one, really, since Tom, my
first and last almost serious boyfriend. As my family never tired
of reminding me. So when Art called a fortnight later and
invited me for a Friday-night drink that turned into two that
turned into dinner that turned into a whole weekend, we fell
into a routine.

It wasn't what my sister would have called a relationship,

at least not at first, but it worked for us. We were both away a lot, we both had our own places (although Art was always on at me to move in with him), but when we were both in London, we were a couple.

22

For the first couple of years everything seemed fine. We were successful, we were in love, we were greater than the sum of our parts, as Art never stopped telling me. We were golden. My career, which had been on the up before Iraq, went stratospheric. I had more commissions than I could cope with and the awards came thick and fast. Art had had his moment several years earlier in Afghanistan, but still, he was enough of a name for it not to be a problem.

Or so I told myself.

The pregnancy changed everything.

I was sick as a dog the whole time I was in Haiti. In itself the nausea wasn't that odd. It had been coming in waves like a migraine's outriders since Iraq. So much so, I'd been put on medication that wiped me out almost as much as the attacks themselves. But this felt like more than that. On my way back through Heathrow, I bought four pregnancy tests in Boots and went straight to the Ladies in Arrivals. But once there, with the packet in my hand and my knickers round my ankles, I couldn't face it.

Instead, I stopped for a long overdue skinny latte in the Starbucks round the corner from my flat, and peeled the foil from one in the loos there. As I hovered over the bowl, I hesitated and looked around me. Not here. The floor was slightly sticky and the basin needed wiping. Do it at home. Talk about delaying tactics.

That was why the first one gave a false positive, I told myself. Carrying it home in my coat pocket, it had become contaminated. The second one? Well, it might have been faulty. I knew it wasn't. Just as I knew the first one wasn't contaminated. I was pregnant and I didn't need a test to tell me. But still I did another, just to be safe; to try to convince myself that what I already knew to be true was a lie. No, not a lie, simply a mistake.

'I don't know how it happened . . .'

I tried the words aloud for Art, my voice puzzled, a little shocked, almost apologetic. I don't know how it happened . . .

It was true; I didn't know how it had happened. We'd stopped using condoms years ago and, thanks to our schedules, hadn't seen each other for a couple of months. But it was his, no question. I hadn't slept with anyone else since we'd met, and the last time we had sex I'd had a migraine the day after and must have thrown up my pill. Thanks to the migraines, I was always throwing up.

It didn't help that we'd argued just before he left. I'd been setting up a small exhibition at a gallery in Shoreditch, my first. Art had been sent to Afghanistan to cover the elections and wanted me to go to Heathrow to see him off. I thought it was obvious why I couldn't. He thought the only thing that was obvious was how selfish I was. 'I thought we were supposed to be a team.' Those were the last words he said before he slammed the door.

Then Haiti had happened and a week later I'd been on a plane out myself.

Art's emails, usually frequent, were infrequent in the weeks we were away. The few there were, were cold and brittle. My replies were friendly at first, coaxing and cajoling, and then cool and finally as terse as his. Until he wrong-footed me by sending me an essay he'd written on refugees. There was no indication who it was for and I wondered if it was on spec, something the agency had suggested he do. I made as many suggestions as I dared, said how much I liked it, how unlike his other pieces it was, but how I'd really liked those too, and got an email almost by return saying he was flying home at the weekend and was looking forward to seeing me.

Would I be back by then too?

Did I mind coming to his? he added. He'd probably need a bath, a shave and long sleep, but then I would too. He didn't mind where he was so long as he saw me.

'Your place is fine,' I replied, adding more xxxx after the H than I'd done in a while, already suspecting I was pregnant and wondering too late whether it was safer to have this conversation on home territory or neutral ground? Maybe, for something like this, I should have suggested we meet in Antonio's, the Italian place in Soho we used to go to in the beginning. Art's concession to my intolerance of the scene at whichever restaurant was of the moment this month, and the way his cronies at the Groucho Club slapped him on the back and looked right through me, unless I dressed up, in which case it wasn't my opinions or talent as a photographer that drew their attention.

'Your face,' Art would say, half-affectionate, half-mocking.

'They're important,' he'd add occasionally. 'They can help you.'

I just grimaced. Said nothing. I'd helped myself this far. I didn't need their help now.

The problem was, I knew that if I suggested he drop off his luggage and come on to Antonio's, Art was more than capable of suggesting we go to the Groucho instead. So Art's flat it was.

I showered, washed my hair, upended my rucksack of filthy clothes into the washing machine and then did one more test in the hope it had changed its mind in the last hour. It hadn't. I would have taken a taxi but there weren't any, and I was between stops when a number 73 passed, so I ended up walking. As I was passing the Tesco Metro on the way I realised Art wouldn't have any milk, let alone food. Filling a basket with Tesco Finest – Art didn't really approve of Tesco – I added a bottle of good Chilean Merlot to the bread, tomatoes, cheese, olives and posh crisps already in my basket.

If Art wanted real food we could call out or drop down to the pizza place on the corner. Art's flat was on the top floor of a sixties block between Soho and Regent Street, an area they'd just started calling West Soho. The porter, a sweet old Irishman with a face like a scrunched-up flannel and swept back white hair too thin for its length, smiled and told me Art was in. He watched me choose a lift, since all three were at the bottom, and smiled again as the doors closed, leaving me to the slow hum of the winch above, my reflection and my bag of shopping. I checked my hair, my clothes, my make-up from habit. I'd made an effort in that I had actually applied make-up, but that was about it. Art could live with me in jeans and a T-shirt and my old black leather jacket. He'd seen them often enough.

'You're . . .' Art paused. 'I was expecting you earlier.'

'I stopped off at the shops.'

He caught me as I slipped past him on my way to his kitchen, wrapping his arms tight around me, so the Tesco bag was trapped at my side, and leaned his forehead against mine. I closed my eyes and when I opened them he was smiling.

'Let me,' he said, taking the bag from me.

Art raised his eyebrows approvingly at the Merlot, which cost more than the rest of the shopping put together, and nodded towards a cupboard when I suggested olives. I knew where the little bowls lived. They were a Christmas present to Art from my mother the Christmas before, along with a cashmere jersey, which he admired at length and then put in a drawer, complete with its label, where to the best of my knowledge it was still languishing. The bowls were Spanish pottery translated by Marks & Spencer. Faux Spanish, Art called them.

I emptied the olives into a bowl and tore off two sheets of kitchen roll to act as napkins. Behind me I heard a slight pop as Art uncorked the Merlot and a clink as he took two glasses from a different cupboard.

'To us,' he said, raising his glass.

As we toasted each other I watched Art suck air through the first slight sip of wine and smile. I returned his smile and drank mine down, aware the wine was smooth and more than drinkable but not appreciating it in the way he seemed to.

'Glad to be back?' I asked.

'Happy to see you,' he said. 'Always happy to see you. But this city . . . After Afghanistan . . . Most of the people here don't know how lucky they are to be alive. You know, over there, tribal feuds are obvious. Someone dumps an IED beside the road and blows up their neighbour's truck, you're not left in much doubt. Where you come from matters. What you believe matters. Here, we're still pretending it doesn't.'

'Still . . .?'

'World's changing, babes.'

He knew I hated 'babes'.

'It's getting harder. We were better off when the wall was up. At least no one pretended the Soviets were our friends. It was tough for the poor bastards they ruled, of course. But they had their rules and we had ours and everyone understood how it worked. America arming the Afghans was bloody stupid. I know it brought down the Russians, but now it's just a mess. And we sit here, letting our boys get killed in the name of democracy, and half the people we've made government ministers out there couldn't run a village council.'

'You don't think they deserve democracy?'

'I'm not even sure we deserve democracy.'

I sighed and didn't challenge him further. It was best not to when he was in this mood.

Perhaps my news should wait until tomorrow.

He nodded towards the Heal's leather sofa which I'd gone to buy with him and ended up wishing I'd simply let him make the choice himself. I was more of a distressed leather, collapsed cushions, sloppy enough to look as if it had been there forever kind of girl. Art wanted chrome and white and let himself be edged into cream and wood. Neither of us was happy with the result, but it was Art's money, and it was a lot of money, and every time I saw the sofa I wished I'd been out of the country that Saturday.

'So,' he said, 'what's been happening in your life?'

I paused too long and Art's eyes narrowed very slightly, his gaze hardening.

'Well?' he said.

He was sitting into the corner of the sofa, his hair in need of a cut and his stubble at exactly the right length to make him look

*piratical. He was wearing chinos and a pale short-sleeved shirt
that looked expensive. It suited him and he knew it. He always
knew it. His clothes were meant to look thrown on while on his
way to do something more important. Art was never one to
underestimate his own attractiveness; and he'd mastered the
subtleties of appearing famous, even if no one could quite put
their finger on who he was. In restaurants, bars and private
members' clubs you could see people feel they should recognise
him and compensate accordingly. It had happened more when
we were first together. He'd thickened at the waist in the three
years since. But he still, just about, had his looks. When I looked
up, he was staring at me and there was a tightness to his eyes.*

'*Thinking about when we were first together.*'

'*What were you thinking?*'

'*All those glamorous clubs and restaurants.*'

'*And all you wanted to do was go to that pizza joint in
Soho.*'

'*They do—*'

'*Yeah, I know. They do pasta too and salads. I half expected
you to suggest we meet there tonight. So, what's been going on?
How was Haiti?*'

'*Grim. I'm pregnant.*' *I stopped. That wasn't how I'd
planned it.*

*Art blinked like someone had just turned on a floodlight.
'How did that happen?*'

'*The usual way.*'

He wasn't amused.

I shrugged apologetically.

'*How pregnant?*'

*I looked at him. 'You left what, eight weeks ago, nine . . .?
That pregnant, I imagine. When I missed the first period I
didn't think much of it. You know I've always been irregular.*'

'And then you missed a second?'

I nodded.

'I thought you were on the pill?'

'I am . . . Well, I was. I stopped taking it when I started to suspect.' I'd stopped the migraine pills too, but I didn't mention that. Art took a dim view of my migraines. 'You remember I was sick the morning you flew?'

'I thought that was . . .'

'An excuse for not seeing you off?' I ventured a smile. He didn't return it.

'Nerves, at the gallery thing. How did that go?'

'Well enough. I had to fly to Haiti almost straight after. I must have thrown up that day's pill.'

I didn't tell him, because why make trouble – and with Art, I was starting to discover, trouble could be trouble – that I'd also forgotten to take my pill the previous day in the stress of trying to get pictures chosen and to the developers before Art took me to lunch and then, inevitably, back to his flat so we could spend the afternoon in bed before going out to supper and returning to bed, which should have been a repeat of the afternoon, but ended up being one of those lying in silence rigid and parallel to the edges of the bed arguments after I told him I didn't have time to see him off at the airport.

And now I've come back to this.

I could see that in his face. I wanted to say I'd thought it through, and I was going to ring a clinic in the morning. Or that I'd thought it through and it was OK, I was going to take responsibility for this and being a single mother wouldn't make that big a difference to my life. Who was I kidding? He'd know that for the lie it was. But at least it would be my lie and it would give him an out if he wanted one and he could live with that. The trouble was, I'd been thinking it through for weeks *and still couldn't reach a decision. In that moment, watching Art watch me, I wished I'd taken the decision earlier and dealt with it ruthlessly enough not to be having this conversation.*

It would have been the end of us, but from the look on his face, it was anyway.

'Hungry?' Art said suddenly, drawing a line under the conversation.

I shrugged, taken aback. 'Can be.'

We ordered takeout pizza, more for something to do than anything else. Art finished his and I ate half of mine and left the other half in the box, carrying both boxes through to the kitchen and hoping he wouldn't look later. I considered going home, I even worked out the words, but when I got back to his living room it was empty. Through the bedroom door I could see the side light was on, hear water running in the en suite.

'Shattered,' he said, wandering through. 'Need an early night. I'll run you a bath if you need one . . .?'

I've never been that good at keeping my thoughts off my face. Certainly not as good as Art, who'd respectfully interviewed people I knew he despised.

'You seem tense, babe.'

'I'm just . . .'

'Worried about stuff?'

I smiled, willing it to reach my eyes.

'I'll run you a bath . . .' Water splashed like a little waterfall from the Italian monoblock he'd found in some magazine and the lights went out, followed by the flicker of a match. When I went through he'd lit the three candles on the windowsill and was sitting on the loo with the lid down, waiting for me. 'There,' he said.

'How was it? You want to talk?'

'I hate doing embedded. They keep us from the real stuff.

How can you be expected to file proper copy if they won't let you write about what matters? It's all colour stuff. Our brave boys. Not that they're not brave,' he said hastily. 'They're bloody magnificent. Better than the moron politicians who sent them out there. But you know . . .'

Yeah, I knew. It was an opinion that used to be mine. One of many.

'You all right?'

'Just thinking about Haiti.'

He smiled sympathetically. I could feel him staring as I stripped off my jeans and T-shirt and reached behind me to unhook my bra. His reflection was watching me intently as I climbed out of my knickers and into the water, wishing Art believed in bubbles. With him sitting there and neither of us in the mood to talk it wasn't possible to stare at the ceiling and simply soak. So I washed in a businesslike fashion, Art staring openly now. 'Here,' he said, handing me a towel.

In the bedroom he hesitated. 'On or off?'

'Off, if that's OK.'

'Whatever you want.' He flicked the room into darkness, considered it for a second and dragged back one curtain, letting in a sliver of communal area lights from the office block behind. He stripped briskly, draping his shirt and jeans neatly over his bedroom chair as always and climbed in beside me.

He reached for me and I rolled into his arms, wrapping my own around his neck and holding him tight. I was glad to see him, I told myself. Glad we appeared to have made friends. Also it stopped him simply grabbing bits before I was ready. He suffered it for a few seconds and hugged me back, before reaching up and gripping my hair to turn my head so he could kiss me. It was hard and deep and fierce.

'Missed you,' he said.

'Missed you too.'

I felt him smile in the darkness before shifting his other hand to my breast, fingers tightening on flesh.

'Gently . . .'

He stilled. 'It's been a while,' he said, not bothering to keep the irritation from his voice.

There was no pretence, no kissing or stroking. He just hammered into me, hard fingers digging into the soft flesh at the top of my arms. In the morning there would be finger bruises. Biting my lip until it hurt, I wondered: Was it the baby? Having put it into me, was he trying to get it out again?

He changed positions a couple of times. I didn't realise at first that I was counting, silently, methodically in my head. Not Art's thrusts. Not anything really. Just crouching outside myself, letting the long seconds pass, like a child playing hide and seek. Finally, he collapsed at my side, gasping like a drowning man.

'You OK?' he asked eventually.

'Fine.'

'Do you want me to . . .?'

My hand found his and I squeezed it briefly. 'Tomorrow,' I said. 'You're tired. I'm tired. It was a long journey. You should sleep now.'

Unconsciousness descended on him almost before the last word was out of my mouth. Slowly his breathing regulated and I slipped noiselessly from the bed, shutting the bathroom door behind me before turning on the light over the basin. I slid the lock as an afterthought, before running a basin of cold water and using Art's flannel to numb myself. In the mirror finger bruises already blossomed on my upper arms and the back of my thighs.

I stepped closer to the mirror and peered at myself. I didn't look any different. I certainly didn't look pregnant. But I would, *and soon, a little thickening at the abdomen, people who didn't know me wondering if I'd put on weight. It occurred to me, belatedly, that pregnancy might be the reason my breasts were more tender than usual when Art snatched at them.*

I wasn't ready to be a mother, I was pretty sure Art wasn't ready to be a father again, and my family sure as hell weren't ready for me to become a single mother. There was only one choice, and by the time I slid myself back under the sheets next to Art, I'd made it. My only regret was that I hadn't made it before he came home.

Art was already dressed when I woke, sitting on the bed, staring at me with a smile on his face. He leaned in and kissed my forehead, a blast of his aftershave making my gorge rise. That and the jam-like smear at the edge of my vision told me a migraine was approaching.

'Wake up, sleepyhead,' he said. 'I called the café. They're keeping us a table.'

The café was on the corner, a zinc and Formica homage to fifties London that was newer than it tried to look but hung with enough original black-and-whites to be interesting. In the week it was full of Soho media types. At the weekend it was used by locals, and people who'd like to call themselves local.

'Come on,' Art said. 'It will do us good.'

I ordered toast, which came with a slab of butter hacked straight from a packet, and Art attacked the full breakfast; stealing a piece of my toast to prop up his baked beans.

'Been thinking,' he said. He looked at me, in that fixed-gaze way he'd made a trademark, and I smiled back to confirm I was paying attention.

'We should get married.'

'Married?' I stopped buttering my toast.

'A child needs a father. A proper father.' He put down his fork and picked up his tea, Earl Grey but in a solid white builder's mug. 'I want to do it right this time. I called Dad first thing and said I was going to propose to you. Mum's delighted. You know it's what she wanted. I thought we'd drive down to tell your parents after breakfast.' He looked at me. 'If you say yes, obviously.'

He grinned and looked round the café, signalling to the Spanish girl behind the counter that he wanted another cup of tea and I'd have a cappuccino. 'I know this isn't the most romantic place to propose . . .'

I looked at the floor, long overdue a good mop. I wouldn't want to kneel there either. Not that Art would kneel, not in public, and not for something where he might get knocked back. I could see from his eyes he wasn't entirely sure he wasn't going to. He didn't like embarrassing himself. He didn't like being embarrassed.

'Art . . .'

He looked at me intently.

'Last night . . .'

'God, I'm sorry, babes. It was too much, too hard and way too soon.' He hesitated. 'It was a bastard, this time. If I'm honest. The fixer wasn't any good. The desk kept changing their mind. It's a bloody mess. We know that. They know that. We're just not allowed to say it.'

Reaching across the table, Art took my hand. 'Let me apologise, OK? Please? It won't happen again. You know I love you. We could be really good together. I mean, we are good. We're a team.'

His brown eyes were full of remorse. He was right, of course. We were a team. Bigger and better than the sum of our parts. He never tired of saying it.

'Yes,' I said. 'OK, yes.'

He grinned his trademark grin and clicked his fingers, not loudly, but just loudly enough for the Spanish girl at the coffee machine to look across and see him make the universal cheque-signing movement of someone who wanted the bill.

'Great,' he said. 'Drink up, and let's go tell your parents the good news.'

23

We married for the best of reasons. At least, I let Art convince me it was the best of reasons. Then the reason went and we remained. Art was furious when I miscarried, even more so than when I told him I was pregnant. As if losing his child was my fault. As if I could have stopped my body rejecting what we'd made. But we'd only been married a few weeks, and already I wasn't sure that, if Art wanted to try for another, I'd agree.

I threw myself into my work. But each commission I got, every overseas job I took, made Art more tight-lipped and resentful. He hadn't had a major by-line for a couple of years and that was eating at him. Afghanistan wasn't the first trip he'd returned from without a front-page story and he was constantly being side-lined in favour of younger, cheaper journalists. Reckless kids with a smartphone, as he put it, who were already on the ground. So when an American news agency asked him to set up a European office for them in Paris, he jumped at it.

The first I knew of it was when I came home to find a brochure from a Parisian estate agent on the kitchen worktop.

'Surprise!' Art said, looking more like his old self than he had in months.

I should have been furious. How dare he make such a big decision without even consulting me? But he was so fired up, so much like the Art I'd fallen for, that all I felt was relief. I had been walking on eggshells for months. Making myself as small and invisible as possible so as not to enrage him.

And the truth was, Paris suited me too. I'd been asked to participate in an exhibition there, so I wanted to be close enough to work on it when I wasn't travelling. It was my first exhibition since Shoreditch. That one had been called children + naked *and caused outrage until the outraged realised every one of the young refugees in the pictures was clothed. It was their surroundings that were bare, their futures. Back then, back when I still took pictures of people, that was my thing, what I was most proud of. That my photographs showed people naked. Not without clothes. No. They were some of the most wrapped-up people on the planet, but naked before the lens, stripped back to fear, emptiness or resignation. Their nakedness was political, financial. Nudity is a first world luxury. Naked is to be without defence, clothes are not the issue, emotions are.*

The exhibition was at the Musée du Luxembourg, one of the city's smaller museums. It was an exhibition of Female War Photographers Since 1965 and I would have a whole room to myself. In fact, they seemed pleased to get me.

They'd opted for 1965, Art said, so they could shame the Americans with Vietnam, Iraq I and II, and Afghanistan. If they'd chosen 1950, which would have made more sense, they'd have had to include Indo-China and the war in Algeria. The French had behaved every bit as badly as the Americans had ever done in those.

I ignored him. I didn't care. A week had gone into choosing the best of my photographs. I'd found a photographic printer who let me stand over his machines while he adjusted contrast at my request. Today was the day I delivered my prints to the museum.

I woke before les enfants des écoles. A rare occurrence. Usually their squeals from the playground behind our apartment permeated my dreams long before I opened my eyes. But today there was silence. I rolled over and fumbled for my iPhone: 7.45. The cacophony never started until eight when the mamans and the occasional papa delivered their offspring on the way to work.

Art's side of the bed was empty, but not yet cold. Lying very still, eyes closed, I listened for telltale traces of life in our small apartment. I'd mastered the art of the understatement in the six months we'd been here. It would have been funny if the flat wasn't so claustrophobic. Deux pièces, plus kitchenette and bathroom. With a bath, the estate agent told us several times. Looking from me to Art and back again, expecting approval. Un bain! Baths didn't come cheap in Paris, apparently. If you could even find one. Especially not in a seventeenth-century square just west of Bastille. Film stars lived here, he said, feigning nonchalance. There was even one in the apartment across the hall.

Art had left for work. If he hadn't, it would be impossible not to hear him, even at his most stealthy. Running water, the groan of our boiler, shoes on rocky tiles. Original, we were told, priceless, not to be damaged at any cost. I listened, just in case;

but heard nothing except next-door's boiler, and a baby wailing below. Always the baby.

Always crying.

Always hungry for something.

There was only one way to escape its wail. I threw back the duvet and dashed across cold tiles to the bathroom, showed my teeth the toothbrush, ran a flannel over my face and avoided looking in the mirror. I knew what I'd see. What I'd seen ever since we'd moved to Paris. Dark circles beneath my eyes, growing daily as sleep became ever more elusive and my migraines more frequent. The last time I'd looked at the clock it was four a.m. Even then, I slept fitfully.

Grabbing my running kit from where I'd dropped it, in a ball in the corner under the basin, I sniffed cautiously at the T-shirt. Not exactly fragrant but it would do. Maybe today, after I'd delivered the photographs, I'd face the laundrette.

The flat was too small for a washing machine. It was too small for a freezer. Even the fridge was tiny. The location, of course, was fabulous, the view into the courtyard below, picture-postcard. We lived right in the ancient heart of the most romantic city in the world. It didn't seem to be rubbing off.

Ramming my feet into my trainers, I did a circuit of the flat, checking the wonky electrics, turning things off, unplugging. Art was obsessed with the flat's electrics, their Europeanness being a serious flaw in his eyes. Ditto the plumbing. Satisfied, I double-locked the door, pulled at the handle to be sure, and ran down the sweeping stone staircase, waving to the concierge, who was dusting the banister as I passed.

Almost as soon as the ancient wooden doors – original, they'd survived the revolution according to the letting agent, he didn't say which one – clicked behind me, my spirits lifted. There was something about the apartment that weighed on me. Not instantly. I usually felt fine when I went to bed, but by the time I woke, assuming I'd slept at all, I could feel its thick stone walls closing in on me. Eight-foot-high ceilings pressing down like a medieval torture chamber. The building had seen a lot in its three-hundred-odd years. I hoped it hadn't seen that.

Place des Vosges was deserted except for two other runners doing circuits and a street sweeper making a circuit of his own in the opposite direction. I crossed Rue St Antoine and wove through the village of St Paul to approach the Seine. Same route every day. Not at first. Initially I'd felt a moral duty to explore. Then it was a different route, in a different direction, each morning. But then I found this one. Through St Paul and across Île St Louis. I liked it, and that way I saw the same faces each morning. I liked the sense of knowing people but not knowing them. Not exactly disinterested, just Parisienne. Anonymous. I liked that. It was something I'd lost since meeting Art.

'Bonjour, madame.'

'Bonjour. Comment allez-vous?'

My first locus of the day; on the Pont Marie, where bridge met island. The elderly woman with the kind of chic grey bob I could only dream of waved her hand in greeting before bending awkwardly to scoop the poop of her ill-tempered over-trimmed schnauzer and dropping the bag daintily into her Chanel tote. One day, I would ask to photograph her. One day. Not today. I would see her again tomorrow. And the next day. And many days after, probably. What was the hurry?

On the Left Bank, I took the steps down to the river two at a time and ran along the cobbled quay, feeling my muscles work harder on uneven ground. The walkway teemed with runners and dog walkers. A silent community of early morning movers.

To me, a relative newcomer, Notre Dame rearing above us was spectacular, to them simply wallpaper. Under the next bridge, red setter woman appeared. Mustard Crombie, dark, cropped hair, flanked by two dogs. As usual, Victor, the more relaxed of the animals ran loose, giving me as wide a berth as possible. Hugo – who could not be let off his leash at the best of times, she'd told me a few weeks earlier – strained, desperate to get to me. I jigged backwards, butting up against the wall as he reared, teeth bared.

'Pardon, madame! Pardon!' *she cried. She couldn't understand it, she said. Hugo was not a good dog, but he did not behave like this. Every day I ran I saw the red setters. Every day Hugo was the same. They weren't alone. There were dogs everywhere at that time of morning and to a terrier they gave me a wide berth. But only Hugo ever attacked. It made no sense. Dogs used to love me. Not any more. It had been that way for three or four years now.*

Beneath the Pont Neuf, I stretched my hamstrings on the blocks that lined the bank. Two sapeurs-pompiers *jogged past, neither breaking a sweat, although their pace was twice mine.*

'Bonjour, mademoiselle,' *the dark-haired one called out. Another ritual. Another locus in my day. I smiled, perhaps a little too readily.*

'Bonjour, monsieur.'

His dark eyes crinkled and I could have sworn he winked.

Beyond the sapeurs-pompiers' *boat, a cluster of houseboats was waking up. An elderly woman and young girl sat shrouded in blankets on a deck, clutching steaming mugs, as they stared across to the Right Bank in companionable silence. At the furthest point of Île de la Cité two lovers sat, locked in embrace. I glanced at my watch. Nine a.m. Either an early morning*

*rendezvous or very, very late. Feelings surged up inside me.
Squashing them, I ran on.*

*At the Pont d'Amour I took the stairs up to the road and
slowed to a jog as I crossed the bridge of locks. I don't know
when the lock thing started but now the bridge was weighed
down with them. Heavy with the hopes and expectations of a
million lovers.*

*It wasn't hard to see why. What was love without superstition?
Names leapt out as I slowed.*

Clemence et Alexis
Simo e Paola
Jens heart Agathe
Helen 4 Tom

*Another Helen and another Tom. Not hard, there were
millions of us. Was she happy with her Tom? I wondered. Was
he happy with her? Did he even know who she really was? If
she said that was it, she was done, after some stupid row about
being late, would he be equally stupid, turn his back and walk
away?*

*On and on they went, the declarations of love indelibly inked
in red, green, black on to the kind of padlocks you bought from
a local hardware store. Or from one of the North Africans who
saved you the trouble of visiting a hardware store by selling
you locks from their holdalls for twice the price.*

*As a symbol of love, a padlock left a lot to be desired. And
yet, it seemed strangely apt.*

*I don't know how long I'd been staring at the locks when
I saw it.*

Cold & Heart

Someone had a sick sense of humour. Then I found another:
S & M. *And another:* Heart & Broken. *Barbs of cynicism
among the hope.*

Their bleakness sapped what little remained of my equilibrium. I'd stood on the bridge too long. It was cold and I felt sick. I hadn't eaten since yesterday lunchtime and I hadn't slept. I'd done a good job of not thinking too much as I ran. But as Paris woke around me, life rushed in. In the last hour, runners and dog walkers had given way to commuters and traffic jams. A woman tutted disapprovingly as I pulled out in front of her. It took all my will power not to give her a very un-French gesture.

Silence enveloped me as I slipped back into the courtyard. There was nothing unusual in that. It wasn't until I pushed open the lift door on the top floor that I knew something was wrong. The dog in the flat opposite was yapping more than usual, and the smell . . . The vaguely stagnant air that hovered in all the public areas, that told of damp towels and two-day-old rubbish, had been replaced by something else. Something acrid. Burnt and black. Like toast, scraped into my grandma's sink, but not. More chemical. A dry, metallic burning like an old light bulb dusty with neglect and grown too hot.

As I turned into our corridor, the odour grew. And there was a sort of haze – like the veil that slowly lifts after a migraine. Only this wasn't in my head, it was hovering, gauze-like beneath the skylights, wafting up from our floor.

My heart pounding I scrabbled the key fob out of my pocket and ran towards the stench. As our apartment drew closer, so did my fear. I fumbled the key, cursing the idiot – me – who insisted on installing Chubbs and window locks on an apartment three floors up.

As the door flew in, smoke burst out.

Only then did it hit me. Our flat was burning. My cameras, my laptop, all my equipment, all my work. My life was on fire. Without thinking what I was doing, I covered my mouth with my sweatshirt and ran in. I couldn't see flames for the smoke that forced me out into the corridor again.

'Madame Martin!' Frantic, I ran to the stairwell, screaming the concierge's name, 'Madame Martin! Fire! Feu! Le feu!'

It was futile. With three floors and countless walls of stone three hundred years old and twice as thick below there was no way she could hear me. I'd have to go back down. But I couldn't leave the flat. Behind me I heard a door open, footsteps.

'Merde!' said our neighbour, still in her dressing gown. 'Stay here. I call the pompiers. And Madame Martin. She must know.'

'I can't just stand here.'

'Stay, Hélène,' she said firmly. 'Or come with me. Do not go in.'

'What the fuck, Helen? Helen? Oh my God! Are you all right?'

I spun round.

'Art! Thank God!'

I took a step towards him, ready to throw myself into his arms.

Then stopped.

'What are you doing here?'

'Is that all you can say?' His face frozen, he dropped his arms to his sides, threw his holdall down by my feet and ran back the way he'd come. 'Call the fire brigade, for fuck's sake.' He yelled over his shoulder. 'Call the fire brigade!'

'I did,' I yelled. 'Eta did.' Tears were streaming down my face, the smoke billowing from our door stinging my eyes.

Within seconds Art was back, a fire extinguisher in his arms. Where had he got that? I didn't even remember seeing one.

Pushing past me, he yanked the lid from the fuse box just inside the door, flipped off the mains power, ripped the pin from the fire extinguisher and aimed it through the living-room door. 'I've told you,' he yelled, face white – with fear or fury, I wasn't sure. 'I've told you the electrics aren't safe. You've seen the wiring. Turn your fucking computer and stuff off before you go out. How many times do I have to say that?'

'I did!' I shouted, trying not to look at the yellow-and-green wires curling from a hole in the wall above our flat door. 'It was the last thing I did before I went out. I swear it!'

He yelled something in response. Something I couldn't hear over the roar of the extinguisher. Then there were footsteps pounding along the corridor behind me and our tiny flat was full of uniforms and my brain went blank. I no longer understood a word they were saying. All I could see were mouths moving and arms waving, pushing me away.

But I knew it had to be my fault. What had happened to me?

Fifteen minutes later I stood in the dripping mess that was our living room. The fire had been surprisingly contained, the pompiers told us as Madame Martin bustled off to call the landlord so the landlord could call the insurers. Once they'd realised the fabric of the building wasn't damaged, everyone lost interest. It was a small, very straightforward fire. Confined to one room and focused on the one corner of it, by the desk and the electric fire. The rest of it was just interior smoke damage.

And burnt wiring, of course. And my photographs for the exhibition.

Whatever fury had gripped Art earlier had passed. The old Art was back. Calm, efficient, in control. He'd dealt with the French firemen and placated Madame Martin, charmed Eta into shrugging it off and smiling as she returned to her own flat. Now there was just him, me and the mess.

'Are you all right?' he said, wrapping his arms round me. My face pressed against the fabric of his shirt. 'God, Helen,' his left hand stroked my hair, while his right hand clamped me to him. My muscles tensed. I felt him feel them tense.

'I was so scared,' he said. 'Don't frighten me like that again.'

'I'm sorry.'

'Promise me, Helen. Promise you'll listen to me about the electrics.'

'I did,' I said, my voice muffled by his smoky shirt. A row was the last thing I wanted, but I knew, I was one hundred per cent certain, I'd turned everything off. Art's hand stroked. My mind raced. I'd played the sequence over and over. I'd turned off the fire, the two electric radiators, unplugged my laptop, the TV, the kettle, checked the window locks, and went out double-locking the door. Short of unplugging the fridge . . .

'I . . .'

'It's OK, Helen.'

'No, Art,' I forced my head from his chest and his hand stopped, poised where I couldn't see it. I could still feel its presence.

If I could just explain, make him see what I could see, we could work out what had happened.

'No, Art, what?'

I forced myself to look up at him. Still clamped against him, I couldn't see the expression in his eyes.

'I did check. I swear. It must have been an accident.'

'An accident?'

'Yes. An accident.'

'There are no such things as accidents, Helen.' The stroking resumed. 'You know that.'

'Sometimes there are. It just happened. Things do.'

'It just happened?'

Stroke, stroke, stroke.

'It just fucking happened?' Calm voice belying the aggression of his words.

Shut up, Helen, I thought, shut up. Shut up now.

'Why won't you believe me?'

'What won't I believe you about?'

'The fire. The electrics . . . It's my stuff, Art. It's my stuff that's gone. OK, the desk's a lost cause and the rug's had it. But it's my photographs. My exhibition.'

His hand paused, lying heavy near the top of my head. Somehow the weight of it was worse than the stroking. Taking a deep breath, I ploughed on. 'It's my first exhibition in years. My first ever in Paris. It won't matter to them why I don't deliver. I'll simply be the English woman who can't be relied on. You know they won't ask me again.'

Yes they will, of course they will – *that's what he was meant to say*. Don't worry. We'll work something out.

Instead, his silence hung like a weight between us. His warm breath heavy on my ear. I could taste bile and chemical fumes from the extinguisher in my throat. I forced myself on. 'Art?'

'What?'

'What are you doing here?'

It had been playing on my mind since the fire brigade left. Before that. What *was* he doing here? Outside, the school bell rang across the rooftops. The playground echoed with children's shouts. Runacross, or whatever French infants played. A ball hit something it shouldn't have hit.

The sharp reprimand of a teacher.

'It's ten thirty in the morning, Art,' I said, forcing my hand further into the flames with each word. 'You've never come back at this time. Not once.' The last words came out as a whisper, fell heavily to the floor.

'I came back.' His voice was flat in my ear, cold. 'To get some peace. Thought you'd have gone to the gallery and I'd get more work done. God knows what would have happened if I hadn't.'

His arm tightened around me.

'I turned everything off before I went out,' I repeated. How many times I'd already said it, I had no idea. But this time I was more certain than ever. 'I know I did.'

He sighed. 'You need to start taking some responsibility for yourself and stop making excuses.'

'So you're saying this wasn't the first fire?' Gil asked, leaning forward. 'That the fire in Paris this time was connected?'

'No,' Helen shook her head, swallowed the rest of her vodka in one mouthful.

Gil waited patiently while she stopped coughing.

'Yes. No. I don't know.' She could hear her voice rising. 'I don't know what happened in the fire last month. Don't you understand? I can't remember.'

24

Syria 2012

After the fire, I found the courage to leave. I'd given up my flat when we married so I ended up at my sister's. She moved Sophie into Jake's room, much to their mutual disgust, and I got two months of every relative I'd ever known telling me what a great guy Art was and what a terrible mistake I was making. My mother, my sister, my sister's husband, Art's parents, Art's friend Mark . . .

Everybody loved Art. What was wrong with me? He was such a great bloke, such a catch, how could I be so heartless? What had he done that was so bad . . .?

How could I possibly answer those questions?

The poor broken-hearted lamb.

It was one long process of attrition. He waged a war to get me back, emails to my friends, emails to friends in common, letters to my mother, my sister, everyone he could think of. I fought to stay away, but his forces were stronger, and in the end his side won.

Eventually, they wore me down.

His timing was immaculate. By the time he came over on the Eurostar and persuaded me to go up to London to meet him, just to hear him out, I'd have believed black was white if he'd told me it was. Despite everything I'd done, everything I'd achieved, he had everyone believing my success was down to him. Was it any surprise if I started to believe it too?

We met at Antonio's, the Italian place we used to eat in at the start. The manager was different, the waiters had changed and so had the décor, the food was twice the price and half as good. But Art was making an effort. He told me how much he'd missed me, how taking a break had been good for him, it had made him realise what he'd done, how bad things had got . . .

He almost blew it by saying it didn't matter whose fault the fire was.

And I used my brief flare of anger to lay down some conditions. The minute we'd moved to Paris, Art had started to object to me being away so much. Ironic, given my travelling was meant to be one of the reasons we'd moved there. That had to stop. I was taking the next job I was offered. Wherever in the world it was. However long I was away. Without a camera in my hands I wasn't me. He could take it or leave it. That was non-negotiable.

He grinned, took my hand across the table and told me this was the me he recognised, the me he'd fallen in love with, the furious one. Afterwards, he delivered me to the station. He didn't try to persuade me to book into a cheap hotel. Didn't even try to kiss me. Instead he stood on the platform and asked me to give his love to my parents and sister and asked me, rather than told me, to think about it and promised he'd really changed.

It had been a wake-up call.

We were a team. A good team. We'd always been a team.

And like a fool I believed him. I moved back and for a while everything was almost the way it had been at the beginning. We went out for dinner, talked, made love. He'd had the flat redecorated and bought me a new computer, much flashier and more expensive than I needed. I did a couple of small European assignments, some photojournalism in Iceland. He admired it. Seemed genuinely proud of me. Then, I was asked to go to Syria. Art didn't bat an eyelid. But the next day he told me head office had pulled some strings and got him a visa. Wouldn't it be great to see our names together on the front page again . . .

There were no seats left on my flight, so we flew out separately. The day after I arrived, when he was still in the air, a French journalist was shot by a rebel sniper. Her name was Helen too. Hélène Graham.

I was there when she died, which sounds more dramatic than it was. We were on opposite sides of the same square, I heard the snap of rifle fire and by the time I'd turned Hélène was dead. It wasn't even that rare an occurrence and it's getting worse. Once the news agencies started arming local teenagers with recording equipment, journalists and photographers began dying weekly. They were cheap and they would take risks no trained Western journalist or photographer was prepared to consider. That, and they brought new meaning to blending in.

What was special about Hélène's death was that she was Western and a woman.

We barely knew each other, but when the man sent by the French embassy learned I also lived in Paris he assumed Hélène and I must have been friends and made me promise to write to her parents to say it was quick, she was wearing a flak jacket and she'd been warned of the dangers. I agreed, simply to get rid of him. But it made the whole thing even more fraught. The next day our original minder vanished and a new one turned up in his place.

'Today will be different,' was his opening gambit. 'No bodies, all right?'

I nodded and he took it as assent.

Ahmed was in his mid-twenties, neatly dressed in a dark suit with a white shirt. He lost his tie the moment the government minder disappeared. Ahmed was also a government minder, but he was younger and spoke English with a Birmingham accent, because that's where he went to university. He wanted to go to university in America, he said, but he wasn't clever enough. I wondered if he knew how rude that was and realised he was too wide-eyed for the insult to be intentional.

He'd been told I was famous, poor boy. The famous English woman photographer he had to impress. I wanted to say it wasn't true. I wasn't famous, at least not in the way he meant. But then I was there for the Herald Tribune so maybe that counted.

I liked the hotel suite they gave me – who wouldn't? – with its sitting room and two bathrooms and a huge television that got nothing except the official channel. It was a cocoon from the outside world. Just as it was intended to be. I liked the sleek black limousine waiting for me outside. To be honest, I liked the lack of a child's cries echoing through the wall and the absence of school children screaming in the playground and the clang of a school bell.

That was how I found myself being nurse-maided round the safe – from Assad's point of view – parts of Syria by a *well-dressed young man with a Birmingham accent and a Marks & Spencer suit.*

'We're agreed . . .?' Ahmed asked, jerking me back to the air conditioning and tinted windows.

He was young and anxious and eager to impress; and on the wrong side of a particularly nasty war, as if all wars aren't nasty; except his side used to be the right side, and he was too young to know what happened to people who used to be on the right side before the rules changed and they became the enemy.

'The jacket . . .'

'I don't need a flak jacket.'

He looked at me, eyes skimming my floppy shirt and jeans, my Converse and the camera bag now hanging from my hand, but which would be on my hip when the limousine delivered us to where the pictures were.

I knew where the pictures were. I could hear them. I also knew we wouldn't be going there. The whoosh of rockets and the crump of tank fire and the small-arms chatter that became as familiar as birdsong in cities like this. Ahmed was impressed I didn't want the heavy jacket he'd brought me. He thought it was bravery. Better that than the truth, which was that I hated the way they made you stand out.

'We have another journalist joining us,' Ahmed said. 'We collect him from an appointment at the Excelsior.' This wasn't in the plan, but I went with the flow. By the hotel entrance, a thickset man, blond hair cropped short, was sheltering in the safety of a doorway. He looked left and right and ran at a crouch to the limousine, sliding himself in beside me.

'You,' he said, grinning.

'Carl . . .! Long time no . . . you know.'

Ahmed was surprised. 'You know each other?'

'Old friends,' Carl said. 'Shouldn't we get moving? Snipers . . .'

'No snipers,' Ahmed said firmly. 'This area is loyal.'

Carl rolled his eyes but said nothing. His hand reached across and found mine, squeezing briefly. 'Good to see you.'

'You're . . . friends?' Ahmed was watching us in the mirror.

'Not that kind of friends,' I said, and behind his stubble and shades Ahmed blushed.

'I knew his—' I began to say.

'We separated,' Carl cut in.

'I'm sorry.'

'Me too,' Carl said. 'We just couldn't make it work. You know how it is . . .'

We exchanged a glance and I decided to leave it there. Ahmed seemed OK for an official Syrian fixer but that was still what he was. Neither of us knew how he'd take to a conversation about Carl's ex, a pretty, high-maintenance Venezuelan boy with a thing for black Lycra. In a bar, in Soho, one time when Art was away, Carl had showed me pictures on his iPhone. He accidentally flicked forward when he meant to flick back and the photograph I saw showed Kris looking very tanned, very nude and very excited . . . We agreed he was fabulous but probably a little too high maintenance for me.

Ahmed was watching us closely in the rear-view mirror, trying to work out what this conversation was about, whether he should be worried by it. He saw me watching and I smiled, shrugged, and went back to business. 'No corpses,' I told Carl. 'Has that been mentioned?'

I could see him wondering what we were doing here.

'What then?' Carl asked.

'Normal life . . . Schools, markets, playgrounds, women shopping, buildings.'

It hadn't bothered me too much, when I'd agreed. Since Iraq

I'd lost my stomach for corpses, preferring my wreckage in the form of bricks and mortar. But I had a bad feeling about this and, as the day unfolded in a round of the Syrian equivalent of Potemkin villages, it was proved right. Ludicrously over-stocked local shops selling fresh goods to neatly dressed women; smiling school children happily astonished to see us while being able to greet us in carefully rehearsed English.

Carl slid a camera on to his lap in the car, changed the lens and adjusted to video. In the old days there'd be the click of the motor drive, but digital is silent; and I knew, as Carl lifted his lens in line with the bottom of the window, while trying to keep it low enough to stay out of Ahmed's line of sight, that he was hoping to snap something, anything to make this day worthwhile.

There was an absurd normality to the life these people were living. To me, this faux normality was worse than outright fear. How could anyone . . .

Hot tears spilled over before I could look away. I shook my head in fury. How dare I compare my life to theirs?

'Helen?' Carl said.

I turned my face to the window.

'Are you all right?'

I shook my head. 'Stop,' I told Ahmed.

He took one look at my face in the mirror and pulled over by a concrete substation. It had the skull for danger and a lightning zap for electricity you'd find anywhere in the world. He looked worried when I opened my door. No doubt there was a child lock but he'd left that too late.

'Where are you going?'

'In there.' I pointed to a blind alley brutally deserted in the afternoon sun. Shadow cut a sharp line down one wall and across the dirt floor. At best, it would smell of hot dog shit,

infinitely preferable to the stench of bodies that had filled my head a few seconds earlier.

'I'll go with you.'

I had expected him to forbid me to leave the car. There were rules. In a situation like this there were always rules. I probably subscribed to them when I scrawled my name across the piece of paper Ahmed thrust in front of me earlier.

'Ahmed . . .'

He blushed.

I've peed in worse places, but that wasn't what I intended. Stumbling from the limousine I pushed myself into the shadows and threw up, only just missing my shoes. I threw up a second time and spat in the dry dust. It was disgusting of me to see my life with Art reflected in theirs. Yet I understood what was happening here in a way I doubted Carl could. I understood why these people were going through their routines, pretending everything was normal. They hoped that in pretending everything was normal they could make it so.

At the end of the alley was an open door. All around was silent, but I could have sworn I saw a flicker of movement, a small boy watching me.

Common sense said go back to the car, go back to the hotel, try again tomorrow. I went through the door all the same, through the door, through a ruined house and into a courtyard. There was no one here. No sign of anyone having passed through. The air was thicker here. It smelt of dog shit and open drains. A burnt-out motorbike lay on its side. I snapped it without thought. Turned to take a second shot as I walked away. At the street corner up ahead I froze. Office blocks had once stood either side. Now the street was a canyon of broken concrete, with sunlight lancing on to rubble. At the far end, the front wall of a bank had a hole blasted through it like a ragged rose window.

My throat tightened and my chest locked as I stood trapped in the cross hairs of something deadlier than a sniper's rifle.

We talk of being frozen by terror. Of being struck dumb by shock. Mostly we keep talking because we don't know how to say what we want to say. Those are the times that pictures say it for us.

I raised my camera to take the shot. I knew I should bracket the exposures, play with the field of focus, and see what changing the shutter speeds might do. I did none of these. I simply took my photograph and headed back to the car.

Carl noticed the splatter on my jeans. 'You all right?'

I nodded, glanced at Ahmed, who was obviously listening. 'Tripped,' I said.

Ahmed wasn't sure what I was talking about and Carl didn't believe me anyway. Pulling his iPhone from his pocket, he opened the message app, set the screen for a new message with the place for the number left blank and slid it across.

I keyed in my own number.

We talked in silence, side by side on the hot plasticised leather of the limousine, and the most Carl did was open the window slightly when Ahmed asked, apologetically, if I might have stepped in something while I was in the alley.

'Thank you,' I said, when I climbed out of the car.

Ahmed smiled, looking young enough to still be at school, and I hoped I wasn't about to get him into trouble. I knew what I had. The photograph said everything and nothing. Some people would simply see a ruined street. Others would see the cathedral.

Carl found me in the hotel bar later, nursing a vodka and tonic that tasted mostly of synthetic quinine. He nodded to the stool opposite, giving me the chance to say, No, I want to be alone.

When I didn't, he took it, ordered a beer, and asked if I wanted to talk about it. I shook my head, inclining it across the room to where Art sat glowering.

'He's pissed off,' I whispered. 'Thinks I should have told him where I was going. He could have come too.'

Carl made a What-the-Fuck? *face and nodded.*

'Won't hang around too long then. We all know how he feels about your gay best friend.'

Leaning over to see what I was looking at, he turned my iPad towards him and flicked through the images until he came to the photograph I'd taken earlier. I had already sent it down the wire to London. Unapproved and without permission. No bodies. And yet it was almost worse.

'Fuck,' he said, then sat in silence for a long while.

Eventually he handed me back my iPad and reached for his beer bottle, raised it to me and took a large swig. 'There are days,' he said, 'when I wonder if I should simply give up. Most of them happen when I look at work like yours.' Then he leaned over and kissed me on the cheek, and with a glance at Art, wandered off.

All the rest of that evening I was aware of Art, on the far side of the bar. More a presence than a person. He appeared engrossed in his work; an in-depth report that his agency hoped would make the news section of a Sunday paper. His story. His big project. He'd seen the picture I took. He knew it would now dominate the front pages. He looked up only rarely. But never at me. Only shaking his head when I asked if he wanted a beer. He hadn't been drinking. Just the one, to be polite. He didn't really drink, not any more. Not like those early days when he could match pint for pint and shot for shot with the worst of them. Didn't like what it did, he said pointedly.

I stared at him defiantly and ordered another. I knew I

shouldn't, alcohol mixed badly with my migraine pills, but it was part of my armoury of tiny rebellions.

Only once, when I glanced across, did I catch him looking my way, his eyes dark, his face full of shadows. Discomfort settling like acid in my stomach.

'Do you even know what a team is, Helen?'

Art's voice coming out of the darkness made my heart lurch.

It was almost an hour since he'd flipped his laptop shut, declared himself knackered and gone to bed. Until that moment, I realised, I'd nurtured a small hope that, if I lingered in the bar long enough, he'd be asleep; but he was leaning against the wall by the window, looking out across night-time Damascus.

Hoping he couldn't smell my anxiety, I hovered just inside the bedroom doorway, not helped by the alcohol fuelling my bloodstream. I'd had more vodka than I wanted just to make a point and had felt sick before I even realised he was awake. Art flicked his half-smoked roll-up out on to the courtyard below and pulled the shutters to, extinguishing what little light the moon provided. The heat of the day had vanished with the sun and the room was as cold as his rage. An icy controlled fury. If I'd been able to see them, I knew his lips would be set in a tight white line, his eyes flat. For a moment, I was glad I couldn't.

I took a tentative step forward. Instinct shrieking at me to step back.

'Answer me,' he breathed.

I tried not to jump. He was close, so close.

Close enough for me to feel his breath on my face. I had neither heard nor felt him move. He didn't touch me, and I didn't reach out to touch him. It wouldn't calm him. He didn't want to be calmed. 'Well? Tell me, the great Helen Lawrence, what is a team? Or is that something else they didn't teach you at school?'

So much malice in one sentence, my head spun. I was drunk. Very drunk. My head already starting to pound. Art was utterly sober.

'A team?' he repeated quietly. Hot breath in chill air.

A team, I wanted to say, is something that never wanted me in it. A team is something I never wanted to be picked for. A good job, because I never was picked. A team is something I have no interest in being any part of. But I know what you think a team is, Art. You think a team is something that has a captain and people who do what the captain tells them. And you think that captain is you.

Rage, alcohol and fear mingled inside me. It was on the edge of my tongue to say those things, to unleash the genie, to shout and scream and yell and see what happened. It was unlikely to be worse.

I didn't. I didn't answer him at all.

'I'll tell you what a team is . . . Helen.'

His tongue wrapped around my name and I shuddered, instinctively taking a step back. Hit wall. Or door. When had the door shut? I hadn't heard it click to.

'A team, Helen . . .' he said, repeating my name, as if in repeating it he owned it. Owned me. '. . . is what we are meant to be. A team. Professionally and personally. In work . . . and in life.' He took one more silent step, I felt the air change this time, closing what little gap I'd managed to open up between us. His body just millimetres from mine.

I stood very still. Said nothing. Waited.

In the courtyard below a raucous yell, followed by a laugh. Tomorrow was another day. Anything could happen, and would. We knew that. We'd seen it. Yesterday morning, Hélène

Graham had been alive. I tried to concentrate. All I had to do was open my mouth and shout. Art hated shouting. Hated embarrassment. But what would I say? And what would anyone say who came running?

Domestic.

Drunk.

Clash of the egos.

All of the above.

Would they even be wrong?

If neither of us moved, neither of us spoke, I told myself, it might yet be all right. We could go to bed, get some sleep, or pretend to, lying side by side untouching in the dark, and in the morning it would have passed. It could happen. It had happened before. But not often.

Then he gripped my upper arms and I felt my feet leave the ground. My tendons shrieked and I knew bruises would have blossomed a livid violet on my pale freckled arms by morning. In one movement, I was face down on the bed. Half lifted, half thrown. My legs thrashed, but there was nowhere to go. A hand heavy on my neck forced my face into the mattress and I felt consciousness begin to slip, peeling away at the edges. Frantically I tried to free my arms, but they were trapped beneath my weight and his knee pinning my spine, his hand working at my jeans. Struggling for breath, I inhaled . . . the unmistakable taste of stale cloth choked me . . . and something else . . . acrid, sour . . . last night's sweat . . . my own rising nausea. I heard him unbuckle himself noisily.

Just as I thought I was going to vomit, light exploded behind my eyes. Then everything bloomed black.

Morning took forever to arrive.

* * *

'It wasn't . . .'

Helen looked up, blinking as if seeing the room for the first time in many hours. The grey of pre-dawn seeped through the gap in the curtains.

'It wasn't the first time. He saved his fury for the bedroom. His bruises for places that didn't show. It wasn't even the most painful. But this was by far the worst.'

'Why didn't you leave before this?' Gil asked.

Helen sighed at the inevitability of the question.

No idea didn't seem an adequate answer.

'I did, remember. And he wore me down I suppose,' she said, twisting the hem of her sweatshirt in her hands. 'Little bits of me got cut away, until I wasn't me any more. When I did leave, that first time, everyone said I was wrong. I didn't have the self-belief not to go back. What he did to me in Syria . . . It flicked a switch in my head.

'Next morning, I pretended to be asleep until he went out, then I packed my case and flew to London. I booked an emergency appointment with . . . A doctor I'd seen on and off since Iraq for migraines . . .' Helen took a deep breath. 'And other things. She knew me, was familiar with the situation. Still is. She'd seen me with injuries there before.'

Helen looked at Gil to gauge his reaction, then down at her feet.

'I stayed here for a few days, in London, holed up in a hotel, healed, I suppose you'd say. Then I went back.'

Gil inhaled sharply.

'No, not *back* back. I mean back to Paris. I waited for him outside his office, somewhere nice and public. Told him it was over. I'd be filing for divorce.'

'How did he react?'

Helen snorted. 'How d'you think? He was contemptuous, mocking. Said I was nothing without him. Worthless. He didn't know why he'd bothered with me. Some people couldn't be helped. Then he just turned on his heel and stalked away. Didn't turn, didn't look back. I know, because I stood and watched until he vanished round the corner. That's why I chose there. I knew he'd never make a scene in the street, never.'

'And then?'

'What do you mean, *and then?*'

'What happened next?'

Helen shrugged.

'Somehow I ended up here.'

PART THREE

The Scar

'There are boys out there who look for shining girls;
they will stand next to you and say quiet things in
your ear that only you can hear and that will slowly
drain the joy out of your heart.'

Caitlin Moran

25

It had been a long time since Gil had done the walk of shame. Best part of forty years and even then he could have counted the times on one finger. But there was no way to reach his house other than through the centre of the village, so he fingered his last B&H, rolling loose in his pocket, for comfort, decided against, and strolled up the high street trying to affect the air of an insomniac on his way back from an innocent early morning stroll.

He had nothing to hide, after all – more's the pity.

It was not yet six a.m. but already the village was waking. That was the trouble with old people, Gil thought, feeling Maude Peniston's curtains twitch as he passed. They didn't know how to lie-in. It would be a few days yet before he could consider the General Stores safe ground. He'd have to make another trip to the wretched garage on the bypass for his supplies.

With the door safely shut behind him, Gil reached for

the coffee, taking the sad-bastard-cafetière-for-one Lyn had bought him from the cupboard. She'd given it to him for his birthday years ago, and been so proud of herself. All Gil had seen was that his barely twentysomething daughter never expected him to have someone to make coffee for again. Turned out she was right.

He was so far beyond sleep he wasn't sure he'd ever sleep again. Images furled and unfurled in his head. Bombed-out buildings he'd never seen and the corpse of a small boy he felt almost sure he had . . . And Helen, dark-haired, watchful-eyed Helen, years younger than him, young enough to be his daughter, in bed. Her naked body was in Gil's mind. Her body, as he imagined it. She was smart and he liked smart, and she was talented and he admired that, and she was strong, somewhere inside the ruins that life and Art Huntingdon had made of her. Assuming he believed her. Against his better judgement, Gil was starting to think he did.

You silly old sod, he thought, as he fingered the lone cigarette in his suit pocket. The last of the twenty he'd smoked through the night. He was being ridiculous and he knew it. Instinctively liking her shouldn't be the same as trusting her. As if she'd have given him the time of day in any other circumstances. What if all this was fabricated and he was being played for a fool by a younger woman who'd murdered one man, and might, quite possibly, murder another? Him. Because, despite everything she'd told him, she still hadn't begun to explain what happened that night.

'She tells a good story,' Gil said out loud. She did too. Such a good story it had to be true, didn't it? Only a psychopath could carry that level of detail plausibly. But then – Gil paused, inhaled and, feeling his head swim, wondered when he'd last eaten – only a psychopath could set fire to her husband and walk away . . .

As he smoked, Gil extracted his knackered old iPhone from his breast pocket and checked the Voice Memos: two hours forty minutes. Not bad, albeit less than half the night's conversation. Better than nothing. He hadn't used it in an age, so he hadn't been sure it would work at all. He'd felt bad, flicking it on in his nearside breast pocket while she was downstairs making coffee, but only a fool would have done otherwise. He was a journalist and, like it or not, Helen Lawrence, as he was starting to think of her, was this close to being a suspect in a murder. Skimming backwards, he picked a point at random and pressed play, jumping as Helen's cool voice echoed round his small kitchen.

'*His eyes were closed and he was curled as if in sleep, a plastic toy in his hand. There was no sign of the talking head now, but he could still be heard, explaining how I took the shot in the immediate aftermath of a car bomb. The photograph faded to be replaced by another shot. The boy from behind . . .*'

Gil pressed stop, trying to work out what it was about her tone that bothered him. That she was calm? Almost indecently so? Her voice steady even as he'd watched tears coat her cheeks as she described the boy. For most of the night he might as well not have been there. It was only when she remembered he was, and smiled – suddenly, incongruously – that he had to remind himself this was someone used to war zones, who'd heard bullets fired in anger rather than on film, who'd seen buildings broken that were places where people lived rather than sets designed with the sole purpose of being destroyed.

He'd seen his share of bodies. Children killed in car crashes. Murder victims. Suicides. He didn't doubt for one minute she'd seen more.

Face it, Gil, he told himself, if she can recount horror so calmly, with no tremor in her voice, what else is she capable of? If she'd been through even a fraction of what she claimed, she was strong. Very strong. She had to be; she was alive and Art Huntingdon was dead.

And whatever she said, whatever she claimed not to remember, she'd had the presence of mind to get herself here. And she was hiding from something.

Gil knew he shouldn't be thinking like that. He should be telephoning the police. If not them, telephoning a paper. Not the *Post*, a national. He'd been turning the idea over and over, ever since he'd worked out who she was. A scoop like this . . . it could give his career a whole new lease of life. Put him back on the radar. He wasn't ready for retirement.

He'd do no such thing though. Not yet, anyway. Not until he was sure she was lying. People did lie. Of course they did. Women lied to men as readily as men lied to women. Lying to journalists was almost as great a tradition as lying to the police. The truth was subjective. Endlessly elastic. God knows, Gil's life through his own eyes bore little resemblance to the version seen by his ex-wife; quite possibly no relationship at all to his life seen through the eyes of his children.

Proof. That was what he needed. Taking his coffee through to the sitting room, Gil turned on breakfast news low in the background for company, flipped open his laptop and put 'Art Huntingdon' and Death into Google News.

Six hours of talking. And in all that time she hadn't even mentioned the fire that killed her husband, had made it clear she had no intention of doing so. Not a single mention. Call himself a journalist?

If she wouldn't tell him, he'd have to dig for himself. He'd start there and work back through Huntingdon's life, see if what he found matched Helen's description. He hoped it would; but then, if it did, there was another problem. If Huntingdon was as vile and controlling as she said, why had someone like her, a grown woman, successful in her own right, stayed with him that long?

Gil understood the reasons in theory.

He'd sat through enough rape trials, usually involving people known to each other, as most rapes did. He'd sat through child custody cases. Restraining orders being issued and appealed against. Injunctions applied for and then applications withdrawn by women too scared of the repercussions to fight. As a student, he'd heard his elder daughter talk with fury about how unsafe the streets were, how bad things could happen to anybody, even someone like her, and there was a thought Gil didn't want to follow.

But he didn't *understand*. He'd never understood, not really.

Right back when he began, when he was office boy, not even old enough to be a copy taker, one of the girls in the office got engaged to a clerk in the classifieds team. The man was tall, charming, played football for the paper on Sundays. One of the secretaries was overheard saying the girl was terrified of him, and the chief sub, a man as old as Gil was now, said, 'You don't marry a man you're afraid of . . .'

And the secretary, a quiet girl who ordinarily wouldn't have said boo to a goose, rounded on the department boss and said, 'Of course you do. That's precisely the kind of man you marry, because how on earth would you say no?'

A teenage typist, flattered by an ad salesman three or four years older . . . Possibly. But someone like Helen?

It seemed unlikely.

Gil thought of that as he drained his coffee. He didn't like where the thought was taking him. If you couldn't walk away, might you . . . Might someone that desperate resort to extreme means? And, if they did, would that make them a murderer? Or something else?

Gil knew he had four choices: sell her story, call the police, help her, or do nothing. Sit back and watch and wait and hope no one else died. Like that was going to happen. Gil had never done *nothing* in his life. So he had three choices, and he had already, in the back of his mind, discounted the first two.

So, you're going to help a murderer?

26

Helen leaned her forehead against the upstairs window and watched him go through the gap in the curtains. The leading was cool against her skin, a chill draught lifting the wisps of hair on her forehead. Through the warp and weft of the centuries-old glass, she watched Gil's loping strides make short work of the large forecourt, his body slightly distorted like a fairground mirror. To her surprise, he didn't turn round. Didn't look back. Didn't even pause as he reached the gate and turned on to the road. She would have put money on him being a looker-backer. Just went to show what a good judge of character she was.

Fatigue closed in the moment he vanished from sight. Allowing her eyes to droop she breathed slowly through her nose, condensation fogging her view as she tried to clear her brain. *Thank God that was over.*

She laughed, a hard bark of a laugh, and opened her eyes.

But it wasn't, was it? It would never be over. Not now.

Art was dead. And Gilbert Markham knew. He knew almost as much as she did. More, possibly. How much more there was to know Helen hardly dared think.

The thought brought her up short. What if Gil *did* have more information than he was letting on? What if he'd already spoken to the police? What if he was toying with her, the way Ghost toyed with tiny rodents in the middle of the night?

No. Helen shook the thought from her head. That wasn't Gil's style. She was sure of it. That was Art's MO. She was transferring.

Helen knew she should try to get some sleep, but adrenalin surged through her. The idea of putting on her pyjamas, closing her eyes and getting seven blissful hours' rest was laughable. It had been laughable for as long as she could remember.

Slumping on the settee, she looked around the drawing room. It reeked of Gil, she realised. She'd got so used to the constant fug of B&H that accompanied him that she hardly noticed. The miasma of smoke that hung in the air wasn't the only evidence of their long night. Empty mugs, vodka bottle three-quarters drained lay to one side on the floor, a saucer overflowing with cigarette butts perched precariously on the arm of the chair where he had spent the last six hours, hardly moving except to light another cigarette or take another shot of vodka. The carpet around his chair was confettied with cardboard. The B&H packet, Helen realised, noticing shards of gold in amongst the white. Shredded into tiny pieces and then shredded again. She could still make out the clear spot on the carpet, where his feet had blocked their landing.

And she was meant to be the anxious one.

As inquisitors went, Gil Markham seemed strangely benign. Even Ghost seemed to think so. Sometime during the night he'd slunk into the room and settled beside Gil's chair, a puddle of black fur barely visible against the dark red of the rug. His presence was strangely comforting.

But Gil wasn't benign. You were either an inquisitor or you weren't. Gil was a journalist. He fell firmly into the former camp. And he would be back, she knew that. And with him would come more questions. Questions that right now she didn't know how to answer.

Dragging the old settee closer to the three-bar fire, Helen lay down and curled her legs up beneath her. Tucking her arm under her head, she waited for sleep to come. Her head throbbed – vodka, smoke, anxiety, exertion – all four, but the headache didn't bear the hallmarks of a migraine. This was a good old-fashioned tension headache.

Gingerly she closed her eyes. The second she did, images crowded in. A small boy, maybe five or six, sitting on a filthy doorstep, surrounded with rubble. Brown eyes huge. Bare legs skinny and bruised, ending in lace-less, too-big plimsolls. In his hand was a red Power Ranger. She squeezed her eyes tight in an attempt to banish him and was rewarded with an orange haze and the over-powering stench of smoke. She could have sworn she heard something crack.

Her eyes shot open.

Just an overflowing saucer of B&H stubs, a three-bar fire and a snoring cat. Nothing more. She rolled over and lay on her back, eyes wide open staring at the ceiling. It had been white once, but now it was cream, faded with age and stained yellow with nicotine. The coving engrained with dust where it met the ceiling.

Now she'd let them in, they'd taken root. Art and the boy. Not that either of them had ever gone away.

A montage of images she'd studiously pushed to some distant corner of her brain began replaying over and over.

Art in the bar in Baghdad, half-empty Bud in his hand, twinkling like he knew how to twinkle when it suited him.

Art looming over her in a concrete stairwell, his breath hot on her face.

Art gazing at her earnestly over a café table in Soho. 'Marry me.'

Art, thin-lipped with rage at something or other she'd done. Got pregnant. Lost it. Got a job. Got a front page. Got an award. Talked to someone he didn't like the look of. Someone like Carl.

Art, holding her close in the debris of her exhibition, stroking.

Outside the window, a crow took flight, wing batting the pane as it did so. Helen jumped, leg shooting out and kicking the vodka bottle. In the corner, Ghost stretched, arching his back and then effortlessly inverting his spine in a way Helen could never have achieved in a million yoga lessons. Yellow eyes stared at her.

'Not yet, cat, I'm sleeping.'

Ghost gave her a look of pure contempt and padded closer, fixing her with his yellow glare.

She closed her eyes, couldn't bear what she saw there and opened them again.

Ghost started up a low-level purr. The frequency went right through her.

'All right!' Helen knew when she was beaten.

The cat allowed her a two-minute detour to her bedroom to put on her running kit and then followed her into the bathroom, where he worked a figure of eight around her legs as she sat on the toilet and then moved with her to the basin while she cleaned her teeth. Like Gil, he had no plans to let her out of his sight until she'd given him what he wanted. At least in this case it was just breakfast.

Too lazy to go via the road, she slipped out through the back door, locking it behind her, and crossed the courtyard, unbolting the gate that led into the gardens beyond and down to the copse. The sun was rising, still low, but unmistakably there, and for a moment or two she allowed herself to wonder if it was a sign of better things to come.

Maybe everything *would* be all right. Maybe talking to Gil would bring her memories back. If she could remember what had happened that night, maybe she wouldn't have to leave after all?

Maybe she would.

'Don't be stupid, Helen,' she muttered, as she slipped through the lychgate and picked up her pace through the shadowy cover of the copse. 'He's a journalist, not a priest.'

The Dales were quiet this time of the morning, like the day she'd arrived. Just sheep, crows and a couple of early morning birdwatchers. Helen gave the twitchers a wide berth and ran in the direction of the Scar, picking up pace and letting the movement of her body, muscles pumping, blood pulsing, push all thoughts from her mind.

Although she didn't usually come at it from this direction, she was starting to know this part of the Dales like the back of her hand. So well, she could almost run it with her eyes closed. To test herself, she did, and immediately stumbled on a crop of boulders that came from nowhere.

'Idiot,' she muttered, catching herself before she hit the ground, and moving off again.

At the bottom of the slope, Helen stopped and looked around. She hadn't been far from here when she'd seen him that time, the small boy, the one with big brown eyes and no coat. It was him, she'd known the second she saw him. If she'd been able to get closer she'd have been able to see the red Power Ranger he always carried in his hand. She'd wanted to tell Gil last night, but she wasn't sure he'd believe her. Silly, considering everything else she'd entrusted him with, but he didn't seem the superstitious type. Mind you, neither was she.

In some cultures, they believe that taking someone's photograph steals a bit of their soul. Helen had always felt that with the boy, that she'd taken a little bit of him with her when she snapped that first shot, a bit that was never meant to be hers . . . A bit that remained with her.

She looked up, half-expecting to see him standing next to her now. Instead, one of the birdwatchers had moved closer, binoculars raised in her direction. Helen looked upwards, following the angle of his gaze, expecting to see a hawk wheeling above. But the sky was empty. Not even a bunch of crows. When she glanced back the birdwatcher in the dark cagoule was still staring.

She looked up again, thinking she must have missed something. But no.

The fine downy hairs on her arms prickled and Helen felt the ground beneath her give.

Steadying herself, she turned and started down the slope, zig-zagging too hastily between boulders, almost tripping. At the fork in the path that would take her back the way she'd come she jinked left towards the road instead. In the distance a jogger, small, probably female, was coming towards her.

Don't be so paranoid, she told herself, slowing as she reached the drystone wall that bordered the road. Lack of sleep, too much vodka, too much thinking about Art . . . They were messing with her head. Nevertheless, she couldn't shake the feeling that the man with the binoculars hadn't been watching birds at all. He'd been watching her.

27

Gil was obsessed, he knew it. He recognised the signs. Had seen them before. He could tell himself it was the story, the thrill of the chase. But it wasn't. It was the woman. He wanted to believe her. More than that, he wanted to *understand* her. And to do that, he would have to get under the skin of Huntingdon.

He started with his Facebook account, unused since the fire, and his Twitter account: 7,500 followers. Somehow Gil had expected more.

Huntingdon's feed was a slow boil of outrage and dislike. Protests that the truly talented were ignored. Sweeping political generalisations. Insults to politicians followed by sycophantic climb-downs to any who bothered to reply. He introduced himself, on Twitter, to Rupert Murdoch as a man with skills to offer. He tweeted a critique of the Royal Family's news handling to a palace account. *Hire me* was his endless unsaid plea. When no offers materialised, his position changed. It was a conspiracy. What society needed was genuine meritocracy.

As someone who started his first job at fourteen and worked his way up only to meet others coming down from university into jobs above him, Gil could sympathise. But Huntingdon came from the generation that went to university almost as a matter of course. From what Gil could discover, the milk round had given him a traineeship on one of the top newspapers. He *started* in Fleet Street. What did Huntingdon think meritocracy could offer that this hadn't already handed him? The tweets stopped, obviously enough, with the man's death. Shutting down the twitter feed, Gil moved on to Google Translate.

The few French news reports focused on the damage to a historic building in one of the city's oldest squares. The fire had been so fierce the whole floor had been cordoned off, and the floor below. When it had finally been declared safe, one body was found. Well, the remains of one, carbonised and twisted and almost beyond identification. Dental records proved inconclusive, DNA tests were to be carried out, assuming DNA could be extracted from a body so burnt. All evidence pointed to it being Art Huntingdon.

When the reports became repetitive, Gil returned his attention to Huntingdon. The man also had a LinkedIn account. After opening one for himself, Gil took a look. Nothing he wouldn't expect. Although, one thing struck him. Huntingdon had begun well, taken in for training by a big organisation, and had changed jobs on the dot of two years. His next job was a putative promotion but meant going down a level in the quality of paper he represented. Two years was when training ended. Gil wondered if he'd jumped ship or been advised to look elsewhere. Clearly 9/11 raised his profile for a while. But the overall pattern was repeated: grander jobs, but at slightly less impressive places each time.

Then the bylines began to dry up.

After the last of the staff jobs came the news agency Helen mentioned: small, unimpressive; Huntingdon had been made head of bureau. Trawling through the *about us* pages of the agency's Paris office suggested Helen had been kind in her description; it appeared to have a senior staff of one.

A trawl of electoral registers showed Art Huntingdon's first wife reverting to her maiden name the moment they separated; despite living alone at the family home, and remaining ostensibly single for the next five years. Reverting to your surname that quickly was never a good sign. Interestingly, his children's surnames changed too. Albeit briefly. If there was a legal battle, the mother lost. The roll gave the children their mother's surname for the year of the divorce. The following year they were back to Huntingdon.

On a hunch, Gil skipped a few years and discovered that in the year Huntingdon's daughter went to university she reverted to her mother's name. The boy, two years younger, was still Huntingdon. His first wife kept the house. That must have hurt.

Gil wondered if that was relevant.

He decided it was and began to make notes the old-fashioned way, using pen and paper. As a hack-free medium it was pretty secure, short of someone nicking your notepad.

As he leaned forward to turn off his laptop, another thought struck Gil.

Clearing the Google search box, he typed 'Domestic violence symptoms' and watched the screen fill. As searches went, it was hardly specific. There were so many pages he didn't know where to start. He was halfway down a long and boring report on clinical characteristics when a phrase brought him up short.

He cleared the search box and typed 'Domestic violence PTSD' instead. Thousands more links filled his screen. Gil scanned them one after another, scribbling notes as he did. *After a period of time*, he read, *it's not uncommon for victims of domestic violence (like victims of all types of abuse and trauma), to develop the symptoms of PTSD, most often associated with wars . . .* As he read on, his shower forgotten, the breakfast news long since replaced by a mid-morning chat show, Gil began a list.

Symptoms:
short-term memory loss
good long-term memory
avoidance
amnesia
nightmares vs insomnia
recurring flashbacks
migraines
later events may trigger PTSD months, even years, after
   source event
need to keep busy
obsessive behaviour like exercise
easily startled
detachment/tendency to dissociate

He forced himself to slow down as his notes grew less legible.

Causes:
fearing for life or life of others
loss of physical integrity
powerlessness/helplessness
witnessing horror
women more likely to experience high-impact trauma like
*   sexual assault*
20% risk of development in women

Gil circled the 20% twice and put down his pen. His head filled with Helen's face, seemingly emotionless as she described in horrific detail the things she'd experienced. Helen had been witnessing horror since she was twenty-three, long before she got involved with Art. But if even half of what she said was true, going to bed with Art in response to a small boy's death had been disastrous.

It was almost lunchtime when Gil realised he'd missed his chance to sleep. He could go to bed now, of course. He was retired, he could do anything he wanted. But he felt more awake than ever. He could go for a walk or visit the café at the other end of the village, which ran almost entirely on tourists, and nurse what passed for their cappuccino while eating a slightly stale croissant. The croissants were always stale, for the most Yorkshire of reasons. Instead of throwing away stale ones and serving fresh ones the owner insisted on selling the older ones first so as not to be wasteful. By which time the new ones had become old themselves. Gil supposed he should be grateful the café sold them at all.

Having talked himself out of all the options, he was left with what he'd been trying to avoid: calling his daughters.

At least, calling one of them.

He thought about what he could say, ran through what had been going on in his life, tried to think of amusing anecdotes. Short of embellishing stuff or making up outright lies, there wasn't a whole lot to say. Except, Hello, how are you . . .

Not giving himself the chance to chicken out, he telephoned Lyn. Once he'd convinced her there was nothing wrong, and he meant that, there wasn't anything wrong: his health was fine, the cottage was fine, he was enjoying retirement as much as could be expected, i.e. not at all; they had a conversation about daytime TV and what a waste of space it was; and, much to Gil's surprise, about how little he knew about her life, and how sorry he was for that.

When he put the phone down half an hour later, Gil felt better than he had for years.

28

'I should warn you: we're having an affair. Which is outrageous, seeing as you're young enough to be my daughter.' Gil shrugged. 'Actually, that's entirely true. You are. But our affair is doubly outrageous because it's barely a week since I took Liza to supper. And why would I have done that if I didn't have designs on her too?'

'Do you?' Helen asked.

'No,' he said defensively. 'Oh, I don't know. She's a nice woman. We had a good time. But I think she, you know, wanted more. My name is mud in the village. Mrs Millward asked Liza how it went, and read between all the wrong lines. Now I'm two-timing her with you.'

'Mrs Millward's saying that?' Helen couldn't suppress a smile.

'*Everyone's* saying that . . . You wouldn't believe the number of people who think I should know every little thing that's being said about me.' Gil's smile was grim.

'And the number who want to know if the rumours about you are true.'

Helen raised her eyebrows. 'You came up here just to tell me that?'

Gil looked at her camera and there was something so wistful in his glance that she handed it over. He held it gingerly, turning it to look at it from the front. 'I wonder if I'd be so impressed if I didn't know it was a Leica?'

'You do know.'

'Exactly. No, I came up here because I've had enough of awkward silences when I walk into a room and people telling me things for my own good. Also, I thought I might see you.' He blushed slightly. 'I wanted to say a few things. Ask a few questions.'

Helen tried not to sigh. She'd been expecting him earlier. Him or the police. The only surprise was it took him so long. In a perverse kind of way she was beginning to find his presence strangely calming. Better the devil you know. Better than the one in her head, certainly.

'Say away.'

'I just wanted you to know I haven't called the news desk,' Gil said. 'I haven't called the police either. I wanted you to know that.'

There was something almost childish about his intensity, something that told her he found not going to the news desk far harder than not going to the police. Helen was grateful all the same.

'Is that all?'

Gil looked uncomfortable, as if there was something he wanted to say but didn't know where to start. She knew the feeling.

'Nothing that can't wait.'

SAM BAKER

Helen had been perched at the base of the Scar when Gil found her, wondering what it would be like to climb. How likely she'd be to fall and whether, well, whether, in the circumstances, that would matter. Around them the Dales were a ragged patchwork of greens and yellows with frayed edges. The occasional hard-edged block showed where a building had intruded. Gil smiled when she said that.

'Ah, the Dales are taking you in,' he said. 'They get everyone who lives here eventually.'

Helen nodded, surprised to find that not only did she live here but she liked the idea of living here. The only question was how long she could continue to do so. Whether or not Gil gave her away, it was only a matter of time before she would have to move on.

'From this distance you can't tell if the house is still lived in or a ruin,' Helen said, pointing to the red-brick sprawl of Wildfell behind a veil of trees.

'Both,' Gil said. He grinned and she couldn't help grinning back.

'You know, you solved a lot of problems for a number of people. That house is listed but only Grade II, the owners are overseas and the council probably couldn't enforce a maintenance order, even if they had enough staff left to issue it. The only way would be for them to issue a compulsory purchase notice – and that won't happen because they'd have to find money out of a shrinking budget and pay for repairs . . . I can get a bit carried away,' he admitted, having reeled off this information, 'when I start digging.'

'What else have you dug up?' Helen asked.

Planting his hands in his pockets, Gil looked out at

296

the horizon. For a few seconds Helen thought he wasn't going to answer. 'Your story . . .' he said eventually. 'It seems to stack up.'

'My *story*?'

He looked embarrassed. 'I don't mean to offend you, but I need to ask a few more questions. What kind of journalist would I be if I didn't?'

Helen nodded, resigned.

'How long have you had PTSD?'

'How long have I *what*?'

'The specialist you told me you saw after Syria. Is that why you see her? Those pills you take, the ones in your kitchen you said were for migraines . . .'

Helen winced. She should have left while she had the chance. Moved on somewhere, somewhere she could be truly invisible. Bangkok, maybe, where she could have blended in with the other backpackers. Although there was the small matter of money. She couldn't get hold of any more without exposing herself. Perhaps Gil . . .

No. She caught herself. *He's not your friend. He's a journalist. Don't forget that.*

He was looking at her, his head to one side, waiting for her to answer. 'Helen?'

'They *are* for migraines,' she said.

'And the migraines . . .?' Gil prompted.

'Are possibly a symptom.' Helen pulled at the grass and stared into space for a few seconds, wondering how much silence would have to pass before he took the hint. He didn't. 'I've always had migraines,' she said eventually. 'But they changed after Iraq. Became part of my life.'

'Like the boy?' Gil asked simply.

Startled, Helen stared at him.

'You mentioned him the other night.'

'Oh.' Helen wished she could remember everything she'd said the other night. Or even half of it. 'Yes, I guess, like the boy . . .'

They sat in silence for a minute. 'Does anyone else know about the PTSD?' Gil asked eventually.

Helen shook her head. 'No. Well, only Caroline. My doctor,' she added when Gil looked vague. 'Art thought I saw her for girl problems. God knows, I've had enough of those. My sister thinks she's my therapist.'

'And they're both right?'

In lieu of an answer, Helen climbed to her feet. 'You like living here?' she asked, making no attempt to disguise the change of subject. She watched Gil wrestle with himself and decide to let her off the hook, for now. He clambered to his own feet to stand beside her, nodding south towards the patchwork moors, his gaze taking in the red brick of the house, the grey stone of the village beyond and the air-soiled shimmer of concrete on the horizon.

'It's complicated,' he said finally.

'Like a Facebook relationship status.'

'I love the landscape. At least, I love it now. When I was younger I barely noticed it. It was just where I came from. The village though . . .' He shrugged. 'I came home, you know. My parents lived here and their parents before them and theirs before them. It had memories. A few good, a few not, but I find it . . .' Gil hesitated. 'Small. Small in every way. I grew up here; I thought I'd belong.'

'So what's the problem?'

'I'm not sure I want to belong.'

'You miss living in a city?'

'I haven't lived in a city for decades. I miss my job. I have a leaving card full of people telling me to enjoy retirement. I want to ring them up and ask if any of them have any suggestions how. It's not like I have hobbies. I don't fish or garden. I don't play golf or take photographs like you. Not that I think photography's a hobby,' he added hastily. 'I've seen your work in the Sunday supps.'

'Someone younger would have said *online*.'

He winced. 'And to think you told me I was too truthful the other night.'

'Did I?' Helen didn't remember. She had little memory of the night. Instead she had the dregs of a two-day hangover that told her she was older than she thought. The dregs of a hangover and no migraine, despite having drunk, despite having slept too little and eaten junk for days. She didn't like admitting the stress link to her migraines. She didn't like admitting to stress at all. But even thinking about Art tightened a band round her forehead. That band had grown so tight in the time she was with him she could barely think at all. She'd spent most of it lost in fog.

'Can I ask you something?' Gil said.

This time Helen did sigh. 'Must you?'

'I think so, yes. I asked you before and you answered, but I want to know more.'

'Do I need to sit down first?'

'Up to you. Why didn't you just leave? I mean, I know you did. Twice. But sooner. The first time he hurt you? The second time? Why did you even marry him?'

The band tightened, her vision blurred. She could feel

the coldness in her fingers and the landscape grow distant. Without even thinking about it, she sat down and clutched her knees to her chest, hugging them. *Ninety-nine, ninety-eight, ninety-seven* . . . When she glanced up, Gil looked frightened.

Ninety-three, ninety-two, ninety . . .

'Helen?'

'Art made sure everyone knew I was difficult. My family already thought so. It became common knowledge I was highly strung. Talent often is. Occasionally, very occasionally, he'd let the mask slip when my family were around and I'd find myself making excuses for him: he'd only just come back from somewhere hot and brutal; other men would be destroyed by what he'd seen.'

Gil said, 'No one ever asked why you weren't destroyed, too?'

She smiled at him gratefully. 'I went everywhere Art went, and more. I was destroyed – only not by that. The friends who took me aside to ask if everything was all right were the ones Art hated. When my personal trainer noticed bruises on my legs when I was pregnant, I simply never went back. If he'd known what I talked to Caroline about he'd never have let me go there.

'It was like being put in a box. How you end up in there is the biggest trick. Maybe you think it's a treasure box at first. You're in there because you're special. Soon the box starts to shrink. Every time you touch the edges there's an "argument". So you try to make yourself fit. You curl up, become smaller, quieter, remove the excessive, offensive parts of your personality. You begin to notice lots of these. You eliminate people and interests, change your behaviour. But still the box gets smaller.

You think it's your fault. You don't realise that the box is shrinking, or who is making it smaller. You don't understand that you will never, ever be tiny enough to fit . . .'

Helen paused, tears leaking down the side of her face and into her hair. She didn't bother to wipe them away. Being lonely was hard enough. Realising just how long you'd been lonely was worse.

'Art said we had a fierce I-feel-like-I've-known-you-all-my-life affair. No one had felt like us before. We were different, unique, a team. I wanted to believe it. I told Caroline we were different, once. She fired up her laptop and talked me through a flow chart of the abuse cycle. It turned out we weren't different at all.

'Art's jealousy ate into everything. Most of my friends, my real friends – and I admit I didn't have many to start with – dropped away. The slightest thing would trigger Art's fury. One night we went to dinner with his new boss. The guy considered himself a serious amateur photographer and grilled me about cameras. I didn't know what to do. If I held forth, Art would accuse me of dominating the conversation. If I didn't, he'd say I was rude and showed him up. So I said as little as I could and still be polite. Yet, when we got home I got the "team" lecture and a lesson . . .' Helen took a deep breath, hoping Gil wouldn't ask what that particular lesson involved.

'Next morning, Art was hurt at what I'd made him do and I had to convince him we were OK, *a team*. As I always did. By the time we got to Paris, my days simply became about working out what it was safe to say.'

Gil nodded, discomfort evident in his eyes.

'Climbed this once,' he said suddenly, leaping to his feet.

Looking at the side of the Scar, Helen tried to imagine it.

'I was thirteen,' he said. 'We came out on a school trip and it seemed like a good idea. Showing off, I guess. Proving just because I read books didn't mean I was afraid. The teacher was at the bottom, shouting at me to come back. I was too terrified to do anything but keep going.'

'It's the looking down that kills you,' she said.

Gil put out his hand to pull her up. To her surprise, she took it. 'Sometimes in life you have to look down,' Gil's face was earnest. 'But it's better not to do it if you're hanging by one hand from a rock.'

He looked at her and Helen knew another question was coming.

'Did you kill him?'

'I don't know,' Helen said. 'I honestly don't. I think I must have.'

Halfway up the mild grass slope, Gil looked back, raising his eyebrows to see her right behind him. What would happen when the grass ended and the rock began was anyone's guess. Gil's done this before, Helen reminded herself. She wasn't so old or scared she couldn't match what had already been done by a thirteen-year-old boy. Not any more. Whether a sixty-year-old man could pull it off again was another matter.

As Gil stopped to get his breath Helen pushed past, stepping up on to a grey rock, reaching for a handhold above and pulling herself up.

'Helen, wait . . .'

She didn't.

Having found a second foothold, she reached again and pulled, feet scrabbling for a footing she couldn't seem to find. One foot turning almost sideways to balance on an inch-wide ledge as she reached up again, clinging to the cliff with two hands and barely one foot. Anyone would have thought she had something to prove.

'Just do it,' she told herself, as she'd been telling herself for years, in the rare gap when her self reappeared. Just leave, move out, tell him it's over.

Just do it.

They'd loved each other at first. At least, Helen thought they must have. Maybe she'd simply liked the idea of him, his charisma and easy charm, his way with people when he wanted something. Maybe she'd simply been lonely with only her camera for company, and everyone settling down and having babies around her.

He'd certainly said he loved her. Art loved her so much he could hardly bear for them to be apart. He wanted her always; he wanted to be with her always; he hated it when they were apart. Especially when her job was the cause of the parting.

'How could you be so gullible?' Helen muttered, clinging to the cliff edge, unable to go forward or back.

But that's all you were. You weren't frigid, you weren't stupid, you weren't useless, you weren't a whore. You wouldn't have fallen to pieces the moment you left. You really didn't need to be grateful he bothered with you at all.

By the time he'd finished all she had left was her ability with a camera. He couldn't take away the one thing she had that other people didn't.

The Helen Lawrence touch.

Photography was an art of observation. When she looked through a lens she saw the world as only she saw it for that second. He hated that, she realised now. Too late, far too late to do anything about it. It was one of the reasons he'd taken her apart, piece by piece, systematically hacking pieces from her soul, trying to snuff out her light. By the time he'd finished, she'd believed him when he told her everything he did was her fault. Art stripped everything from her except the thing he wanted to take more than anything.

What she'd rediscovered by coming to Wildfell.

When she picked up a camera she was her again.

'Are you all right?' Gil was behind her, uncomfortably close.

Helen lurched dangerously and clutched at a rock above. 'I'm fine,' she said, forcing herself to breathe as she found a handhold that dug deep into her fingers. Ignoring the pain, she dragged herself up, kicking her foot into a gap that was barely there and reaching for a better handhold, pulling herself higher.

'Sorry I made you jump. Thought you were stuck.'

'For a while I was,' she said. 'I'm not any more.'

Gil grunted and Helen could hear him behind her, his breath laboured and his brogues showering the grass below with gravel as their leather soles scrabbled for purchase. 'This was a bloody stupid idea,' he said. In his voice there was amusement and pride, and a hint of resignation. Maybe he'd expected her to argue him out of the climb. He certainly hadn't expected her to join in.

For a moment Helen let herself look down; wished she hadn't.

Look, Ma. No hands. Except then she'd be down there,

instead of clinging for dear life to sun-warmed rock that smelled slightly acrid as it pressed against her face. There were tiny weeds dug into the cracks of the Scar. Her fingers crushed them and they sprang back up. Helen wracked her brain. Something was wrong. Not about the climb. The climb was wonderful. She was used to the amnesia, the blackouts and fog, they'd been there ever since Iraq. But this was different.

This was a black hole.

Smoke . . . sourness . . . chemical burning, stinging her eyes. Rolling out of bed, brain so foggy it almost defeated her. The shock of landing barely waking her before vomit splattered across tiles . . .

Suddenly the memory was there, just a flicker, but more than before.

Migraine, she thought, her gaze sliding out towards the Dales. But the colours were true. No migraine. Not this time. This was different.

Arms and legs barely finding the strength to drag herself through the blazing living room . . . somehow reaching up to find a door handle . . . flinging herself through on to the cold stone landing beyond . . . leaving Art's body to the flames behind her . . .

'Helen . . .'

'Just getting my breath.'

'You're almost there. Look above you.'

The edge of the Scar was a couple of handholds away. The rock face was not so steep here and she dragged herself on to a slope that lessened as her foot found a hold and raised her on to more level ground. Collapsing on her back, Helen stared at the sky, gulping in big breaths. Below her she could hear Gil's ragged breathing.

'You need to move,' he gasped.

Rolling over, as she'd rolled over to roll off that bed, she made space for him. He dragged himself on to the rough grass beside her and then, obviously deciding he was still too close to the edge, crawled over her, and collapsed on the far side.

'That was stupid. You trying to kill me too?'

He was joking, she thought.

'There was a body.'

Gil rolled on to his side to look at her. His face suddenly serious. 'You don't mean just now . . .? No, you don't. Where did you see it?'

'In the flat. I was there, Gil. I should have told you sooner, but I wasn't certain until now.

'It was Art. I'm almost sure of it.'

Gil rested his head on his arm and let the tension go out of his body, his face smoothed and at least a decade dropped away. When he spoke his words were careful, his voice neutral. 'Of course it was Art.' He looked slightly shame-faced. 'I've checked the reports,' he said. 'Well, some of them. They're doing DNA tests, but they seem pretty sure it's him.'

He hesitated. 'They're looking for you, you know.'

Helen nodded.

'You really were telling the truth when you said you didn't go online?' Gil asked.

'I did for a while. I set up a VPN so that if the police had filters set to capture anyone showing excessive interest in the case it looked like I was in America.'

'That's possible?'

She smiled. 'Yes, Gil, it's possible. Anyway, then I went to London. I had to. I had to see Caroline . . .' Helen hesitated. 'It was a huge mistake. I haven't really felt safe since, so I stopped using it. I know he's dead, the police say he's dead, the papers say he's dead. I saw the body. But ever since I got back, I can't shake the feeling I'm being watched.'

She told him about the birdwatcher and a flash of concern crossed his face.

'Journalist?' he suggested. 'Private investigator?'

'Could be.'

'What will you do?' Gil asked. 'I mean, long term.'

Helen shrugged, clambered to her feet. 'I don't know,' she said. 'You catch your breath. I'm going to take some photographs. Then we need to think of a way to get down.' She looked at the flat slab of rock under her feet, a ruined liner in the yellow-brown sea of gorse and grass around them. It felt so solid that she stamped, imagining the sound waves travelling almost forever.

'Everyone does that.'

'Really? Why?'

'Some places are more real than others. I've never been anywhere more real than this. Have you ever read Alan Garner?'

Helen looked blank.

'You should. He writes about places like this. Children's books, supposedly. For very sophisticated children. He'd have a field day with the cave systems under the Scar. Miles and miles of twisting tunnels and shafts. Used to play in them when I was a lad.'

He grinned at her. 'Pre health and safety, naturally. Most of them are shut off now. They're unsafe. Limestone's like that. Though I don't doubt a person could get lost in there if they really wanted to.'

She gave an involuntary shudder.

'Don't worry about getting down. The nearest path's over there. It's not that steep.'

'Now you tell me.'

'Which would you rather have done? Walked the path or climbed the cliff? I'll wait here while you take your photographs. Then tell me again about the body. I want to know everything you can remember. No matter how insignificant.'

Opening her mouth to say something, Helen stopped.

'Go on,' Gil said.

'All I know is there was a fire and I saw Art's body. But I don't know what I was doing there. I'd moved out of the flat. I hadn't been back since Syria. I swore I'd never go back. I know my track record isn't great on that. So it's possible I'm as stupid as Art said. But I'm pretty sure even I couldn't both go to sleep and set fire to the flat. Not even a flat I'm meant to have set fire to twice.'

29

Gil's suit jacket was sodden by the time he reached the General Stores next morning. Another sleepless night full of images of Helen, Art, and the dead child had left him ragged and in need of nicotine and coffee. Nothing else would have persuaded him into the lion's den. Just as he pushed at the door, it burst open from within, its ancient bell clanging overhead. Clutching at the frame, Gil narrowly avoiding being mown down by a tourist.

''Scuse me, mate.' His sarcasm was wasted.

The man grunted from inside the hood of his navy cagoule and barged past with two plastic bags. No walking sticks though, Gil noticed. Mind you, who could blame him? It wasn't exactly walking weather. Bracing himself for a tirade about tourists' manners, with a side order of meaningful looks and leading questions, Gil pushed his way inside.

To his relief there was no sign of Margaret Millward.

The young woman behind the counter smiled sympathetically as Gil wiped rain from his face. When had
he turned into the kind of man that pretty shop assist-
ants could smile at with no danger of either of them
misunderstanding the smile? Truth was, he'd probably
been that man for decades. Was that why Helen
Lawrence seemed so relaxed with him?

It was an uncomfortable thought, and Gil dismissed
it. Smiled again at the girl as she handed him his paper.
He had a feeling he'd known her mother. Then realised,
with a lurch, seeing exactly how young she was beneath
her make-up, that it might have been her grandmother.
Glancing at the paper, he almost handed it back and
chose another simply to prove he wasn't that predictable.
Only, he was. Here he was, sodden wet in the General
Stores, buying a paper that mostly contained news he'd
read already online, for no reason other than that he
always bought it.

His had been the glory days. Fleet Street as Fleet
Street, strong local papers with strong local views. He
knew he was lucky. He knew things changed. Gil simply
didn't feel he was sufficiently old to be taking it this
hard. Handing the girl the exact change – how sad was
that? – he wiped more rain from his scalp, smiled his
goodbye and pushed his way back through the squeaking
door into the rain. Unscathed by gossip for the first time
in days.

He hadn't bought cigarettes.

He hoped she noticed he hadn't bought cigarettes.

The Bull would be open and Bill already perched on
his stool by the bar. There would be the die-hard walkers
too, drinking coffee admittedly. Gil couldn't see the point

of drinking coffee in pubs. It was like being celibate in a brothel. If you're celibate, don't go there in the first place. Not that he'd ever been to a brothel. It was just something his old news editor used to say.

The front window of The Café on the Corner was steamed up, with seven sodden members of the Wednesday book club gathered inside. They stopped talking when Gil came in, but they didn't stop looking. He had a pretty good idea they hadn't been talking about books. He chose a corner, as far away from them as possible, and draped his suit jacket over the back of the chair opposite to dry. Pulling his phone from his pocket, he began rechecking the sites he'd checked yesterday, and the day before, and the day before that.

To test his newfound digital prowess, Gil had set up Google alerts on 'Art Huntingdon' and 'Helen Lawrence' the previous night. Nothing was flagged, and there was nothing new on Art Huntingdon's Twitter feed, Facebook page or entry on LinkedIn. Why would there be?

All the same, he checked a couple of search engines. He hoped Helen was wrong about police filters or he'd be right up the Swannee. Mind you, he was a journalist. Journalists were meant to show excessive interest in things that weren't their business.

Gil smiled at the girl who brought his coffee and she seemed surprised, then smiled tentatively. She was new. Within days she'd be bringing the regulars their cappuccino without them having to ask. Gil wasn't sure how they stood it. He picked up a local paper someone had dumped on the next table. A smattering of global news, carefully linked back to Yorkshire. Its quick crossword was too easy and the cryptic one too hard. He hated sudoku and the chess problem stared back at him for so long his cappuccino went cold. He couldn't live like this, not long term. At least holidays were eventually over. He needed to find something that interested him or return to work in one way or another. He'd die of boredom else.

But maybe he'd already found it. One call was all it would take and he'd have a commission. A big one . . .

'You busy, Mr Markham?'

One of the younger members of the book group was hovering near his table. Gesturing to the chair with his jacket, Gil invited her to sit and saw her glance at what remained of the group behind her. One of them nodded.

'It's just, you're, uh, friends with . . . the French woman?' She blushed. 'You know? She's renting the big house . . .'

He nodded. Here we go.

'Thought so. Someone's asking after her.'

'Someone?' Gil's stomach lurched.

'He said he was an old friend and he had a photograph. She had different colour hair in the picture but it was definitely her. Me and Katie thought he could be a journalist . . . No offence. Or a private detective. So we said we hadn't seen her. We don't think he believed us though.'

'What was he like?' Gil hoped he looked calmer than he felt. He was pretty sure he knew the photo she meant. But that didn't mean a thing. Anyone could have downloaded it.

The girl thought about his question, shrugged. 'Oldish . . . Bit fat. Well, not fat exactly, more not thin. Going a bit bald, you know.' She patted the crown of her head to show Gil where she meant. 'He was wearing a dark green jacket. Bit like a Barbour, but not. You know the kind.'

Gil did. 'Is he still here?'

'Got into a blue car. Said he was going to try the next village.' The girl thought about it. 'We think he'll be back. It was a hire car,' she added.

'How do you know?'

She looked at Gil as if he was simple. 'It had a Hertz sticker in the window.'

'There was a man,' Kath said.

Gil waited while the landlord's daughter-in-law pulled his first pint without being asked and reached behind her for a packet of salt-and-vinegar crisps. He could demand prawn cocktail instead, but he didn't like prawn cocktail and what was the point of eating crisps you didn't like just to prove you weren't predictable? His hand already itched for the B&H he hadn't bought for the same stupid reason.

'What was he like?'

'Don't you want to know what he wanted?'

Sliding coins across the bar, Gil said. 'I know what he wants. He was in the café this morning asking about Mademoiselle Graham.'

'Then you know what he's like.'

'Middle-aged, slightly balding, wearing a Barbour.'

Kath sniffed. 'Tell whoever told you that not to bother applying to join the police. He wasn't nearly middle-aged. Probably only a few years older than me. Good-looking bloke. Still had his hair, for a start. Well, most of it. And it was a Belstaff, not a Barbour. They're not even the same colour.'

Waving away his change, Gil said, 'He had a photograph?'

'Of your friend? Yes.'

He considered saying Helen wasn't his friend, but perhaps she was, if not in the way Kath meant.

Gil sighed. He wished he was a bit younger. A bit more modern.

'This photograph?' he prompted.

'It was a few years old, you know. She looked—'

She broke off as a tourist approached the bar. While Kath turned away to serve him, Gil got out his phone to call Helen. It was only when he started to flick through his contacts that he realised he didn't have her number. Perhaps he should skip his pint and go out there and warn her? Two sightings – three, if you included Helen's birdwatcher, and Gil wasn't sure he did – couldn't be a coincidence.

Kath wandered back with a bar towel to wipe away crisp crumbs and the ring left by Gil's glass. 'Sad's not the right word,' she continued as if she hadn't stepped away. 'Exhausted, maybe. There was something about her eyes. If you said she'd been ill – you know, seriously – I wouldn't be surprised.'

'What did you tell him?'

'Oh, I said she'd been in. He asked if she was a regular and I said not really. She'd come in once that I could remember.'

'Did you say where she was living?' Gil's fist was clenched tight around his pint glass.

'He didn't ask.'

*　　*　　*

314

Wind howled through the trees and stripped rain from the leaves on to his head and into his face as if it knew he was coming. The sky was dusk dark, although it was not yet four. He should have brought a torch. Anyone with any sense would have brought a torch, but then people would have been seen him coming up the lane from the village to the house and Gil didn't want to be seen in case somebody was watching.

And for once he wasn't worrying about the village gossips. He only wished he was.

Stopping at the rusty gates to the house, he unzipped and pissed the pint he'd just drunk against a red-brick pillar, keeping one eye on the road that led past the gates and turned off towards an abandoned sheep farm further up. Follow the road beyond that and it would deliver you to a village on the far side of the saddle where the houses were mostly weekend cottages, incomers or holiday homes.

The rain slowed enough for him to check the road was deserted; and then stopped entirely, just as he opened the small gate in the big wrought-iron one, and prepared to take himself somewhere dry. A sliver of light behind a curtained upstairs window went out the moment he leaned on the bell push. Gil waited for another light to appear, one on the landing or on the stairs or in the hall. It didn't. All he got was darkness inside the house, and gloom without. Rain pattered from the trees mimicking the way it had fallen from the sky until moments before.

A gargoyle high on a corner of the oldest part poured water in a steady stream on to gravel. There should have been a butt below. There undoubtedly was back in the day when the house had gardeners and servants, and probably an old butler so infirm it was all he could do to manage the door. Gil had picked apples in Wildfell's orchards when he was barely a teenager for a pittance an hour. Picked apples and tried to get his hand up a girl's skirt. The skirt was washed-out denim, short enough to be barely there. It had still been enough to keep him out, no matter how he wrestled or pleaded.

'Who is it?'

Helen's voice was hoarse, almost disguised. Loud enough for Gil to realise she was standing on the other side of the locked door.

'It's me. Gil.'

'Is anybody with you?'

He looked round stupidly at the wet gravel and sodden trees. He wasn't sure which would be the right reply but answered truthfully. 'No. I came alone.'

A bolt shot back and the door slipped open a little, with Helen out of sight behind it. 'Come in then,' she said. She sounded cross, or maybe just tired.

In her hand was a pencil torch she used to light her way, only turning it off when they reached the upper sitting room. She shut the curtains before turning on the light. Her laptop was on. A picture of a ruined street filling the screen. *Ruined street* hardly did the picture justice. There was a desolation to the photograph that made it almost painful. 'I started going through my USBs,' she says. 'Seeing if I've still got the picture files to put the Paris exhibition together. Not that it's much use to me now. It's more the principle.'

'This was one of them?'

'No, this is Syria. The picture I told you about . . .'

'Are you all right?'

316

She glanced up, her face lit from the side by a table lamp placed low, and given an unhealthy glow by her screen. She looked like a different woman from the day before, hollow-eyed and haunted.

'Helen . . .'

'I feel watched,' she said. 'I thought it was you. I thought it was this bloody village. It's not. Ever since I came back from London I've felt watched. Art would have said it was paranoia. That I needed to get a grip on myself. Stop being hysterical. I shouldn't have gone to London, but I needed the pills. It was stupid of me. And then, that birdwatcher . . . standing there, with his binoculars, just staring . . .'

Gil started to speak but she put up a hand to silence him.

'Don't tell me it's nothing, a coincidence. Someone's out there. I can feel it. Even the bloody cat's freaked out.'

'Where is Ghost anyway?' Gil looked around.

'This is the point you're meant to say I'm being stupid. That, obviously, there's no one out there watching me. I'm imagining it. Not start me worrying about the missing cat too.'

Gil took a deep breath. Best just to come out with it. 'Someone is looking for you, Helen. I only just heard about it. That's why I'm here.'

Helen clapped a hand to her mouth and, for a moment, Gil thought she was going to vomit. It obviously took an effort to force her hand away.

Removing his suit jacket, he shook it on to the floor, then sat in the armchair without thinking to ask. He watched Helen clock the over-familiarity and decide to let it go.

317

'I've been thinking about it,' he said. 'On the walk here. It's not the police. If they'd found you, they'd be outside with their sirens on. And if they were looking very hard, believe me, they *would* have found you by now. So they're not. It's someone in a hire car. My money's on another journalist, or a private detective. Neither of which is great, obviously.'

'What if it's Mark Ridley?' Helen said suddenly.

'Who?'

'Art's friend. You know, from the Admiral Duncan.'

'Ah,' Gil nodded. 'Why would it be him, after all this time?'

Helen looked slightly sheepish.

Was he going to lose the story to someone else? Gil raised his eyebrows. 'Something you want to tell me?'

'He's been in touch,' Helen said. 'With my sister, by email. And he called my doctor, Caroline, trying to find out where I was.'

'You didn't think to tell me that?' Gil didn't bother to conceal his irritation. 'Anything else, while we're on the subject?'

Helen swallowed, and Gil leaned forward. He was a tolerant man – laid-back enough to be horizontal, Jan always said – but Helen was testing his patience.

'I forget what I've said and what I haven't . . .' she started. 'But yes. You should probably know about Tom.'

'Tom?' That name rang a bell. 'Ex-boyfriend Tom?'

Helen nodded.

'Been in touch with him too?'

'No!' Helen looked indignant. 'Well, yes, actually, but not how it sounds.'

'How is it then?' Gil patted his pocket for his B&H

and cursed himself for not buying a packet. All because he had to make a point.

'I called him, apparently. And no, I don't know why and I don't remember doing it, but he told my sister I called him after the fire, and . . . he emailed me.'

'He emailed you?!'

'Don't worry, I didn't reply. I'm not entirely stupid.'

Gil turned away. He hadn't felt this riled up since the last days of Jan.

They sat in silence for a moment, listening to the drip, drip, drip of the guttering straight on to gravel outside while Helen gnawed at her cuticle. Gil had to resist the urge to slap her hand away.

'So, that's two suspects: Mark Ridley and Tom . . . Anyone else I need to know about?'

Helen shook her head and then stopped, colour draining from her face.

'Art.'

'What about Art?'

'What if it's Art?'

Gil sighed. 'He's dead, Helen. You said so yourself.'

'But what if he's not?'

'They've got his bloody body. Or what's left of it. You saw it yourself . . .'

'I saw *a* body.'

Gil looked at her.

'I can't remember *anything*,' she said furiously. 'Doesn't that strike you as odd? There's a whole day missing. At least a day, if not more.'

'What are you trying to say?' He wasn't irritated any longer. Either she was a bloody good actress, or she believed it.

'I don't know.' She scanned the room wildly, as if expecting to see a face staring in the first-floor window behind her. 'I thought I saw Art's body. But what if it wasn't Art? He could still be out there, watching me.'

Gil tried not to sigh. She was yanking his chain, playing the hysteric to throw him off the scent. But her body language . . . the way she hunched up, knees clutched to her chest like a child . . . What had she said before about trying to make herself as small as possible?

'Helen, think about it . . . Why would he hide? And who was in Art's flat if not Art?'

'I don't know. But you don't know Art. You don't know what he's capable of.'

'Helen, you told me.'

'I told you a fraction of it,' she said fiercely. 'There were other things.'

'Worse things?' asked Gil, remembering how hard it had been to listen to her describe what happened in Syria.

'*Similar* things,' she said. 'Lots of similar things. It's possible to forget, you know. In between. You can fool yourself it's not that bad. That it was your fault. That it won't happen again.'

She stared at him bleakly.

'It's like war. It always happens again. Only, if you're going to accept that, why would you want to stay alive?'

30

Gil's phone bleeped, breaking the silence that hung over them, and he glanced down. A Google alert in French filled his screen. The words *Arthur Huntingdon* leapt out at him.

'Everything all right?'

Gil glanced up, startled. 'Uh yes, yes,' he said. 'All fine. Just a, uh, text. From my daughter. But I need to speak to her. I should go.'

Helen's face lost a little of its weariness. 'You called her? Great, Gil, that's really great. Call her now if you want.'

But Gil was already on his feet, shrugging his way back into his soggy jacket. 'I should go,' he repeated. 'Really.'

'But everything's . . .?'

'Yes, yes. All fine. I just need to—'

'Of course,' Helen sounded confused, but he could hear her feet on the treads behind him as he took the stairs two at a time. 'I'll be fine,' she said, overtaking him at the bottom to unlock the door. 'You know how I am with locks.'

'I'll be back,' Gil promised. The only truthful thing he'd said in the last two minutes. 'Lock up safely in the meantime.'

Helen forced a smile, and Gil felt a pang of guilt as the door swung shut, locks clicking into place one after another behind it.

He knew it looked odd, leaving like that. But he had to get away.

As he approached the outskirts of the village, Gil passed the old bus shelter. Pulling over, he covered the phone's screen with his jacket, slid the link open and pasted the first line into Google Translate:

Place des Vosges fire body no longer believed to be that of journalist Arthur Huntingdon. Paris police now urgently seek a man and woman to assist with their enquiries . . .

He read it again and then a third time. Had she been playing him all along? Setting herself up as Huntingdon's victim when really she was his accomplice?

A twig snapped somewhere to his left and Gil spun round. For the first time it occurred to him that he might be the one in danger. Behind and ahead stretched the empty road, the shadow of hedgerow looming on either side. Dusk had fallen fast. Anything could be out there. Any*one*.

There was an alternative view, of course.

That Helen was telling the truth. That her fear of Art

was genuine, the look on her face in the glow of her laptop screen when she'd asked 'What if the body wasn't Art's?' looked real enough. If everything she'd told him about Huntingdon was true and her husband was alive, she was in real danger.

'Fuck,' Gil shouted into the night. He wasn't a big curser, but swearing seemed the only sane response. 'Fuck, fuck, fuck.' His words were swallowed by sodden hills and vanished into the night. If the body wasn't Art, whose was it?

The high street was dark except for an occasional streetlight. Not that that meant anything when it came to curtain twitchers. Still, he shut the door quietly, stepping out of his sopping suit on the landing and threw himself into a shower in the hope of steaming his brain to life. Drying himself roughly, Gil shrugged on the ancient towelling robe that hung on the bathroom door and went to make coffee.

The milk was off. Again. Black, then.

This was becoming a pattern, he thought, as he started skimming news sites. It was early days for the new story. So far only a couple of French sites carried the news. But it would be only a matter of time, hours even, before the man and the woman sought by French police were named. Then there would be nothing Gil could do to protect her. Gil caught himself. Why the hell did he still think she needed protecting? The things she'd seen, the things she'd done . . . She was tougher than she looked, tougher than him by a long chalk.

The only thing protecting her was living here, in the middle of nowhere, using another name – but at least one person had managed to find her.

The aspirin packet in the bathroom cupboard was eighteen months out of date but Gil washed a couple down with coffee anyway, then grabbed his notepad and added two names to the list he'd begun earlier in the week. There were four now, not including the scratched out Hélène Graham.

Caroline – PTSD
Tom – ex-boyfriend
Mark Ridley – journalist
Carl – German photographer, Syria

'Caroline PTSD' typed into the search engine brought him a host of names, when he narrowed it down by searching UK pages only. There were several leads, most based in London. The medical qualifications meant so little to Gil, he hardly knew where to start. He noted down a few likely names, numbers and websites to revisit later and moved on. Opening another tab he typed in 'Mark Ridley' and journalist and found himself back on more familiar turf. Like Huntingdon, Ridley had Facebook, Twitter, LinkedIn . . .

In his late forties, Ridley was still a journalist and running a news agency in the south-west. No call to be chasing down a story in the north then, Gil thought. Unless there was a south-western connection to make it viable, and to his knowledge neither Helen nor Huntingdon had history down there. More likely the interest was personal. He was Art's friend, after all. Hadn't Helen said something about Ridley getting involved when she left Art the first time? Reaching for his recorder to play it back, Gil realised that was pointless. The recording stopped long before she reached that point in the conversation.

The pictures of Ridley didn't tell Gil much. The description of the man asking after Helen could fit him, but then it could fit half the men Gil knew between thirty-five and fifty. Gil circled his name twice in black Biro to indicate further research was needed. He could contact the man on Facebook, but that would take time. Twitter was too public. And he hadn't got the hang of LinkedIn for anything other than snooping.

Unless, of course, unlike Karen's, the man's Facebook account wasn't locked? Quickly, Gil set up a different Facebook account using a variation of his Gmail address, drumming his fingers impatiently on the coffee table as he waited for a confirmation email so he could prove he wasn't a bot. Once his new account was live he sent Ridley a friend request. On a whim, he added a private message. It was risky, but what the hell?

I hear you've been looking for Helen Lawrence?
I may have information.

Although he wasn't sure the message would go, it uploaded the second Gil clicked send. Clearly Ridley hadn't reset his privacy settings in quite some time.

Gil loved this bit of the job and hated it too. The frustration of getting nowhere fast made his brain bleed; but the adrenalin rush of knowing he was on to a lead was what had kept him going for the last forty years. He still preferred the old methods, door-knocking and legwork. But he couldn't deny the Internet was handy. Even if it had made journalists into desk jockeys. Turning his attention to the last two names on his list, Gil groaned. Two first names to choose between; he didn't hold out much hope. Why hadn't he thought to ask Helen for Tom's surname?

Carl or Tom? Tom or Carl? Might as well just toss a coin.

Next to Carl he'd written 'German photographer, Syria'. Next to Tom it said simply 'ex-boyfriend'. So Carl it was.

It turned out to be the work of ten minutes to find Carl Ackerman, German photographer. His website was at the bottom of the second page, at the top of the third was a link for his agency. Like Helen, he specialised in reportage. So, Gil assumed, it followed that they'd know each other. The link below this was for a German news story. One word leapt out: *Syrian*.

Opening the link, Gil put it through Google Translate.

According to a German newswire, Ackerman was missing. He hadn't been seen since he boarded a flight from Damascus to Paris. Gil skimmed the appalling translation, adjusting words for sense as he went, his blood racing, his head pounding. Neither had anything to do with his headache.

This was Helen's Carl. It had to be. Gil knew Carl was a common name, but no way were there two German photojournalists in Syria this summer called Carl. *Except* . . . Gil re-read the article. The dates didn't add up. Carl had been reported missing less than two weeks ago. Gil's heart sank. It was a duff lead. A coincidence. A huge one, but a coincidence all the same.

Gil groaned and threw himself back in his chair.

There had to be more to go on. Leaning forward, he cleared the search box and typed in '**Carl Ackerman**' photographer Paris instead. Several more snippets scrolled up; two in French, about a war photography exhibition; two more in German. The first German one was in purple, to show he'd read it. Gil clicked on the second.

Again those incongruous dates.

'Got you!' Gil slammed his palm on the coffee table, his half-full mug slopping cold coffee on to his notes. Ackerman hadn't been reported missing by his agency until 18 September because before that he was on annual leave. But records showed he'd been booked on to a flight from Paris to Berlin on Saturday 1st. The day after the fire.

What if he'd never boarded it?

31

'This is becoming a habit.' Her voice was wry, but Helen was pleased to see him. It had been a rough night, most of it spent lying on the sofa in the upstairs drawing room, jumping at the smallest noise. Ghost's absence had only added to her disquiet.

'How's your daughter?'

Gil coloured. Helen scrutinised him. Had she caught him in a lie?

'She's OK, thanks,' he said. 'Thought I might find you here.'

'Where else would I be?' she shrugged.

Helen was out on the Dales most days. Usually twice; once in her running kit, once with her camera, sometimes both. The fact she'd taken to using a different route hadn't thrown Gil. The back gate through the copse at the bottom of the land surrounding Wildfell brought her out on the Dales more quickly and cut out the road and the tourists. Gil seemed to think she hadn't realised that the easiest way for him to reach the Dales by the lychgate was trespassing through her garden.

'You're not usually up this early,' she said. 'Couldn't sleep either?'

Gil glanced at his watch. He looked shifty, and his discomfort was making her nervous. 'Didn't go to bed.'

That much was obvious, he was a wreck.

'Me neither.'

'Migraine?' he asked.

Helen shook her head. 'Nightmares. The waking kind.'

She could tell he wanted to ask what her nightmares were about, whether she'd remembered something, but he stopped himself.

If not that, then what was he doing here?

She started to walk backwards, taking the path that led towards the Scar at a gentle pace, her eyes fixed on Gil. When Gil followed she turned and began to jog. He jogged incongruously beside her for what felt like minutes.

'Spit it out,' she said eventually.

'What?'

'Come on, Gil, there's something, there's always something. We could start with why you left in such a hurry last night.'

She turned, expecting to see him looking uncomfortable. Instead, his face was serious.

'You'd better sit down first.'

There was nowhere to sit but water-logged grass. Helen laughed. Her laugh was cut short when he didn't join her. 'What, Gil?' she asked, half irritated, half scared. 'Just tell me, what?'

'OK,' Gil said. He put out a hand to touch her arm and Helen felt herself flinch involuntarily.

'But I really think you should sit down. Art's not dead.'

The first Helen knew of blacking out was the ground coming up to meet her. The soft squelch of rain-sodden mud as her face hit grass. Someone tried to shake her awake and she shrugged them away. So they kept shaking.

'Helen, Helen. Are you OK?'

Gil was crouched beside her, his body folded like a paper clip, his face crumpled in concern. She struggled up, her bare elbow slipping in the mud.

'Let me help you . . .'

Helen shook her head. She didn't trust herself to stand, let alone walk. Instead, she patted the boggy grass and Gil made a face he'd probably been using since his gran force-fed him porridge of a morning. Trying not to glance at his clean suit, he folded his lanky frame on to the wet ground beside her.

Her head was swimming. She thought she was going to vomit, right there on the Dales.

'How can you be sure?' said Helen. 'Last night you were adamant he was.'

'Our good friend Google.'

Helen scrutinised him. 'Would that be our good friend Google alert masquerading as a text message from your daughter . . .? It doesn't matter,' she added. 'I don't blame you. Most journalists would do the same. What did it say?'

'I don't know that much,' Gil said. 'Only what I came up with online. But the body at the flat is definitely not Art. The French police are looking for both of you.'

Helen gazed at the haze of clouds above the top of the Scar, a promise of sun to come. An optimistic day, she'd thought, when she left the house minutes earlier. The nightmares slipping away with every step. She waited for the clouds to roll in along with the news that Art was alive. That he was out there somewhere. She wasn't surprised they didn't. She preferred the version where she'd killed him. Whoever came up with pathetic fallacy hadn't a clue.

'What else?' she asked.

'Nothing else.'

'Why do I think you're lying?'

'I'm not sure you're in a position to talk about people lying.'

Gil's voice was sharp. He sounded like someone else. And though the air was warmer than it had been in days, Helen shivered involuntarily.

Do you even know what a team is . . .?

'Here are the facts,' Gil said, his tone was so formal Helen almost expected him to produce his notebook and read her Miranda rights.

'One: there's a body.

'Two: it's not Art. There's no doubt. I have a theory about who it is, but, for now, we're talking facts.

'Three: someone is looking for you. That's also a fact. It should be the police. It will be soon. But right now I'm pretty sure it isn't.'

'Go on,' Helen said.

'If you know where Art is, then tell me. If you tell me where he is, I can find him before he finds you. Unless, of course . . .' Gil paused. 'You're in this together.'

Until now Helen hadn't taken her eyes off the horizon, the Dales beginning to fill up with tourists brought out of their beds by a break in the bad weather. Turning to look at Gil to see if he was serious, she saw only suspicion.

How could he think that, after everything she'd told him? The idea of her and Art as some kind of journalistic Bonnie & Clyde made her want to vomit.

'Helen,' Gil repeated. 'Do you know where he is?'

'I swear I don't, Gil. I only wish I did.'

She didn't know which was worse. The disappointment in his eyes or the disbelief on his face. Closing her own eyes, Helen swallowed, images from last night's nightmares imprinting themselves on her eyelids.

'You have a theory about the body?'

'It's just a theory.'

'But you think you're right?'

Gil nodded. 'Yes, I think I'm right.'

'Then tell me,' Helen said. 'It can't make things worse than they already are. In return I'll tell you what I started to remember last night. I was going to call you after my run. Once I thought you were up.' The look Gil gave her hurt. He wanted to believe her, it said. He just wasn't sure he could. 'Please?' she said.

'OK. Tell me about Carl.'

Helen stopped pulling at the grass. 'What has this got to do with Carl?'

'You mentioned him the other night. You were talking about Syria.'

'He's a friend. German photographer. East German,

originally. Don't go getting ideas – he's gay,' she added, before Gil could say anything. 'Very gay. More's the pity.' Helen looked briefly troubled, then shook her head. 'Why are you asking?'

'I think it's Carl's body.'

'Carl Ackerman?' Helen reeled, hands clutching the ground as if she could slip off. 'My Carl? You think he's dead?'

Gil's voice softened. 'Like I said, conjecture. Your turn.'

She sat in silence on the wet grass, lost inside herself as she remembered Carl Ackerman, one of the sweetest men she'd known. Drunk, often. Promiscuous, unquestionably. More talented than he thought in an industry filled with people less talented than they believed. 'I don't know where to start now.'

'Begin with what you remembered last night. We can talk about Carl later, if you can remember anything.' He wasn't being sarcastic. At least, Helen didn't think he was.

'Since Iraq I've had blanks in my short-term memory. My mind's way of dealing with horrors, according to Caroline. Things I've seen. Things I've . . . experienced. It's fairly normal, apparently. But they tend to be brief. The night of the fire . . . The way whole days were blank never quite made sense. Ever since I started talking to you, the fog's been lifting. Remember I told you I thought I saw a body?'

Gil nodded.

'Last night I had a full-on migraine flashback. Only when I came to, it wasn't a migraine. No cold hands. No strange lights. Simply flashback.' She looked at him, as if noticing something. 'No cigarettes?'

'Ran out.' Gil shrugged. 'Figured I might as well go cold turkey. It probably won't last. Go on.'

'I don't know how accurate this is. I never do. But I'll tell you what I remember if you promise me one thing.' She paused, waiting for Gil to make eye contact before she went on. 'Whatever you think of me. Whether you believe me or don't believe me, believe this: if Art is alive, I'm in danger. So, if you do decide to tell someone where I am, make it the police. Because if he sees a piece about me in a paper and finds me first, he'll kill me.'

'That's emotional blackmail,' Gil said.

Helen shrugged. 'Maybe. It's also true.'

She told him what she could of the fire. All the fragments she'd remembered put together as coherently as she could manage. The smoke, the flames, the fear. The lag between what she knew she had to do and what she could manage. She ended with the body, curled away from her, in the corner. Naked, except for his jeans.

'Art . . .?'

'I thought so. Even though I knew Art and I had split up, that I shouldn't have been there, that he was meant to be away, I just assumed . . . Gil, I swear I have no recollection of going to that flat. It was weeks since I'd left him. Weeks since I'd last seen him. But I must have gone there. He must have come back and we must have had a fight. A bad fight, even by our standards.'

'But it wasn't him, was it?'

'It doesn't look like it, no. Shall I go on?'

Gil nodded.

'The fog in my brain was thicker than the smoke blinding my vision. But I remember – in my dream I remembered – wondering, as I crawled towards the door, what if he was still alive? If he was, I should drag him with me.

'I glanced behind me and as I did, flames erupted, singeing the rug and scorching my heels. It was him, or me, Gil. For the first time in five years, I chose me.'

'And then?'

'I woke up on the sofa in the upstairs drawing room. It was about three in the morning, I'd only been out about half an hour, and I was gagging and choking, and I swear I could smell burning. I couldn't get to sleep again after that.'

'Nothing else?'

'Flashes, glimmers. Fragments as I dozed.'

'And you believe your . . . flashes and fragments?'

'I've learned to. It always happens like this. My memory will come back eventually.' Helen sounded sad. 'It always does.'

'So tell me . . . the fragments.'

'I grabbed my camera bag from the entrance hall, and a trench coat. Art's, it turned out. Don't worry, I ditched it as soon as I could.'

'Your camera bag was there?'

'Always. I never go anywhere without my camera bag. That was the first lesson my picture editor taught me. If you want to play with the big boys, behave like the big boys. Always be ready to go at a moment's notice. I even used to go down to the Monoprix to buy my baguette with a bag full of Leicas, a Nikon D4 and a Canon 5D, plus five thousand dollars – still just about universal currency – in a battered wallet in the inside pocket, next to my passport with its collection of visas for places most people in their right minds don't go.'

'Obsessive,' Gil muttered.

'I've been called worse.' Helen managed a smile. 'Then I was stumbling down the stairs, great, sweeping seventeenth-century things that swirled up the centre of the building. I was pulling on clothes as I went, so that by the time I reached the courtyard I could pass for dressed. I don't know what I was thinking, if anything. But I remember a weird chemical calmness that kept me moving even though I didn't know where I was going. Where *do* you go when you think you've just killed your husband? Your ex-husband. Your technically not yet ex-husband.

'The flats were almost empty. It's one of those blocks where rich people stay during the week. Art and I were often the only ones there at weekends. Plus it was the last weekend of August and you know what Paris is like in August . . .'

Gil shook his head.

'A desert. Thank God. Because it meant all the flats around ours were empty. If they hadn't been . . .' Helen shuddered. 'There'd be more than one body.' She paused. 'Maybe not. Maybe if the building hadn't been empty the fire wouldn't have been able to get out of control the way it did. Maybe there wouldn't have been a body at all.

'I had no shoes on and I remember the feel of the cobbles in the courtyard under my feet. The courtyard door thick, heavy and painfully slow, I remember waiting, anxiety eating at me, for it to creak closed. It would never be rushed and I knew I had to wait, make sure no one followed me in or out.

'Although that memory could be from another time. It was always the same, that door.'

'You're sure nobody saw you?'

'As sure as I can be. It wasn't yet dawn and the colonnades were deserted. Not even stragglers from the clubs that fill the basements of the Marais . . .'

'CCTV?'

Helen laughed. 'This is Paris we're talking about.'

'So?'

'Do you know how many CCTV cameras there are in France? Twenty thousand tops. And most of those in Marseilles, which is where the immigrants come in. In the UK, there are what? Five million?'

Seemingly satisfied, Gil nodded. Helen went on.

'After that it's blank. I know I must have returned to the flat where I was sleeping – it belonged to a friend of a friend – to collect my things.'

'How do you know that?'

Helen shrugged. 'I've got my things.

'And I know I called Tom.'

Gil suddenly looked alert. 'You remember that?'

His voice was tense, he looked . . . Jealous? No, Helen shook the thought away; he was just annoyed at the thought she might have told someone something she hadn't told him. 'No, remember, I told you my sister said—'

'Why do you think you called him?'

'I've been wondering about that . . . subconsciously I must have felt I could trust him. Apparently, I woke him at five a.m.'

Gil looked quizzical. 'What's the number?'

Helen reeled it off without thinking.

'That's Tom's number?'

'No, his parents'. He just happened to be there.'

Gil was silent for a while. 'He must have been some

boyfriend if you can call him at five in the morning nearly twenty years after dumping him.'

Helen smiled. 'He was.'

Something flickered on Gil's face. 'How did you get out of Paris without the border force recording your passport?'

'I didn't. Hélène Graham did. I had her wallet in my camera bag. Press card, driving licence, passport. The consul gave it to me . . . I'd been meaning to send it on. We didn't look that different, at a glance. I just said I'd dyed my hair and they let me through without a second glance.

'I'd forgotten about her wallet,' Helen said suddenly. 'Do you think I should send it on to her parents,' she looked at Gil, 'or is it too late?'

'Are you asking me as a parent or a journalist?'

'A parent, I guess.'

'In that case, I'd say it's never too late.'

'I sold my cameras,' Helen told him. 'To a second-hand dealer north of Oxford Street that I found on the Internet. He couldn't believe his luck.'

'And you remember all this?' Gil asked.

Helen shook her head. 'Just barely. Like I said. Fragments, glimmers, flashbacks glued together with logic and a fair amount of conjecture.'

'That won't stand up in court if it comes to it.'

Leaning over, Helen rested her hand briefly on his elbow.

For a moment neither of them spoke, but Gil didn't shrug her hand away.

'And Art?' he said eventually breaking the silence. 'Where was he, if the body isn't his?'

Helen took a deep breath. 'If you'd asked me that twenty minutes ago, I'd have said he was dead. Now?' She shuddered and looked out across the Dales, as if scanning the clusters of people, sheep and crows stretched out below them.

'Now, he could be anywhere.'

32

'What are you going to do now?' Gil asked as Helen unlatched the lychgate and he followed her into Wildfell's gardens.

'I'm not planning to run out on you, if that's what you're afraid of?'

'It's not . . .' Gil started, then stopped.

That was precisely what it was.

'Where would I go?' Helen said. 'I can't go to my sister's or my mother's – it wouldn't be fair on them. I could leave the country, I suppose, on Hélène Graham's passport. Perhaps I will eventually. But for now, I guess here is as safe as anywhere.'

The words hung unspoken between them.

Not very.

A stranger was looking for her, Art was missing presumed alive and her only ally was a journalist who couldn't decide whether to believe her. Helen almost laughed. She knew the feeling.

She handed Gil her key and he unlocked the back door, locking it again behind them.

'What about the man who was asking around after you yesterday?' he said. 'The journalist. Assuming he was a journalist?'

Helen sighed. 'If he's a journalist, let him come.'

Gil looked put out.

'If he's a journalist, you can call the police, like you promised.'

It didn't seem to appease him.

Gil paused. 'And Art?'

Helen looked at him, saw her own concern reflected back in his eyes.

If Art was out there, there was no point running.

'What I still don't understand is where Carl fits in,' Gil said as Helen made more tea and tipped the last of the milk into Ghost's saucer in the hope of luring him back. While he waited, Gil patted himself down in a futile search for a stray cigarette.

She sank down at the table and pushed a mug towards him.

'No biscuits, I'm afraid. No nothing.' She couldn't remember the last time she'd even been hungry. The hollowness was comforting.

Helen felt strangely calm. Calmer than she had for days. The fear was exhausting, but the possibility of Carl's death had drained every last bit of emotion. If Carl was dead and Art was alive, the world was as she'd always suspected; there was no justice.

'That's what I'm trying to work out. I know I texted him the morning after I left Syria, apologising for not saying goodbye. I didn't say why, just that I'd tell him next time he passed through Paris. There's probably a record of that in a central phone log somewhere, if you want to check.'

'I'll take your word for it,' Gil said, not without a trace of irony.

'We arranged to meet for supper,' Helen told him. 'At a bar in Bastille one Saturday night a few weeks later.'

'*The* Saturday night?'

She thought about it. 'Could have been, yes.'

'Do you remember how long was he staying in Paris?'

Helen hesitated. 'Overnight, I think. He had annual leave coming up and a hot new lover back in Berlin he wanted to spend it with.' She frowned. 'He said he'd stop over on the way. That was it.'

'Not so hot the lover bothered to investigate when Carl didn't turn up,' Gil said.

'True.' Helen shrugged. 'That's Carl for you.'

'Remember more,' Gil said.

'Gil . . . I can't just conjure it on demand. Don't you think I would if I could?'

'I'm serious. Try. Where did you go?'

Helen wrapped her hands around her mug and closed her eyes, trying to picture the last time she had seen Carl, feeling fragments coalesce.

'A bar in Bastille I liked.' She thought some more. 'It was a hot night and we chose a table on the street so Carl could smoke. Camels, always Camels. He'd buy

342

them by the crate in duty-free. For a while he had a South Korean boyfriend and afterwards he swore that what he missed most was the cut price cigarettes.'

'What did you talk about?'

'I don't remember.'

'Helen. He was an old friend. A dear friend. He's *dead*. You owe it to him to remember.'

Slamming her mug on the table so that tea sloshed on to the wood, Helen glared at Gil. How dare he?

'*I don't remember.*'

'You do,' Gil said. 'You know you do. It's in there somewhere. You just have to dig.'

They sat in silence listening to the crows chattering on the Dales, the floorboards creaking. Out on the main road, Helen thought she heard a car. 'I told him I was getting out,' she said eventually. 'Had got out. Carl thought I meant out of photography. He was outraged. Told me I was a natural. I said, "Why would I leave this behind?" Something like that.

'And Carl said, "If not this, then what?"'

Helen hesitated. 'He must have seen the answer in my eyes, because he emptied his beer and said, "I thought you were meant to be *really good together*." His words dripped sarcasm. "*A team*."

'"Who told you that?" I asked.

'"You did. Don't worry. I never believed you. No one believed you. I think, we just thought . . . Well, if you stayed that long you must have some reason we didn't know about. You must like . . ." Then he told me he'd been in the next room that night in Syria. The night we had the *argument* . . .

'And he told me it wasn't an argument. He said, "Walls

can be thin even in five-star hotels. I heard him rape you. It sounded endless. To be .honest, I considered coming round, but then I thought . . . well, you know."'

'What did he mean?' Gil asked. *'You know?'*

Helen swallowed hard. 'I guess he thought, each to their own.'

Gil nodded, put his mug back on the table and picked it up again when he realised he didn't have anything else to do with his hands.

'He asked me if I loved Art.'

'Did you?' Gil asked.

'No,' said Helen. 'I did. Once. At the beginning. Very much, I think.

'Carl wanted to know about my plans. Not that I had any. I was sleeping on floors, taking the occasional cheap hotel room while I decided which city to live in. To be honest, I wasn't sure I wanted to stay in Paris if Art was there. Same went for London I suppose. I was biding my time, waiting to see what Art would do. I'd heard he was in New York seeing a man about a job. I said as much to Carl.

'Carl just snorted. Said he'd heard something of the sort from a friend and made it pretty clear what he thought of Art's chances. Art wasn't big on gays. Carl called Art the *war junkie*. They'd never exactly been each other's biggest fans. Carl was just the one friend of mine Art never managed to see off.

Helen hesitated 'I told him that, in the short-term, I needed to go back to the flat, unless Art had changed the locks. Carl nearly choked on his beer. Asked if I was completely fucking mad.

'Not *back* back, I told him. Just in and out, to get my

stuff – most of my things were still there. Assuming Art hadn't trashed everything. It was too much of my life to leave.'

Helen stopped, mug poised in mid-air. She stared at Gil.

'He offered to come with me.'

Gil inhaled sharply. 'Are you sure?'

'Yes, I don't know . . . Yes, I think so. Oh God. I shouldn't have let him, but I was too grateful and too scared to go alone. I was probably even hoping he'd offer.'

'You're saying you think he was with you, that night in Paris?'

A tear dripped off her chin to the kitchen table and Helen wondered when she'd started crying. When she admitted she'd once loved Art, probably. He'd never been the man she thought he was. And it was a very long time since she'd been the woman she was back when they met. How could she have brought Carl into the middle of that?

Gil hadn't said anything or even appeared to notice. Even now he didn't comment.

'You really think Carl was at the flat with you?' he said. 'It's not just because I suggested it?'

Shaking her head, Helen put her head in her hands. Tears seeped through her fingers. 'I can see him in my head, almost. Putting my key fob against the courtyard door to open it. The big old door swinging open. I thought Art was away, but he must have been there when we got there or come back before I'd finished packing . . .'

Helen sat there sobbing, not caring if Gil stared.

Everything she'd ever had, every friend, everyone and everything that mattered, Art had to try to take it away. She hadn't killed him, Helen knew that now, if only because Gil said she couldn't have done. But she wished she had.

33

Dusk was beginning to settle by the time Gil got up to leave. Before he did he followed her from room to room while she checked the windows, and shut and locked every door she could. If he thought she was mad, he didn't show it. It wasn't as if he hadn't seen her do it before or heard the locks on the front door shift, one, two, three times whenever she shut that behind him.

They started on the ground floor where all the windows had sash locks.

Helen shot the bolt on the back door and did the same for the side door into the pantry. The French windows in the main drawing room were already locked top and bottom, although the wood was so rotten a good kick would cave them in. The door locked from either side so she locked it from the hall and took the key with her before heading upstairs to check the windows to her little drawing room.

All the bedrooms on the first floor had locks, but only on the inside. Helen made do with checking their windows and shutting each door firmly behind her. At the next stairs, Gil saw her hesitate and slipped ahead. The servants' quarters had horizontal windows high in the wall so they couldn't look out on whatever the family were doing in the gardens. There was a huge bath with curved legs that ended in ball claws sitting in the middle of a bathroom. China bowls were inset into a wide oak shelf like basins in a row.

'This place should be properly listed,' Gil muttered. He caught Helen's look and shrugged. 'How can this not be Grade I?'

Helen rolled her eyes and Gil grinned sheepishly. 'Don't retire,' he told her.

'Photographers don't.'

'Journalists shouldn't either.'

They came to a halt at the bottom of the attic stairs, where the door was locked and firmly bolted from their side.

'Do you want me to check?' Gil asked.

'Would you?' She didn't want to admit she hadn't dared explore before. She tried a light switch inside the door and nothing happened. So Gil led the way with the torch on his iPhone. A skylight was partly open and a rolled carpet beneath dripping wet. There was probably a matching stain on the ceiling of a servant's room below.

'Been open for ever,' said Gil, shutting it and wrestling the bolt as close to locked as he could get it.

He played his torch over the darkness around them, revealing mementoes of lives forgotten. A huge rocking horse grinned back, made piebald by peeling paint. A large painting, torn in one corner, showed a ringletted girl in a green dress peering at a monkey in a cage. On her shoulder sat a parrot. There were chairs stacked one upside down on the other. Rotting velvet revealed the horsehair of their seats. There was a mahogany prie-dieu, a walnut bureau so buckled with damp it looked like dented metal. A dozen paintings in cheap gilt frames leaned against a leather trunk, which would sell for thousands in a chichi London shop. The paintings were of the Dales, mostly. The Dales and Wildfell.

'Satisfied . . .?' asked Gil, when they'd done a more comprehensive circuit than Helen would have dared.

'I'm sorry.'

'I don't blame you.' He hesitated. 'Are you sure you don't want me to stay? On the sofa, I mean. Or in the bedroom, if the sofa's already taken. By you, that is.' He smiled, to make it clear he was joking.

'I'll be fine, really.'

'Or come with me. There's a spare room at the cottage. Stay there tonight.'

'That'll get them talking,' Helen grinned.

'Sod the lot of them,' he said with feeling.

Helen shook her head. 'And tomorrow? And the day after . . .?'

'What will you do?'

'Leave. Stay. Think about it.'

'You can't live like this, not indefinitely.'

'I've been living like this for years. I can barely remember any other way. Thank you for humouring me, though. I'll be fine now.'

She waited for him to realise that was his cue to go.

It was still early, but she was shattered and needed to lie down, even if she knew she wouldn't sleep. Too many memories, too many bad dreams, too much adrenalin in her blood. She'd take her laptop to the drawing room, tune the radio to something soothing and leave the light on while she dozed. Ghost would be furious. If he bothered to come back at all.

At the front door, Gil lurched slightly towards her, planting a kiss on her cheek. His hand squeezed her arm gently.

'Call me,' he said. 'If you need me.'

'I will,' Helen said. They both knew she wouldn't.

He was so embarrassed that he didn't look at her as she let him out; and he headed down the drive with his shoulders hunched, shaking his head as if cross at his own clumsiness. Killing the outside light, Helen locked the door and turned for the kitchen, with plans to fetch her laptop on the way upstairs, when a knock behind her made her stop. Cursing Gil, she unslid bolts and unlocked the door.

'What did you forget?'

A shadow, definitely not Gil.

She was pushing the door shut when the figure jammed its foot in the gap. If she'd been thinking straight, she'd have opened it a fraction, very quickly, then slammed it hard and hoped it hurt enough to make him step back. She didn't think of that in time. Instead she pushed hard, throwing her weight against it.

'Helen . . . Wait.'

Stopping, she opened the door slightly and peered at the silhouette. Forcing herself to focus through the blood racing in her head. 'Tom?'

'Who did you think it was?'

Helen shuddered, glanced over his shoulder and he turned, following her gaze to see what was there. Only wind in the trees, wet gravel and the outline of rusty gates. Needs a padlock, Helen thought, then laughed out loud at her own absurdity.

Tom looked uncomfortable. 'Can I come in?'

'What are you doing here?'

'I've been looking for you.'

'Here? In the last few days? In the village?'

'Yes.'

Helen laughed again, high-pitched, hysterical.

'That was you?'

'Yes.'

She sagged against the door jamb in relief.

'Why are you looking for me?'

'For God's sake.' Tom sounded almost furious. 'Why do you think? You called me from Paris, remember? In the middle of the night. You called me from Paris and when I asked if you were all right you didn't answer. When I asked where you were, you put the phone down on me.'

'I shouldn't have called.'

'Yes, you should. We had a deal.'

She looked at him blankly. He was too relieved to have found her, too busy trying to decide what to say next, to notice.

'Deal?'

'If either of us was in trouble, the other would help.'

Helen laughed. 'We were *sixteen*.'

'What difference does that make?'

Helen looked at her first serious boyfriend, standing

on the doorstep in front of her. The first boy she'd ever loved, if not the first she slept with. Although he should have been. The boy she'd walked away from over a stupid row about her being an hour late for no good reason. Getting her dumping in before he dumped her. Mistake. The first of many. Twenty years older now. Twenty years more lived in.

She felt herself smile. 'How did you find me?'

'Your sister. Well, your sister initially. She told me about the psychiatrist in London. Said if you'd go to anyone it would be her. It was a process of elimination to find Ms Harris. There aren't many with her specialisms and fewer still called Caroline. The clinic refused to tell me whether you'd been in touch so I visited and played the doctor card. Don't worry,' he added, seeing Helen's expression. 'She didn't tell me anything – well, nothing medical I couldn't work out for myself.'

'How *did* you find me then?'

Tom grinned. Still the same Tom grin, slightly lopsided, slightly more crinkles around his eyes. 'A huge outcrop of rock staring down over a patchwork landscape?'

'What?'

'That's what you said to Ms Harris. "A huge outcrop of rock staring down over a patchwork landscape." That, and the fact you told her receptionist you'd be coming into King's Cross. Come on, Helen. You always wanted us to come up here when we were kids. You were obsessed with the bloody Brontës. It took a while, but once I narrowed down the area, talk of the incomer was like a breadcrumb trail right to you.

'You know the weird thing? I found a picture on the Internet from a few years ago to show round. Now I'm here, I can see it doesn't look like you at all. Hair, eyes, nothing. I should have just used one of my old ones.'

Helen didn't know whether to be impressed or horrified. Given away by a shared teenage memory.

'Can I come in?'

She glanced over his shoulder.

'The police don't know I'm here,' he said, stepping into the hall.

'It's not that. I'm not afraid of the police. I just don't want to be found by Art.'

'Helen, Art's dead. He died in the fire.'

'You're wrong. He didn't.'

Without comment, he watched her lock and bolt them into Wildfell and turn the lights off in the hall before leading him to the kitchen. 'Coffee . . . or something stronger?'

Tom inclined his head towards the packet of pills on the worktop. 'How long have you been taking those things?'

Helen shrugged and filled the kettle. 'Too long and not long enough.'

Tom sighed.

'I hope you're not hungry,' she added, loading coffee into the jug, and picking up two mugs, 'because my culinary skills haven't developed in the last twenty years either. It's bread and cheese or cheese and bread. Except I'm out of cheese and I've only got sliced.'

Tom shook his head. 'I'm not hungry.'

They talked for hours, up in the little sitting room that Helen was aware had become something of a confessional. Well, Helen talked and Tom listened, occasionally prompting her with another question. He reminded her of Gil like that. Doctors and journalists obviously shared a few tactics. Well, the good ones did. As she spoke, reprising everything she'd already told Gil, her memories started to solidify. When the coffee went cold, Tom headed downstairs to make more while Helen sat on the old settee listening to the comfortable sounds of human existence below. It occurred to her as she listened that he was talking to someone. Murmuring to himself? A thought slipped in that he was on the phone to someone, and she pushed it away.

When he returned, not with coffee, but two mugs and a bottle of red under his arm, Helen was surprised to see Ghost pad in behind him. Back for the first time in days.

'Wow,' she said. 'That's impressive. He doesn't like anyone.'

'This one?' Tom said. 'You're kidding? He's been all over me.'

'Who were you talking to, down there?'

Tom inclined his head towards his ankles. 'Him. Who else? He has some things to say about the level of service around here.'

Helen looked at Tom, at the cat winding itself around his legs and then back at Tom. Then she pushed herself out of the chair, took the mugs from his hands and set them on the floor. It was time, in fact it was long past time. 'Can we talk about this later?'

'If you want . . . Where are you going?'

'To bed. Are you coming?'

Sun was pouring through the window, long lancing shafts that brightened crumbling plaster on the wall. Her eyes adjusted and she looked up to see Tom resting on his elbow, looking down at her. His smile was wry. 'I'm sorry,' she said. 'I haven't slept properly in months. Years.'

'It's all right,' he grinned. 'I've waited twenty years, what's another night?'

When he slid from the bed, Helen couldn't help noticing he was massaging his upper arm.

'Me?' she asked.

He grinned ruefully. 'Lost all feeling in it at about three a.m. Didn't want to move and wake you.' He smiled, glanced towards the Dales and smiled again, then headed for the loo. When he came back, Helen took her turn, aware of him watching her slip from the bed as she'd watched him.

He was older than she remembered, obviously.

He grinned in the wintery sun.

'You were my first' she said. 'The first to touch me. The first to do most things.'

'Except the one that counted.'

'The one I wish I'd given you.'

He smiled. 'Do you mean that?'

'Totally. It took me years to work out it's not the age you first sleep with a boy that matters. It's who you sleep with. I couldn't even get that right.'

34

Gil had coffee and banana bread in the new Costa that used to be the antique shop and then a picture framers and finally a card shop that closed when Gil was still enough months away from retirement to believe he hadn't decided where to live. The site had lain empty for a while, and everybody had made a huge fuss when they heard the chain was moving in. Who knew, people said darkly, what would be next. It was the first chain in the network of villages that surrounded their part of the Dales. If you ignored the Co-op in the next village along, and that big bank the Chinese owned, and the Tesco Metro at the garage on the way to Keighley.

That's different, Gil was told.

It was pretty crowded at 8.30 a.m., given the number of villagers who'd claimed they'd never step through its door. Taking his coffee and cake to a corner table near the window, Gil opened his laptop and logged on to next door's Wi-Fi, which wasn't locked, and began to work his way through that day's papers.

In between he checked his phone in case he'd missed a call from Helen when he wasn't looking. He'd been doing it for the last twelve hours.

After the papers, Gil went through his usual routine, checking Huntingdon's Twitter, Facebook and LinkedIn profiles, scouring Google for Huntingdon, Lawrence and now Ackerman, despite the absence of any further alerts. He didn't expect to find anything and his expectations weren't disappointed. But the silence bothered him nonetheless. If Huntingdon had gone to ground, where the hell was he?

Gil glanced out of the window, half expecting to see the deformed face of a monster staring in. Instead he saw a small child in a red anorak fighting to get out of his buggy.

When he'd finished, he checked his own Facebook page.

A few friend requests from people he'd never heard of and had no friends in common with; nothing from Karen. Then he remembered the page he'd set up in order to friend Mark Ridley. Unsurprisingly, the friend request hadn't been accepted but there was a message, a terse one-liner: **Don't know who you are, mate. But you must have the wrong Mark Ridley. I haven't been looking for Helen Lawrence.**

Frowning, Gil opened Ridley's profile on Facebook, compared it with the one on LinkedIn and everything else he knew about him. It was the right Mark Ridley, he knew it.

So either Ridley was lying . . .

Or he wasn't.

Gil bought another coffee, extra shot this time, and drank it to a soundtrack of hummable songs from the eighties for which he mostly knew the words or at least the choruses. Occasionally he'd snap awake to the early notes of something from the seventies and feel for a second how he used to feel when the tracks were new.

It's a rat trap Judy, and we've been caught.

So, what were the alternatives? Ridley was lying: in which case he *was* looking for Helen but wasn't about to tell any random chancer on social media his business. Fair enough, Gil thought, protect your leads and all that. It was what Ridley planned to do if and when he found Helen that bothered him. It wasn't losing an exclusive that scared Gil – he'd long since given up on that, he was surprised to realise. He was scared for Helen. But if Ridley was telling the truth, if he really hadn't been looking for Helen . . .

Then someone else was.

Someone who was using Mark Ridley's name.

Gil could only think of one person who would have the inside knowledge to do that.

When what remained of his second coffee was drunk, Gil folded down his laptop lid and transferred to The Café on the Corner, where the cappuccino was more expensive and the music classical, courtesy of Classic FM. Helen still hadn't called and without her number the only way of contacting her was to turn up on her doorstep. It was doubt that stopped him. What would he say when he got there? Either he'd upset her, or she'd just think he was making excuses to see her. He needed more detail before he went again.

Gil was glad when the clock reached twelve and he could relocate to The Bull. Ordering a pint, he settled himself in his corner. Then he went home and watched bad afternoon television with one eye on his laptop and read a chapter of a crime novel he barely remembered. He was back at the door of The Bull on the dot of six.

Conversation dipped the way it always did whenever a stranger walked in; not so much unfriendliness as watchfulness; as everyone waited to see if the newcomer was one of those who'd smile and want to talk. This man walked to the bar carrying a bag of shopping from the General Stores and ordered a pint, and while it was pouring asked a question. The girl holding the fort behind the bar glanced over his shoulder to where Gil sat. She turned her head away before the man had time to turn to see where she was looking.

He said something low and serious and she seemed troubled. This time when she looked across Gil nodded and the girl pointed him out. She did it discreetly, with a jerk of her chin towards the table Gil now thought of as his.

'Mr Markham?'

'Who's asking?' Gil had heard it used in a film, and then several times in a row on different television shows. It seemed to work, though; because the man blinked and immediately adjusted his expression.

'Tom . . . Tom Bretton. I'm a friend of Helen's.'

'Who?' Gil picked up his pint and stared at the beer moodily, hoping the man hadn't caught the flicker of recognition when he announced himself. The beer was

cloudy as ditchwater with flakes of yeast. He was learning
to like it. Well, he told himself he was learning.

'I know you know Helen, Mr Markham.'

'Don't tell me what I know.'

The stranger gestured at the spare chair opposite and,
when Gil didn't react, he took it anyway. He ran his
hand through his hair and sighed. He looked tired, and
worried, and uncertain. What he didn't look, at least to
Gil, was remotely dangerous.

'What did you say to May?'

'Who . . .?'

'The landlord's granddaughter.'

'I told her I was a doctor. That I had something I
needed to discuss with you but that I didn't know you
by sight.'

'How much of that is true?'

'All of it.'

'Just not in the way she thought?'

The stranger shrugged.

'What do you want?' Gil asked. He could see the
stranger, he supposed he should try to think of him as
Tom, choosing his words with care. When they came,
they weren't what Gil expected.

'Someone's slashed the wheels of my hire car.'

Gil shrugged.

'My hire car,' Tom repeated. 'They slashed all four.'
He glanced at the pint in Gil's hand. 'You fit to drive?'

'You've come in here to ask me for a lift?' Gil sounded
incredulous.

'I'm meant to be seeing Helen.'

'Call her. Whoever she is. Presumably you have a
number?'

'I forgot to ask her for it.'

Gil looked up at this.

'I was out there until an hour or so ago. I should have got her number then.'

'She didn't suggest you take it?' Gil asked, more jealous than he dared admit.

'We, uh, no she didn't and I forgot to ask.' Tom looked uncomfortable.

'You went out there this morning?' Gil said, forgetting to pretend he didn't know where there was.

'No,' Tom said. 'I went out there last night.' He nodded. 'I waited until after you left. That was you, wasn't it?'

Gil didn't answer.

'Mr Markham,' Tom said. 'I'm not the enemy. I'm a friend of Helen's. An old friend. And if the things she's told me – things I know she's told you – are even halfway true, I'm scared for her. I was scared even before someone slashed my tyres.'

'Could be kids,' Gil said. 'They don't like tourists or incomers.'

'And you don't either?'

'I'm an incomer. Well, sort of. Never really belonged.'

'I don't think kids did it. Too neat. Too professional.' Gil could see the impatience on Tom Bretton's face, the difficulty with which he made himself answer Gil's time-wasting comments.

'Call the police. If you're scared for her.'

'And say what? I've found a woman French police apparently want to eliminate from their enquiries? That I think she's being hunted by someone who until last night I thought was dead?'

Gil pushed back his chair so hard the squeak of wood

361

on stone brought the pub to sudden silence. He shrugged his apologies, half on the edge, but not yet out of, his chair.

'Huntingdon?'

'I think she's mad to have talked to a journalist . . .'

Gil rounded on him. 'I think she's mad to trust someone she hasn't seen in twenty years.' Then he caught himself, heard the jealousy talking. 'If I was going to anyone it would be the police and I'm starting to wonder if I should. Come on. We can talk in my car.'

The entire Bull stilled to watch them leave.

On the way out, Gil stopped to talk to the landlord's granddaughter, who was looking anxious.

'It was OK me saying?' she asked.

'Of course.'

'I thought, him being a doctor and all.'

'It was fine, I promise.'

'Good. Someone else was in here asking.' She blushed. 'About the French woman. He asked where she lived. Granddad said I was to tell you.'

'You didn't tell him?'

'No, but I think one of the incomers did.'

The stone bridge over the burn had been there long enough for everyone to say for ever, although 1787 carved into the side said it was nothing like that long. It was the width required to let two riders pass in opposite directions or a single coach cross if there was no other traffic. An old metal sign gave its width in feet and inches and warned that it was unsuitable for lorries. The size and shape of the lorry on the sign hadn't been seen on the road for years.

'Shit,' Tom said.

Heading towards them from the far side of the bridge were a flock of Swaledale, all off-white wool and curling horns. The first crested the bridge at a trot and the wave carried the rest behind him. Gil dragged on the wheel of his old Golf and pulled as tight to the drystone wall as he could manage, car half on the road and half on the bank.

'Can't you get past them?'

Snorting, Gil asked, 'How am I meant to get past that lot?'

At the sight of the car some of the sheep broke away and Gil restarted his engine and reversed until the stone wall was no longer beside the car and he could pull off the road entirely. The sheep who'd broken away rejoined the herd.

'We wait,' he said, before Tom had time to say anything else. 'Driving through that lot isn't an option.' And wait they did, while seemingly endless sheep trotted past the car until all that was left were the dawdlers, a collie and a girl not much out of her teens who raised her hand in passing. 'Seen a car?' Gil asked her.

'What kind of car?'

'Any kind.'

'No,' she said.

35

Ghost sits across the lintel of the kitchen door, scowling when she returns from putting out rubbish. Standing, he arches his back, bends his spine in the opposite direction so his head is flat to the ground and sits down sulkily.

'Move then.'

When she's certain he has no intention of doing any such thing, Helen steps over him, shutting the door behind her, bolting it top and bottom. If Ghost wants to come in he can damn well use the water butt, and the missing pane in the pantry window, which she dutifully uncovered for him. The plates she and Tom used for toast are still in the sink, along with several mismatched glasses and mugs. Knowing the water from the hot tap won't be hot enough on its own to wash up, she boils a kettle first, and later puts the newly clean dishes neatly on the rack, running the mugs and glasses under a dribble of cold before upending them. The knives and teaspoons she dries with a tea towel and puts in a drawer that contained beetles and a desiccated bat when she first moved in.

She's humming, something from when she was younger.

Something really dated. The Cranberries, quite possibly. From habit, she pours herself a glass of water, and wanders up to the little sitting room with the water in one hand and her laptop in the other. Putting the water on the table, she plugs in her laptop and reaches for the lamp.

'Leave it.'

Helen jumps so hard she knocks the water over. It drips in the half-light on to synthetic carpet.

'Now look what you've done.'

Instinctively she drops to her knees, not knowing what to use to wipe it up. Art sighs.

'Fetch a towel from the bathroom.' He says it like she's stupid, like she'd lose her own head if it wasn't screwed on.

She does as he says, hurrying to grab a towel from the rail and mopping frantically at the wet carpet.

'Start with the table.'

Lifting the lamp, she remembers to dry its base before putting it down on a dry patch of carpet. She wipes the table top, returns the lamp and dabs at the carpet below the table as best she can. Then, with the room and the corridor in near darkness, she replaces the now damp towel on the rail and returns to where Art waits, in Gil's armchair. She could run for the front door and wrestle its bolts open, but there's no point. By the time she's unlocked it he'll have caught up with her. And that would be worse. In trying to lock the monsters out, she's locked herself in. The irony doesn't escape her.

'Strange place to live,' Art says, conversationally.

'The flat burned down.'

'I know, Helen. How did that happen?'

Helen shrugs, before remembering how much he hates her shrugging. 'I don't know,' she says truthfully. 'I woke up on the bed and there was smoke. Flames were licking up the curtains. The red ones on the long window.'

'The red ones on the long window . . .' he mimics.

'I managed to get out.'

'That was clever of you, Helen . . . Why did you run away?'

'Why did I . . .?'

'Helen . . .'

'I don't know. There was a body. I saw a body. I thought it was you. There were flames.' She's talking too fast.

'You thought it was me, and you didn't check to see if I was alive?'

She hesitates long enough to feel the air chill. Art never likes having to wait for answers. He doesn't like having to wait for anything. Being *made* to wait, as he put it. In the year it went wrong, after the miscarriage, her chief rebellion had been walking too slowly.

'Art, there was a body. The police found a body.'

Carl, she wants to say, it was Carl. Art, why did you kill Carl? She forces herself to stay silent.

'And you saw it?'

'Not clearly.' She can see it now, in her head, though. She can see it through an orange haze. She can see what she couldn't see before. That the body is too short and thickset, the torso too muscular, to be Art. 'Yes . . . yes, I saw it.'

The atmosphere crackles around her uninvited guest, she can almost hear it. 'How do you think this fire started, Helen?'

'I don't know. I don't remember anything at all.'

'You don't?'

'It's all blank.'

'Shock,' he says thoughtfully. 'That stress thing you get.'

He gets up and walks towards her and Helen feels her body still.

'You must have been terrified,' he says. 'So terrified, you didn't think to go to the police.'

Helen opens her mouth, shuts it again, brain rushing to work out what she's supposed to say next.

'They're looking for you, you know. The police. Must be frightening for you.'

His breath is hot on her neck as he comes to stand behind her. Helen forces herself not to freeze, to wait for whatever comes next. The worst thing is she has no idea what that might be. He puts his hand up to the back of her neck and squeezes slightly. He could be massaging the muscles there. He could be seeing how tense she is. He could be about to strangle her. Very slowly he begins to stroke her hair.

'I don't like your hair like this, Helen,' he says. 'The cut's terrible. The colour's wrong. You should dye it back.'

The action is precise, agonisingly repetitive.

'Aren't you glad to see me, Helen?'

She nods, gets away without answering properly because he can feel the nod beneath his fingers.

'I'm glad,' Art says. 'So glad I've found you. It hasn't been easy you know.' He puts his arms around her, hugging her tight. She can feel him go hard against her. His hands grip the side of her thighs, thumbs digging into the front as he holds her in place. There will be bruises. They both know there will be bruises.

'We should go to bed,' he says. 'It's been a while. I've missed you so very much.'

Helen swallows. She doesn't know what to say. Except, she does. With Art there is only ever one answer.

'Of course,' she says.

He knows where her room is. Just as he knew there was a bathroom on this floor when he sent her for a towel. She tries not to wonder how long he's been in the house. How long he's been watching. Did he get in when she put out the rubbish? Or before? A long time before, waiting silently for the right moment? She pushes the thought away. When he flicks on the light in her bedroom, pulls back the blankets and looks at the bottom sheet she wonders what he thinks he knows.

'Undress then.'

She kicks off her trainers. Remembering at the last minute to put them together neatly.

Art smiles, watching as she pulls her T-shirt over her head and folds it before putting it on the chair. She hesitates and his smile freezes, then she reaches behind to undo her bra. 'You always did have a good body,' he says, and she makes herself remain still as he reaches for her breasts.

'You like that, don't you?'

His eyes are fixed on hers in an unbroken stare. It always was one of the most unnerving things about him.

'You like everything I do . . . Touch yourself.'

His fingers tighten when she doesn't immediately obey. The slight smile sliding from his lips, his gaze hardening.

'I-I need to use the loo,' says Helen.

'*I need to use the loo . . .*'

She hates the mockery with which he repeats her words, she always has.

He examines her, as if looking at a curious object, his grip just this side of properly hurting as he leans in close for a better look. She refuses to shiver. Her bladder will not empty itself. It will not.

'When did you last have a bath?'

'This morning.'

'Helen . . .'

'Yesterday. I had one yesterday.'

'Morning or night?'

'Morning.' It's the right answer. Sighing, Art releases her. 'Wash well when you're done. All over. And clean your teeth.'

In the bathroom the shakes set in, where Art can't see them and decide he'd like to amuse himself by deepening her fear. After she's peed, she catches sight of herself half-naked in the mirror. There is such fear in her eyes. A look that wasn't there this morning.

It has been there as long as Art has.

'Don't,' she tells herself. 'Either wash and get back in there or think of something else.' But what? That's the problem. What else?

369

She flushes the loo again, very loudly this time. Holding the handle to drain the cistern.

See, I have been doing something.

Running the tap, she splashes water on her face and looks up to see tears. On holiday with Art, a belated honeymoon at a hotel in Turkey he chose from a boutique website – Just us, babes, help us get over it, what more could we want? – an argument on the first night left her with bruises impossible to hide beneath bikini bottoms. A middle-aged woman climbing out of the pool behind her came up to Helen later, when she was waiting for Art in the bar, and told her to get out now because it would only get worse. She was trying to be kind, Helen knew that now. At the time, two days into a two-week holiday, two months married, one month miscarried, it felt like cruelty.

Being with Art wasn't something she knew how to get out of.

'Don't get yourself killed,' the woman had whispered, squeezing Helen's arm, her expression a mixture of exasperation and despair.

Don't get yourself killed.

What was it Art said? *You didn't check to see if I was alive.*

Only, the body wasn't him, was it? And then his next question. 'How did the fire start?' When she'd replied that she didn't know, he'd said, 'You don't remember anything at all?'

Was that why she was still alive? She didn't remember anything at all . . .

Helen has pushed open the bathroom window without realising.

The roof of the outhouse slides away towards the ground. Flushing the loo one final time, she turns on both taps to the basin, grabs a filthy T-shirt from the laundry pile and drags it over her head before clambering on to the cistern and squeezing through the window, pulling it to behind her.

Bare feet slide on filthy tiles, slip over the edge and she tumbles down, almost managing to land upright, until she buckles at the last minute, feeling rose-thorns rip her arm.

Up above, there's a crash as the bathroom door is booted in. Art slams open the window and peers down as she scrambles into the hedge out of sight. He hates getting his nails dirty. He'll regard kicking in the door as getting his nails dirty. She waits for as long as she dares, and then crawls along the side of the outhouse, down past the stables and ducks inside a square of rotting and overgrown boxwood topiary just as Art appears round the side of the house.

Far from looking angry, he's smiling. As if her presumption in trying to escape amuses him. Helen feels nausea rise. Pushing back into her shelter, she watches him hesitate as he looks around the ruined garden and his gaze seems to settle on her. It's lighter outside than in the darkened house but sunset has been and dusk is soon.

There's a rustle and Art swings round in time to see Ghost jump from the pantry window. Art loathes cats. He steps towards Ghost, who stares him out. Art takes another step and the cat eyes him contemptuously. When Helen sees Art dip for a rock, she crawls from her hiding place, her pale T-shirt catching his eye in the twilight.

'Helen . . .'

She hesitates.

'Don't make me come after you.'

Turning, she sees him begin to move towards her.

Suddenly the cat streaks across wet grass as if he's spotted prey and passes just in front of Art, who trips. A howl of fury bursts from Ghost, who hisses and then yowls again, his anger echoing in waves off rotting walls. Still down, Art kicks out and misses.

Breaking cover, Helen runs. Through the lychgate, which slams behind her as she heads up the path towards the Dales. In the distance she can hear Art calling her name. Seconds later, the gate slams again and she knows he's behind her.

36

The front door stands open and the black cat Helen has adopted, although it was probably the other way round, lies across the step. It glares balefully, which seems to be its job, and looks not remotely surprised when both of the newcomers step over him.

'Helen . . .' Tom's shout is loud enough to fill the house. He looks in the kitchen, tries the door to the downstairs drawing room, which is locked, and races upstairs towards the small sitting room. Gil follows. He'd have been more careful; called from the front door, taken longer to search downstairs, kept calling Helen's name as he went upstairs. He finds Tom standing in the doorway of Helen's bedroom, an unreadable expression on his face.

In his hands are a T-shirt and a bra. A slightly muddy pair of women's plimsolls sit neatly on top of a discarded magazine.

'There's a tap running.'

Tom keeps looking at the T-shirt and bra.

In the bathroom there are two taps running into the basin, the hot tank has run entirely cold. Turning them both off, Gil instinctively mops up splashes with the bath mat. He looks at the wide-open window, the scattered pile of filthy clothes, and the unexpectedly clean track down the middle of otherwise filthy roof tiles.

'She got away.'

Tom glances up from the clothes he's clutching as Gil comes back into the room.

'She escaped through the bathroom window. You can see how she got to the ground. It has to be Huntingdon. It was never Ridley. It was always Huntingdon.'

Tom opens his mouth as if to ask what the hell he's on about and then says, 'I'll call the police.'

Gil shakes his head. 'They'll tell you to wait here until they arrive. Do you want to wait here until they arrive?'

'They'll have a helicopter.'

'Which will take hours to get airborne.' He sees that Tom is about to object and cuts him off. 'The paperwork, not the actual take-off. Call them when we know what's happening. Of course, you'll have to work out what to say first . . .' Together they go downstairs. It's Tom who discovers blood on the roses. He looks for more and is relieved when he doesn't find it.

'Gil, we need the police.'

'And you'll say what? Someone back from the dead is trying to kill someone the French police want to eliminate from their enquiries?'

Tom looks at Gil. 'But you said the body wasn't his?'

'It isn't. And Helen didn't start the fire. It seems the Paris fire brigade now suspect it began in an empty flat below.' Gil can almost see the thought behind Tom's eyes. 'Spit it out. We haven't got time to waste.'

'You're right. We need to go. I should have gone after her once before.' His face sets. 'Hang on. I'll be back in a sec.' When he returns, he's clutching a hatchet taken from the outhouse.

'We'd better find her before Huntingdon does.'

'We will,' Gil says. 'I know the Dales like the back of my hand, and I know where she's going.' He hesitates. 'Although I doubt she does. Not yet.' Without waiting to see if Tom will follow, he heads for the lychgate and hears it shut as Tom comes through behind him.

The sun was setting as they drove up to Wildfell, dusk is drawing in as they go through the gate and the Dales are in darkness by the time the ground under their feet gives way to gorse, bracken and the wild grass that grows faster than the few feet using the path up from Wildfell can keep trodden.

The previous days' rain has emptied the sky and the afternoon sun burned off what remained of the clouds. Above them, stars spread in a huge bowl, only fading at the edges where the light of distant cities intrudes. The Dales flow before them like a wild sea and in the distance like a floundering ship stands the Scar, sharp in the darkness. As always, when he looks at it, Gil feels himself drawn by its mass.

'She'll go there,' he says.

'How do you know?'

'I just do.'

'We should shout as we go.'

Gil shakes his head. 'No. We should listen. Shouting

will warn him we're coming and if he's got her already he'll keep her quiet until we pass.'

'You're a journalist?'

'Most of my life.'

'What else did you do?'

'Short-term commission.' Gil saw Tom's blankness. 'Three years in the army. Not for me, I discovered . . . We should speed up.'

'You're sure that's where she'll go?'

'I think so.'

'You said—'

'That's where she'll go.' He lets Tom push ahead; he can hardly lose his way since there's no way to lose; all he has to do is keep heading for the Scar looming in the distance. The young man – well, probably not that young, younger – walks with his head down and his body bent slightly forward. When he slows, Gil thinks he's heard something.

'Last night . . .' Tom says. He hesitates and Gil knows that's somewhere neither of them really wants to go. 'Helen said something I didn't get about a boy. But there's no sign of a boy at the house. And her sister didn't mention anything.'

'He's Iraqi,' Gil says.

'She adopted him?'

Gil shakes his head, almost invisible in the looming darkness. 'He's dead.'

Tom stops, and Gil jerks his head to say they should keep going. He wants to hate this younger man with his vague good looks, hesitation and quiet intensity. Gil doesn't doubt that in some way, Tom has a claim on Helen's affections; although you aren't meant to think

like that these days. The way Tom stared at the bra and
T-shirt, his shock was almost physical. The way he dashed
outside to grab the hatchet now hanging loosely from
his hand. Even though Gil can see that going after
psychopaths in the dark is the last thing Tom is cut out
to do.

'She took his photograph. In Iraq,' Gil says, not so
much for something to say as to help keep thoughts of
Tom and Helen at bay. 'You probably saw it in the papers,
just didn't make the connection. He died right before
she got together with Art. The shock of it was probably
why she got together with Art. She more or less said as
much.'

Tom stares at him, confusion evident on his face.

'How much did she tell you?' Gil asks.

'Enough,' Tom shrugs.

'Syria?'

'I'm not sure she got as far as Syria. We . . . She
crashed out, she was tired.'

'It was bad,' Gil says shortly. 'It's been bad for a long
time.'

'Why did she tell you all this?'

'She needed someone to talk to. I was there . . .' And
she was buying my silence with confidences and secrets,
Gil doesn't add.

'If he was hurting her, why did she stay?'

'Ask her.' Gil catches himself. 'Actually, don't. I think
she's had enough of that question. She'll talk about it if
she wants.' He hesitates, then says it anyway. 'I thought
I saw the child once. Staring from the back of her car. I
had a grandmother who saw things. That said, I'm not
sure I believe in things like that.'

'You're saying he's a ghost?' Though Gil can barely make out Tom's face in the gloom, he knows he's looking at him as if he's mad.

Gil sighs heavily. 'He haunts her, if that's what you mean. It's not the same. As for me, I was probably just seeing things.'

'We need to speed up,' Tom says.

Nodding, Gil increases his pace.

The Scar looks closer than it is, so obvious and visible in the night-dark sea of gorse and grass. A couple of miles? Surely not that far . . . Tonight it feels centuries distant and sharper than he remembers. The moon is halfway to being a sliver but it lights the Scar's edges with a tallow glow and muted light from a distant urban sprawl beyond makes it stand out against the sky. She will go there. Gil knows she will go there. She will go there, and her tormenter will go there, and he and Tom will follow after and should any come out of this alive they won't believe the Scar was calling.

He's beginning to sound like his grandmother.

Keep up, Gil tells himself. That's all he's ever been trying to do. Gorse drags at his suit trousers and thorns scratch his wrists and he barely lets himself notice. When this is done – however this is done, he thinks darkly – if he is still alive, he will call Liza and he will ask her out for dinner and if she offers he will sleep with her, because he likes Liza and he wants to sleep with her, and he will make his peace with his daughters, if that is possible, and with their mother and her no-longer-new partner. Her *husband*, however much he hates that word. He will not let, he cannot bear to let, what has happened to Helen happen to them. He should never have let the gap grow to the point where he couldn't be certain they'd tell him if it did.

'You're out there,' Gil whispers.

Even he doesn't know if he means Helen, her attacker, or the Scar. They stop to listen in case they can hear Helen calling for help or her attacker blundering through the gorse. Although Art doesn't seem the type to blunder. He seems the silent stalker type. Gil has come across more than a few of those in his life. Mostly standing in the dock, being glared at by the hollow-eyed family of their victim. It's the ones who never go to court, whose violence and cruelty are hidden that are the most dangerous.

Helen called Art the master of the unseen bruise. She said it with a shiver. Gil hadn't been sure whether or not to believe her. He believes her now.

37

'Helen. Stop NOW.'

Helen does. She stops dead on the path from the lychgate, heart pounding behind her ribs, wrists burning from where they've been torn by thorns. The pain feels familiar, not welcome but expected. She stops and turns and he's not even running after her now. He's slowed to a steady walk. When he sees her looking, he stops altogether.

'Come here.'

Years of obeying lift one foot from the ground. What is the worst he can do? Short of killing her, there isn't much he hasn't tried already. Why not let him do that? A sense of relief courses through her at the thought. As if she always knew this was how it would end. That what the woman said to her in Turkey was bound to prove true.

'Faster. You pathetic little fool.'

He shouldn't have spoken. All the he-shouldn't-have-spokens collide.

Would you like to go out for dinner? Why don't you stay? Let's move in together. I think we should marry.

For a second she would have gone to him; habit, obedience and a crushed spirit delivering her to his cold, waiting anger. He shouldn't have spoken because his voice unexpectedly wakes her, she hesitates mid-step. For a moment she'd forgotten how much she hates it. He sees her begin to turn, and there's just enough moonlight to reveal his fury. Art will never forgive her this. No amount of cajoling, of obeying, of curling up into a ball, will be enough.

This time when she runs, she runs.

Behind her he stumbles and curses viciously. Then she hears the sound of him running and runs faster. Too late, she realises she should have headed for the village or thrown herself on the mercy of the first car to sweep along the road and catch her in its headlights. This path leads up to the Dales, which stretch like an ocean until she expects to feel water splash around her knees. The gorse drags against her ankles and she struggles to run faster, feeling thorns whip as air scalds her throat and her heart hammers. She can't run this hard for much longer; and she can't afford to slow down or risk turning to see how far he is behind.

There's nowhere safe out here. No forests to hide in or trees to climb. There are ditches and dips, old drystone walls and new ones, but nothing that will provide enough shelter for her to hide without the man who follows knowing where she's hidden. So she runs, and keeps running, until her throat is as tight as if it's been gripped, and her breath is raw. Her ribs hurt, and there's a stitch in her side as brutal as the after-effects of any punch.

'Helen. Enough . . .'

Keep shouting, she thinks. *Shout every time you see me falter or seem about to stop. I can run from that voice for ever. I can run from it faster and for longer than you can try to keep up.* She wants to believe that. She knows she can't afford to stop, that her fear creates the adrenalin that keeps her running, and lactic acid is what burns in her muscles, making them want to lock. Her thoughts splinter. She's watching herself run as if from a distance. She's watching as she pushes herself over the edge of what she can stand.

She's been here before many times: outside herself, watching some pathetic snivelling thing face down on a bed, curled around its whimpers and misery on the floor. What comes next is darkness, and waking with tears and bruises she doesn't remember acquiring.

She's always grateful for that.

A drystone wall appears and she runs beside it until she realises she's being herded into a corner. So she swings herself up, rolling clumsily over and tearing her jeans on flint before landing on the other side. Run, she tells herself. Run.

He grunts as he rolls himself on to the wall, grunts louder as he lands. She can hear his ragged breath in the silences between hers. This is every nightmare from which she's ever woken in a glaze of sweat. Hunted from room to room, running blindly for her life. Which came first? The fear or the dreams?

She's underwater, drowning, lungs burning and throat tight from trying to drag in enough air to keep moving.

As she puts one foot in front of the other, running blind, at the mercy of the first stone to send her sprawling, the first rabbit hole to break her ankle, she knows her body is shutting down everything except what it needs to survive. She's seen it a million times.

God knows she's seen it.

In famines and battle zones and places where badly built buildings fall in on those inside. Her mind is slowly separating from her body. She will run and run until she drops, until the darkness pulling at the edges of her mind takes her. If she goes down this time she won't wake. The last thing she'll see is Art standing over her. The last thing she'll remember is his face.

The ground goes soggy beneath the grass, her toes suddenly cold from water. Before she knows it, she's crossed a stream. Seconds later Art does the same. The ground is hard beneath her feet again, the rough grass dry enough to lacerate her ankles.

She runs on despite the pain.

A ripped knee and lacerated ankles are nothing to what Art will do. Out here, alone, with no thin walls to make him snap at her, no need to worry about people in the flat below, what's to stop him? She wonders if she should shout for help. But why waste the breath when there is no one out here to help her?

In the middle of a moor in the early hours of the night, chased by the man who once pledged to love and cherish her above all else. Behind her, she hears a curse and turns before she can stop herself, to see Art tumble over a grass hassock she somehow avoided. Grabbing a mouthful of cold night, she shouts.

'*Help me. Anyone. Please, help me.*'

Art's face lifts and she sees her death in his wild eyes as clearly as if it has happened already. She's running again before she realises it, bare feet pounding on dirt that echoes hollow beneath, lungs grateful for the briefest possible break. Ahead is the Scar, closer now than she remembers. It juts from the dale like a black iceberg. The moon is a thorn bright enough to light her way. The stars are high and cold, clear and singing in a way she can't describe. The Dales are suddenly almost luminous. So unexpectedly different she fears her heart is failing, her body giving way, these are the seconds before she drops with exhaustion.

The Scar was always where she was heading.

She simply hasn't realised it before.

Art is closing in. He's so close that if she trips or hesitates he'll be on her. The ground slopes up from here to the Scar. As if black rock pushed up the dirt hundreds of yards all around. She's been here before with Gil, this is where they climbed, but it feels older, more familiar than that. Scrambling on her hands and occasionally knees, she climbs a dirt bank with the dark rock rising over her.

'Helen. Don't be stupid.' Art's words are broken, breathless. But from further behind than she expects. When she glances back she sees him, bent slightly forward, hands resting on his knees as he grabs breath. He's stopped at the bottom of the earth slope as if he can't be bothered to clamber up it after her.

'There's no escape.'

'There never was,' she says.

Art looks at her and his face is yellow with moonlight, his hair lank with sweat. He was beautiful once. At least she thought so. But it was a mean kind of beauty and she should have known better. There's nothing left of even that. His cold smile, once so confident, now seems less certain. Helen sees Art properly for the first time and wonders, if she saw the old version on the street, would she even take a second look?

He thinks she's trapped by the curve of Scar that folds around her.

The rock face is behind and to both sides. Art believes there's nowhere for her to run. For years she's believed the same. Now that he thinks he has her trapped the malice returns to his face. His words when he gets his breath back are cold and low and meant to crush her.

'Enough stupidity. Come down here now.'

I could do that, Helen thinks. I could keep my silence and hope to live through what will come. But I'm not that stupid or scared or small, not any more.

There are no doors here to walk into, no stairs to trip down, so it would have to be a proper fall. They could get a helicopter out to collect her if there was anything left to collect. Turning, she looks up at the rock and sees a handhold that wouldn't have been visible without moonlight. She looks around for somewhere to put her foot and finds that too. Rock digs painfully into the soft underside of her lacerated foot and she forces herself to ignore the pain, reaching for the handhold and instantly spotting another above. Her other foot scrabbles for traction and Art hurls himself up the slope, shouting.

Art never shouts. He's never needed to.

She reaches for the higher hold and Art grabs her

ankle before she can clamber further. For a moment she feels the full force of his muscles, and then stamps down with her other foot, heel slamming into his face. When he doesn't let go she does it again so hard she feels something should break. He shouts with pain and she scrambles higher the moment he lets go, her feet finding places to put themselves, handholds seeming to appear where she needs them.

At twice her height, she stops and risks looking down. Art stands with his hand to his nose, which streams blood. One of his eyes looks puffy.

'I'm going to kill you,' he says.

'Third time lucky?'

'You're deranged. You've always been deranged.'

'Two fires in Paris, now this. I'm not the one who's deranged. You drugged me.' She knew the truth now. *'Let's have a drink, Helen. No hard feelings, Helen.* You drugged us, killed Carl and left me to die. You couldn't even get that right.'

'Helen—'

'There's nothing you're really good at, is there? Lots of things you'd like to do well and nothing you can quite manage. Is that what this is about? The fact I can actually do something. And you can't?'

'You can't prove anything.' He spits his words, blood flecks accompanying them. 'You're nothing. Without me you're nobody.'

Helen smiles and sees how he hates her for it. He won't stop now. He will come after her but the Scar won't welcome him. He will have to fight for handholds, scrabble harder than he's ever had to scrabble for anything to find a place to put his feet.

If she dies here, then so does he.

She can accept that price, but she doesn't want to pay it unless she has to. For the first time, she knows what Art doesn't. If she has to, she can kill.

38

Her hand reaches for a grip and slides into a horizontal crack, grit sticking to her fingers. She lifts a foot and her toes scrabble and then there's a narrow ledge that she can use if she turns sideways before reaching for the next handhold.

She is utterly calm. Maybe this is what you find on the other side of fear.

An emptiness so vast winds could blow through her. The fear has turned to fury and the fury to an icy certainty. It ends here. Him or me . . . There should never have been an *us*.

Reach and drag, scrabble and step.

Helen climbs and Art begins to climb after her. He's not good with heights; not as fit as he was. Uncertainty is eating into his anger. He makes the mistake of looking down and she sees him hesitate. Her hand reaches for its next grip and the rock it finds is loose. For a moment she panics. Then, as her fingers close around it, she wonders if it's meant to be loose.

It comes away with a rattle of falling gravel that makes Art look up.

She waits for his gaze to find her. Then raises the fist-sized chunk of rock, waits for his eyes to focus on it and hurls it as hard as she can. It only just misses and he looks so shocked she laughs.

'Go back,' she shouts.

Art hangs there looking up.

She tugs at another rock that protrudes; it shifts but won't come free, so she climbs some more, fingers tugging at chunks that look likely. Suddenly the fear is back. Her chest tightens and her foot slips as she reaches for a rock, and she has to scrabble to keep her grip.

The third time a rock fails to come free, Art begins climbing again.

As her fear grows, so his anxiety lessens. His movements become more confident. Her failure to find something to throw is making him stronger. That's how it works, she realises. That's how it's always worked. To be strong Art needs her weak. Everything he's taken from her he's added to himself. For her to be strong she must take it back. She stops scrabbling and breathes, as she hangs there daring him to come closer. Her heart settles slightly. The fear leaves her throat. Below, Art hesitates and comes to a halt.

When he restarts it's with less confidence.

She knows what she must do. If he tries to grab her she'll kick him first. If he does grab her then she'll let go and they'll go down together. It's not what she wants but it's a price she'll pay. If she goes, then he does too. The next chunk of rock she reaches for sheers from the Scar with a clean break. Had she put her weight on it she'd be dead. Instead she has her next weapon.

This time, her aim is careful.

No anger, no fear, simply intent.

She throws as hard as she can and gravity helps. Art flinches at the throw and shifts just enough to avoid taking the rock in his face. It clips the back of his shoulder and she sees a glint of blood in the moonlight. The Dales, vast around them, hold their breath. In the silence, Art's swearing seems blasphemously loud.

'Next one kills you,' she warns him, her quiet voice carrying into the night.

'Helen . . .'

'What?'

'We should talk about this.'

'Like we talked about things before? You tell me what I'm doing wrong, I listen?'

'It's not like that.'

'It was always like that.'

The moonlight shifts and a shadow falls across them.

Fixing her grip, Helen risks taking her eyes off Art and looks up. A small figure stands on the edge above them. Backlit by the slivered moon, a single star bright beyond. Her heart stops in her ribs. It's him. He's always been there, she just didn't know that until now. He looks so solid he could be rock. Is he still clutching his Power Ranger? She'd like to know, but she can't see through her tears.

All that happened in Iraq and beyond comes back in a wave that rolls tsunami-like across the Dales and breaks around her against the massive heart of the Scar. 'Of all the things . . .' she says, her voice crashing on the cliff face. 'Syria was the worst.'

It wasn't the first time, it wasn't the most painful. It was simply the worst.

Art looks up at her, his eyes unfocusing to fix on the Scar above her. He doesn't see what she sees, but he knows she sees something. Art doesn't say anything, he simply shuffles backwards slightly, looking for a crevice, a protruding rock, anything to grip while he finds a new foothold. Helen knows she wouldn't trust the one he chooses, but he grabs it anyway, feet scrabbling for purchase. It's that that decides her. Swiping at each eye in turn, she releases her hand, swipes her eyes again, returns her hand, then starts towards him.

It's not as easy climbing down, she discovers. You can't see the handholds in advance. It's not like climbing up. You can't remember places to put your feet for the move after next or the one after that. You have to find them blind. She watches him do it and almost feels his body tense with each risk he takes. He glances up, suddenly alert, when she moves and seems more put out that she's starting to climb down than if she'd been about to hurl another rock.

The rock he would understand.

How high is a four-storey house? That's how high they are.

Well, she's four storeys and he's little more than three. He finds a handhold and somewhere to put one foot, a lower handhold and somewhere to put his other foot. Helen does the same. He takes it as mockery, a physical reflection of his habit of repeating her words back at her. That's what she reads from the tightening of his face. Not that far above, she sees the small silent boy still watching and waves to him shakily.

A long second later, he waves back.

Art looks at her, looks above them and looks at her again. She knows he sees nothing. He never did. When he stops, she stops and watches him speak. What he says she doesn't know, because she's ignoring it. She didn't know that was possible. When he stops speaking she hears things again.

A bird calling in the distance. Wind rises suddenly and stills as fast. A little pitter of falling stones tells her Art's foot is slipping slightly. He seems to be waiting for a response. She stops listening when he repeats whatever he said the first time, and when she starts again she can hear the same bird and, in the distance, the sound of someone calling her name.

Art seems to have heard it too. He doesn't like it. They're collecting witnesses, complications. He was always very careful to make sure there were no witnesses, and complications were always somehow Helen's fault, so she avoided them.

There's a shout from above.

Two shouts that echo over the Dales and shock the wind and the bird into silence. Gil's Yorkshire accent. Tom's voice, southern, metropolitan, and very, very dear. Sudden movement takes her by surprise and she realises Art is scrambling towards her. She grabs a rock that looks ready to come free but it stays where it is. She tries another and that won't come free either. In despair she begins to climb.

Too late. Art's fingers tighten on her ankle, locking her in place. His other hand digs into the back of her knee as he clambers up, using her leg as his climbing frame. He's below her now, hissing to himself, his fingers vicious as they dig into her flesh. He can't resist folding his hand into a fist and punching unseen between her denim-covered thighs.

Vomit rises and she swallows hard.

'Stupid little whore. You think I don't know you've been fucking someone else? You think I wouldn't find out?' He's right behind her now, pressed tight. A hand grips the rock beside her face, the other grips her neck as waves of darkness sweep through her. Through the darkness she hears shouts.

'You really think they can save you?'

His hand tightens when she doesn't answer. He edges his leg hard between hers. His face is next to her, his whisper in her ear, his hot breath brushing her face. When he releases her neck and brings his hand up to stroke her hair the tears come. She's been here before. She knows what comes next. This time, she won't let it.

'Well?' he says.

He's insane. That's her last thought before she lets go of the rock face with both hands and suddenly Art's single hand is the only thing holding them in place.

'Helen . . .!'

Art grabs with his other hand for a better grip, any grip, but she's leaning back, and as his fingers tear frantically at rock, she pushes off. The last thing she sees is the boy standing on the top of the Scar looking down. He grows distant, and then there's a blast of bright, bright light.

39

'Helen . . .'

Someone loomed over her made blurry by tears and pain. There was a prick at her arm and the pain lessened almost immediately. The tears kept coming. A hand came up to brush them away and she flinched.

'It's all right,' Tom said. 'Everything's going to be all right.'

'Where's . . .?'

Fingers tightened gently on her wrist.

'Gil? He's over there. They wouldn't let him through. They only let me through because I'm a doctor. You could have been killed, you know. Out here alone like that. What if Gil hadn't worked out where you'd gone . . .?'

He looked behind him, muttered to whoever was there. Police or ambulance, Helen's eyes wouldn't focus enough for her to find out. The man said something and Tom nodded. 'They're going to airlift you to hospital

now. I'm going to come with you. If that's all right? Help
look after you on the way.'

'It's bad?'

'A few bits broken.'

'They always were.'

Tom shook his head sadly.

'He was here. You know.'

'Helen . . .'

'I saw him.'

'You should save your strength.'

'At the top of the Scar.'

'At the . . .?'

'He was there. I saw him.'

The man behind Tom said something and Tom shook
his head. He knelt beside her stretcher, which was on
the ground at the bottom of the Scar. 'Who did you
see?' he asked gently.

'The Iraqi boy with the Power Ranger. He was standing
there. Right at the top.'

'Helen, that's impossible. He's dead. He's been dead
for years.'

'But I saw him. He waved to me.'

'What did you do?'

Helen smiled. 'I waved back.'

Tom bent and kissed her forehead, very gently, and
then he stood up. The helicopter crew lifted her aboard
and they took off carefully. When she started crying, really
crying, someone who wasn't Tom crouched beside her,
there was another pin-prick on her arm and she slept.

She remembered nothing of the two or three days that
came after that. Shortly after she woke on the fourth

day, Gil arrived with grapes and a card and roses. He wasn't to know Art always gave her roses.

He had a striped jacket over a black T-shirt and was wearing jeans for the first time she could remember. He put the card on her bedside cabinet, placed the roses in a jug he seemed to have acquired on his way through the hospital, and began eating his way through her grapes.

'Date,' he said, seeing Helen eye his outfit. 'Thought I'd see if I could persuade Liza to give me another go. For some mad reason she said yes. Lyn said I ought to prove I was serious by making an effort.' He made a face. 'She took me shopping.'

Helen grinned. Winced at the movement. 'It shows.'

'How do you feel?' he asked, sitting on the bed beside her.

'Dreadful.'

'You'd feel a lot worse if not for those.' Gil pointed at an array of tubes and catheters running in and out of her body. Told her which was saline, which drip fed her morphine, which machine monitored her heart, which recorded her blood pressure hourly. There was no mention of the catheter vanishing over the edge of the mattress to take all the liquid out of her.

'How do you know all that?' she asked. 'Is there no end to your journalistic prowess?'

'Tom told me.'

'He's here?'

Gil smiled. 'Yes,' he said. 'He's here. I offered him a room at the cottage, but here is closer. He persuaded them to give him a bed. Well, he is a consultant. Quite a good one, apparently.'

'A consultant?'

'Paediatrics. He's been helping out. I believe they'd like him to stay. Smart London surgeon and all that.'

'Gil . . .'

He knew what she was going to ask because he tried to shake her question away. For someone who claimed to like silence he talked a lot. He'd been to see his grand-children and his younger daughter had finally accepted him as a Facebook friend. She was a teacher in London in an inner-city school.

'Gil . . .' Helen tried to interrupt, but he was in full throttle.

'I'm thinking of writing a book. Did I tell you that? I thought of writing about the cave systems under the Dales. Miles and miles of twisting tunnels and shafts. Then I thought, why not write a book about the Scar itself? It has the most amazing legends, you know. The Victorians found bones at the bottom of the drop. They decided it must have been used for sacrifices. That's prob-ably not true. Unless it is. So that's what I'm going to do. I'm going to write *the* book.'

He ate the last of the grapes and looked apologetically at the skeleton of stalks on her bedside table. 'The Scar sits on top of limestone shafts you know. Much too dangerous to explore, but I don't doubt some of those contain bones too. Human bones, quite possibly.'

Helen looked up. The sudden movement hurt her head, and her neck, and several other bits. She closed her eyes until the pain subsided. Was Gil saying what she thought he was saying?

She opened her mouth to speak, but he held up his hand.

'The police want to talk to you. Tom's managed to fend them off so far, but he'll have to let them in eventually. In my experience, not that I have much, it's best to keep things simple . . . Apparently, the night you fell, you said you saw the boy. The one who died in Iraq? He was standing at the top. You waved to each other?'

She nodded and Gil glanced away, embarrassed.

'The police are taking that as proof of a breakdown.' Gil took a deep breath. 'Your husband died in a fire. Well, so you believed. Now he's just missing. The police think, well, they think he might have been involved. You've seen terrible things. Some people in the village are saying you couldn't take it. You threw yourself from the top. That's made it into the papers.'

Helen looked at him.

He smiled. 'Now I know, for future reference, that if I ever find myself in the middle of a media firestorm, then drugged out of my head is a good place to be. Every amateur psychologist in the country has analysed your mental state. Personally, I'd stick with grief, memory loss and that post-traumatic stuff you're not keen on. Because that's what everyone else has already decided.'

He kissed her carefully on the cheek, let his hand very slightly brush hers and told her Tom would be along in a moment. At the door, he turned and grinned. 'You might not want to look at yourself in the mirror for a while.'

It hurt to grin back but she did.

Gil was wrong though. For the first time in years she felt able to face herself. She was her. Her, with damage and experiences and a portfolio good enough to land her a job anywhere she wanted. All the same, this new her felt as if those years had never happened. Or, if they had, they happened to someone else. Someone she quite liked, but wouldn't want to admit being slightly afraid of . . . So now she waited, and even the drugs being dripped into her weren't enough to still the butterflies in her stomach, or take away the feeling that she was waiting beside the war memorial, on time this time, and about to turn seventeen.

June 2014

Reports that English journalist Art Huntingdon, wanted for murder of Carl Ackerman, seen in Belize prove unfounded French police say.

February 2015

@TimeOutLondon *Putting my Hand in the Fire*, the first major retrospective of reportage by Helen Lawrence, opens at the ICA on Monday.

Acknowledgements

In no particular order, I owe a huge debt to . . .

The authors of the many books I read in the course of my research. They suffered so I didn't have to leave the comfort of my spare room:

Journalism Joe Sacco

The Place At The End Of The World Janine Di Giovanni

Ghosts By Daylight Janine di Giovanni

On Photography Susan Sontag

It's What I Do: A Photographer's Life Of Love And War Lynsey Addario

On the Front Line: the Collected Journalism of Marie Colvin

The much-missed Marie Colvin for the quote that precedes Part Two, taken from a speech made at St Bride's in London on November 10, 2010 in honour of the war wounded. Her untimely death in Syria on February 22, 2012 was one of the inspirations for this book.

The ever-generous Caitlin Moran for permission to use her quote about Shining Girls from *The Times* magazine, July 13, 2013. And to my brave and brilliant friend, Lauren Laverne, for the 'box' analogy. I couldn't have put it better myself. Which is why I stole it wholesale.

The man who, when called upon for advice on how long a body had to burn to eliminate all traces of DNA said, 'Where's the body?'

The woman whose professional expertise and generous help enabled me to write the character, Caroline.

The far-too-many women whose stories mirror Helen Graham/Lawrence's own. Friends, friends of friends, people I met through social media or my work as a journalist – who generously shared their own experiences with me.

Sandra Horley, the tireless powerhouse behind domestic violence charity, Refuge, and whose book *The Charm Syndrome*, has been invaluable.

The very patient Mark Ridley who, in 2011, bid to have his name in one of my novels as part of an author's fund-raising campaign after the Japanese earthquake. Neither of us knew he would have to wait quite so long.

My agent, Jonny Geller, editor Lynne Drew, publicist Louise Swannell and all the teams at Curtis Brown and Harpercollins. You have the patience of several saints.

Almost last, and definitely not least, Anne Brontë's *The Tenant of Wildfell Hall*. In my opinion, the most original and radical of the novels written by the Brontë sisters. This is in no way an attempt to rework that great novel of 1848, more a stepping off point for looking at the many ways in which the social and economic status of women has changed in the last 170 years. And the ways in which it hasn't.

And finally, Jon who's been living with this project and its repercussions for far too long. I'm sure he'll be delighted to see the back of it. Thank you.

Reading Group Questions

1. How much, if at all, do you think Gil's fascination with Helen has to do with his estrangement from his daughters?

2. Do you think it would be easy to disappear from your own life and leave no trace in the digital age?

3. What do you think makes Helen decide to trust Gil? Should Gil have rung the police once he worked out who Helen was?

4. Helen and Art's marriage is a difficult one. Did you believe that she would stick with him – and go back to him? What did the book highlight about domestic violence?

5. What do you think the significance is of the little boy in Iraq?

6. Did you notice parallels between the main themes of this book and Anne Brontë's *The Tenant of Wildfell Hall*?

Author Q&A

A Q&A with author Sam Baker

Where did the starting point for this book come?

I have long been fascinated by *The Tenant of Wildfell Hall* and never really understood why, whilst still read, it hasn't endured in quite the same way as *Jane Eyre* and *Wuthering Heights*. One theme I really felt had endured was the issue of control within relationships. Also, someone I admired hugely as a journalist was killed covering the early years of the Syria conflict and that person's courage and dedication made a huge impression.

How easy or difficult was it to use a classic novel as an inspiration?

Extremely difficult, as I found out. I tried only to take the themes I felt still resonated and the structure of the original. I wanted to look at what had changed for women and what hadn't. More than we think, less than we know.

What research did you have to do for this book?

An enormous amount of research – far more than I banked on if I'm absolutely honest. I learned about photography and studied the lives of several war photographers, researched the historical incidents that form the linchpin of the plot points and obviously interviewed countless strong women who have emerged from all kinds of abusive relationships, as well as doing endless reading around the Brontës. Not to mention having to research how to go off line, or at least keep as low a digital profile as is now possible.

How much, if at all, did your background as an magazine editor contribute to your decision to give these characters the careers they have?

Not particularly. In the case of the original Brontë Helen, she is an artist who had the temerity to not even paint in watercolour but in oils. Her art not only gives her a possible income source at a time when a married woman was not legally entitled to one, but she chose to do so with the most masculine of materials. I chose the role of war photographer for Helen because I wanted a reflection of that, a role that felt very male in a man's world. As for Gil, he had to have a profession (or have had a profession) that gave him the necessary investigative skills and made his 'investigation' of Helen not too stalkery – either a retired journalist or a policeman. The introduction of digital into press photography and the changes that technology wrought in journalism over the last decades played into the other digital themes in the novel.

Do you have a routine when you are writing or is every day different?

Because I have also launched a digital platform for women called The Pool, every day is different. Weekends, when possible, are spent writing in a cafe with my partner.

What's next?

I plan to stick with this new darker approach for the next book.

For more from Sam Baker, including her answers to the Reading Group Questions, go to www.sambaker.co.uk